About the Authors

Nicole Helm grew up with her nose in a book and the dream of one day becoming a writer. After a few failed career choices, she gets to live that dream writing down-to-earth contemporary romance and romantic suspense. From farmers to cowboys, Midwest to the West, Nicole writes stories about people finding themselves and finding love in the process. She lives in Missouri with her husband and two sons, and dreams of someday owning a barn.

Melanie Milburne read her first Mills & Boon at age seventeen in between studying for her final exams. After completing Bachelor's and then Master's Degree in Education, she decided to write a novel and thus her career as a romance author was born. Melanie is an ambassador for the Australian Childhood Foundation and is a devoted owner of two cheeky toy poodles who insist on taking turns sitting on her lap while she's writing.

A typical Piscean, award-winning *USA Today* bestselling author **Yvonne Lindsay** has always preferred the stories in her head to the real world. Married to her blind-date sweetheart and with two adult children, she spends her days crafting the stories of her heart and loves to read or travel when she's not working. Yvonne loves to hear from readers, contact her via yvonnelindsay.com or yvonne@yvonnelindsay.com or on Facebook YvonneLindsayAuthor

Romance On Duty

March 2025
Irresistible Sparks

May 2025
Undercover Passion

April 2025
Love in Action

June 2025
In Pursuit of Love

Romance On Duty:
In Pursuit of Love

NICOLE HELM

MELANIE MILBURNE

YVONNE LINDSAY

MILLS & BOON

All rights reserved including the right of reproduction in whole or in part in any form. This edition is published by arrangement with Harlequin Enterprises ULC.

This is a work of fiction. Names, characters, places, locations and incidents are purely fictional and bear no relationship to any real life individuals, living or dead, or to any actual places, business establishments, locations, events or incidents. Any resemblance is entirely coincidental.

Without limiting the author's and publisher's exclusive rights, any unauthorised use of this publication to train generative artificial intelligence (AI) technologies is expressly prohibited. HarperCollins also exercise their rights under Article 4(3) of the Digital Single Market Directive 2019/790 and expressly reserve this publication from the text and data mining exception.

® and ™ are trademarks owned and used by the trademark owner and/or its licensee. Trademarks marked with ® are registered with the United Kingdom Patent Office and/or the Office for Harmonisation in the Internal Market and in other countries.

First Published in Great Britain 2025
by Mills & Boon, an imprint of HarperCollins*Publishers* Ltd
1 London Bridge Street, London, SE1 9GF

www.harpercollins.co.uk

HarperCollins*Publishers*
Macken House, 39/40 Mayor Street Upper,
Dublin 1, D01 C9W8, Ireland

Romance on Duty: In Pursuit of Love © 2025 Harlequin Enterprises ULC.

Badlands Beware © 2020 Nicole Helm
Flirting with the Socialite Doc © 2014 Melanie Milburne
Tangled with a Texan © 2019 Harlequin Enterprises ULC

Special thanks and acknowledgment are given to Yvonne Lindsay for her contribution to the *Texas Cattleman's Club: Houston* series.

ISBN: 978-0-263-41738-8

This book contains FSC™ certified paper and other controlled sources to ensure responsible forest management.

For more information visit: www.harpercollins.co.uk/green

Printed and Bound in the UK using 100% Renewable Electricity
at CPI Group (UK) Ltd, Croydon, CR0 4YY

BADLANDS BEWARE

NICOLE HELM

For the family secrets that never get told.

Chapter One

Rachel Knight had endured nightmares about the moment she'd lost the majority of her sight since she'd been that scared, injured three-year-old. The dream was always the same. The mountain lion. The surprising shock and pain of its attack.

Things she knew had happened, because what else could have attacked her? Because that was the truth that everyone believed. She'd somehow toddled out of the house and into the South Dakota ranchland only to have a run-in with a wild animal.

But in the dreams, there was always a voice. Not her father, or her late mother, or anyone who should have been there that night.

The voice of a stranger.

Rachel sucked in a breath as her eyes flew open. Her heart pounded, and her sheets were a sweaty tangle around her.

It was a dream. Nothing more and nothing less, but she couldn't figure out why twenty years after the attack she would still be so plagued by it.

Likely it was just all the danger that her family had been facing lately. As much as she loved the Wyatts, both sturdy Grandma Pauline and her six law enforcement grandsons who owned the ranch next door, their connection to a vicious biker gang meant trouble seemed to follow wherever they went.

And somehow, this year it had also brought her foster sisters into the fold time and again. Putting them in jeopardy along with those Wyatt brothers—and then culminating in true love, against all odds.

All of their tormentors were in jail now, and Rachel wanted that to be the end of it.

But something about the dreams left her feeling edgy, like the next dangerous situation was just around the corner.

And that you'll get thrust into the path of one of the Wyatt boys and end up...

Rachel got out of bed without finishing the thought. Just because four of her five foster sisters had ended up in love with a Wyatt didn't mean she was doomed. Because if she was doomed, so was Sarah. Rachel laughed outright at the thought.

Sarah was too much like Pauline. Independent and prickly. The thought of her falling for *anyone*, let alone a bossy Wyatt, was unfathomable. Which meant it was inconceivable for Rachel, too. She might not be prickly, but she had no designs on ending up tied to a man with a dangerous past and likely even more dangerous secrets.

So, that was that.

Rachel went through her normal routine of showering and getting ready for the day before heading downstairs. She didn't have to tap her clock to hear the time to know it was earlier than she usually woke up.

She was—shudder—becoming a morning person. Maybe she could shed that with the coming winter.

It was full-on autumn now. Twenty-three was creeping closer and while she knew that wasn't old, she was exactly where she'd always been. Would she be stuck here forever? In the same house, on the same ranch, nothing ever changing except the people around her?

Teaching at the reservation offered some respite, but she was so dependent on others. If she moved somewhere with more public transportation, she could be independent.

And yet the thought of leaving South Dakota and her family always just made her sad. This was home. She wanted to be happy here, but there was a feeling of suffocation dogging her.

Maybe *that* was why she kept having those dreams.

Weirdly, that offered some comfort. There was a reason, and it was just feeling a little quarter-life crisis-y. Nothing…ominous.

She held on to that truth as she headed downstairs. Inside the house she never used her cane, even after the fire this summer. They'd fixed the affected sections to be exactly as they had been, which meant she knew it as well as she knew Pauline Reaves's ranch next door, or her classroom, or Cecilia's house on the rez where Rachel stayed when she was teaching.

She wasn't trapped. She had plenty of places to go. As long as she didn't mind overprotective family everywhere she went.

Rachel stopped at the bottom of the stairs, surprised to hear someone in the kitchen. Duke's irritable mutterings alerted her to the fact it was her father before she could make out the shape of him.

Big, dark and the one constant presence in her life, aside from Sarah—who was the opposite of Duke. Small, petite and pale. She couldn't make out the details of a person's appearance, but she could recognize those she loved by the blurry shapes she could see out of her one eye that hadn't been completely blinded.

"Daddy, what are you doing?"

"What are you doing up?" he returned gruffly.

Rachel hesitated. While she often told her father everything that was going on with her, she tended to keep things that might worry him low-key. "I think my body finally got used to waking up early," she said, forcing a cheerfulness over it she didn't feel.

"Speaking of that..." He trailed off, approached her. His hand squeezed her shoulder. "Baby, I know you've got a class session coming up in a few weeks, but I think you should bow out. Too much has been going on."

Rachel opened her mouth, but no sound came out. Not teach at the rez? The art classes she held for a variety of age groups were short sessions and taught through the community rather than the school itself. She only instructed about twenty weeks out of the year, and he wanted her to miss a four-week session? When teaching was the only thing that made her feel like she had a life outside of cooking and cleaning for Dad and Sarah.

"Just this session," Dad added. "Until we know for sure those Wyatt boys are done bringing their trouble around."

It felt like a slap in the face, but she didn't know how to articulate that. Except an unfair rage toward the Wyatts.

Rachel took a deep breath to calm herself. She never let her temper get the better of her. Mom had impressed upon her temper tantrums would never get her what she wanted. "I don't have anything to do with their trouble."

"I might have said the same about Felicity and Cecilia, but look what they endured this summer. It won't do."

"Dad, teaching those classes—"

"I know they mean a lot to you. And I am sorry. Maybe you could do some tutoring out here?"

"I'm an adult."

"You're twenty-two. I know this is a disappointment, but I'm not going to argue about it." His hand slid off her shoulder and she heard the jangle of keys.

Rachel frowned at how strange this all was. Maybe she was still dreaming. "Are you *going* somewhere?"

There was a pregnant pause. "Just into town on some errands."

Her frown deepened. Sarah took care of almost all the errands now that it was just the two of them left living with Duke. Her father almost never ventured into town. And he never gave *her* unreasonable ultimatums.

"What's wrong, Dad?" she asked gravely.

"I want my girls safe," he said, and she heard his retreating footsteps as though that was that.

She fisted her hands on her hips. Oh, no, it was *not*. And she was going to get some answers. If they wouldn't come from her father, they'd just have to come from the source of the trouble.

TUCKER WYATT HAD always loved spending nights at his grandmother's house. Though he kept an apartment in town, he'd much rather spend time with his family at the Reaves ranch.

Until now.

He sighed. Why had he ever thought his current predicament was a good idea? He was *terrible* at keeping secrets.

Case in point, he was about 75 percent sure his brother Brady had figured out that Tucker *accidentally* stumbling into a situation where he could help save Brady's life from one of their father's protégés wasn't so accidental. That it was part of his working beyond his normal job as detective with the Valiant County Sheriff's Department.

And, since their youngest brother had been kicked out of North Star Group just a few months ago, it didn't take a rocket scientist to figure out what group Tucker might also be working for.

He was going to have to quit. The North Star Group had approached him because of his ties to Ace Wyatt, former head of the dangerous Sons of the Badlands, and a few of Tucker's cases that involved other high-ranking officials in the Sons.

Cases Tuck had been sure were private and confidential. But those words didn't mean much to North Star.

They'd wanted him on the Elijah Jones investigation, but then Brady and Cecilia Mills, one of the Knight girls, had gotten in the way.

The only reason Tucker hadn't been kicked out of North Star, as far as he could see, was because the North Star higher-ups didn't know his brother and Cecilia were suspicious of Tucker's involvement.

Which didn't sit right. Surely they didn't think his brother, a police officer, didn't have questions about a mysterious explosion that took Elijah Jones down enough to be restrained, hospitalized and, as of today, transferred to prison.

It had been a mess of a summer all in all, but things would assuredly calm down now. Ace was in maximum-security prison and Elijah was going to jail, along with a variety of his helpers.

But as long as Tucker was part of North Star and their continued efforts to completely and utterly destroy the Sons of the Badlands, he wouldn't feel totally settled *or* calm.

The back door that came into the kitchen swung open—not all that unusual. Grandma Pauline always had people coming and going through this entrance, but Tuck was surprised by the appearance of a *very* angry looking Rachel Knight.

She pointed directly at him, as if he'd done something wrong. "What's going on with my dad?"

Tuck stared at Rachel in confusion. She looked... pissed, which was not her norm. She was probably the most even-keeled of the whole Knight bunch.

While her sisters had all been fostered or adopted by Duke and Eva Knight, Rachel was their lone biological daughter. She didn't look much like her father—more favored her late mother, which always gave Tuck a bit of a pang.

His memories of his own mother weren't pleasant. He'd had Grandma Pauline, who he loved with his whole heart. Her influence on him and his brothers when they'd come to live with her meant the world to him.

But Eva Knight had been a soft, motherly presence in the Reaves-Knight world. Even if she'd been next door and not their mother, she'd treated them like sons. He'd never seen anything that matched it.

Except in her daughter. Tall and slender, Rachel had Eva's sharp nose and high cheekbones and long black hair. The biggest difference were the scars around Rachel's eyes, lines of lighter brown against the darker skin color on the rest of her face.

She could *see*, but not clearly. It always seemed to Tuck that her dark brown eyes were a little too knowing.

At least on *this* he wasn't keeping a secret—and failing at it. He had no idea why she'd demand of him anything about Duke Knight.

"Well?" she demanded as he only sat there like a deer caught in headlights.

"I haven't the slightest idea what's going on with your father. Why would I?"

"I don't know. I only know it has something do with *you*."

By the way she flung her arms in the air, he could only assume she didn't mean him personally but the whole of the Wyatts.

"Why don't we sit down?" He took her elbow gently to lead her to the table. "Back up. Talk about this, you know, calmly."

She tugged her elbow out of his grasp, clearly not wanting to sit. "He doesn't want me teaching this fall. He's worried about our safety. I know it doesn't have to do with *my* family. So, it has to do with yours."

Tucker held himself very still—an old trick he had down to an art these days. Letting his temper get the best of him as a kid had gotten the crap beaten out of him. Routinely.

Ace had told him his emotions would be the death of him if he didn't learn to control them. Hone them.

Tucker refused to *hone* them or be anything like his father. Which meant also never letting his temper boil over. He pictured a blue sky, puffy white clouds and a hawk arcing through both.

When he trusted his voice, he spoke and offered a smile. "I guess that's possible." He didn't allow himself to say what he wanted to. *Your sisters seem to be getting my brothers in trouble plenty on their own.* "I'm not sure specifically what it could be that would have Duke worried about you teaching at the rez. Did something happen? Maybe Cecilia would know."

"What would I know?" Cecilia asked, walking into

the kitchen. She was in her tribal police uniform, likely on her way to work. Though she was still nursing some wounds from her run in with Ace's protege and hadn't been cleared for active duty, she'd started in-house hours this week.

Though Duke and Eva Knight had fostered Cecilia, like Rachel she was a blood relation—Eva's niece. But she had been raised as "one of the Knight girls" as much Rachel's sister as her cousin.

"Has there been any new trouble at the rez that might make Duke nervous about Rach teaching her upcoming session?" Tucker asked.

Rachel scowled at him. "I wasn't going to bring her into it, jerk."

Cecilia's brow puckered. "I haven't heard anything. Dad doesn't want you teaching? Kind of late to have concerns about that, isn't it? Doesn't your session start the first of the month? And why didn't you want to bring me into it?"

Rachel sighed heavily. "Yes, it does, and yes, it's late." She looked pointedly in Tucker's direction, but when she spoke it was to Cecilia. "I wasn't going to bring you into it, because obviously it's not about *you*. I don't think it's about the rez, either. I think it's about the Wyatts."

"Look, Rach, I know the Wyatts are an easy target, no offense, Tuck. But if something bad was going on over here, Brady would have told me."

Because Cecilia and Brady now shared a *room* at his grandmother's house, a simple fact Tucker wasn't used to. Four of his brothers all paired off. And with the Knight girls of all people. It was sudden and weird.

But he just had to keep that to himself. Especially when Brady and Cecilia lived here now. "Well, I'll let you ladies figure this out. I've got a meeting to get to," Tucker said, quickly slipping past Rachel even as she began to protest.

Whatever was going on with Duke and Rachel was not his business, and he had to meet with his boss at North Star to nip this whole mission in the bud. It wasn't for him. He was a detective, and a damn good one, but he would never become adept at lying to his family.

He got in his truck, and drove to the agreed upon location. A small diner in Rapid City. Tucker had never met Granger McMillan, the head of the North Star Group. He'd been approached by field operatives and dealt with them solely.

Until now.

Tucker scanned the diner. Granger had said he'd know who he was, and Tucker had thought that was a little over-the-top cloak-and-dagger, but the large man in a cowboy hat and dark angry eyes sitting in the corner was *quite* familiar.

The man he was sitting across from turned in his seat, looked right at Tucker and gestured him over.

Tucker moved forward feeling a bit like he'd taken a blow to the head. Why was Duke here? What *was* this?

"You two know each other," the man, who could only be Granger McMillan, said. Not a question. A statement. "Have a seat, Wyatt. We have a lot to discuss."

Chapter Two

Rachel didn't get anywhere with Cecilia. Falling in love had certainly colored her vision when it came to the Wyatts. It was a disappointment, but one that was hard to hold on to when Brady had come in and he'd exchanged a casual goodbye kiss with her sister.

She would have never put Brady and Cecilia together, but when they were together, it seemed so *right*. Two pieces clicking together to mellow each other out a bit.

But even if that softened her up, Rachel wasn't ready to give up on being mad at the Wyatt brothers. So, she sought out someone she knew would back her up.

Sarah wiped her brow with the back of her arm. She'd been hefting water buckets into the truck to move them to a different pasture while Rachel laid out her case.

"Yeah, it's weird Dad took off, but what do you want me to do about it? I'm kind of running a ranch single-handedly here while he's doing whatever." Dev Wyatt's dogs raced around Sarah and Rachel. "My biggest concern is why I suddenly have two dogs. I did not consent to these dogs."

Rachel patted Cash on the head. Sarah talked a big game, but Rachel had overheard her just last night loving on the very dogs she was currently irritated over.

With a pang, Rachel missed Minnie, her old service dog. She knew she should start working on getting another one, or maybe even work on training her own, but it just made her sad still.

"What do you need help with?" Rachel asked, feeling guilty about unloading on her sister when she was so busy. The Knight ranch wasn't the biggest operation in South Dakota, but Duke and Sarah had to work really hard to make it profitable, and with all the danger around lately, hiring outside help felt like too big a risk.

"It's fine," Sarah replied, hopping off the truck bed and closing the gate. "Dev's coming over this afternoon to help. Maybe he'll take those stupid mutts back with him."

Even if Sarah could convince the dogs to go back with Dev, Rachel knew Sarah was all talk. She'd be bribing the dogs back over by suppertime.

"Well, I'll go make up some sandwiches for lunch. Want some pasta salad to go with it?"

"Yes, please."

Rachel walked back to the house over the well-worn path along the fence that led her to and from the stables. She moved through her normal chore of preparing lunch for Sarah and Dad, though Dad still wasn't home.

Rachel set the water to boil for pasta salad and frowned. It wasn't like her father to run errands on a ranch morning, even more unlike him to be gone for hours at a time. Cecilia had seemed concerned, but not enough to miss work. Plus, now she was going to tell Brady and he'd talk about it with his brothers and Rachel was fed up with Wyatts interfering.

Ughhh, those Wyatts. Rachel let herself bang around in the kitchen. She supposed Cecilia was a *little* right and Rachel was *maybe* projecting some feelings on them because it was safer than being upset with her father.

But Rachel didn't really care about being fair or balanced in the privacy of her own thoughts. Pasta salad and sandwiches made, she set them in the fridge and went to handling the rest of her normal chores, grumbling to herself the whole way.

Duke and Sarah were terrible housekeepers, so Rachel was often the default cleaner in the house. She didn't mind it, though. Having things to do made her feel useful. She tidied, swept, vacuumed, even dusted. She went upstairs and made the beds. Once she was done, she tapped her clock for the time.

The robotic voice told her it was nearly noon. Still no Sarah and even worse, no Dad. Rachel headed downstairs, wracking her brain for some reason her father would be gone this long without telling her.

She stopped halfway down the stairs. A horrible thought dawned on her. What if he was sick? Like Mom. What if he was at the doctor getting terrible news he wanted to hide?

The thought had tears stinging her eyes. She couldn't do it. She couldn't lose her mom and her dad before she was even twenty-five. Before she found a significant other. Before she had kids. Dad had to be around for that. Mom couldn't, so Dad *had* to be.

Rachel marched toward his room, propelled by fear masked as fury. If something was wrong, she'd find evidence of it there.

She stepped inside. He'd moved down to the main floor with Mom when she had gotten sick. He'd never moved back upstairs. Sometimes Rachel worried about him wallowing in the loss. Now she worried the same fate was waiting for him.

No. I refuse.

She tidied up, deciding it was an easy excuse to poke around his things. Which wasn't out of the norm. When she deep-cleaned the house, she took care of Dad's room. She didn't find anything out of the ordinary, though she wouldn't be able to read any of the medicine bottles to tell if there was something off there—but based on the number and size there didn't seem to be anything more than the usual over-the-counter painkiller and heartburn medicines.

She'd need Sarah to read the labels to be sure, but then she'd have to bring her sister into this and Sarah had enough to worry about with the ranch.

She pondered the dilemma as she made Dad's bed. As she adjusted the pillows, she felt something cool and hard. She reached out and touched her fingers to the object. It was a black blob in her vision, but she quickly realized she was touching a gun.

Rachel stood frozen in place for a good minute, pillow held up in one hand, her other hand grasping the gun. It wasn't that her father didn't have firearms. He had a few hunting rifles, kept in the safe in the basement. He had one hung above the back door because after reading the *Little House* books to her, he'd decided that's where one needed to go.

But this was a small pistol. Like the ones the Wyatt boys carried when on duty. And it was under his pillow. Carefully she picked it up and felt around some more, getting an idea of the gun model before she checked the chamber.

Loaded, which seemed very unsafe in his *bed*. Rachel didn't know what to make of it, but his whole talk about safety sure made it seem like he was worried about some kind of threat.

What on earth kind of threat would Duke be facing?

"Rachel?"

She nearly dropped the gun at Sarah's voice. Luckily, it came from the kitchen, not from right next to her. She quickly slipped the gun back under the pillow, left the bed unmade and tiptoed into the hallway.

"Coming!" she called, trying to steady her beating heart. Sarah didn't need to know about this. Not just yet. First, Rachel had to figure what was going on.

"So, what you're telling me..." Tucker raked his fingers through his hair, not knowing whether to look at Duke or Granger "...is Knight ranch was a witness protection hideout."

Duke's gaze was patently unfriendly, which was odd coming from a man he'd always looked up to. Tucker had grown up in a biker gang surrounded by nothing but bad. Ever since he'd gotten out, Duke had been there. Grandma Pauline and Eva had been mother figures. Duke had been the father figure.

But Duke clearly didn't want Granger letting Tucker in on his past. His *true* identity. How did Duke Knight of all people have a *true* identity?

"And the girls don't know?"

"Why would they know?" Duke asked, his voice a raspy growl. "I left that old life behind over thirty-five years ago. Met Eva two years later, and we built this family on who I was *now*, not who I was *then*. Then was gone, and has been for a very long time."

"A cop." Duke Knight had been a cop. A cop who, in his first year on duty, had taken down a powerful family of dirty police officers. And then had a bounty put on his head and had to be moved into WITSEC.

A ranch in the middle of nowhere South Dakota sure

made sense, and feeling safe enough to find a wife and build a family here made even more sense. But Tucker didn't know how to accept it.

"Grandma Pauline... She had to know."

Duke shrugged. "Don't know if she did or didn't, but Pauline never asked any questions. Never poked her nose into my business." He looked pointedly at Granger.

Granger, who was here for a current reason. That somehow involved Tucker. "Why would this group want to come after you when thirty-five years have passed? Wouldn't it be water under the bridge?"

"You're Ace Wyatt's son and you really have to ask that question?"

Tuck was chastened enough at that. When fear was currency, the years didn't matter so much. Only proving your strength, your ability to destroy did.

Tucker turned to face Granger across from him at the diner table. "And how does this connect to North Star?"

"We've been working under the assumption Vince MacLean was casing your grandmother's ranch because of the Wyatt connection, which is why we brought you in," Granger said. Facts Tucker was well aware of.

Granger was a tall man, dressed casually. A layperson might not think anything of someone like him, sitting in a diner, having a friendly cup of coffee. But Tucker saw all the signs of someone on alert. The way his gaze swept the establishment. The way he filed away everyone who entered or exited.

"We couldn't quite figure his role out. But the information you've passed along to us, plus what we already had, started to point to the fact there might be a different target." Granger nodded toward Duke. "We started looking into not just who Vince was directly reporting to, but who the people he was reporting to passed information to and so on. What we found is a connection to the Vianni family."

Tucker didn't need to be led to the rest. "Who were the family of dirty cops you took down?"

Duke nodded.

"We started digging into the family, into possible connections, and figured out Duke's. Since he was the target, we brought him in. And now we're bringing you in. The Sons connecting to the Vianni family is an expansion. It gives both groups more reach, and makes them stronger than they were."

"The Sons have been weakened."

"You can keep throwing their leaders in jail, Wyatt, but that doesn't end their infrastructure or ability to regroup."

"What does?" Tucker returned.

Granger's gaze, which had been cool and controlled up to this point, heated with fury. But his voice remained calm as he spoke. "We need Duke to help us. Which means he has to disappear for a little while. Duke's not too keen on leaving his ranch or his daughters."

"Nor should he be," Tucker snapped, his own temper straining. "Have you been paying attention these past few months? Duke being gone doesn't make the threat go away." He turned to Duke, who was sitting next to him in the booth. "You're leaving them to be a new target, that's all. And you—" Tucker faced Granger "—you're caring about your own North Star plots and plans without thinking about innocent lives."

Tucker didn't wilt when Granger lifted his eyebrows regally. "Watch your step, boy. I know more about protecting innocent lives than you could even begin to imagine. But Duke is our key between the Sons and the Viannis, and without him, more innocent people get hurt. A lot more."

Tucker whipped his gaze back to Duke, too angry to be chastened by Granger's words. "You didn't tell any of us? This whole time you knew you were a target and you didn't think to give us a heads-up so we could help?"

"I didn't want to bring you or your brothers into it. I don't want my daughters brought into it, and that's all your brothers seem capable of doing." Duke nodded toward Granger. "His father is the reason I have the ranch I do. The life I do. When Granger here came to me… I might not like it, but I owe the McMillan family, and I owe it to the other people the Viannis have hurt after I bowed out."

Tucker snorted in derision. Maybe he should have felt sorry for Duke, but all he could think about was Rachel already coming to him worried about her father. "You think your girls are going to buy you *leaving*?"

"It'll be your job to convince them," Granger said matter-of-factly, like that was a mission anyone could accomplish. He pushed a manila envelope over to Tucker. "This includes a letter to the daughters from Duke, a packet of fake vacation itinerary. You'll take it to Sarah and Rachel and say you found it—where and how is up to you." Then Granger slid a phone across the table. "You'll also take this. It's been programmed with your cell number, as well as a secret number that will allow contact with someone at North Star directly. We'll reach you through this if we need you. It's also got access to security measures set up around the Reaves and Knight ranches, thanks to your brother. He has no idea you have access to any of this, and no one in your family or Duke's can know, either. Is that understood?"

Tucker looked at the folder and the phone. None of

this made sense, and how on earth was he going to convince Sarah and Rachel—and the rest of either family for that matter—that Duke, who'd barely left the ranch even for errands throughout all their lives, was going on vacation. Suddenly, and without warning. "You can't be serious."

"Oh, I'm deadly serious, Wyatt. And so is this."

Chapter Three

"Something has to be wrong." Rachel stood in Grandma Pauline's kitchen, Sarah next to her. She could hear the dogs whining outside, but Grandma Pauline did not allow dogs in her kitchen.

"If he'd come home before dinner, I wouldn't think *too* much of it. But he still isn't back and he won't answer his cell," Sarah said, wringing her hands together.

"I called Gage," Brady offered. "He's going to head over to Valiant County and see if he can sweet talk them into putting some men on it before the required hours for a missing person. Then he'll look himself. Cecilia said she's going to ask around town after her shift, too. If he's around, one of them will find him."

"What do you mean *if*?" Sarah demanded. "Where else would he go?"

Which echoed the fear growing inside of Rachel. "Do you think something happened to him?" she asked, straight out. Because if Brady Wyatt thought something had happened to him, his instincts were most likely right.

Brady's response was grim. "Duke left the ranch of his own volition, but you were concerned about him being worried about danger. Maybe there's something he wasn't telling us."

The door opened and Tucker entered. Aside from Brady and Gage, Rachel could tell the difference in the Wyatt brothers by general shape. Even though they were all tall and broad, they had a different presence about them.

If she took a lot of time, she could figure out Gage and Brady, but being twins made it a bit more difficult, and she could always tell from their voices.

But Tucker was always a slightly...lighter presence. His hair wasn't so dark, his movements were always a little easier. But something about the way he entered the kitchen now was all wrong.

"Hey, all. What's going on?"

Rachel frowned. He did *not* sound his usual cheerful self. Something was weighing on him, and that was clear as day in his voice.

"Duke's missing," Sarah said plainly.

"Missing?"

"We can't find him. He hasn't come back to the ranch since this morning."

"You're sure he's not out in the fields?" Tucker asked.

"No. I'm worrying everyone because I didn't look around the ranch," Sarah replied sarcastically. "Don't be an ass, Tuck."

"I'm sure there's a rational explanation. If you're all worried, I can—"

"We've already got Gage and Cecilia on it," Brady said.

There was something off about Tucker. Something... odd in the way he delivered his responses.

"Oh, I picked up your mail," he offered as if it he'd just remembered. "It was falling out of the box."

Rachel assumed he put it into Sarah's hands before he moved over to the table. "I didn't have a chance to get dinner. You got any leftovers, Grandma?" He moved farther into the kitchen, still acting...strangely. But no one else seemed to notice, so maybe she was taking her worry about Dad and spreading it around.

There was a thud and the flutter of papers. "There's a letter from Dad," Sarah screeched. The sound of the envelope being ripped open had Rachel moving closer even though she wouldn't be able to read it.

Sarah read aloud. "Dear girls, I know you probably won't be able to believe this, but I've decided it's time for a break. If I don't go right now, I know I never will. I've included my vacation itinerary so you don't worry, but this is something I need to do for myself. Take good care of each other. Love, Dad."

"There's no possible way," Rachel croaked, panic hammering at her throat. "Maybe he wrote that, but not because he wanted to take a vacation. Not of his own volition." Nothing would drag her father away from the ranch, away from his daughters. Not even temporarily.

"And he'd never leave without someone here to help me," Sarah added, her voice uncharacteristically tremulous. "I can't handle the ranch on my own."

"We'll work it out," Dev said gruffly. "Don't worry about the ranch. Brady—"

"We'll tell Gage the latest development," Brady said before Dev could instruct him. "He can—"

"Let me look into it," Tucker said. "I'm the detective. We don't need to get Valiant County involved or have Gage and Cecilia asking around."

"We can *all* look into it," Brady said evenly.

"Yeah, but if we all start looking into it, and something *is* wrong, we've alerted everyone we know. But if I look into it, pretend like I'm just researching one of my cases, we might be able to unearth whatever trouble there actually is without causing suspicion. *If* there's any trouble at all."

"My father did not go on a *vacation*. Period. Let alone without telling us. What kind of trouble would he be in?"

"I don't know, Rach. Let me look into it. If there's trouble, we'll find it."

"Yes, you're very good at finding it," she replied caustically.

"Now, now," Grandma Pauline said, and though the words might have been gentle coming from most grandmothers, from Pauline it was a clear warning.

Rachel blew out a breath.

Tucker's voice was very calm when he spoke, and she could easily imagine him using that tone with a hysterical person on a call. He would promise to take care of everything no matter how upset the person was.

She swallowed at the lump of fear and anxiety in her throat. Tucker could do that because he wanted to help people. She wanted to blame him for all the trouble right now, but deep down she knew it wasn't his fault or his brothers' faults.

The Wyatts were good men who wanted to do the right thing, and she had to stop sniping at them. Division was not going to bring her father home.

"What can we do? While you're looking for him?" she asked of Tuck. "We can't just sit around waiting."

"Unfortunately, I think you *should* sit and wait. If there's danger, and we're not sure there is, we want to know what kind before we go wading in. What we do know is that even if he is in danger, he's alive. He left of his own accord. He's made *some* kind of decision here."

"He could have been threatened to leave," Sarah

pointed out. "Blackmailed. Though over what I don't have a clue."

"Yes," Tucker agreed equitably. "If that's the case, someone wanted him to leave of his own accord. Think how easy it would be to ambush a man like Duke. How often he's out in the fields or barn or stables alone. This is more than Duke being in life-threatening danger. It's deeper and more complicated. *If* it's anything other than a mid-life crisis."

Rachel scoffed simultaneously with Sarah.

"He's not wrong," Grandma Pauline said. "Duke hasn't been himself lately. Wouldn't be unheard of for someone in their late fifties to have a bit of a personal crisis."

Rachel felt like the world had been upended. Why were her and Sarah the only ones freaking out about this? How could Grandma Pauline stand there and say her father was having a *personal crisis*?

"I'll head back into the office right now. Get the ball rolling on an investigation. I'll update you all in the morning."

No one spoke, not to argue with Tucker or demand more answers. Rachel had to believe they were in as much shock as she was. This couldn't actually be happening.

And Tucker wasn't acting right. She couldn't put her finger on what was wrong, just that something *was*. She heard him exit, the normal conversation picking back up. Sarah and Dev discussing ranch concerns, Brady on the phone with Jamison, the oldest Wyatt brother, giving him an update, and Grandma Pauline fussing around the kitchen cleaning up.

Didn't any of them feel it? Didn't any of them… She shook her head and slipped out the kitchen door.

She couldn't make out Tucker's shape in the low light of dusk, but she didn't hear a car engine so he hadn't made it that far yet.

She took a few steps forward until she could make out the shape of him. "What aren't you telling us?"

She could tell he turned to face her, but she didn't have the ability to read his expression. Still there was a lot in that long careful pause.

"If there was anything I could tell you to make sense of this, I would."

She wasn't sure why that made her want to cry instead of yell at him. Which left her unsure of what to say.

He stepped close, then his hands were giving hers a squeeze. "I'm going to do everything I can to bring him home safe, Rach. Whether he's in trouble or not. You believe that, don't you?"

She wasn't sure what she believed in the midst of all this insanity, but in her heart she knew Tucker was a good man and that he loved her father. Maybe none of this made sense, but he wouldn't promise to do everything he could and then not.

"Yeah, I do."

He gave her hands one last squeeze, released them. "Good. I'll have an update in the morning. I promise." Then he left her standing in the cool evening, unsure of how to work through all her emotions, and all her fears.

IT WAS A lot of work. Not looking for Duke, and trying to undo all his brothers had already set in motion. Tucker couldn't very well have the entire Valiant County Sheriff's Department out searching for Duke. Even if North Star hid Duke or used him for whatever their plan was, having people sniffing around just wasn't going to be good.

Tucker scrubbed his hands over his face. Granger hadn't given him much to go on. Just that he had to make sure the Knights thought Duke was on vacation while they did the hard work.

When North Star had first approached Tucker, it had been through a lower operative. The woman had told him they had reason to believe Vince MacLean was gathering intel on the Wyatts, and to do whatever he could to find out who Vince was reporting to.

It had been a simple mission, straightforward and in Tuck's own best interest to help his family. And it had, in fact, helped his family a great deal as his following Vince had led him straight to Brady and Cecilia when they were in trouble.

Tucker locked up his office and headed for his car. He'd have liked to head back to the ranch, but it was two in the morning and he needed to catch a few hours of sleep.

He didn't know how he was going to face Rachel. He hadn't lied to her. He *would* do everything he could to bring Duke safely home. Tucker just didn't know how much of a say he had in things. But the one thing he *did* know? That he was never going to convince her Duke had taken a vacation of his own accord.

He headed for his car. The night was dark, the station mostly deserted. Still, the feeling of being watched had him slowly, carefully resting his hand on the butt of his weapon strapped to his belt.

"No need, Wyatt."

He didn't recognize the female's voice, but when she materialized out of the dark, he recognized her as the woman who'd originally contacted him about North Star.

"What now?" he muttered. Instead of stopping, he kept moving for his car. He wasn't too keen on being accommodating to the North Star crew right now, considering they were making his life unduly complicated. He kept one hand on his gun for good measure.

"There's chatter. Some people know Duke's missing."

"Yeah. Like his entire family? They're worried about him, because no one in their right mind is going to believe Duke Knight left South Dakota to go on *vacation*."

"Like the Sons. From what I've been able to gather, they think the Viannis got him. While they think that, there are certain parties who are going to be interested in friends of the Wyatts being unprotected, so to speak."

Tuck tossed his bag in the passenger side of his car. He was tired and irritable and this wasn't helping. "And who's fault would that be?"

"Look, I'm trying to be friendly here. I know enough about the setup from your brother. Someone needs to keep an eye on the Knight ranch. Just because the Viannis are focused on Duke, doesn't mean the Sons won't focus on a weakness in the Wyatts' armor if they can find one. Last I heard, the Knights are a weakness."

"I'm pretty sure I told your boss to be just as worried about Duke Knight's daughters as he was about Duke. He didn't seem too concerned."

"Yeah, because his concern is the mission."

"And what's your concern?"

She muttered something incomprehensible under her breath. "Watch their backs, huh?"

"Why don't you go talk to my brother about it?"

"Because your brother got kicked out, pal. You, on

the other hand, are in the thick of things. So, grow a pair." She melted back into the dark shadows before he could retort.

Which was for the best. No use taking his nasty mood out on someone who was trying to help.

Especially when she was right. Sarah and Rachel alone in the Knight house, even with Dev's dogs, just wasn't a good idea. He wouldn't be surprised to hear that Cecilia had decided to spend the night over there herself, and she was trained law enforcement.

She'd also been injured not that long ago, and Brady still wasn't on active duty due to his injuries. They'd saved an innocent child from being taken into the Sons, but they hadn't come out unscathed.

So, sending him over there to spend the night with Cecilia wasn't enough of a comfort. Dev would be helping out with ranching duties, but he'd been a cop for all of six months before he'd sustained serious injuries that left him with a limp.

Thanks to dear old Dad.

Jamison and Cody both lived in Bonesteel, and while he knew they'd all pitch in to help, it'd bring Cody's young daughter and Jamison's even younger sister-in-law into the fray and they deserved to be as far from danger as possible after what they'd endured when Ace Wyatt had come after them and their families. The only other option was Gage and Felicity, who both worked almost two hours away. Not to mention, Felicity was pregnant.

Which left him. He didn't mind that. He was happy to protect whomever needed protecting. It was the convincing the women involved they *needed* protecting that was going to be the headache. On top of the one he already had.

Tucker slid into his car. There was no going to his apartment now. Even if it was the middle of the night, he needed to head to the ranches. He had to figure out a way to convince Rachel and Sarah it was best if he stayed with them for a while.

As he drove through the thick of night, he considered just telling everyone the truth. What could the North Star Group do to him? He didn't owe them silence. And with the whole Wyatt clan in on things, wasn't it possible they could help take down the Viannis and the Sons themselves?

The list of reasons not to have his brothers spend the night at the Knight house went through his head. Because for all the same reasons, it didn't feel right to bring them into this. They'd built new lives, survived their own near-death injuries. And what had he done? All this time, all these months of danger and threats from Ace and the Sons, and he'd *investigated*. Between his brothers and their significant others, they'd all been tortured, shot, temporarily blinded and more.

Tucker had fought off a few Sons goons, but had mostly emerged unscathed.

So, no, he couldn't tell them. It was his turn to take on the danger, take on the Sons. His turn to protect his family, and the Knight girls.

Whether they wanted protecting or not.

Chapter Four

Rachel woke up from the nightmare in a cold sweat. The recurrence so soon after the last one made sense. She was stressed and worried. Of course, she'd have terrible dreams to go along with those terrible feelings.

But there'd been no mountain lion in this nightmare. She sat up and rubbed her eyes and then hugged herself against the chill.

The mountain lion had been a man. She could still visualize him. Blue eyes glowing, burn scars all over the side of one face. She could hear his voice in her head, rough and growly with an odd regional American accent she couldn't place.

She shuddered. It was a *dream*. Yeah, a creepy one that was still lodged in her head, but it was fiction. Dreams weren't real.

Though this one had felt particularly, scarily real.

She got out of bed even though it was still dark. She didn't bother to check the time. Too early. She'd just go downstairs and get a drink of water. Hopefully, it would help settle her.

She was safe. Maybe Dad wasn't, but she was. Here in this house, with Cecilia and Sarah down the hall. Though she felt a little guilty that Cecilia had insisted on spending the night since Brady had to stay at Grandma Pauline's due to his leg injury.

She wished she could say her and Sarah could handle it, but while they could manage anything around the ranch, they weren't trained law enforcement, and they didn't have any background or experience in fighting off bad guys.

Cecilia did. In fact, *everyone* else did. Rachel blew out a breath as she tiptoed downstairs. She stopped at the bottom, frowning at the odd sound. Like the scrape of a chair against the floor.

Her breath caught, pulse going wild as panic filled her. Someone was in the kitchen. Someone was—

"What are you doing up?"

Tucker's voice. Coming from the kitchen table. The *Knight* kitchen table. Long before sunrise.

"What are you doing here? It's…dark still."

"Honestly? I got a little tip that I shouldn't be letting you two be here alone. A friendly tip, but still. I thought it was better if I headed over here rather than stayed the night in my apartment."

"You didn't need to do that. Cecilia's here. We have our law enforcement contingent."

"Good." But he made no excuses to leave. Instead, they stood there, together in the dark.

"Which means you don't have to stay," she continued. She wasn't sure why she'd said that. It was a nice thing he was doing, and she should be thanking him. But she was braless in her pajamas and Tucker Wyatt was in her kitchen. She crossed her arms over her chest.

"Unfortunately, I don't agree."

She scowled in his general direction, whether he could see it or not. "A penis is not the protector of womankind, Tucker."

He sighed heavily. "I never said it was, but Cecilia is still recovering from her injuries. It's good she's here. She'll be able to notice and address a threat, but will she be able to neutralize it? No one heard me pick the lock, did they?"

"You picked the lock?" she screeched.

He immediately shushed her, which did not do anything to make her feel better about the situation. "It's just a precaution. Regardless of what's going on with Duke, the Sons know he's missing. We don't want them looking at you as easy pickings."

"Because I'm blind," she said flatly.

"Because we don't know where this threat is coming from, if it's coming. I don't think Sarah should be out in the fields alone, and I don't think you should be in this house alone. And before you lecture me about sexism, it isn't about your gender, it's about numbers. When there's danger, two is better than one."

"Then I can accompany Sarah out in the fields, and *you* aren't needed."

"What do you have against me, Rach?" His voice was soft. Not sad exactly, but there was a thread of…hurt in his voice. "I thought we were friends, but you seem to have something very specifically against *me* right now."

"I don't."

"You're sure acting like you do."

"I…" She felt like an absolute jerk, which wasn't fair. She wasn't acting like she had anything against Tucker. He was just…

She felt him approach and his hands rested on her shoulders. "I know it's a tough time. I'm not trying to make it tougher. I'm honestly just trying to help. Can you let me do that?"

There was no way to say no and maintain that she

was a reasonable human being, which she *was*. Plus, he was giving her shoulders a squeeze—a kind, reassuring gesture. He smelled like stale coffee and she wondered if he'd been up all night worrying over Duke and his girls.

It made her heart pinch. Here he was, doing all he could to find out what was going on with her father, and she was taking out her fear and anxiety on him. She sighed. "Of course I can," she said gently. "I'm not trying to be difficult. I'm just scared."

He gave her a light peck on the temple. It was something he'd always done. Tuck was the sweet Wyatt brother, if you could call any of them sweet. He had an easy affectionate streak, and he often comforted with a hug or a casual, friendly kiss.

But his hands lingered, even if his lips didn't. Rachel didn't know why she noticed…why she felt something odd skitter along her skin.

Then he cleared his throat, his hands dropping as he stepped away, and she didn't have to think about it any longer.

"I think it'd be best if I stay here," he reiterated. His voice had an odd note to it that disappeared as he continued to speak. "It'll help my investigation, and after the fire, we can't be too careful about threats that can get through Cody's safety measures. Everything I've found points to Duke leaving of his own accord."

Before Rachel could object to that, Tucker rolled right on.

"I'm not saying he left because he wanted to. I'm just saying he did it on his own two feet. No one dragged him away. Even if he didn't take a vacation like he's saying, there might be a reason. One that doesn't mean he's in immediate danger. It could be he's trying to protect you girls."

"You don't really think that."

"Actually, so far? It's exactly what I think. You don't have to agree with me, Rach. You just have to give me some space to stay here and keep an eye on things, and maybe go through Duke's room."

"And if I say no?"

"Well, I'll go through the rest of your sisters until someone agrees."

She huffed out an irritated breath. Of course he would, and one of her sisters would. But he could have barged in there and done it without any permission, so she would have to give him points for that. "I guess you could stay in his room, and if you poke around, it wouldn't be any of my business."

"Great," he said, sounding a mixture of pleased and relieved. "Hey, you should go back to bed. It's three in the morning."

"Yeah, I just came to get a glass of water."

"Here, I'll get it for you."

"I'm perfectly capable of getting my own water, Tucker."

"I know you are, but there's nothing wrong with letting someone who's closer to the glasses and the sink do something for you, Rach."

Rachel didn't know what to say to that, even when he handed her the glass of water. So she could only take it, and head back upstairs, with those words turning over in her head.

TUCK WAS NOT in a great mood. Usually when he felt this edgy, he kept himself far away from his family. He wouldn't take his temper out on anyone. Ace Wyatt might be his father, but he didn't have to be like the man. He got to choose who he was and how he treated people.

He was very afraid he wouldn't treat anyone very nicely in this mood, and quite unfortunately he had to deal with Wyatts and Knights all day long.

Tuck hated lying to his brothers. He didn't relish lying to the Knights, either, and last night with Rachel he'd felt like a jerk. She was afraid for Duke and Tucker knew he was fine, but couldn't tell her.

Then there was that odd reaction to touching her bare shoulders and inappropriately noticing that Rachel's pajamas were not exactly *modest*...

Nope. He wasn't thinking about that. Rachel was and always had been off-limits. Him and Brady had always felt like any attraction to a Knight girl was disrespectful to Duke. A good, upstanding man, great rancher, excellent, loving father, helpful and compassionate neighbor. Next to Jamison, Duke had been the Wyatt brothers' paragon of what a man should be.

Of course, Brady had broken that personal rule. Now here he was, in love with Cecilia. Planning a future together once they were healed.

Tucker shook his head. Brady might be the most strict rule follower Tucker knew, but that didn't mean Brady slipping up on one personal tenant meant Tucker would. Or could.

He focused on the fact Brady was coming up to the Knight house, which no doubt meant Tucker was in store for a lecture from his older brother.

"You look rough," Brady commented, limping toward the porch where Tucker was standing, trying to get his temper under control.

"Yeah, you, too," he replied, then immediately

winced. Brady had been shot in the leg just last month. He'd made great strides—this wound healing a lot quicker than his previous gunshot wound had.

Because Brady had been beaten to hell and back over the course of this dangerous summer, and what had Tucker done? Not a damn thing. "I updated Cody."

"I'm not here for an update." He took the stairs with the help of his cane. "I'm here to see Cecilia before she heads in to the rez."

"Shouldn't she be going to you?"

"Walking is part of my physical therapy, Tuck," Brady replied mildly, standing in front of him and putting all his weight on one leg. "What crawled up your butt?"

Tucker scraped his hands over his face. "Running on no sleep. Sorry. Dev's out with Sarah, but I've got to stick close for Rachel. Making me a little antsy."

"How are you going to stick around when you've got work?"

"I've got a call with the sheriff this morning about doing some remote work, and leaving field work to Bligh for the time being."

His brother frowned. "I can help out around here. Just because of the bum leg doesn't mean I can't be of some use."

Tucker could easily read Brady's frustration with being out of commission. He couldn't imagine the feelings of futility, especially since Brady had been dealing with months of healing, not just weeks. "A lot of it's just research and following leads from the computer. Once I've got a decent thread to tug on, I'll share it with you." Which ignored the fact his brother could help with the watching out around the ranch, but Tuck didn't want to go there.

Brady nodded, then studied him a little too closely for Tuck's comfort. "I'm trusting you, Tuck." He nodded toward the house. "I always have. It hasn't changed."

Tucker shoved his hands in his pockets. He knew Brady was referencing last month when Tucker had called in backup to get Brady and Cecilia out of a dangerous situation. There'd been some aspects of that rescue mission that Tucker had had to lie about to keep his involvement with North Star a secret, and he knew Cecilia hadn't trusted him at all. But when push had come to shove, Brady had. It meant a lot. "Well, good. You should."

"I haven't said anything, and I won't. But maybe you could talk to Cody..."

Tucker couldn't let him finish his sentence, since he had a feeling it was about North Star. "This is my thing, Brady. Let it go."

Brady opened his mouth to say something, but the door behind them swung open.

"I thought I heard you." Cecilia came out in her tribal police uniform, smiling at Brady. She crossed to Brady first, gave him a kiss.

Tucker looked away from the easy affection. It wasn't that it bothered him. His brothers deserved that kind of good in their lives, and if they were happy, Tuck didn't have any problem with their choice of significant other.

He just didn't really want to...*watch* it. It caused some uncomfortable itch. At first when Jamison and Cody had hooked up with their ex-girlfriends, both Knight fosters, he hadn't felt it. But something about Gage and Brady falling for Felicity and Cecilia respectively made things...weird.

Rachel stepped out onto the porch, and Tucker's gut tightened with discomfort. Something he *refused* to acknowledge when it came to Duke's daughter who was a good eight years younger than him.

"Who all needs breakfast? I'm making omelets."

"I got fifteen minutes before I need to head out," Cecilia said. She patted Brady's stomach. "Don't tell me you actually snuck away from Grandma Pauline without getting stuffed full of breakfast."

"Mak was doing his crawling demonstration. Grandma was distracted, so I made a run for it." He had his arm casually wrapped around Cecilia's waist. An easy unit where one hadn't been before. They'd helped Cecilia's friend keep her infant son, Mak, safe, and now both lived at Grandma Pauline's, as well.

"All right. Tucker, since you're our sudden houseguest, you can come help me with setting the table." Rachel smiled sunnily, then turned back into the house.

Cecilia and Brady's gazes were on him, a steady, disapproving unit.

"Whatever is going on, she needs to stay far, far away from it," Cecilia said solemnly. "I'll give you the space to handle it, Tuck, because it seems that whatever's going on needs that, but I'm holding you personally responsible if anything happens to Rachel."

"She's not so helpless as all that," Tucker replied, trying not to let his discomfort, or the weight of those words, show.

"You know what I mean, whether you admit you do or not. Now you better get in there and help out."

Tucker had a few things to say in response, but he'd get nowhere against these two hardheads. Better to just save his breath. He had enough of a fight ahead of him—he'd just avoid the ones that were pointless.

He stepped into the kitchen as Rachel sprinkled a ham, cheese and pepper mixture into a pan.

"Let me guess, Cecilia was saying how you need to watch out for me or she's going to leave you in the middle of the Badlands chained to a rock with no water."

Tucker couldn't help but smile—at both the colorful specificity and how well she understood Cecilia. "It was a little less violent than all that, but the general gist."

"I don't need to be babied."

"Believe it or not, that's what I told her."

Rachel made a considering sound and said nothing else, so Tucker set out plates and silverware. He couldn't understand why she was cooking for everyone. "Why do you go to all this trouble?"

"It isn't any trouble to make breakfast."

"You and Grandma Pauline. Cereal isn't good enough. A frozen pizza is an affront. I happen to subsist just fine off of both when I'm at my apartment."

"That's because you have us to come home to."

Come home to. He didn't know why those words struck him as poignant. Of course, Grandma Pauline's was home. It was the place he'd grown up after escaping the Sons. It was the first place he'd been safe and loved.

"I guess you're right."

"Grandma Pauline taught me that you can't solve anyone's problems, but you can make them comfortable while they solve their own."

"What about when *you* have problems?"

She paused, then expertly flipped an omelet onto a plate next to her. "We aren't the ones out fighting the bad guys," Rachel said, and he could tell she was picking her words carefully.

"That doesn't mean you're without problems."

She inhaled sharply, working on the next omelet with ease and skill, but she didn't say anything to that.

Like Grandma Pauline, she was so often at the stove

it seemed a part of her. Yet she'd been blinded at the age of three, lost her mother at the age of seven. Maybe she hadn't survived a ruthless biker gang like he had, but she had been scarred. Now he had to stay under the same roof as her and *lie*.

Not just to protect her, though. He was also protecting Duke, and the life he'd built. As long as North Star brought him back in one piece, did the lies matter?

Still, he stood frozen, watching her finish up the omelets, as Cecilia and Brady strolled in, still with their arms around each other. A few moments later, Sarah and Dev came in from the fields, bickering with the dogs weaving between them.

The North Star worked in secrets, in following the mission regardless of feelings, and he'd made a promise when he'd signed on with them. He wouldn't break it.

But it was a promise to be here, to be part of these families, too. He couldn't break that, either.

So he had to find a compromise.

Chapter Five

Conversation around the breakfast table flowed the way it always did when Wyatts and Knights got together. Rapid-fire subject changes, people talking over each other, Sarah and Dev constantly disagreeing with each other.

They avoided the topic of Duke, though it hung over them like a black cloud. Still, Rachel appreciated how hard they all tried to make it seem as though this were normal. In a way it was. They'd eaten hundreds of meals together over the years. Usually not in her kitchen, though.

"You going to eat that, Tuck?" Sarah asked through a mouthful of omelet.

Rachel frowned. Why wouldn't Tucker be eating? "I can make you a different kind if you'd like."

"No, it's fine."

She heard the scrape of fork on plate and was sure Tucker had just taken a large bite. He needed to eat. He hadn't slept, that much she'd known when she'd woken up and there'd been coffee before Sarah had even come down.

"I'm just thinking," he continued. "Something about this whole Duke thing doesn't...match."

Whatever chatter had been going on around the table

faded into silence at the mention of her father. Rachel's appetite disappeared and she set down her fork.

"Duke left of his own accord," Tucker continued. "Maybe he's being blackmailed in some way, but he left on his own two feet. With everything that's happened this summer, I'd assume it has to do with the Sons, but there's no evidence that it does."

"What else could it have to do with?" Cecilia demanded.

"That's what doesn't jive. Maybe there's something in Duke's background we're missing."

Dad's *background*. "Just what exactly are you suggesting about my father?"

"Nothing bad, Rach. Just that there's more to the story than we've got."

"I don't see how we can rule out the Sons," Cecilia returned. "Not when four of Duke's foster daughters are hooked up with four of Ace's sons."

"I'm not saying rule it out. You can never rule out the Sons. I'm saying, look beyond them, too. Look at *Duke*. Not just where he's gone, but why. He wasn't taken. His house wasn't set on fire. This is different than the times the Knights have been caught in the crossfire of the Sons."

Rachel heard the voice from her nightmare echo in her head. Silly. It was just a dream, and it had nothing to do with what Tucker was talking about.

"What could Duke be hiding? We've been underfoot forever," Sarah said. "Wouldn't we know if he had some deep dark secret?"

Secrets always hurt the innocent.

Rachel squeezed her eyes shut, trying to push the dream out of her head. It had no bearing on the actual real conversation in front of her. That voice was made up, born of stress and worry and an overactive imagination.

She stood and pushed away from the table, abruptly taking her plate to the sink.

"Rach—" But Cecilia was cut off by someone's phone going off.

Cecilia muttered a curse. "I have to get to work."

There was the scraping of chairs, Dev and Sarah arguing over what work they had to get back to, Brady offering thanks for the breakfast as he left with Cecilia. The voices faded away, punctuated by the squeak and slap of the screen door.

And though he didn't make any noise, Rachel knew Tucker was still there. Likely watching her as she cleaned up the breakfast mess.

"Do you have something to say?" she demanded irritably, which wasn't like her. Nothing about the past week or so felt like *her*. She wanted to yell and rage and punch somebody and make her life go back to the way it was.

Weren't you just complaining about your life staying forever the same?

Rachel stopped washing the pan she'd used to cook the omelets and let out a pained breath. She'd wanted change, yes, but on her terms. Not the kind of change that put her father in danger.

"Did something I say upset you?" Tucker asked carefully. Like she was fragile and needed careful tiptoeing around.

"Do you assume everything is about you? That's pretty self-centered of you."

He was quiet for a long time, then she could hear him stacking dishes and placing them next to her so she could finish loading the dishwasher.

"It's just a theory, that this has something to do with Duke and not the Sons. It's not the only theory. I'm just struggling to find any evidence that ties to the Sons."

"I'm sure that struggle has nothing to do with how little you want to tie your father's gang to my father's disappearance."

"Don't be a child, Rachel," he snapped, with enough force to make her jolt. And to feel shamed.

"I wasn't—"

"I'm more aware of everything my father has done than you'll ever know. He's also in maximum-security prison because my brothers put their lives on the line to make it so. And so did some of your sisters. Let's not pretend I'm under any delusion that I could ever erase the effect my father has had on your family, through no fault of your family's."

The shame dug deeper, infusing her face with heat. "I'm sorry. I didn't mean—"

"You meant to slap at me, and I get it. You want to take out your fear and your frustration on me and I'm usually a pretty good target. But not today. So back off."

Fully chastened, Rachel reached out. She found his arm and gave it a squeeze. "I am sorry."

She could hear him sigh as he patted her hand. "I am, too. I didn't sleep worth a darn, and I'm not handling it well."

Silence settled over them, her fingers still wrapped around his arm, his big hand resting over hers. It was warm and rough. Despite being a detective, Tucker helped out at the ranch as much as he could, which was probably where he'd gotten the callouses. The big hands were just a family trait. All the Wyatts were big. She was a tall woman, but Tucker's hands still dwarfed hers. If she flipped her hand over, so they were palm to palm—

Why was she thinking about that? She pulled her hand away from under his, and only the fact she was at the sink kept her from backing away. She had dishes to finish, so she turned back to them, ignoring the way her body was all…jittery all of a sudden.

"My theory about Duke seemed to upset you," he said, in a tone she would have considered his detective voice. Deceivingly casual as he tried to get deeper information on a topic. "Do you know something about what's going on? About Duke's past?"

She laughed, with a bitterness she couldn't seem to shove away. "No, I don't know anything."

"You're acting like you do."

She blew out a breath. Mr. Detective wasn't letting it go, so she had to be honest with him even if it was embarrassing. "I had one of those nightmares last night that felt real. I can't seem to shake it."

"Why don't you tell it to me?"

She shook her head. How embarrassing to lay out her silly, childish dreams for him to hear. He'd tell her they were natural. She'd had a traumatic experience as a young child and her brain was still dealing with it and blah, blah, blah.

"Grandma Pauline always said if you explain your nightmare, it takes away its power."

She couldn't help but smile at that. Grandma Pauline had something to say about everything, and wasn't that a comfort? "Did that work?"

He was quiet for a minute. "With the things that weren't real."

The word *real* lodged in her chest like a pickax. Sharp. Painful. Both because Tuck probably had plenty of real nightmares after almost eight years raised in a terrible biker gang, and because hers wasn't real. No matter how much it felt that way. "It wasn't real," she insisted.

"Then lay it on me."

Tucker had never seen Rachel quite so…wound up. He understood this situation was stressful, but they'd been in stressful situations all summer, and she'd kept her cool.

Did she know something? Was the dream some kind of distraction? Something wasn't adding up.

He'd brought up Duke's past because it was a possible answer. If Brady or Cecilia stumbled upon those facts on their own, without him telling them specifically what, then he wouldn't have betrayed his promise to North Star.

They probably wouldn't see it that way, but the more he felt the need to comfort Rachel as she came slowly unraveled, the less he cared about North Star's approval.

They'd put him in an impossible situation. All because he wanted to do what was right. Well, getting some of his own answers was right.

Rachel hesitated as she did the dishes. Finally, she shrugged. "It's silly. I just… I've always had nightmares about the night I was attacked by that mountain lion."

"That makes sense."

"It does. Usually they're few and far between. Especially as I've grown up. But something about the last few weeks has made them an almost nightly occurrence, and they're morphing from memory into fiction. But the fiction feels more real than the memory." She frowned, eyebrows drawing together and a line appearing across her forehead.

She really was beautiful in her own right. Much as she could remind him of Eva, the older she got, the more she was just… Rachel. He knew her sisters sometimes saw her as the baby of the family, the sweet girl with no grit, but that was her power. A softer Grandma Pauline, she held everyone together. Not with a wooden spoon, but with her calm, caring demeanor.

And *why* was he thinking about that? He should be thinking about what she was saying. "Well, what's different? Between the real dream and the fiction dream?"

She took a deep breath and let it out slowly. She looked so troubled that he wanted to reach out and hold her hand. He curled his fingers into his palm instead. Touching seemed…dangerous lately.

"Instead of a mountain lion, there's a man. He has blue eyes, and half his face is scarred. Not like mine. Not lines, but all over. Like a burn, sort of. He's carrying me. We're…" Her eyebrows drew together again, like she was struggling to remember. "It was the hills in one of the pastures. I don't know which one, but that's where the mountain lion attack happened. Outside one of the pastures."

"Do you remember if that's where the mountain lion attack happened or is that just what you've been told?"

She stopped rinsing a plate. "What does it matter?"

"For the purpose of your dream. Is that part real—what you actually remember when you're awake. Or is it what you've been told so that's what your subconscious shows you?"

"I… I guess I'm not sure." She put the plate in the dishwasher then turned to him.

He'd hoped getting it off her chest would ease her mind some, but she seemed just as twisted up. Like the more she talked about it, the more it didn't add up.

"Mom and Dad didn't like to talk about it, but I remember sometimes they'd mention something and it didn't...match with what I thought had happened. But I was only three. Their memory would be more accurate."

"Okay, so in your dream the mountain lion usually takes you somewhere?"

"No. I'm already there. He jumps out of nowhere. I see the glint of something sharp and then I wake up before it swipes at me. But...the dream last night was more involved. I was being carried away. The man's talking. And the thing glinting in the moonlight isn't claws. It's some kind of knife."

She whirled away abruptly. "It's a *nightmare*, Tuck. It's happening when I'm asleep. It's nothing and I'm tired of it making me feel so unsettled."

He watched her agitated pacing, decided to hold his tongue and let her get it out. Maybe she needed a full-on breakdown to be able to find that center of calm that was so inherent to her.

"But I can't get that *fictional* man's voice out of my head. The way he talks. There's an accent. Like New York or Boston. Why is that so clear to me? What can't I shake this stupid dream?"

She raked her fingers through her hair, and Tucker desperately wanted to offer her some soothing words and a hug, but over the past day any physical offers of comfort had gone a little weird. He needed to keep his hands to himself.

"Secrets always hurt the innocent." She dropped her hands, wrapping them around her body instead. "I keep hearing this voice say that. *Secrets always hurt the innocent. Curtis Washington is going to learn that the hard way.*"

Tucker's entire body went cold. He didn't know that

name, but having a specific name, a specific voice in her dreams...

Dread skittered up his spine.

"Who's Curtis Washington?"

"I don't know. I've never heard that name before. It's just in my head."

Tucker had to work to keep his breathing even. To maintain control and a neutral expression rather than let all his theories run away from him in a jumble of worry.

She gestured toward him. "Say something."

He had to be careful about his words. About how he approached this horrible possibility. "Mountain lions aren't particularly aggressive."

"No, but I was three. Who knew what I was doing."

"You were three. Why were you so far from your parents? Duke and Eva weren't exactly hands-off parents."

"They...they didn't like to talk about it. I probably wandered off. Accidentally. Not because they weren't paying attention. You know how toddlers are. It's possible... It just happened."

She didn't seem so sure.

"This voice...this man..."

"It's stupid. All my life the dream has been a mountain lion. The man is a recent change, Tuck. It's a new morph on the old nightmare. If something else happened that night, why would I only dream about it now?"

Because Duke was in trouble, in danger. And this was his WITSEC life. Which meant he had another name.

Could it be the name in Rachel's dream?

Chapter Six

Tucker made himself scarce after Rachel had told him her dream. She could hardly blame him. Why was she coming so unglued over a nightmare? It made no sense, and if it was irritating to her—she could only imagine how annoying it was to the people around her.

She wouldn't bring it up ever again. Not to Tucker, not to anyone. Her dreams were her problem.

She went through the rest of the day without seeing him, though she knew he was there. Then he popped in for dinner, chatting cheerfully though she could tell he was distracted. He helped clean up after dinner, then he disappeared into Dad's room.

Door shut.

She had to admit, she didn't feel babysat, even though that's why he was here. Still, it helped that he wasn't hovering. Which meant she had the space inside herself to recognize Sarah's irritation simmering off her in its usual fraught waves.

Rachel had never been to the ocean, but she always associated Sarah's moods with the slapping waves and whipping winds of a hurricane.

While Sarah's moods were often operatic in nature, Rachel couldn't blame her right now. She was carrying the entire ranch on her shoulders, even with Dev's help.

"How about an ice-cream sundae?"

"I'm not a child, Rach," Sarah replied grumpily. But Rachel heard her plop herself at the kitchen table.

Rachel got out all the fixings for a sundae. Her conversation with Tucker from breakfast repeated in her mind.

Grandma Pauline taught me that you can't solve anyone's problems, but you can make them comfortable while they solve their own.

What about when you have problems?

She supposed her comfort was making other people food, and she supposed she'd gotten that from Grandma Pauline. She'd never fully realized how much she'd adopted the older woman's response to stress or fear, or wondered why before.

It wasn't hard to put together, though. Grandma Pauline was the last word around here. You didn't cross her, but everyone loved and respected her. They spoke about Grandma Pauline with reverence or loving humor.

"What do you think about what Tucker said?" Sarah asked.

Rachel blinked, remembering she was supposed to be making a sundae. Heck, she'd make one for herself, too. "Which part?"

"This being more about Dad than the Sons?"

Rachel scooped the ice cream, poured on chocolate syrup and sprayed on some whipped cream. She set one bowl in front of Sarah, then took her seat at the table with her own bowl.

They were the two youngest Knight girls, often sheltered from danger. Not just because they were the youngest or because Rachel was blind, but because they hadn't come from the dire circumstances their sisters had. Rachel had been born happy and healthy to Duke and Eva, their miracle baby. Sarah had been adopted at birth, so Sarah didn't remember or know anything about her birth parents.

Neither Rachel nor Sarah had ever left home. No tribal police or park ranger jobs for them. Rachel's part-time job as an art teacher was a challenge, and Sarah being a rancher was definitely hard work, but they were home. Still sheltered from so much of the *bad* in the world.

So, if Rachel could be honest with anyone, it was Sarah, because more than everyone else they were especially in this together. "I really don't know what to think of it."

"He's a detective," Sarah said.

"It doesn't make him infallible."

"No, but it gives him some experience in putting clues together. He also knows the Sons, and much as I hate to agree with Dev, he's right. The Sons have left Duke alone for all this time." Her sister released a breath. "So why would they start poking at him now? Especially with Ace in jail. Ace is the one with the vendetta against the Wyatts, not the Sons in general."

"I don't imagine they feel kindly toward the boys who escaped, or the men who put their leader in jail."

"Maybe not. I'm not saying it can't possibly be the Sons. God knows almost all our problems this summer have come from that corner of the scummy world. But... Dad never talks about his parents."

Rachel frowned at that. Surely that wasn't true. But no, she couldn't remember any stories about Dad's parents.

"It never really dawned on me that it was weird since we had Grandma and Grandpa Mills. And I always *assumed* this ranch was passed down, Knight to Knight, because Dad's so proud of it, but...wouldn't there be stories? Heirlooms?"

"What are you trying to say?" Rachel demanded, panic clutching at her.

"We don't actually know anything about Dad, and we never asked. As far as stories I've heard, and just being around Dad, his life started when he met Mom. And that can't be true."

Rachel couldn't eat another bite of ice cream. What was there curdled in her stomach. Sarah was right. She couldn't think of a thing Dad had ever told her about his life before he'd met her mother.

"So, you think he's running from something in his past?"

"Or running *to* something in his past."

Rachel thought of the gun under his pillow. About Dad not wanting her teaching. "He didn't want me to teach this session. He blamed it on the trouble with the Wyatts, but I taught all summer through all that danger."

"So, he was afraid. Something was *making* him afraid. I can't imagine Dad leaving us if he thought we were in danger. Unless..."

"Unless what?" Rachel demanded.

"What if he did something wrong? What if there isn't danger so much as... I mean, he could have run away from something bad."

"Dad would never. He wouldn't... No, I don't believe that."

"He wouldn't have left us in danger, Rachel. So one of these things he would never do *has* to be what he's done."

What a horrible, horrible thought. Maybe it was true, and maybe she was naive, but she refused to believe it of the father she loved. This man who had been a shining example of goodness and hard-working truth. "What if he thought only he was in danger? Just like Cecilia and Brady when they were trying to save Mak. They thought staying here would bring trouble to our doorstep, so they took off trying to draw the danger with them."

Sarah didn't respond to that. They sat in silence for ticking minutes.

"We have to tell Tucker he was right," her sister finally said. "That we don't know anything about his life before Mom. The answer is somewhere in there, and Tuck can find it. He's a detective. He has to be able to find it."

Rachel wasn't so sure. If her father had kept this secret for over thirty years, maybe no one could find it.

"Rach." Sarah's hand grasped hers across the table. "We have to help in whatever way we can. We're always swept off to the sidelines. But who put out that fire last month? We did. Who always holds down the fort? Us. And we're damn good at it. But Dad's gone. He can't protect us like he's always trying to do. Whether he's running away or hiding or *whatever*, it's just us. We have to step up to the plate."

Rachel knew Sarah was right, and she didn't understand the bone-deep reticence inside of her. It felt like they were stirring up trouble that would change *everything*, and she didn't want everything to change. Maybe she'd wanted a *little* change, but not her whole world.

"I can talk to Tucker myself. If you don't want to—"

"No...you're right. It's just us. We have to work together. It's the only way to make sure Dad's safe."

"He's a tough old bird," Sarah said firmly, and Rachel knew she was comforting herself as much as trying to comfort Rachel.

"He is. And we'll bring him home."

TUCKER CALLED EVERY North Star number he had in his arsenal over the course of the day, and no one would answer. He was too annoyed to be worried that was a bad sign. He needed to know if Curtis Washington was Duke's real name.

It would change things. For North Star, too. He barked out another irritable message into Granger's voice mail, then threw his phone on the bed in disgust.

He'd searched Duke's room, too. No hints to a secret past. There'd been plenty of guns secreted throughout the room, which led Tucker to believe Duke was a man who'd known his past would catch up with him eventually.

No. He'd fostered five girls, raised one daughter of his own. Duke had been certain he'd left that old life behind. Something must have recently happened to lead him to believe he was in danger.

And it tied to the Sons. It shouldn't make Tucker feel guilty. Just because he'd been born into the Sons didn't make him part of them. His life had nothing to do with Duke's secret past.

But the guilt settled inside of him anyway. Luckily, a knock sounded at the door and he could pretend he didn't feel it.

"Come in," he offered.

Sarah poked her head in. "Hey, can we talk to you in the kitchen for a second?"

"Uh, sure."

He followed her out of the room and down the hall. Rachel was already in the kitchen, washing out some bowls. He wondered if she ever stepped away from that constant need to cook and clean for everyone. He wondered if anyone offered a hand, and doubted it very much. He knew from experience how little kitchen work held appeal after a long day ranching.

Maybe that explained it. This was her way of helping her family, the ranch. It was how she felt useful.

When she heard them enter, she turned and smiled. "Did you want some dessert?"

"No, thanks. What did you want to talk about?"

Rachel took a seat at the table, but Sarah paced, wringing her hands together. "We were thinking about what you said. About Duke's life, and the truth is…" She looked at Rachel, so Tucker did, too.

Her expression was carefully blank, calm, which told him all he needed to know. Inside, she was anything but.

"We don't know anything about his life before he married Mom," Sarah continued. "He never talked about parents or siblings. Where he was born or if this ranch was passed on. We just…assumed. And we had so much family, and everything with losing Mom, and Liza and Nina disappearing and… Well, you know. It just didn't come up. Until now."

Liza's stay with the Knights had been brief, but her returning to the Sons had hurt all of the Knights, and Jamison. Liza and Jamison had since patched things up after saving Liza's half sister, but it had taken a long time.

Nina's disappearing had been the only time in Tucker's life where he thought Duke might actually cut all ties with the Wyatts. He'd personally blamed Tucker's youngest brother Cody, Nina's boyfriend at the time. It had taken a long time for Duke to get past it. When Nina had returned—injured and with her daughter in tow—Tucker had been sure Duke would be furious all over again, but the reconciliation of Cody and Nina had soothed some of his anger.

Some.

There was the guilt again, darker this time. Tucker *knew* Duke had a secret life. He'd put the idea in their heads. Now he was going to lie to them as if he didn't know what it was.

Where does your loyalty lie? North Star or your friends?

Two very different women stared at him. Rachel, dark hair, eyes and skin. Tall and slender. Sarah, petite, curvy, with baby blues and flyaway blond hair.

He wanted to tell them the truth. He couldn't think of a good reason not to, except Granger had told him not to. Duke hadn't argued with it. There might be a very good reason Sarah and Rachel should be kept in the dark.

What might they do if they knew the truth?

"I'm...looking into it. His past, that is. Best I can. To see if it connects to anything that's going on." He did his best not to cringe, not to show how utterly slimy he felt for the flat-out lies. "I haven't gotten very far because I don't have a lot to go on. I don't suppose you have any ideas?"

Sarah shook her head sadly. "That's just it. Who *never* talks about their parents? Or where they're from. Dad's got to be from South Dakota. How else would he end up with all this?"

Tucker really hated that he knew the answer to that question. He forced himself to smile reassuringly. "I'll keep digging. I—"

He was interrupted by his phone going off. It wasn't his regular ringtone. He frowned at the screen. It must be a North Star number. "I have to take this," he said, pushing away from the table.

Both women looked at him with frowns, but he lifted

the phone to his ear and stepped out of the kitchen. "Wy—"

Granger was barking out questions before Tucker even got his last name out of his mouth. "Where'd you get that name?"

Tucker felt shattered, and he didn't even fully understand why. He looked back at the kitchen. No one had followed, but he still slid into Duke's room and closed the door. "So, it's true. That's his real name."

Why was Rachel dreaming about Duke's real name? A man instead of a mountain lion?

"I asked where you got the name, Wyatt."

Tucker hesitated. He had the sinking suspicion if he mentioned it was in Rachel's dream, she'd be dragged into this. Maybe North Star would keep her safe. Maybe they even needed to know that she knew something. But…

He couldn't bring himself to utter her name. It felt wrong, and beyond that, he doubted very much Duke wanted his daughter dragged into this even if she did know something.

And his loyalty *was* to his friends over the North Star Group. Even if they were doing something good in trying to take down the Sons, and that *was* important. But so was safeguarding Rachel.

So, he lied instead. "I did some research on dirty cops in Chicago. You did give me enough information to go on to make an educated guess."

"Wyatt. Your job is to keep your families from getting suspicious while we handle the real threat. I don't need any misdirected people wading into this. Keep your side out of it. No more digging. Do you understand me?"

Tucker wanted to say *or what*, but he had a feeling

Granger McMillan was dangerous enough to make *or what* hurt. "All right, but it seems to me it'd be more helpful if I knew the whole story."

"I don't need your help. I need you to keep your families out of it. That's it. If you can't do that, I'll bring in someone who can, and you will be dealt with accordingly."

Tucker opened his mouth to tell Granger to jump off a cliff, but the line went dead.

Probably for the best. He let out a long breath.

Rachel knew her father's real name without knowing that's what it was. Which meant, she'd had *some* encounter with *someone* who'd been a part of Duke's previous life.

If that someone was still out there, if that someone was behind this connection to the Sons, it meant Rachel was as much of a target as Duke.

Chapter Seven

Rachel didn't have the dream. She woke up feeling rested for the first time in days. It might have put her in a good mood, but as long as her father was missing, there was no real good mood to have.

Tucker had promised to look into Duke's past, but she had to wonder if it wouldn't end up being…catastrophic somehow. She didn't want to believe her father was involved in something bad, but how could she ignore facts?

He'd left of his own accord, sort of. She still believed he'd been forced to leave, but he hadn't been carted off or held at gunpoint. His little disappearing act and fake vacation *had* to be born out of threats, or something like that.

Rachel got dressed, trying to remind herself there wasn't anything she could do about it. She had to trust Tucker and the Wyatts to look into her father's disappearance. And Cecilia. Cecilia wouldn't sit idly by. None of her sisters would. Sarah would ranch, Nina and Liza were busy with their children but would probably help Cody and Jamison in whatever ways they could. Felicity should be concentrating on growing her baby, but she would likely discuss with Gage what was going on.

And Rachel would be left to cook and clean. She tried not to be disgusted with herself. After all, if it was good enough for Grandma Pauline, it was good enough for her.

But Grandma Pauline was eighty. Rachel also had no doubt she'd pick up that big rifle she kept hidden in the pantry and take care of whatever intruders might deign to invade her ranch.

What could Rachel do? Scream?

No. That really wasn't good enough. She needed to learn some basics about getting away or fighting back.

She'd insist Tucker teach her. If he had to be underfoot, the least he could do was be useful. She headed downstairs and to her normal routine of making breakfast, but she stopped short at the entrance to the kitchen.

Tucker was in her kitchen. She couldn't tell what he was doing, but she could make out his outline. She could hear the sounds of…cooking.

"What are you doing?" she demanded, maybe a little too accusatorially to be fair.

"Thought I could take breakfast duty since I'm staying here," he replied, continuing to move around *her* kitchen as if she were just some sort of…bystander.

"But… I always make breakfast."

"Don't tell me you've completely morphed into Grandma Pauline and can't stand someone else carrying some weight?"

"That isn't…" She had to trail off because it was silly to be upset someone had beaten her to breakfast. She'd been complaining for years that Duke and Sarah never even tried to figure out their way around the kitchen.

She should be grateful someone was lending a hand, even if it was Tucker. But mostly she felt incredibly superfluous and useless. "I guess I'll—"

"Have a seat. It's almost ready. I don't want you picking up after me. I can do my own laundry, keep Duke's room tidy and all that. I'm not your houseguest, so you don't need to treat me like one. I'm here to help. That's all."

"Being here to help does technically make you a guest," Rachel muttered irritably.

"Well, this guest can take care of himself." As if to prove it, he slid a plate in front of her. "All I did was bake some of Grandma's cinnamon rolls you had in the freezer and cut up a melon. Hardly putting myself out."

"But what if your coffee sucks?" she asked, trying to make light of how small that made her feel. When did she get so pathetic that she needed to make a meal to feel worthy of her spot here?

He slid the mug in front of her. "It doesn't. And, I already doctored it. You're welcome."

The coffee didn't suck. She might have made it a little stronger for Sarah, but he had indeed put in cream and sugar just how she liked it. She wanted to make a joke about keeping him around, but it sat uncomfortably on her chest so she couldn't form the words.

It was a little too easy to picture. She knew it would be…difficult to find a significant other. Not so much because of her scarring and lack of sight, but because she just didn't get around much and lived in a rural area. But she'd always had that little dream of a husband and kids in this kitchen.

To even picture Tucker filling that role was *embarrassing*. So she shoved a bite of cinnamon roll in her mouth instead. Even after being frozen, Grandma Pauline's cinnamon rolls were like a dream.

"You know, Sarah and Duke would mess up even reheating frozen rolls," she offered, trying to think of anything else than what was currently occupying her brain.

He took the seat next to her, presumably with his own plate of food and mug of coffee. "If that's what you want to tell yourself, Rach, but I don't think you give them much space to figure out how."

She frowned at that.

"I'm sorry," he said. "I wasn't trying to be a jerk. Maybe you're right and they can't."

But she could tell he didn't think so, and worse she knew he was right. She complained about how little they did, while never ever giving them even an inch to do it for themselves.

She ate her feelings via one too many cinnamon rolls, then started on the fruit. She could wallow in…well, everything, or she could do something. She could act. She could *change*.

"Tuck, I want you to teach me how to fight."

"Huh?"

"I can't shoot. But I could fight." She pushed the plate away, ignoring the last few bites of melon. "I want to be able to defend myself. Maybe nothing bad happens here, but I want to be ready if it does."

"Rach, you don't have to worry about that. We're all—"

"Tucker." She reached across the table, found his arm. She needed that connection to make sure he understood this was more than just…a suggestion. She needed it. Needed to feel like she could contribute or at least not make a situation worse. "I could fight. I want to be able to fight." She gave his arm a squeeze.

He hesitated, but he didn't immediately shoot her down again. "I'm sure Cecilia—"

"Isn't here. You are. Didn't you teach some self-defense class at the Y for a while?"

She could hear him shift in his chair, a sense of embarrassment almost. "Well, yeah, but—"

"But what? What's different about that and this?"

After a long beat of silence, he finally spoke. "I guess there really isn't one."

"Exactly. So, you'll do it." She didn't phrase it as a question, because she wasn't taking no for an answer.

"I guess I could teach you and Sarah a few things." He didn't sound enthused about it, but she'd take agreement with or without excitement.

Rachel heard Sarah stepping into the kitchen, and then her small bright form entered Rachel's blurry vision.

"What things are you teaching me?"

"Self-defense. Rachel wants to learn how to fight."

Rachel noted that, while he didn't sound sure of teaching her anything, he didn't seem dismissive or disapproving. Maybe he didn't like teaching was all.

Well, he'd have to suck it up.

"Good idea," Sarah said around a mouthful of food. "But I can shoot a gun. And kick your butt, if I had to."

"Kick *my* butt?" Tucker replied incredulously. "You're five foot nothing. If that."

"I also wrestle stubborner cows than you, Wyatt. I could take you down right here, right now."

"All right." There was the scrape of the chair against the floor. "You're on."

"Oh, you don't want to mess with me."

Rachel could see the outlines of them circling each other. "You aren't really going to…"

There was the sound of a grunt, a thud and then laughter. It was a nice sound. Comforting. Like having her family home. Except Dad wasn't here, and they were pretending to fight.

"All right. Sarah gets a pass," Tucker conceded. "Though I maintain you did not kick my butt."

"Whatever you gotta tell yourself, Tuck," Sarah replied cheerfully. "Dev's truck is already out there." The cheer died out of her voice. "I could wring his neck. I told him to wait for me. Leave me a cinnamon roll to heat up," she called, already halfway out the door.

The door slammed.

"Did you let her win?" Rachel asked.

"It wasn't about winning. I just wanted to see what she's got. Good instincts and a nice jab. She's scrappy and mean, which is good in a real fight. Besides, she's right. She can shoot."

"Are you saying I'm not scrappy and mean?"

Tucker laughed. "I wasn't saying that, but we both know you're not. Which is why I'll teach you a few self-defense moves, if it'll make you feel better."

"It will. When do we start?"

AUTUMN IN SOUTH DAKOTA meant anything could happen. A nice sunny day. A sudden blizzard. Today was a pleasant morning, thank God. The yard in front of the Knight house would be as good a place as any to teach Rachel a few moves.

Rachel had changed from jeans and a T-shirt to something…he couldn't think too much about. It was all stretchy and formfitting, so he kept his gaze firmly on the world around him and not on her.

"Shouldn't we have padding or something? I don't want to hurt you."

The fact she wasn't joking was somehow endearing. Before he'd moved to detective, he'd been on the road.

Fought off the occasional person too high on drugs to feel pain, quite a few men larger and meaner than him, and more than one criminal with a weapon.

"We're just doing a few lessons. Learn a few rules and moves. You're not going to be beating me up quite yet."

"But shouldn't I be able to?"

"Sure. But we'll have to work up to it. You can't learn everything there is to know about self-defense in a day."

She wrinkled her nose. "Is it *that* complicated?"

"It's not about being complicated. It's just…something you practice, so it becomes second nature. So you're ready to do it. But listen, Rach. You're not going to need to, because I'm here and—"

She shook her head. "I don't want to feel like the weak link. Like the person everyone has to protect. Maybe it isn't much, but I just want to be able to land a punch or get away from someone if I need to. That's all."

She more than deserved that. He just wished he didn't have to be the one to teach her. It would involve touching and guiding, and she was… Hell, exercise leggings and a stretchy top were not *fair*. He was *human*.

Human and better than his baser—and completely unacceptable—urges. Because he'd shaped himself into a good, honorable man. One who did not take advantage of a young woman who meant a lot to his family.

And to you.

Because what he could forget when he didn't spend too much time one-on-one with Rachel was that they had a lot in common. What she'd said inside about wanting to feel useful echoed inside of him. Her surprise and irritation that he'd help out around the house made him want to do it all the more.

Take care of her and—

He cleared his throat, forced himself to focus. To treat this like any other lesson. "Rule number one. Always go for the crotch."

She made an odd sound. Like a strangled laugh. "I'm not going for your crotch, Tucker."

Jesus. He could *not* think about that. "Thanks for that. I just meant, in real life, that's your target. Crotch. Eyes. The most vulnerable points." He hated the thought of her needing to do *any* of that.

"Okay."

"You have to be mean."

She fisted her hands on her hips. "I know how to be mean."

"*Really* mean. Channel your inner Sarah."

"I'm going to channel my inner Grandma Pauline and whack you with a rolling pin."

Tucker laughed. "All right, killer. Show me how you'd punch."

He walked her through the proper form for a punch. Tried to talk her through aiming even though her sight was compromised. He instructed about grabbing anything she could make into a weapon. How to kick with the most effect.

Her form wasn't bad, and it got better the more she practiced. He offered to quit or take a break at least five times, but she kept wanting to go on. Even as they both ended up breathing heavily.

"The problem is I'm not going to be in a boxing ring. If *I'm* going to be in a fight, it's probably going to be because someone's trying to hurt me or someone I love. But they'd underestimate me. Either by ignoring me or just grabbing me."

"Maybe, but you have to learn the basics."

"But I can practice punching and kicking form on

my own. We need to practice like...how to get away if someone grabs me. I know you don't want to hurt me, and I don't want to hurt you, but it has to feel more like an actual fight."

"You don't have to worry about hurting me."

"Because I'm that weak?" she demanded.

"No, because I'm a professional at dodging a punch, Rach. I've been a cop for almost nine years. I've been learning to not get hit my whole life." He hadn't really meant to say that last part, or wouldn't have if he'd known she'd get that...sympathetic look on her face.

Nothing to be sympathetic about. He'd survived eight years of Ace Wyatt and the Sons of the Badlands. All his brothers, except Cody, had survived more time than him. Jamison hadn't gotten out until eighteen, after working hard to get Cody out before his seventh birthday. Tucker had followed not much later when he'd been eight. Gage and Brady had been eleven, and Dev twelve.

Tucker had gotten off easy, like he usually did.

She opened her mouth to say something—likely something he didn't want to hear, so he spoke first. "Come on then. If I'm coming at you, land a punch."

She got in the stance he'd taught her, made a good fist. As he moved forward, she swung out. He easily pivoted so she didn't land it.

"That's good."

"I didn't hit you!"

Tucker laughed. "Don't sound so disappointed." He took her still-clenched hand by the wrist and held it up. "This is your dominant hand, so you want it to do the big work." He took her other hand and brought it up. "But this one needs to do the work, too. Make a fist."

He walked her through using both hands to punch. Using her arms to block. He let her land a few punches.

She wasn't going to ward off any attackers with her fists—she'd have better luck kicking a vulnerable area or grabbing something to use as a weapon. Still, if it made her feel as though she was more prepared, that was what mattered.

It wasn't so bad all in all. It felt good to teach her something useful. A little *uncomfortable* teaching her to break holds by holding on to her against her will—but an important skill nonetheless.

Until he had the bright idea to teach her how to get away from someone who grabbed her from behind. Which necessitated…grabbing *her* from behind.

They went through the drill a few times. Slow, with pointers, and he tried very hard not to think about anything related to his body. He told her how to position her hands, how to maneuver her body. All while pretending his was made of…ice. Or plastic. Whatever kind of material that was not moved by a woman's body.

She was…lithe. Graceful.

Hot.

That was a really, really unacceptable thought when it came to Duke's daughter. Duke's daughter who's safety he was being entrusted with.

The strangest part was he'd scuffled with Sarah just this morning, and it hadn't felt any different than wrestling with his brothers. Familial. Funny.

But this was *none* of those things and he hadn't the slightest idea why.

"Do that again."

"I don't think—"

"Do it again," she insisted. "Come at me from behind."

He allowed himself to curse to his heart's content silently in his head. Rachel turned her back to him.

He just needed to enact a quick, meaningless grab around the waist.

The problem was he didn't like putting himself in the mind-set of an attacker. And he didn't like staying in his own mind-set, which was way too aware of how the exercise clothes she wore molded to every slender curve.

But who else could he be?

He gritted his teeth and tried to think about times tables as he wrapped his arm around her waist. She lifted her right hand to keep it from being held down by his grab, but he used his free hand to ensnare her arm.

She mimicked a kick to the insole and twisted in his grasp. He gave a little, as if stepping away from her kick. It gave her room, but kept his arm slightly around her, palm pressed to her stomach.

He wanted to tell her to pull her arm down in the way he'd shown her earlier, but he was afraid his voice wouldn't come out even. Or that he could manage to unclamp his jaw.

But she paused there, in this awkward position. His hand was on her abdomen, the fingers of his other hand curled around her wrist. He could feel the rise and fall of her breathing because her back was against him, her butt nestled way too close to a part of him he could *not* think about right now.

She tilted her head, and though he knew she couldn't see out of one eye and only general shapes out of the other, it felt as though she were studying him.

And then there was her mouth. Full and tempting. She wasn't trying to get out of his grasp, and she definitely wasn't putting any distance between their bodies.

She smelled like a meadow, and everything they were doing faded away. There were two aches inside of him—one he fully understood, and one that didn't make any sense. They both grew, expanded until there was only his heartbeat and the exhale of her breath across his cheek.

The sound of people arguing interrupted the buzzing in his head. He dropped her abruptly, moving away clumsily.

"Tucker..."

He didn't like the soft way she spoke, or the way her breath shuddered in and out, or that look in her eye, which he could not in any circumstances think about or consider.

"Hey, there's Sarah and Dev. We've been at this a while, huh? How about a break? I'm starved, you know?"

Sweet hell he was *babbling*. He cleared his throat. He was a grown man. A grown man with an inappropriate attraction, but that just meant he knew what to do with it. Scurrying away and babbling were not it. Getting himself together and *handling* it was what he needed to do. Would do. Absolutely. *Obviously.*

The dogs raced over first, so Tucker focused on them, squatting to scratch them both behind their ears. He spoke to them in soothing tones and tried his damnedest to get that *ache* coursing around inside of him to dissipate.

"How goes the self-defense?" Sarah asked.

"Great," Tucker said, far too loudly. "Going to take a break now."

"Yeah, us, too."

When Tucker looked up, Dev was frowning at him, but Tucker reminded himself that his brother's resting face was frowning disapproval. That was all.

Besides, he had enough frowning disapproval for himself. He didn't need anyone else's.

Chapter Eight

Rachel went through the rest of the day with an odd… buzz along her skin. Like the precursor to getting poison ivy. It was uncomfortable. Not quite so painful as a rash, but uncomfortable. Definitely.

She knew it was all Tucker's fault. Though she couldn't figure out why. Had he read her mind? He had been horrified that she'd kind of enjoyed him manhandling her. Or, had he enjoyed manhandling her and was horrified?

Either way, there was some horror. And then locking it all away and acting his usual genial self.

Except that he avoided her at all costs.

Which was probably for the best. Or was it? She got ready for bed, edgy and worked up. There was just too much going on. Her father was missing. She was having recurring nightmares. She was apparently attracted to a man she'd always looked at as family. Sort of. And worse than being attracted to *him* was the wondering if he was attracted to her right back. Or oblivious.

She groaned and flopped onto her bed. She needed to talk to someone. With most problems, she confided in Sarah or Cecilia. Sarah would be no help with this one, and Cecilia… She'd be too blunt. Too…forthright.

Rachel needed someone with a softer touch. So she called Felicity.

"Hey, Rach. Everything okay?"

"Yeah. Nothing new to report on our end."

Felicity sighed. "I really hate all this waiting. Gage keeps fluttering around me, trying to distract me from my stress, but all he is doing is stressing me out even more."

Rachel smiled. That was sweet. And also the perfect segue. "How did you end up involved with Gage?"

"What kind of question is that?"

"Not a mean one. I just… I wondered." Rachel rolled her eyes at herself. She sounded like an idiot. A transparent one. But at least of all her sisters, Felicity would never call her on it.

"Is this about Tucker?"

Rachel forced out a laugh. She was afraid it sounded more like a deranged array of squeaks. "What? No."

"You're a terrible liar. And even if you weren't, this is completely transparent."

Rachel pouted in spite of herself. "Of course it is. But you weren't supposed to call me out on it!"

Felicity laughed. "Sorry. Normally I wouldn't, but you're strung tight. I know Dad's whole disappearing act is scary, but you're usually calm in the midst of a crisis."

"I'm calm." Aside from the dreams. Aside from Tucker *touching* her. "Tucker believes Dad left of his own accord. Whatever prompted it, he doesn't think he's in any immediate danger and I have to believe that."

"I do, too. And so does Gage for that matter." Felicity paused. "So…why are you wound up?"

Rachel could blame it on the dreams. Some of it *was* the dreams, and the possibility of Dad being…far more complicated than she wanted him to be. But she didn't want to lay either of those things at Felicity's feet, where she'd worry needlessly.

"I think there was a moment. With Tucker. When he was teaching me some self-defense moves."

"Define *moment*."

"I don't know. Like…like…an awareness of each other. As a man and a woman. Not…family friends. As people who…"

"Might want to have sex?"

Rachel squeaked, her face getting hot, even though she was alone in her room and no one but her sister had heard that word. "Oh my *God*, Felicity."

"Sorry. It's just that's what moments usually lead to with the Wyatt boys."

"Why? I don't get it. I don't get why we're falling like dominoes for that lot of…"

"Really good guys who also happen to be hot and smart and caring? Who want to protect you, not because they think you're weak or need protecting, but because it's just who they are. On a cellular level."

Rachel expelled a breath. "I don't… I'm twenty-two."

"Is that commentary on the age difference or on being too young to have a serious relationship?"

"Neither. Both. I don't know! Why are we talking about relationships? It was like a moment of…lust. Fleeting lust. Very fleeting."

"Let me tell you this, Rach, lust over a Wyatt is never fleeting. I wasn't exactly planning on doing this whole baby thing yet. But then Gage came along and…boom, lust. And love."

Love. That was *terrifying*. "Just because you four did it, doesn't mean I will."

"Of course it doesn't. You're your own person, and

so is Tucker. I'm just trying to say it's normal to be attracted, and to be confused by it since you haven't always had those feelings. Danger and worry has a way of...stripping away our normal walls. When it does that, we can see someone as they actually are instead of how we've always perceived them to be."

"I don't have any walls."

Felicity was quiet for a few seconds. "Okay." She did *not* sound like she agreed. "But Tucker does. Even knowing how awful that childhood before Pauline must have been, I don't think I fully understood it until I saw Gage in that cave with Ace. Knowing Ace would have killed him and felt...justified. It isn't just viciousness and abuse they were raised with, it was...well, insanity."

Felicity paused, and Rachel shuddered. She hated to think about what Gage would have gone through. As a child and as a man. Tucker seemed so...not as afflicted as the others. She knew the older ones had spent longer being at the mercy of Ace Wyatt, but Tucker's eight years were nothing to ignore.

"The point is, being scared churns things up," Felicity continued. "That's okay. It doesn't mean you're weird. It doesn't mean you're not worried about Dad. It just means you're human. And Tucker is hot."

That shocked a laugh out of her. "Aren't you supposed to only have eyes for Gage?"

"Heart and soul for Gage. Eyes for anyone else. Things will be clearer when this is over, and Tucker and the rest of them are working hard to figure out what's going on so Dad can come home."

Rachel wanted to believe her. More than belief, though, she heard something in her sister's voice she wasn't sure she fully ever had before. Felicity had grown up nervous and shy, and she'd slowly come into her own the past few years. But Gage and this pregnancy had really given her an even bigger strength that she'd been afraid to believe in growing up. "You sound happy, Felicity."

"I am. And I'm mad at Dad that he's adding worry to my happy, but that's life. Happy and worry and even attraction can all pile up on each other in the same moment. I'm learning to accept that. I think the the thing is…we were raised right. We've got good instincts. Don't question your instincts."

Rachel let that settle through her. Wasn't that what she'd been doing? Or maybe she'd been questioning her worth or usefulness but it all kind of added up to the same thing. "Thanks, Felicity. This helped."

"I'm glad. Try to get some rest, Rach."

"You and baby, too."

They said their goodbyes and Rachel climbed into bed. She didn't feel any more clear on the whole Tucker thing, but she felt…more settled.

Don't question your instincts.

She'd be thinking about that a lot over the next few days.

She fell asleep, hopeful for another restful, uninterrupted night. But in the shadows of night came the noise. The rustle. The unearthly glow of cat eyes.

Were they cat eyes? They weren't human but…

Secrets always hurt the innocent. Curtis Washington is going to learn that the hard way.

He had her. He was holding her too tight and she couldn't wiggle away. The eyes weren't his, but they followed. Animal.

The human who had her was someone entirely different. She could hear the hum and scuttle of night life. Could see the moon shining bright from above. But she couldn't see the shadow who carried her too quickly and too easily away from everything she loved.

She squirmed and tried to scream, but she was squeezed too tight—both by the man's grip and her own fear.

When he stopped, it was worse. He wasn't squeezing so tight, but she couldn't breathe at all as he lifted the thing he always lifted, glinting silver in the moonlight. Some kind of...pronged knife. Slashing down at her face.

Run. Wake up.

She always did. Until now.

This time she felt the searing pain of the knife. But a growl, and a thud kept the knife from scoring too deep. It was painful. So painful she thought she might die. She was bleeding and her eyes felt like they were on fire, but the man didn't have her anymore.

TUCKER TOOK THE stairs two at a time, the safety already off on his gun. Rachel's blood-curdling scream had woken him from a fitful sleep, and he'd immediately jumped out of bed and run upstairs.

"Tucker." Sarah stood in the hall in her pajamas, holding a baseball bat.

"Go back to your room," Tucker hissed at her. The screaming had stopped. He inched toward Rachel's room, keeping his footsteps light. He controlled his breathing, pushed all the fear away and focused on the task at hand.

Save her. Now.

He could bust the door open, which was his first instinct. But he didn't know who was behind it, and if he could go for stealthy, he had to. Carefully, he reached out and placed his hand on the door. He willed the slight tremor away with sheer force.

He couldn't afford to be emotional right now. He had a mission. Slowly, carefully, he turned the knob and eased the door open inch by inch.

The room was bathed in light. Rachel sat in the middle of her bed, head in her hands, but Tucker didn't see anyone else.

He immediately swept the room. "Where is he?"

"Tucker." She wrapped the blanket around herself. "What are you doing?"

"I... You screamed." He slowly lowered the gun, belatedly realizing she wasn't in trouble at all. All the fear drained out of him until his knees nearly buckled. "Hell, Rach. That scream could have woken the dead."

"I'm sorry. I'm..." She inhaled shakily and he finally realized she'd been crying. Tears tracked down her cheeks even as she spoke calmly. "I had a bad dream, that's all. I didn't mean to scare you. I..." She shook her head. "Did Sarah wake up?"

"Yeah, but—"

She picked her phone up off the nightstand. "Text Sarah. I'm okay. Bad dream." She dropped her phone, and Sarah burst into the room a few seconds later.

"Oh my God. Rach. How awful. What do you need?"

"Noth—" She seemed to think better of it. "I think I could use a drink."

"I'll be right back." Sarah scurried away.

Tucker studied Rachel. She was shaking, and though she made no noise, fresh tears leaked out of her eyes.

"I'm sorry to have woken you up. I—"

"Stop apologizing," he said, and he knew his voice was too harsh when she winced. But he felt...ripped open. That scream and all the most terrible scenarios that had gone through his mind even as he'd shoved them away to do what needed to be done had taken years off his life.

He let out his own shaky breath. She was okay. Well, not okay. She was crying. Upset. He moved for her bed. "Are they all like this?"

She shook her head, pulling the blanket up to her chin. "No. Usually I wake up before…" She took a steadying breath and he just couldn't take the fear still in her eyes, in her voice. He sat on the very edge of the bed, putting his hand on her shoulder.

She took a deep gulping breath. "It's just I usually wake up before he hurts me. But tonight the knives slashed across my face."

He rubbed his hand up and down her arm. She seemed to need to talk about it, and he had some suspicions now about these dreams. "Knives?"

"A man. He had me. He had this knife or knives with multiple points. He…" She couldn't seem to swallow down a hiccupped sob. She shuddered, so he pulled her closer until she leaned into him.

She let out a little sigh, and some of the shaking subsided. "I could feel it. The pain. The blood. I don't know if it was a memory or made up, but it felt real. And I was small. I had my adult brain, but he could cart me around easily. It was a man, but there was also an animal. I don't think it was a mountain lion. It was more… doglike. And he jumped on the man when he hurt me. That animal saved me, I think."

She shook her head. "It doesn't make sense. I don't want it to make sense." She buried her head in his shoulder. "I want the dreams to go away and I want Dad to be home."

"Of course you do, sweetheart." He rubbed his hand

up and down her back. "So do I." He tried to keep the grimness out of his voice. But this situation was grim. The more she explained the dream, the more he had to wonder if Rachel knew more than she understood.

And he had to wonder if *Duke* knew that. If that was half of why he'd agreed to disappear with North Star on such short notice. To keep Rachel out of it.

"I heard that name again. Curtis Washington. Do you think that's a real person?" She pulled back from him, her gaze meeting his. Her complexion was a little gray, and the faded pink of her scars seemed more pronounced against the brown of her skin. She looked at him earnestly, even though he knew she couldn't see him clearly. "Why am I dreaming this name? I've never thought my dreams were real, but..."

"It keeps repeating. And getting worse."

She nodded. Her face was close to his. Their noses would touch if he leaned just an inch forward. His arm was still around her and she was leaning into him.

In her bed.

Tucker let his arm slip away from her, though he stayed seated at the edge of her bed. He inched even closer to that edge so that, though he was close, their bodies were not in danger of touching, and berated himself for even the second of inappropriate thought that gripped him.

She was shaking, crying and scared.

And very close to a truth he wasn't supposed to let her know about.

"I think we need to look into that name. Don't you? Maybe it has something to do with Dad. Maybe—"

Sarah bustled into the room carrying a tray full of glasses. "I didn't know what kind of drink so I just kind of brought..."

"Everything." Rachel smiled indulgently. "Thank you. I think I'll take the water."

Tucker slid off her bed. He needed to let Sarah take care of this. Comfort her. He needed to escape before she asked him to do what he wasn't supposed to do.

He eyed Sarah's tray, took the shot glass off it and downed the whiskey. He put the glass back, then tried to disappear.

"Tuck, I want to look into the name. I think we have to."

How could he say no to her? "I'll see what I can do."

Chapter Nine

Rachel knew that Tucker would look into the name Curtis Washington, and he was a detective so he'd be able to do far more than her. Still, that didn't mean she couldn't aid him in his search.

If the name connected to everything that was going on, that meant it connected to Dad. And if the dream connected to everything that was going on...

She didn't know what it would mean.

It scared her. That it might be terrible. That it might be buried deep in her subconscious...

"There's a lot of junk up here, Rach. I don't know how we're going to go through it all," Sarah said.

Rachel could tell Sarah was antsy to get outside, to do her work on the ranch, even if it was a rainy, dreary day. But when Rachel had mentioned going up to the attic, Sarah had insisted on helping.

"I know it's overwhelming, but I can't sit around waiting for Tuck to figure it out. I know it was a dream. This is probably insane, but—"

"Look, that's some dream. Maybe normally I'd brush it off, but everything is off right now. Dev is being *nice* to me." The horror in her tone had Rachel smiling.

"That's sweet of him."

"It's creepy as hell." Sarah moved through the attic,

and Rachel figured she was doing what she had asked—reading labels of boxes and pulling out anything that seemed relevant. "Speaking of creepy, Tuck was totally checking you out last night."

Rachel nearly stumbled over what she assumed was a box. *"What?"*

"One hundred percent checking out your rack, sis."

Rachel sputtered, and she could feel heat creeping up her face. "Geez, Sarah…"

"I can tell him to knock it off if you want."

"What? No. Oh my God, don't do that!"

"Why not?"

Rachel tried to work through this insane turn in the conversation. "Because that's embarrassing and weird."

"So, not because you'd *like* Tucker to be checking you out. Tucker Wyatt."

"I know who Tucker is," Rachel replied, all too shrilly.

"That doesn't answer my question."

"Did you actually have one?"

"Yeah. Are you creeped out Tuck was looking at your boobs, or do you like it?"

Rachel opened her mouth but no sound came out. She wasn't creeped out, but she wasn't sure if she liked it, either. She was just… "I don't know."

"I mean, in fairness it wasn't like super creeper ogling. It was like…noticing. Your boobs."

"I need this conversation to be over," Rachel muttered. Her face was hot, her heart was hammering and they had way more important concerns at hand. "Whatever we're looking for, it's not going to be in a box. If it's such a secret that Dad had to disappear, it's going to be somewhere…like in the wall. Or out in the stables or something. It'd be hidden."

"But who would go through all this stuff? Wouldn't hiding it in plain sight work just as well?" Sarah asked, thankfully moving away from the subject of Tucker.

"Not if you expected someone to go looking for your secret stuff. If Dad *had* secret stuff—the kind you run away from so your children aren't in the middle of it—it'd be hidden somewhere. Which means there's not going to be a box labeled *secret stuff*. It's going to be harder than that. Sneakier than that."

Sarah blew out a loud breath. "I really hate this."

"Yeah, me, too."

They worked in silence for a while. Sarah went through reading labels on boxes and checking the contents of those unlabeled. Rachel went around the attic perimeter feeling the walls, trying to determine if there was any place that could be hiding something.

She was about to give up when her hands landed on something metal in the corner by the door. It was some kind of box, but instead of cardboard or plastic, it was a heavy metal.

"What's this?"

"Huh." Sarah stepped closer. "It's a locked cashbox type deal, but there's a little piece of masking tape on it that says *buttons*."

"Who would lock up buttons?"

"Mom loved collecting buttons, but I don't think there'd be any reason to lock them up. Here, give it to me."

"If it's locked, how will you—" Rachel began.

There was a squeaking sound and then a crash—like tiny buttons falling across the floor.

"Oops," Sarah said. "Lock was a little easier to break than I thought. But it is just…buttons. Everywhere now. Here, take the box so I can pick up the ones that fell."

Rachel took the box back. She let her fingers trail over the buttons. Mom had loved to collect them. Old grief welled inside of her, though it had been enough years now that she knew how to push it away.

Still, touching something of her mother's had her eyes and nose stinging with unshed tears. She blinked them back as she dug her fingers into the buttons—and touched something with a sharp edge. She cradled the box in her elbow and pulled the item out of the buttons. Using both hands, she felt around the edge of it. Much bigger than a button. Maybe an oddly shaped belt buckle?

"Sarah?"

"Wh— Oh my God."

"What? What is it?"

"It's a police badge." It was snatched out of Rachel's hand. "It says *Officer. Chicago Police.*"

"Chicago? Why would there be a Chicago police badge in a box full of buttons?"

"A *locked* box full of buttons," Sarah pointed out. "If we're looking for secrets, I think we might have found one."

"Are you guys up in the attic?" Tuck's voice called from below.

Rachel felt Sarah press the badge back into her palm. "Your call. You want to hide it, I will. You want to tell him, I'll be right behind you."

"Why are you leaving it up to me? He's your father, too."

"They're your dreams, Rach. And Tucker seems to be your thing. Let's face it, you're the calm, rational one between the two of us. Whatever you want to do is what we should do."

Tucker's form appeared in the doorway. "Hey. Dev's looking for you, Sarah. What are you two doing up here?"

Sarah didn't answer him. Because she'd put it all on Rachel.

"We wanted to poke around and see if we could find something of Dad's. Get some idea of what he might be keeping a secret." She held the badge behind her back, the box of buttons in the crook of her arm. What else might be in there?

And did she want Tuck to know about it?

"I'll go find Dev. See what he wants."

Rachel heard Sarah's retreat as she let her fingers trace the outline of the badge. Chicago Police? Could she picture her father as a police officer?

Or had he had some kind of run in with a police officer? Was this darker? More awful? Should she *want* to hide it from everyone so they never knew?

But how could she bring her father home without help? Without *Tucker's* help. Why wouldn't she trust Tucker Wyatt with everything she found? He was…a Wyatt. He was a good person. He didn't lie. He was a detective who searched for the truth, who's father's sins weighed on him even when they shouldn't.

He was a good man.

Tucker was totally checking you out last night.

"You okay?"

She nodded and cleared her throat. "We found a box of my mom's buttons."

His hand was on her shoulder, giving her a friendly squeeze. "That's a nice thing to have. Even if it makes you sad."

She nodded, because she agreed. Because she knew he didn't have anything from his mother, whatever complicated feelings he might have had about her. And he wouldn't want anything from his father. She had two good, supportive, loving parents who hadn't just loved *her* but had fostered or adopted five other girls over the years and made them all a family.

"I miss her most around this time of year," Tuck said, his voice gentle. "She was always rounding us up, trying to help Grandma Pauline get us ready for school rather than show up the first day looking like feral dogs."

"She used to say you boys needed love, education and a hardheaded woman to keep you on the straight and narrow."

He laughed. "Grandma Pauline did all three. So did your mom."

It was strange to talk to Tucker about her mom. She knew Eva Knight had considered the Wyatt boys part of her own brood. She'd helped Grandma Pauline corral them as much as she could. Mom had loved them. She'd cared about people who needed help, and love, and she'd given hope to those in the darkest places.

Rachel didn't have any dark places. Not really. Even her dreams were just dreams—even if they were pointing to *something*. She wasn't like Liza and Jamison who had survived the Sons, or Felicity who'd survived an abusive father both as a child and then as a woman. She wasn't any of the Wyatt boys with the horror they'd grown up with and escaped.

She'd had a good, mostly easy life. So, Mom had always tasked her with helping, providing for, being the hope.

If there was any hope in this situation with Dad, it was that they could get him home. Secrets wouldn't do that. Being suspicious of Tucker wouldn't do that.

Rachel took a deep breath, feeling around the edge

of the badge one more time. Then she held it forward. "I found this in the box of buttons."

TUCKER STARED AT the badge held out in Rachel's hand. Chicago PD. He didn't know how to react. He knew, of course, that it was Duke's, though Rachel probably didn't. Wouldn't.

He wanted to tell her. Not just about her father's past but about everything. North Star and where Duke was.

An equal part of him wanted to laugh it off, stop her from probing into this, from entwining herself in trouble. He wanted to wrap her up in a safe bubble so she didn't have to worry about all this.

But he remembered all too well that terrifying scream that had woken him in the middle of the night. Some of this mystery and danger was inside her subconscious somewhere. No matter what he did—he couldn't protect her from that.

"It's a police badge," he said, his voice a shade too rough.

"Yes. Sarah told me it says *Chicago Police*." She pressed it into his palm. "It has to mean something."

Boy, did it. "Did you check the rest of the box?"

"I haven't had the chance. We'd just found this when you came up."

He frowned over that. "Why didn't Sarah say anything?"

"She said she'd give me the choice whether to tell you or not."

"Why wouldn't you tell me?"

Rachel shrugged. "I did tell you, though."

He wasn't sure that was much of a comfort, but he supposed it had nothing to do with the issue at hand. He set the badge aside, then took the box of buttons from her. He found an empty mason jar to dump the buttons into. As he poured them into it, he let the buttons fall over his fingers. There was nothing else big, but as he came to the end of the buttons, a key fell into his fingers.

He held it up, looking at it on both sides. "Nothing else in there except a key."

"A key to what?"

"I don't have a clue. It's just a key."

"It can't *just* be a key."

"Well, no. It was in with the buttons and the badge so it has to be something, but there aren't any hints as to what." Tucker examined the box. It was a rusted out cashbox, nothing special about it. No space for any kind of false bottom.

"A badge and a key. A missing father. Dreams that feel way too close to real." She blew out a breath. "Anything else life wants to throw at me?"

"Please don't go taunting the universe like that."

Her mouth curved. "You don't honestly believe in curses and jinxes?"

"*Believe* might be a strong word. Let's say I have a healthy respect for the possibility."

Rachel shook her head, though she was still smiling. A beam of sunlight shone in front of her, making dust motes dance around her face. He'd always *known* she was pretty, but something about doing all this made him *feel* it.

Maybe he wholeheartedly believed in curses and jinxes, because his sudden attraction for Rachel felt like both.

She frowned. "Did you hear that?"

He hadn't heard much of anything except his own stupidity. "What?"

"I'm not sure. Like an engine, but..." She trailed off and he strained to hear what she heard. Everything was silent, but he felt the need to hold himself still, and continue to strain to hear long after the moment had passed.

Creak.

Rachel's frown deepened, and she opened her mouth, presumably to say something, but Tucker laid his hand gently over her mouth.

She'd heard an engine. He'd heard the creak of a floorboard under the weight of someone. If it was any Wyatt or Knight, they would have announced themselves—or they'd know which boards to avoid.

Tucker scanned the attic. Maneuvering Rachel to hide her would make noise. Everything would make noise, and whoever or whatever had creaked the floorboard had gone silent again. He was too far from the tiny window letting in the light to see through it and scan the surroundings.

He didn't wear his gun around the house because he was afraid it would make Sarah and Rachel nervous, and now he mentally kicked himself for caring more about feelings than safety.

He'd have to fight off whoever was at that door. He'd need the element of surprise. And to do it all while keeping Rachel out of the way.

There was only one way to do it, since once the attic door opened it would open this way and give whoever was on the stairs clear sight of Rachel.

But if he hid on the other side of the door, he could come at whoever it was from behind. They might know he was up here, but Rachel would be a momentary distraction he'd use.

He pressed his mouth as close to her ear as he could. Spoke as softly as humanly possible. "You're going to stay right here. Don't move unless I tell you to. Squeeze my hand if you understand."

When she squeezed, he squeezed right back. He was loathe to let go of her, to do what he knew he needed to do. He wanted to promise her things would be okay. He wanted to be a human shield between her and hurt.

But he had to stop doing what was most comfortable, and start doing what was the safest. He moved in absolute silence to the opposite side of the door.

He waited, counting his heartbeats, keeping his breathing even. Rachel's life rested in his hands, so he could not focus on panic or worry or that heavy responsibility. He could only focus on eradicating the threat.

The door squeaked, the narrow opening slowly growing. He saw the barrel of a gun first. It was pointed down at the ground, but he couldn't take any chances.

He waited until he actually saw an arm, then pushed the door as hard as he could. The gun didn't clatter to the ground as he'd hoped, but the intruder had stumbled back onto the stair.

"Get down, Rach," he commanded, moving through the door and closing it behind him. A figure in all black was on the stairs. The figure didn't raise the gun, but that didn't mean it wasn't dangerous.

The figure struck out, and Tucker managed to block most of the blow. They grappled, exchanging punches and elbows and kicks. Eventually they both stumbled, crashing down the first flight of stairs and onto the landing that would go down to the second floor.

Tucker banged up his elbow pretty good, and he'd landed on the side with his phone in his pocket so not only did a shooting pain go through his hip, but he was pretty sure the phone was crushed.

He swore, and so did the figure. Tuck frowned. It

was a woman. He noticed blond hair had escaped the black ski mask she wore. He scrambled to his feet, recognizing her as the woman who'd first approached him on behalf of North Star, then again outside his office.

"You." Why was the woman from North Star sneaking through the house? Pointing a gun and fighting with him?

The woman glared up at him, then landed a kick to his stomach, and he cursed himself for being caught off guard. She made a run for it to go up the stairs, but Tucker got his breath back quickly enough to grab her by the foot. He heard her let out a curse as she crashed into the stairs.

"Why are Wyatts always ruining my life?" she demanded, kicking back at him.

"What the hell are you doing? North Star is supposed to be the good guys."

She stopped kicking and fighting him off and gave a derisive snort before rolling onto her back. Tucker had the sense she could easily kick him down the stairs and there wouldn't be much he could do about it.

"I have my orders, from those *good* guys." The woman jerked her chin toward the attic "She knows something. She needs to come with me or our mission is compromised. Granger knew you'd be difficult about it."

"How do you know she knows something?" Tucker demanded. How on earth could they know about Rachel's dreams?

The woman gave him a withering glare. "We know everything, Wyatt. Haven't you caught on?"

It didn't matter. It couldn't. "Screw your mission. She's got nothing to do with it and you know it. You're going to drag an innocent into the midst of this? Via kidnapping?"

The woman's expression went grim, but Tucker thought he saw a flash of conscience. "I have my orders," she repeated.

Which told Tucker she didn't particularly want to follow those orders.

"Excuse me?" Both he and the woman he'd fought looked up at the top of the stairs. Rachel stood with her arms over her chest, expression furious. "Maybe one of you could tell me what's going on and I, the woman in question, can decide for myself?"

Chapter Ten

Rachel was shaking, but she'd wrapped her arms around herself to keep it from showing. She was at the top of the stairs and from what she could tell, Tucker and…some woman he knew were on the landing in the middle of the stairs having an argument about her.

"Rach."

"No, I don't think I want you to tell me," she said, holding on to her composure by a very thin thread. Tucker had been lying to her, that much was clear.

"Listen. My name is Shay. I'm with the North Star Group. Tucker and Cody Wyatt have worked for us. Your father's past connected to ours, so we're helping him out. If you come with me—"

"What a load of bull. You're not helping him. You're using him," Tucker said disgustedly. "If you're taking her against her will, you're not in this to protect anyone."

"No one said it was against my will, Tucker."

She heard him take a few stairs. "She was damn well going to, Rachel. She snuck in here, and she fought me—"

"You started that," Shay interrupted.

"She was going to kidnap you. Because you know things about your father's past. Not because she wants to protect you or Duke, but because they'll do anything to bring down the Sons. Including letting innocent people get hurt."

There was a heavy, poignant silence.

"Don't have anything to say to that?" Tucker said scathingly to the woman.

Who still didn't say anything. Rachel didn't understand any of this, but she understood one thing. "You have my father."

"We're helping your father," this Shay person said. "It's what we do."

"What does this have to do with the Sons?" she asked. Because of course it did. Tucker had lied to her and her father was in danger because of the Sons of the Badlands.

What else was new?

"Rachel, listen to me—"

"You knew where he was, who he was being protected by and *why*, but you didn't think to share that with me?" Her throat closed with every word, until the last one was a squeak.

"Rach." He sounded pained, hurt.

But she couldn't have any sympathy for him. He'd lied to her. Let her worry and fear and... He'd used her. Even if he was right about this North Star Group using Dad instead of helping him, Tucker had used her. Knowing...everything.

"If I go with you, what happens?" she said, addressing Shay.

"I'd take you to your father."

"Oh, that's low," Tucker said sourly. "She would not. They would interrogate you about your dreams until they got the information they wanted. If you give them what they want, they *might* let you see Duke, but considering they're using him as bait, I don't think that's happening anytime soon. They need him. They need the information they think you might have. What they don't need is a father–daughter reunion. And who knows, they might use you as bait, too. You can't go with her, Rachel."

"She's coming with me. Whether she does it willingly or not, my mission is to bring her back. So I will."

But Rachel noted they were standing in the attic staircase having this conversation. Shay wasn't making a move to fight Tucker anymore. She hadn't yet attempted to take Rachel against her will like she was saying she would.

"Can you promise my father will be okay if I go with you willingly?"

There was a hesitation. "I...can't promise that. Your father's in a dangerous situation."

"Think, Rachel," Tuck implored her. "I know you're mad at me. Maybe you'll never forgive me. I get it. But think about your father. What would he want you to do?"

"I don't care as much about what he'd want me to do as what I can do to protect him."

"They'd use whatever you gave them to complete their mission. You and Duke would be collateral damage." Tucker sounded so...desperate. So intent. It wasn't his usual self.

But his usual self had been lying to her. Should she have seen it? There had been hints. Hesitations. A carefulness.

The woman was suspiciously silent at Tucker's accusation. "Is that true?" Rachel asked quietly.

There was a long silence. "It's not...untrue."

"So, you're both liars who don't care about anyone?"

"Your father wanted you safe," Tucker said, and while he was being contrite, so to speak, there was a thread of steel in his words. "You and Sarah. Why do you think I'm here? He—"

"You saw him. Before he disappeared. You saw him and you lied to all of us."

She couldn't see his expression, but she knew all those accusations landed like blows. Unless he was a completely different man than she'd always believed. Which maybe he was.

"He wanted you and Sarah protected," Tucker repeated, and his voice was rough. She wanted to believe that was emotion. Guilt.

She just didn't know what to believe about him anymore. He'd seen her father. He'd let her worry.

He'd comforted her after her dreams. Stepped in and made meals, cleaned up. He'd taught her self-defense and...maybe he'd tried to ease some of her fears. She thought of the badge, the key.

"Were you lying about looking into the name?"

Tucker was silent for ticking awful seconds where she wanted to curl into herself and cry. Just...disappear from this world where the man she trusted was such a liar.

"I wasn't lying. I looked into it. I was told to leave it be."

"In fairness, he didn't leave it be," Shay said. "Which is why I'm here."

"You guys are keeping some kind of tabs on me?" Tucker growled as if he was both surprised and disgusted by the information. "What the hell is this?"

"It's business, Wyatt. The business of taking down the Sons."

"I'm so tired of people trying to take down the Sons,"

Rachel said, her voice growing louder with every word. "I'm so tired of people getting hurt because of the *Sons*. My father and I have nothing to do with them. Why can't you leave us alone?"

"Listen, you can dismiss me and all, but neither of you actually have a say. If I don't take you, they'll send someone else. You're a part of North Star's mission now. They won't just take no for an answer. It'd be easier if you just came with me."

Rachel didn't know why that was the straw that broke the camel's back. "And I am really done doing what's *easier* for everyone else."

TUCKER HAD TO ignore the searing pain in his chest. The slick black weight of guilt. He had to focus on getting Rachel out of this mess. Once she was safe... Well, he could self-flagellate and she could hate him forever.

He rubbed at his chest.

"If you don't come with me of your own volition," Shay said in a careful, emotionless voice, "I'll take you by force."

Tucker had already positioned himself between Shay and Rachel. He was ready to fight. He didn't think Shay would use the gun against him. At least he hoped not.

"She is an innocent bystander. Whatever she knows is wrapped up in nightmares she can't untangle." He thought about the badge, the key he'd slid into his pocket. He could give that to Shay as a peace offering. It might even help Duke, and it wasn't that he thought North Star was evil—they just didn't care about people. They cared about their mission.

As for him, he cared about too many people involved to let this go so far as to touch Rachel. The key might be some kind of insurance if he kept it. So, he had to.

Tucker turned to Rachel. She held herself impossibly still, her expression mostly blank. Except her eyes. They were hurt. Betrayed.

And he'd done the betraying.

He had to get her out of this. Maybe she'd never forgive him, but if he could get her out of this, maybe he could forgive himself.

"Your father wanted me to protect you from this. Keep you separate."

"But I'm *not* separate. If they're here about my dreams, there's something real in them." Her eyebrows drew together. "It has to be real."

"That doesn't mean you have to put yourself in danger. It doesn't mean you have to go with this group who doesn't care about you."

"This group has my father."

"You going there doesn't help him. It helps *them*." He wouldn't let her go. Even if she wanted to. But maybe he could assuage at least some of his guilt if she'd just understand the truth here. A truth he hadn't fully understood until now.

Maybe North Star wanted to take down the Sons, but they didn't care enough about the innocent collateral damage involved.

"Oh, just someone punch me," Shay said with no small amount of exasperation.

"What?" Tucker demanded, turning from Rachel to face her.

"In the face." She pointed to her nose. "Make it good, too."

"What are you talking about?"

"I can't go back to Granger unscathed *and* with you having gotten away. You need to make it look like you beat me. Literally and figuratively."

Finally, what Shay was saying got through. She was...letting them go. "I... I can't punch a woman."

She rolled her eyes. "I can punch you first if it gets you going."

"That's not—"

"I'll do it," Rachel said, walking down the stairs. She stopped on the stair right above Shay.

"No offense, but—"

Rachel squared like he'd taught her, curled her fist and landed a blow right to Shay's face.

Swearing in time with Rachel, Shay gingerly placed her palm on her jaw, working it back and forth. Rachel shook out her hand, then cradled it.

"Well, that'll work," Shay said. "Hell."

"You really think one punch is going to convince them?"

"I can handle the rest, but I couldn't punch my own self in the face." She gave Rachel a once-over. "Not half bad. Keep working on that and you might be one hell of a fighter." She moved as if to leave, but Tucker stepped in front of her on the stairs.

"I should take your gun."

She grimaced, clearly loathing the idea of losing her weapon.

"They can't think you got back in one piece still armed, can they?"

"Yeah, yeah, yeah." She handed over the weapon.

Still, Tucker couldn't move out of her way. "Will they kick you out?"

She shrugged. "Not if I quit first."

"Why would you do that?"

"Because you're right, Wyatt. I'm not in the business of hurting innocent people for the sake of a mission. North Star didn't start out that way, but lately...

Doesn't matter. It's getting old and maybe this is my last straw. You're going to need to run, though. Whether I get kicked out or quit—they'll keep coming for her. She knows stuff." Shay let out a sigh. "That phone Granger gave you?"

Tucker pulled it out of his pocket. It was in a couple pieces after his fall down the stairs.

Shay nodded. "That's good. Leave it here."

It dawned on Tucker that meant Granger had been tracking him, maybe listening to him. He'd know about everything up to the fight on the stairs. He nodded grimly at Shay, tossing the phone onto the ground. He smashed it once more under his heel for good measure.

Shay looked back at Rachel, then leaned close to whisper to Tucker. "Get her out of here ASAP. Whatever she knows, they'll use it. Not to help or protect Knight, but to get the Sons. I want the Sons destroyed as much as anybody, and I imagine you do, too, but good people shouldn't be used as bait to take them down."

"If you don't quit, if you don't get kicked out, you could help keep Duke safe. From the inside."

She smiled wryly. "That's a lot of ifs."

"Like you said, we both want to bring down the Sons. We just don't want innocent people hurt in the process. We could work together on this."

She shook her head. "You and your brother. Two peas in a dumb, naive pod."

"Is that a yes?"

She blew out a breath. "Look, I'll do what I can. That does *not* mean we're working together. Be clear on that."

He wasn't sure he believed her, and when he held out a hand for a shake, she shook her head. "We are *not* partners. Be best for you both if you get out of here before I do."

Tucker nodded and looked up at Rachel. Her expression was grim. But Shay was right, they had to get out of here. He didn't know where yet, but he'd figure it out.

What he wasn't so sure he was going to figure out was how to live with what he'd done.

Chapter Eleven

Tucker stole a horse.

Maybe it was harsh for Rachel to consider it stealing, considering it was *her* horse, and she was one of the people riding it, but it felt like stealing. It felt like lying and scaring the people she loved by disappearing.

Like Dad did?

She didn't even have time to wallow in the betrayal of it all because Shay was absolutely telling the truth, no doubt about it. Someone else would come for her, because her dreams were true.

True.

They rode Buttercup away from the ranch—in the opposite direction of the pasture Dev and Sarah were working in this afternoon. It felt really stupid to be riding a horse named Buttercup when trying to escape a group that was trying to bring down the Sons—which was what she wanted.

How could two groups of people want the same thing and disagree so fundamentally on how to get there?

She didn't speak as Tucker explained everything from the beginning. His helping out North Star. Being ready to quit before he walked into a diner with the North Star guy and her father.

Her father. Who'd brought down dirty cops as a

young man and was somehow paying for it over thirty years later.

Her father wasn't who she'd thought. Tucker wasn't who she'd thought.

Oh, that probably wasn't fair. In fact, it was really quite *Wyatt* of Tucker to want to save the day without telling her. Still, no matter how justified, the fact he'd lied to her and she'd bought it hook, line and sinker... It hurt.

Maybe his deception was necessary, but how easily he'd fooled her made her feel stupid. And weak. Now she was riding a horse, with Tucker's hard body directly behind her, through the rolling hills of southeastern South Dakota like she was some kidnapped bride on the prairie.

Rachel didn't say anything as they rode, and after he'd told the whole story, neither did Tucker. She didn't know how many hours they rode in silence, how many miles they covered. She didn't know where they were going and she didn't ask.

Because she was too afraid he'd offer another lie, and she'd believe it as gospel.

"Sun's going down," Tucker said, his voice rusty with disuse. "We should camp."

"Camp," Rachel echoed. Up to this point, she hadn't been afraid, not really. In the moments Tucker had been fighting Shay, yes, but after that there'd been too many other feelings. Sadness, fury, hurt and the ache in her hand from punching Shay had taken up too much space to be truly afraid.

But now the idea of camping had those beats of panic starting in her chest.

"I'm sorry. It's the only way," Tucker said gently.

He brought the horse to a halt and he got off. Since she couldn't see the ground, she had to let him help her dismount.

Rachel immediately pulled away from his grasp, though she kept her feet in the same place since she couldn't be sure she wouldn't trip and fall.

"So, what's the plan?" she asked flatly.

He handed her something. Her cane. It took her a moment to register that and to take it. They'd left in such a hurry, but he'd thought to grab her probing cane.

After lying to you about everything.

"Right now? The plan is to keep you away from North Star."

"For how long?" she asked.

"As long as we need to."

"We're just going to camp in the hills until someone magically alerts us to the fact North Star no longer needs me?"

"You still have your phone," he reminded her.

"It doesn't have service out here." She was completely alone in the wilderness with a man who...who she'd trusted and who'd lied to her. About the most important things. "Sarah is going to be worried sick."

"She would be worried sick if you'd stayed—because Shay would have taken you, or someone else would have come and finished the job. At least she'll know you're with me."

It was true, but that didn't make it comforting. Maybe because she knew Tucker would have stood up for her. He would have fought and protected her against all the people North Star sent. Liar that he was. "I don't camp."

"I know," he said, with enough weight that she figured he understood it was because it reminded her of that night. Of her memories or dreams. She'd been alone in the wilderness when the mountain lion had attacked, or at least that's what she'd believed until lately.

"I'm sorry this has touched you, Rachel. I wish I could make it not."

She wanted to ask him if that was another lie, but she understood in that statement that while Tucker had lied to her about facts, he'd never lied to her about feelings. He'd promised to try to keep her father safe—and he had been working to do that. He'd promised her father to keep her out of it.

He'd failed, and likely was busy heaping all sorts of guilt on himself. She wished that made her feel better, but it actually deflated some of her anger.

"He's my father. It was always going to touch me no matter what you did, Tucker."

He didn't respond, and she could hear the sounds of him making camp. He'd gotten her out of the house so quickly she didn't know how he'd had time to gather supplies, but he seemed to have enough.

"I know you don't want to camp. I wish there was another way," he finally said, so grave and... It wasn't fair. She couldn't be mad at him when he was beating himself up.

"You know, the same thing would have happened even if you'd told us the truth from the beginning. Didn't Shay basically say that phone North Star gave you was tracking everything?"

"Maybe if I'd been a better liar, you'd be just fine at home."

"Is that what you want? To be a better liar?"

He expelled a loud breath. "No."

"That's why you were going to quit. Well, Dad threw a wrench in your plans, and so did my dreams."

"That sounds a lot like absolution. And misplaced blame."

"It's neither. You did what you had to do. And I can't control my dreams."

"You should be mad at me."

"Oh, I am," she told him. "I'm mad at you. I'm irritated with myself. I'm downright furious with Dad. I don't want to camp. I don't want to run. I don't want any of this."

"I'm sor—"

"I don't want your apologies, either. I want the lies to end. And I want Dad back in one piece. So, we have to figure out how we're going to do that. We can't wait. We can't play the hide-Rachel-away-in-a-safe-corner game. We have to fight. For my father. We have to help him. However we can."

RACHEL SOUNDED FIERCE, and looked it, standing there in the fading daylight, probing cane grasped in one hand, the other clenched in a fist. Her expression was hard and determined.

He wished he could agree. Immediately support her. "If I knew how to do that, I would have already done it."

It was humbling to admit. He'd seen no real way to help Duke except protect Rachel and he'd failed. He'd brought her more into the fold by not suspecting McMillan might be listening in.

The bastard had listened in on private conversations. Rachel's dream aftermath. Talking about her mother and the buttons.

He fingered the key in his pocket. Duke already knew his past. There were no secrets to be uncovered.

Whatever the key unlocked, Duke knew about it. Had locked something up. It wouldn't help him now. In fact, it was probably best if it stayed buried.

"Dad's being threatened by this Vianni family, through the Sons, according to North Star."

"It's not just North Star's story. Your father was there when McMillan told me about it. It's true."

She nodded sharply. "Okay. It's true. North Star is supposed to keep him safe, but both you and Shay acted like they're trying to use Dad as some kind of bait to get enough evidence on the Sons. But to what end? To arrest them all? Kill them all?"

"I'm not privy to North Star's plans."

"No, but Shay said that it's gotten too mission focused. They're not caring about people. I don't want Dad to be collateral damage."

"I don't either, Rachel."

"I know you don't." She moved forward using her cane to avoid the dips and bumps in the ground.

Tucker had found the flattest, most even ground he could, but he'd wanted to stay in the hills and trees as much as possible.

"But North Star knows everything about Dad, and presumably they know a lot about the Viannis and the Sons. They don't *need* him there."

"They're protecting him."

"Are they?" she returned. "Or did they say that to you, maybe even to him, but what they really meant is they're using him?"

It was a horrible thought. Even if he didn't agree with everything North Star had done, he believed in their mission. "Your Dad went to them willingly. He had some connection to their leader. Or the leader's dad. Something about him being the reason he had this

WITSEC life here. He had to believe they were going to...fix things or he wouldn't have gone."

"But I don't. I don't believe that at all. When one of their own, a woman sent to take me, let's us go instead... Something is very, very wrong. I want my father out. Screw their mission. *You* said that."

"I did. And I meant it in regard to Shay's particular mission of kidnapping you. But I don't want to sabotage North Star. Even if I don't approve of their methods, I approve of what they're doing. I *support* what they're doing." How had this gotten so messed up? "Bringing down the Sons is important."

"It is. Should my father die for it?"

"I don't think North Star would let that happen." But their attempted kidnapping of Rachel made him uncomfortably concerned.

"You don't *think*."

Tucker raked his hands through his hair. "People are after him. Dangerous people. Regardless of the Sons or North Star, your father was a target."

"Because he did something right. Don't you know what that's like?"

It snapped something in him. That leash on his temper and his emotions he fought so hard to keep tethered. "Yeah, I do. I know it's living your life in fear, wondering when it shows up to take you down. I know it's watching your brothers get hurt over and over again by this thing you escaped, while you can't do a damn thing about it. Knowing you don't even rate to be a target because apparently you're not that much of a threat to their kind of evil. I know what it's all like, Rachel, and I'm telling you, *we* can't do anything about it."

She blinked. "Tuck—"

He was so horrified by his torrent of words that had

nothing to do with her or this situation, he turned his back on her. "No. It's not about me. It's about Duke."

"Tucker—"

"I said no. I won't steal your father out of the North Star's hands, not with you. I can't protect you both from all the different forces after you. I got you out of there so they can't use you, can't use your dreams. Because Duke would have wanted me to keep you safe and because it's the right thing." Because the thought of putting her in any more danger just about ripped him in two.

He had to stop this…*emotion*. It was weak. It was…

Wasn't that what Ace told you? Emotion is weak? Caring is weak?

"Would you do it without me?" Rachel asked firmly, breaking through those old memories of his father.

He'd promised to not let himself lose control. The whole tirade about the Sons and his brothers was bad enough. He wouldn't say anything else stupid. But how could she say that? How could she think he'd leave her behind? To think he'd ever, *ever* let her be a target.

He moved to her, telling himself to keep it locked down. He didn't lose his temper. He didn't lose control. Not because emotions were weak as Ace had always said, but because he had to handle this.

But he wanted to grab her by the arms and shake her. He wanted to do all manner of impossible, disastrously ill-advised things.

Instead, he stood in front of her, maybe a few inches too close, and kept his voice ruthlessly controlled. "Let's make one thing very, very clear. There is not a damn thing I will do without you right now."

She stood very still. The sun had disappeared behind the hills, though there was enough light to still make her out. She wouldn't be able to see anything, even shapes in this light. Still, she moved unerringly into him, wrapping her arms around him.

A hug. A comfort.

He couldn't return it. He couldn't push her away. He could only stand there still as a statue, her arms around him and her cheek pressed to his chest.

"Hell, Rach. Be mad at me. Hate me. I can't stand you being nice to me right now."

"I guess it's too bad for you, because I can't stand to be mad at you right now." She pulled back, tilted her head up toward his. "If you told me right now, promised me right now, that you won't lie again, I'll believe you."

Even knowing he shouldn't, he placed his palm on her cheek. "I'm sorry. I can't do that."

Chapter Twelve

Rachel didn't move away from his hand, even though Tucker's words were...not what she'd expected. At all. She liked the warmth of his calloused palm on her cheek, and she liked how close he was as night descended around them.

She shouldn't be concerning herself with warmth. Or how nice it felt. When he was telling her that he wouldn't promise not to lie.

"Why not?" she asked, and the fact it came out a breathy whisper surprised her, as much as the fact he didn't remove his hand. Instead, his thumb brushed back and forth over her cheekbone.

A sparkling heat shimmered underneath her skin, in her blood. She didn't understand it. Not when it was Tucker touching her, but she could hardly deny it existed. The feeling was too big and real and potent.

His voice was low and rough when he spoke. "I can't promise to never lie. I lied to Brady and Cecilia last month. It was one of the hardest things I've ever done—to lie to my brother like that. Knowing they were both suspicious of me. But I'd do it all over again. I'd have to. Because I was trying to accomplish something good and right. If I had to lie to protect you, Rachel, I would. Any of you. Your sisters. My brothers. Your father. Anyone."

She might not have believed him, except she knew from Cecilia he had definitely lied to Brady. His own brother. Even when Cecilia had been convinced he'd been turned into a Sons member, Brady had trusted him. Even with the lies.

If his own brother could—did—how could she not?

"Okay." She didn't dare nod because he might take his hand away. "Okay."

"We'll camp tonight, and maybe in the morning we'll have a clearer idea of what to do. I managed to grab enough supplies for a day or two for us and Buttercup. This is temporary. Until we figure out how to fix this."

She had no idea how they were going to do that, but it didn't feel so impossible with Tucker touching her. Despite everything, she believed in him. He'd gotten them this far. He'd fought off Shay. Convinced her to let them go.

"I want my dad to be safe. I don't want this awful thing to come back and hurt him. He did the right thing, and he had to give up his whole life. It isn't right that he managed to build a new one and they want to take it away from him."

"No, it isn't. If I knew what to do… If I had any clue, I'd do it. *That* I can promise you."

She nodded, the scrape of his rough hand against her cheek a lovely, sparkling distraction from the fear and confusion roiling inside of her.

He didn't need to promise her anything, but of course he would. She had a plethora of *good* men in her life, and it often insulated her to the fact that bad people like Ace Wyatt and whoever was after her father existed. She so seldom remembered what an enormous miracle it was that Tucker and his brothers had escaped the Sons and become…them.

Good men, determined to do good in the world. Maybe not perfectly. He had his issues. That whole spiel about not being worth the Sons' notice because he wasn't a threat.

If anything underscored all her hurt, it was *that*. Tucker put on a face for the world that he was perfectly adjusted, a good detective, brother, man. And he was those things.

But he didn't think he was.

She didn't know how to make him believe he was all the things *she* thought he was. She could only lean into his hand, lean into *him* and this feeling.

She still didn't know how she felt about being attracted to Tucker, about the possibility he felt the same way. She didn't want to be a domino of Knight girls falling in a line for the Wyatt boys.

But everything swirled inside of her obscuring what she didn't want. She could only think of what she did.

"If they don't think you're a threat, they don't understand you. Caring about people isn't a weakness, Tucker." She placed her hand on his chest when the moment didn't evaporate like she'd been afraid it would. "You don't need to be in North Star or putting yourself in mortal danger to be as strong as your brothers, as important. You solve problems. You take *care* of people. That's just as important as putting your life on the line."

He inhaled sharply, but his hand was still on her face. He was so close, their bodies brushing in the increasing darkness around them. "Rach, I don't know what to say to all that."

His voice was as rough as his hand. He was as strong as she'd said, standing there so close. She couldn't resist tipping her mouth up…wishing for something she'd promised herself she couldn't possibly want.

Then his mouth touched hers. Featherlight. No one had ever kissed her before, and she'd always figured it would take some miracle—getting off the ranch, away from her overprotective father and sisters, into a life that was independent and hers, and when would *that* ever happen.

But it was Tucker Wyatt. She didn't need to convince him she was independent—even when he was protecting her, it was only because that's what he *did*.

It ended far too quickly. The kiss. His hand on her cheek. The sound his footsteps made had her thinking he stumbled back and away, as if he'd realized whom he'd kissed.

"We should get some sleep," he said, his voice tight.

She barked out a laugh, couldn't seem to help the reaction. He'd *kissed* her and he was talking about going to sleep. He was ignoring it. Coward. "You kissed me."

"Forget it. It was... Just forget that."

"Forget it? Why would I?"

"Wrong place. Wrong time. Wrong everything."

She frowned at that. Intellectually, he was probably right. Wrong time certainly, which went along with place. But... "It didn't feel so wrong."

"Well, it was," he said firmly.

So firmly that she thought maybe she was missing something. "Why?"

"*Why?* Because..."

She waited impatiently for him to come up with this reason she was missing. "Because?" she demanded when he was just silent.

"Because you're...you're like a sister to me."

She snorted. It was such a pathetic grasping at straws. "Then you're a pervert, Tucker. You don't check out your sister's boobs and then kiss her."

"I didn't! I never…"

"Sarah said you did."

"I…"

"Maybe you can't promise to lie to me, but if you lie to me about *this*, I won't forgive you. Period."

He was quiet for a long stretched-out moment. "I don't know what you want me to say."

"Why did you kiss me?"

"You want the truth? Here and now of all places? Fine. Maybe I owe that to you after all this. Yeah, I'm attracted to you. I don't have a clue as to why…why *now*. I just am. It's just there. Then you had to go say all that stuff, looking up at me like you meant it."

"I can't see," she pointed out, hoping to lighten the moment.

"You know what I mean," he replied gruffly.

"Yeah, I think I do." Unfortunately that made her all the more gooey-hearted when they had much more important things to deal with. Still, truth for truth was only fair. "I meant it, Tuck. I did. And I…guess I'm attracted to you, too."

"You guess," he muttered disgustedly.

Which almost made her smile. "I'm still working through all that. I haven't exactly had a lot of experience with this."

He groaned. "Please God, tell me that wasn't your first kiss."

"Okay, I won't tell you."

He swore a few times, and she had no idea why that made her want to laugh.

"Look. We need to…go to sleep. Tomorrow, we'll come up with a plan. No more of…this stuff."

"This *stuff*?"

"Whatever this is, we'll figure it out when we're not

camping in the South Dakota wilderness, with absolutely no plan on how we're going to accomplish what we want. For now, we get some rest and focus on the important things."

She nodded as though she agreed with him, and let him lead her into the tent.

TUCKER WOKE UP in his own personal nightmare. He had to come up with a plan to save Duke, to keep Rachel safe. To outwit North Star, the Sons and some other group of people out for blood.

All knowing he'd kissed Rachel. And now she was curled up next to him. Because he'd only had time to grab the pack out of his truck—which was outfitted for one person. A tiny tent and *one* sleeping bag.

It was edging far enough into fall that nights were cold, so he'd had to let her cozy up next to him and fall asleep. All while pretending that kiss had never happened.

It was the only way to survive this. Put a brick wall around his own personal slip-up. Seal it off and forget it.

But he'd never in a million years be able to forget the feel of his lips on hers. Simple kisses weren't supposed to…do that. Make you forget who you were and what was important: safety. Hers most of all.

But he'd forgotten everything except her for those humming seconds—not just the kiss, but her talking to him like she understood him. When it felt like no one did.

He knew his brothers saw him as an equal. They couldn't understand that he didn't *feel* like one.

Right now in this warm tent, Rachel's hair curling against his cheek, the soft rise and fall of her chest matching time with his… Well, he supposed Rachel seeing through his issues was a better line of thought than how good she felt here against him.

She shifted, yawned, her eyes slowly blinking open. Even though she wouldn't be able to see in the dim light of the tent, he could see. The sleep slowly lift. Realization and understanding dawning.

And the way she definitely did not try to slide away or disengage from him, but seemed perfectly content to cuddle closer.

There was a very large part of him that wanted to test it out, too. To see what it would be like to relax into her. To touch her face again. To recognize the soft curves of her body as they pressed to his. To kiss her and—

No. Not possible.

Carefully, he disengaged from her arms and scooted away from her as best he could in the tiny tent.

"Maybe we should go back. I've got nothing. My brothers might have some ideas. They're better at this than I am."

She was quiet for a while as she pushed herself up into a sitting position. "Are they better at it, or were they just put in a position you weren't?"

"You don't need to keep defending me. I don't have low self-esteem. I—"

"You've got issues, Tuck. Good news is, we all do. Better news, you have someone around who's not going to let you believe the crap you tell yourself. So..." She yawned. "I don't suppose you have any coffee?"

He didn't know how to stay in this tiny tent with her looking sleepy and rumpled and gorgeous, talking about how everyone had issues. "I've got some instant. I'll go warm up some water." He didn't *dive* for the tent opening, but he got outside in record time.

The sun was just beginning to rise and the grass held

the tiniest hint of frost. It was cold, made colder by the fact that the tent had been so warm. He shivered against the chill as he zipped the tent back up.

A piece of paper fluttered to the ground next to him. Tuck whirled around, scanning the area. But there was nothing except the soft whisper of the wind against the rolling hills of ranch land.

He crouched down, studied the note on the grass. It was wet from the dew, and all he could figure was that it had been left on the tent, and opening the flap had knocked it off.

He looked around, scanning all he could see for any sign of human life or movement. But the world was quiet, with only the interruption of birdsong.

He picked the paper up and opened the fold. Water had smudged the first word, but Tucker could figure it out and read the rest clearly.

Rachel knows the key and the lock.

Tucker flipped the paper over. Nothing on the back. Nothing else on the front. Just one sentence. That didn't make any sense.

The key and the lock? He thought of the key in his pocket. But what did it unlock? And Rachel definitely didn't act like she had any idea what the key was to.

"Rach." He unzipped the flap again and stuck his head in. She was crouched over, rolling up the sleeping bag. He could tell she'd already tidied what few things were inside. "I found something."

She yawned again. "I take it not coffee." She sighed. "What is it?"

"A note. I... I think this is Duke's handwriting." He frowned, studied it. He wasn't a handwriting expert, and he'd never spent much time scrutinizing Duke's writing, but it certainly looked like his typical slanted scratch.

Tuck looked around the campsite again. He hadn't heard anyone so it was near impossible Duke had left the note for them. He was a big man, and even if he'd been a cop in a former life, stealth was not Duke's current skill. "It was on the tent, then when I opened the flap it fell to the ground."

The only one who knew enough, and had enough access to Duke to get a message to them, was Shay. "Shay must have gotten it to us. She must have."

"Is there any way it's a trap or a trick?" Rachel asked.

"It wasn't addressed to us. There's no signature. It's written in *some* kind of code. So, it might not be from your father, but it's Duke's handwriting." He cleared his throat. "As of yesterday, North Star still had Duke. It could be from North Star. They could have made him write it, but I have to believe if they went through the trouble to track us down, they would have just taken us. You especially. Or written a more specific note."

"Here. Let me see it."

He handed her the paper, though he wasn't sure what she was going to do with it. She felt the corner of the paper. "It's Dad. And not like someone made him write it, either. That's an actual note from him."

"How can you tell?"

"We developed a little system when I was in school. If he had to sign something and he'd done it, he'd poke a little hole in the corner. If there was no hole, I knew I needed to ask him again." She held up the paper, and sure enough there was a small hole in the corner. "What does it say?"

"Rachel knows the key and the lock."

Her eyebrows drew together. *"Me?"* She shook her head. "I don't know anything about that key we found. Let alone what it would unlock."

They were silent for the next few minutes, Rachel frowning as if searching her mind for an answer. Tucker studied the note again, wondering if there was more to it. Something he wasn't seeing. Something more... abstract.

He looked up at Rachel. She'd gone back to tidying up the tent. It was less smooth than how she did it at home since she was going by feel rather than lifelong knowledge of a place. Still, she had the inside of the tent all packed up in no time.

Duke thought she knew what he was talking about, Tucker assumed. Rachel didn't think she knew anything about the key or its lock.

"Maybe it's about your dream. If you know, but you don't actually *know*, maybe the answer is in your subconscious."

Chapter Thirteen

Her dream. Rachel's arms broke out in goose bumps. As much as she was slowly coming around to the idea her dream might be more reality and memory than fiction, she wasn't comfortable with her subconscious knowing something she couldn't access.

Especially when it came to this.

"Dad doesn't know anything about my dreams changing. He still thinks they're about a mountain lion."

"Did you tell him about your dreams?"

"When I was a kid. When I first started having them. He…" An uncomfortable memory had her chest tightening, like she couldn't breathe.

Tucker was immediately at her side. He rubbed a hand up and down her back. "Hey, breathe. It's all right, sweetheart. Take a deep breath."

She managed, barely. The panic had been so swift, so all encompassing, it was hard to move beyond. "I don't know if this was the first time I had the dream, but I remember being little. I still… I may have even still had the bandages on my face. Dad would sleep on the floor of my room. Mom would try to get him to come to bed, but he would insist. He said he was afraid I'd wander away again."

Tucker kept rubbing her back, and it gave her some

modicum of comfort as her body seemed to chill from the inside out.

"I remember telling him about the nightmare and he told me not to tell Mom. That whenever I had nightmares or felt scared, I should tell him. Only him. He said so Mom wouldn't worry, but…"

"If your mother didn't know…"

"How…how could she have not known? How could he have lied to her? How could he have had *me* lie to her?"

"He was in WITSEC, Rach. I'm not saying it was the right thing to do, but you're supposed to leave your old life behind. Entirely."

"It's his story. The mountain lion. He made that up." The horror of that almost made her knees weak. He'd pushed her into the mountain lion story, made sure he convinced her the dreams were of that.

Even when they weren't.

"Are you sure?" Tucker asked gently.

"No. How can I be sure?" Her throat closed up and she refused to cry, but how was she expected to have an answer from a dream? "Everything is wrapped up in a dream that suddenly changed on me!"

"Hey. Maybe it's not about your dream. Maybe I've got this all wrong."

She shook her head. "You know you don't. You're a detective. You know how to piece things together." She wrapped her arms around herself. "What else would I know that I don't think I know? You're right. It's something about my dream, but I don't know *what*."

"Okay, then let's work through this like I'd work through any case. We start at the beginning. What's the very first part of your dream you remember?"

"Do you really think the answer is in my dream?" she asked.

"I don't know. I really don't. But it might help. To lay it all out."

Rachel didn't think that was possible. She'd spent most of her life knowing this dream might pop up. Except the dream had morphed. From what Dad had pointed her to—to the truth? It was impossible to know for sure.

Maybe she'd never get rid of the nightmares, but maybe she could find the truth in the way it had changed… Maybe.

"I'm not sure I know where to start," she said, her voice rough and her chest tight.

Tucker's arm came around her shoulders and he gave her an affectionate squeeze. "Sit. No use crouching around."

"No, no. I need to…to move. To be doing something."

"Okay, so we'll go out and break down the tent while you talk. Sound good?"

She nodded. He helped lead her outside, then led her to the first stake.

"Do you mind if I do it myself?"

"Whatever you need, Rach."

She nodded once and pulled out the stake. Then she felt around the tent, slowly taking it apart. She didn't like to camp, but she and Sarah had often put tents up and down around the ranch as forts or playhouses, so she was familiar with the process of breaking down the tent even without her sight.

Tucker didn't push. He didn't ask questions. Nor did he jump in to help take down the tent. He waited until she started to speak herself. "I'm not sure I know exactly where it starts. When I wake up, when I try to remember, it's just that I'm suddenly aware I'm being carried away."

"Carried away from where?"

"Home. I don't see home, but I know he's taking me away from home." Even knowing she was safe with Tucker, the fear and panic clawed at her. She focused on the tent. "He's taking me away from...lights. I think there's a light behind us and he's going into the dark."

"Lights on in the house maybe?"

"I think so." Even though it was silly since she couldn't see anyway, she closed her eyes. She tried to bring the nightmare back to her. She'd seen for the first three years of her life. There were things she could remember, and this dream had always been one of them.

"Or maybe it's the stables." She opened her eyes, frowning. She could tell light was beginning to dawn in the here and now, but she still couldn't fully make out Tucker's shape. "It isn't windows. It isn't a glow like if it was home at dark. It's more one lone beam of light. I think it's the light outside the stables."

"So, he's taking you away from the stables," Tucker said. His voice was calm and serious and believing. He took everything she said at face value and put it into the puzzle they were trying to work out. "The light on the stables is on the north side. If you're moving straight away from it, that's heading into the north pasture."

"Or toward the highway." She felt how *right* it was, more than saw or knew. Going away from one lone light, heading for the dark of the highway. "The new dream, the changed dream, he's holding me so tight I can barely breathe. I'm too scared to scream. He's talking, but I can't make sense of the words. In my head, they're just a jumble. I just want my mom."

Tears welled up because she still just wanted Mom

and couldn't have her. Couldn't find comfort in her. She'd been gone for so many years now. Rachel folded the tent poles and blinked back tears, fought to make her voice steady. She appreciated that Tucker didn't rush her.

"At some point I notice eyes watching us. They glow a little."

"Mountain lion?"

"At first, that's what I thought. As me. Adult me." She frowned. "I think Dad convinced me that's what I was seeing when I told him about the dream. But when I think about how I saw the eyes move, how it jumps out… I think it was a dog. We used to have dogs then. Lots of them."

"Yeah, four or five, right?"

Rachel nodded. "If this is all real—if it isn't my three-year-old brain getting things mixed up, or dreams mixing with reality, I think it was one of the dogs."

"And it just follows you while the man is carrying you away?"

"Yes. I'm not scared of the eyes. I'm scared of the man. He's holding me too tight, and he has…" She trailed off. This was where she didn't want to go, even knowing she had to.

"Last time, you said he had some kind of knife."

Rachel nodded, folding the tent with shaking hands. "It's either a knife with prongs, or multiple knives. It's sharp, and it keeps flashing in the moonlight." She brought a hand to her scars, and could feel the smooth lines. "It could have made this. Not claws, but this special knife he's carrying." Her breath whooshed out of her. "How is it possible?" she whispered. "And what does any of that tell us about a key?"

"I don't know yet, but let's focus on what you do remember. On the dream."

"That's all I remember. The last one I had, the one where he actually cut me? That's the first time I remember getting that far. Even when I was a kid, he never hurt me in my dream. I woke up before. But in this one, the dog jumps out. The man slashes the knife down and it cuts into me. I can feel the pain and the blood, and hear the dog—barking and snarling. But the dog isn't the one hurting me."

Tucker collected the tent and the poles. She could hear him wrapping it all up and putting it into his backpack. He said nothing.

"Thank you for letting me take down the tent."

"Thank you?"

"Most people can't stand to watch me do something myself, at a slower pace than they would go. They have to jump in to help to speed things up."

"We've got all the time in the world right now, Rach."

But Tucker didn't understand that time didn't always matter. People's compulsion with accomplishing tasks made it hard for them to step back. So, she'd just appreciated that he hadn't needed to do that.

He didn't press about the key, or if she remembered any more of her dream. He simply gave her the space to work through it.

"Do you know where my father is? Where they're keeping him or hiding him or whatever?"

"No."

"Would Cody know?"

Tucker hesitated. "It's possible."

"I don't have the answer to this, Tuck. And Dad clearly wants me to, or thinks I do. He sent us a message, and if Shay was the messenger, it probably wasn't sanctioned by your group."

"No, probably not."

"I need to talk to him. It's the only way."

Tucker couldn't let his own personal feelings or issues, as she'd call them, rule his thoughts or actions. Though it was hard to ignore how much it hurt, he couldn't do this without bringing his brother into the fold.

His brother who'd actually fought the Sons. On multiple levels. And won. Beat Ace. Beat those who would have hurt Cody and his daughter.

Cody. His *baby* brother.

"Tucker?"

"Sorry. I'm just trying to figure out how that would work. We'd have to get to a place that has cell service, and we don't know for sure that North Star doesn't have ways of tracking your phone, too."

"Maybe we should head back to the ranch. Surely North Star doesn't think we'll go back. They'll think we're on the run. We go back. Get word to someone without phones, and have Cody meet us somewhere? We could hide on the ranch. That's smart, don't you think?"

Tucker had to pause and work very hard to keep the bitterness out of his voice. "Yeah, smart."

"Unless you have a better plan?"

"No, Rachel. I don't." How could he?

He continued to clean up the campsite, leaving Rachel standing there with her cane. She ran her fingers over her horse's mane.

She made quite a picture there, dark hand moving through the cream-colored mane of the horse. Her hair was a mess, but it haloed her face. The sun was rising behind her, making the rolling hills sparkle like some kind of fairyland. Her, the reigning queen of it all.

She made a face. "I can tell you're staring at me."

"Maybe I'm staring at the scenery."

"Maybe. But I don't think you are. Why are you staring at me, Tuck?"

"Maybe I think you're pretty, Rach." Which wasn't what he should have said, even if he meant it. Even if her looking pretty was something akin to a punch in the gut. There wasn't room for this—not just because of the current situation—but because of the *always* situation.

"You could kiss me again," she said, very seriously.

She had no idea what it cost him to sound unaffected. "I could, but I don't think that's such a good idea."

"Why not?"

"I can't imagine what Duke would say if I happened to mention it took us so long to help him because I was busy making out with his daughter after spending the night in a tent together."

"After keeping me from being taken by this North Star Group, who are supposedly good guys but condone kidnapping." She huffed out a breath. "I don't understand why you joined them in the first place. Why you worked for people who made you lie."

"Sometimes lies aren't the worst thing in the world."

"I suppose not, but you're not comfortable with them. The weight of that guilt weighs a little heavier on you."

She was right, somehow always seeing right through him. Which meant it seemed honesty was the only option—especially if it kept him from talking about kissing.

"I've been working with them because... I thought I could do something. My father never thought much of me. Not as a threat or as a successor, and mostly

I've been grateful for that. But I thought I could do something, like Cody and Jamison did. Like Gage and Brady did. Hell, even Dev stood up to him." He scowled. It hadn't ended well for Dev at all, but he'd tried. "I've done nothing. I thought I could be a piece of what brought my father down, so I did what North Star asked even though it hurt."

She dropped her hand from the horse, used her probing cane to move forward until she was close to him. Too close. "Until they wanted to take me." She looked up at him, her eyes dark except where they were damaged.

To think it had been a man not a mountain lion made it all worse somehow. The end result was the same, but someone had done that to her on purpose. When she'd only been three. All because her father had done the right thing decades ago.

"You didn't deserve to be dragged into this."

"No. I'm not sure you did, either." She reached out, resting her hand on his arm.

He wanted to touch her hair, her face. He wanted to somehow take those scars away from her, which was a stupid want. This was the life they had. He could only make the right decisions now.

Which meant he had to keep his hands off her. "The Sons connect to me. They connect to this. Don't they always?"

"Only if you let them." She moved onto her toes, leaned into him. She brushed her lips across his jaw, though he imagined she'd been going for his cheek or mouth. Still, it rippled through him. No matter how he told himself to block it away.

"Dev'd probably be a better option for all this," he

said, voice tight. She'd be good for Dev. All light and hope to his dark and hopeless.

She wrinkled her nose and fell back onto her flat feet. "Dev's even older than *you*. And so grouchy. Dev is better suited for a life of inherent bachelorhood. Grandma Pauline told me once all her uncles were bachelors, and she wouldn't be surprised if the lot of you ended up just like them."

"Did she now. Well, four out of six proved her wrong, didn't they?"

"You won't be a perennial bachelor, Tucker. You're too sweet."

"Gee. Thanks."

"You think that's some kind of slight, but it's a compliment. It's a miracle, actually. The way you were brought up. To have any sweet. I think that's pretty amazing."

She almost made him believe it.

"We should get back. Time isn't on our side. The North Star Group has a lot of skills, technology and reach. We can only avoid them for so long, even with Shay's help."

"All right, but you're not getting out of this so easy."

No, he didn't think he was.

Chapter Fourteen

The ride back to the ranch was quiet. Not tense, exactly. There was a certain comfort to just riding Buttercup, Tucker's strong body behind her. A companionable silence as they both thought through what was next.

She had to believe Cody would know enough about North Star to figure out where they'd be keeping her father or what they'd be doing with him. She had to believe he'd give them the location, Tucker would find Dad, and they'd get him away.

Then what?

Well, the key. Dad would know what the key opened and maybe it would...end everything.

Of course, she thought if it would end everything Dad would have handed it over to North Star, told *them* about the key and the lock. But maybe he just didn't trust them. Maybe he could only trust her.

Rachel wished she had any idea what the key was for. There was nothing to unlock in her dream. There was only darkness and fear. Pain and relief all mixed into one powerful, messy, emotional experience.

Tucker zigzagged through rolling hills. "I'm going to head up along the north pasture, come down to the stables that way. Maybe the route will remind you of something."

"I can't see, Tucker."

"I know, Rachel," he said with an endless patience that dug at her. "But I'll tell you where we are, what I see. It can't hurt to try to reenact the moment. And if it doesn't jog your memory, all we've done is add a little time I would have probably added anyway to make sure we aren't being followed."

She didn't say anything to that. Going through the dream once already had left her emotionally drained. Then there was the fact Tucker had refused to kiss her.

Though she wasn't convinced it was because he didn't *want* to. She figured there was something more about honor or loving her dad or something twisted up. Because he watched her. She couldn't see and she could *tell* he looked at her in ways he hadn't before.

She could feel the tension in him when she'd touched him. That quick little sigh of breath he'd tried to hide when she'd tried to kiss his mouth and ended up just touching her lips to his jaw.

Maybe she'd missed, but that had been nice, too. The rough whiskers against her lips. There had been an exciting friction in that.

Tucker Wyatt and exciting friction. She might have laughed at the thought of those two things going together, but it just seemed...right, when it never had before.

"We're on the hill outside the north pasture gate. I can see the top of the stable. From here I can see the light. If it was dark and the light was on, it'd be visible this whole stretch."

Even though she didn't want to, she brought to mind her dream. The light. "Where's the highway in relation to where we are?"

"We're facing south. The highway is due east."

"And how far would you be able to see the light in that direction?"

He clicked to the horse, and they moved. "Let's see. If you were headed for the highway, but looking back toward the house or stables..." He trailed off and the horse moved in a gently swaying motion beneath them. "Most of the way. The main gate is just coming into view and I can see the very top of it. Which means if the light was on, I'd be able to see it clearer."

The main gate led to a gravel road, which led to the highway, but it all made sense. The light had gotten smaller as the man had taken her. Like it was slowly being enveloped—or in this case, hidden by distance, direction and hills.

"I think that's where he was taking me."

"On foot, right? So, probably heading for a vehicle. Then the dog saves you."

Rachel brought a hand up to her scars. Her mother had never let her feel much self-pity over the loss of sight, over the scars. Rachel supposed her age helped with that. She didn't remember all that much before, so it wasn't a comparison or ruminating over what she'd lost.

But the dog *saving* her felt like too strong a word. She hadn't been saved fully. She'd lost something that night.

"Tuck..." She swallowed at the sudden emotion clogging her throat. "Why do you think he did it? Lied to me. To my mom. Made us think something had happened when it hadn't. I know he had to keep his former life a secret, but... I love him, I do. Nothing changes that, but I'm having a really hard time not being mad at him for warping my nightmares to keep this secret."

"Can you imagine how he feels? He did something right. *One right thing.* He did his job, and he had to leave his entire life. Then he starts a new one and this right thing he did not only haunts him, it hurts and permanently injures his daughter. I lied to you, Rach. Because I thought it would protect you. You and Sarah and... everyone. I can't imagine his lies were any different."

"But they are. He made me think something completely different happened than actually did. It wasn't just a lie of omission or hiding something. He *warped* something I actually experienced."

"What's worse? Believing a random act of Mother Nature hurt you, or that your father's past was out there, just waiting? I know what that's like. To know at any point your past could pop up and ruin your life. I mean, Grandma Pauline gave us a good life, a good childhood once we got out of the Sons. But we always knew Ace could pop up—hurt us, hurt her. We always knew Jamison sacrificed eighteen years to get us out of there. It's a hard, heavy weight."

Rachel didn't know what to say to that. She certainly couldn't argue with it, and as much as it hurt that her father had lied to her in such a devious way, she understood that Tucker thought Duke had given her a gift. Maybe he had. What would life have been like if she'd always been afraid?

Tucker had come through it okay, but she was realizing he had deeper scars than he ever let on.

Tucker's body went suddenly tense, not just behind her but his arms holding the reins around her. Everything in him was iron and she was encompassed in all that strength. "We're going to get off the horse."

"What? Why? What's happened?"

"There's a man watching us." He'd slowed down Buttercup, but they were still moving. "We have to do this quickly. I'm going to swing you off with me. I'll point you in the right direction. Then you run for the stables. I'll send Buttercup off as a distraction, and I'll run for him. Three different directions, and he'll either focus on the horse or me."

"Is it North Star?"

Tucker was quiet for a long moment. "I want you to run to the stables. Hide in there. That's it."

"But—"

"I need you to do it, Rach. If I need help, I'll yell, okay?"

He wouldn't. She knew he wouldn't. But he couldn't protect himself, or her, if she didn't listen to him. He'd try to play the hero even more than he already was.

If he wasn't answering her question about North Star, well, that was worse. So, she'd run. If she made it to the stables, she could make it to the house. She could call for help. She didn't have her cane, but once she got to the stables she'd know where she was. She'd be able to move around the ranch without it.

As long as she didn't fall on her run to the stables.

"On my count. One, two, three." She let him swing her off the horse, and he helped her land a lot more gracefully than she might have alone. He turned her by the shoulders in the right direction.

Then, she ran.

TUCKER POINTED RACHEL in the right direction, gave Buttercup's reins a flick, then ran himself. There was no cover until he got a lot closer, so he couldn't pretend like he was doing anything but going after the man behind the fence.

Who had a gun. If it was North Star, he wouldn't shoot.

If it wasn't...well...

The sound of the gunshot had him hitting the ground. When nothing hit him, he took a chance to look toward Rachel. She was still running, as was Buttercup, so no one had been struck.

Tucker got back to his feet, went back to running toward the man, but this time in a zigzag pattern. If he could get to the copse of trees that followed the creek, he could use some cover to get closer.

Another gunshot. Tucker didn't dive for the ground this time. Based on the angle of the gun, he was almost certain the man was shooting at him, not the horse or Rachel. He didn't have time to pause and look, though. He had to keep going.

He reached the cluster of trees and pulled his gun out of its holster. Clicking the safety off, he gave himself a moment to hide behind a tree and steady his breathing. His chest burned with effort, his heart pounded with fear and adrenaline.

The creek was nearly dry, but the trees were thick and old. When the third gunshot went off, it hit a tree way too close to Tucker for comfort.

The fence the man had been crouched behind was due east of the tree Tucker was behind. Still, moving enough to see and shoot would put him at risk.

It was only a gut feeling, not fact, but Tucker sincerely doubted the man was part of North Star. As much as they might prioritize mission over innocent life, they weren't the type to shoot first and ask questions later.

That was more Sons territory. But what would they be doing just lurking around waiting for Tucker and Rachel to appear? How would they know they'd disappeared in the first place?

Unless it was coincidence.

Tucker couldn't mull it over much longer. He had to

act so whoever the gunman was didn't get it in his head to go after Rachel.

He slid from one tree to another, working the angles to keep as much distance between him and the shooter as possible.

Another shot went off, but it was way more off target than the last one. Tucker got the glimpse of movement out of the corner of his eye, quickly changed direction to get behind a tree. The gunman was coming toward him just as Tucker tried to move toward the gunman.

He was somewhat hesitant to shoot someone not knowing where they came from or why they were shooting at him, but when the next bullet hit the tree he was standing behind, he figured it was time to do what needed to be done.

Tucker used the tree as cover, listened for the man's movements, then when he thought he had a clear idea of where the man was, stuck his arm out to shoot. He didn't need it to hit, just needed to catch the man off guard.

Immediately after the first shot, he peeked out from behind the tree. The shooter had ducked behind a bush, but as he slowly rose again, gun aimed, Tucker managed to get off a shot first.

The man stumbled backward. Tucker immediately charged. He didn't think he'd hit anything vital, which meant he had to get the gun away from him.

The assailant had lost his gun—a long high-powered looking model—after Tucker had shot him, but he was curling his fingers around the barrel as Tucker approached. He had to lunge to get to it before the man could lift it.

It was narrow timing, but Tucker managed to grab a hold of the handle. They grappled, pulling and jerking like a life-or-death game of tug-of-war. Which gave

Tucker the idea to take the dangerous chance of letting the gun go.

Since he'd been pulling hard, the attacker fell backward, the gun winging out of his grasp as Tucker had hoped. Tucker immediately leaped on him.

Even with the gunshot wound, the man fought hard. The bullet must have only glanced his side, even with the amount of blood staining his shirt. Tucker had to fight dirty to win, so he landed the hardest blow he could at the spot with the most blood.

The man howled, grabbing the injured section and rolling away. Tucker managed to pin him, face down, hands pulled behind his back. With pressure on the injured side to keep the man from fighting back, Tucker looked around for something to tie the man's hands.

Which was when he noticed the man was wearing a utility belt. Tucker went through the pockets, found a phone and tossed it as far into the creek bed as he could. Next he discovered a plastic bottle of some kind of clear liquid wrapped in a cloth—he disposed of that in the same way—and then happened upon the perfect answer to his problems. Zip ties. He quickly got them on the man's wrists, then had to fight to get another one around the man's legs.

The man swore and spit and kicked, but there wasn't much he could do with his arms tied behind his back and his legs bound together. Tucker got to his feet and rolled the man over onto his back.

Tucker didn't recognize him—not that he'd recognize every Sons goon. Still, there was something different about him. About the way he dressed and held himself, as though he wasn't quite used to the rough terrain.

Sons members were too local, too used to living in the elements and outside of society. This man didn't even have a knife on him. Just the high-powered gun, some zip ties, the phone and a tiny bottle of something Tucker assumed was a knockout drug.

All the tools for kidnapping.

Tucker's stomach roiled, but he didn't let it show. He sneered down at the man.

"I assume you're with Vianni."

The man spit at him.

Tucker didn't flinch, didn't jump away, as the spit missed him entirely. He kept his sole focus on the assailant. "Who are you here for?"

"Not you."

"I guess I could just leave you here, all tied up, and never let anyone know." Tucker looked up at the sky. "Might be fall, but sunny day like this? Going to get pretty hot."

"Bud, so much worse is coming for you if you don't let me go. I don't even care *what* you do."

Tucker leaned in, smiled. "Oh, you're going to care."

Chapter Fifteen

The gunshots had Rachel pulling out her phone. She was afraid to speak too loudly, but her phone was having trouble picking up her voice with her shaky whisper. "Call Cody," she finally said with enough force.

"Rachel? Where are you?"

There was a sharp command in his voice that calmed her. Because he would know what to do when she didn't.

"I'm in the stables at our ranch. Tucker saw someone and went after them. There's been gunshots. I know you're in Bonesteel—"

"I'm going to get off the line and call Brady. He's right next door."

"No! Listen. I mean, you can call Brady, but you have to know North Star is mixed up in this somehow. They have Dad. Tucker was working for them. Then this woman helped us—helped *me* not get taken by North Star and... I don't understand what's going on."

There was a brief pause. "I'm calling Brady to help Tuck. As for North Star..." Another pause that had Rachel holding her breath. "The woman? Was her name Shay?"

"Yes."

"All right. You stay put. I'll get back to you on the North Star thing." The connection clicked off and Rachel slipped her phone back into her pocket. Sure, Brady could maybe take care of things, but he was hurt, too. Likely Dev was out in the pasture somewhere with Sarah.

Would they have heard the gunshots? Surely, they'd have had to. Wouldn't they come running? Call their own reinforcements?

She couldn't just stand here, though. Tuck could have been the one shot.

She heard the door creak open and she pressed herself against the corner.

"Rach?"

"Tuck." She raced forward too quickly and tripped, but arms grabbed her before she could fall face-first. She was too relieved he was okay to be embarrassed. She held on to him as he helped her back to her feet. "You're okay."

"Yeah. We have to get out of here."

"No, it's okay. I phoned Cody. He was calling Brady and figuring out the North Star thing and—"

"What did you do that for?" he demanded, his voice sharp and unforgiving. He released her and she stood in the middle of the stable, feeling unaccountably chastened.

"What do you mean, what did I do that for? A man was out there. I heard gunshots. What was I supposed to do?"

"Just hide here like I told you to."

"You don't get to boss me around, Tuck. Certainly not when there are *guns* going off. We agreed to talk to Cody about—"

"About where your dad might be. Not drag my brothers into a lethal situation."

"Why not? You got dragged into Brady's thing.

Brady was dragged into Felicity's. It's what we do. Get dragged into each other's dangerous run-ins. And it always goes a little better with help, doesn't it?"

He was silent.

"Besides, it's too late. Cody is calling Brady and he's going to look into the North Star thing. He knows Shay."

"Well, he used to work for them."

"But he knew who she was even before I said her name."

"Sit tight," Tucker said, like he was about to leave her alone again. *Oh, no. Not going to happen.* She lunged forward and managed to grab his shirt.

"You will stop this right now." He tried to tug her hand off his shirt, but she only held on tighter. "I don't know what the damn key unlocks, Tucker. I don't understand anything Dad said in that letter. Now there's a man after us. Don't brush me off. Don't tell me to sit tight, and don't act like a child because we need help. I can't even do the *one thing* Dad seems to think I can." Emotion rose up in her throat, making her words squeak when it was the last thing she wanted. "If we need help, it's because of me. Not you."

"Rach." Instead of tugging her hand away again, he drew her close and smoothed a hand over her hair. "None of this is your fault."

Wouldn't that be nice? She leaned into Tucker, wondering if she'd ever fully believe that when the letter had said she was the key. It helped that he'd said it, though. That he'd take the time to give her a hug.

Someone cleared their throat from over by the door. "Uh, sorry to interrupt but I was just wondering if I should ask why there's a guy in zip ties lying next to the creek?" Dev said.

"What are you doing here?" Tucker demanded, releasing her abruptly.

"What am I doing here? You know how sound travels, right? Gunshots ring out while I'm tending to my cattle, and I'm left figuring out who the hell is shooting things. I sent Sarah over to Grandma's to round up help."

"Tucker's being very childish about help."

Dev made a sound that *might* have been a laugh, if he wasn't perpetually grumpy Dev who almost never laughed. At least not without a sarcastic edge. "Yeah, we Wyatts get that way sometimes. Should I leave the guy where he is?"

"Yes," Tucker said.

"And there aren't others?"

"Not yet."

"Who is he?" Rachel demanded.

There was a pause and Rachel didn't have to see to know *something* passed between brothers.

"I guess I'll go head over and stop Sarah and Brady and whoever else off at the pass."

"Have Brady call local police—ones he'd trust to keep it as quiet as possible—to pick up the guy."

Dev didn't say anything to that, but she heard him retreating so she assumed it was some kind of assent.

"What exactly are we going to do?"

"We're going to follow the original plan. Sort of. The next step is getting Cody to see what he might be able to tell us about North Star and Duke, but I want to keep the rest of the family out of it as much as we can. Not because I need to do this on my own, but because the more people we drag into this, the more targets they have. The wider it gets, the harder it is to fight."

She supposed that made sense. A gunman had been

waiting on the ranch. What if Sarah had happened to drive by on her way to town? Or what if Dev had come that way instead of across the pasture where Knight land butted up against Reaves land?

If she and Tucker went off on their own, maybe they'd be able to keep the focus on them, not their families.

"So, we're heading to Bonesteel on Buttercup?"

"Not exactly. The guy has to have a car around here somewhere. And it just so happens, I grabbed his keys."

TUCKER LED RACHEL toward the front gate. He imagined Vianni's man had hidden the car somewhere on the gravel road. There weren't very many places to hide a car, so it should be easy enough to find.

"It still doesn't make sense," Rachel said, one arm hooked with his as he helped her walk. Though this ground was a little more familiar than not, she didn't spend a lot of time walking this far past the main buildings.

"What doesn't?"

"Dad's note. I've gone over and over my dream. There's never been anything about a key. Or a lock. Not in old dreams and not in the new ones. Dad wouldn't even know about the new ones. I never mentioned it to anyone until you. In fact, the more I think about it, the more I don't think he knew I still had the nightmares. I didn't tell him. I didn't wake up screaming. For all he knew, they went away."

It made Tucker's chest ache that she'd continued to be tormented by the dreams and hadn't told Duke, or anyone else. Just dealt with them. As they slowly morphed into something real.

"What else could it be?"

She shook her head as they walked. "I don't know,

but we've only focused on my dream. Maybe it's something else…"

"Okay, so the note said you know the key and the lock. We've been focusing on the key, since we found that. Maybe we should think about locks. Are there any locks in your dream?"

She shook her head. "No keys. No locks. Nothing even symbolic of a key or a lock."

"So let's think about Duke. Do you remember anything about keys and locks you specifically associate with him?"

They reached the gate and Tucker looked down the gravel lane. He wanted to get out of here before the police arrived. Avoid answering any questions they'd have so he and Rachel could move on to the next step.

He wasn't looking forward to bringing Cody into this, but there didn't seem to be another option. Brady was involved now. Dev as well, to an extent.

It ate at him that he'd failed so spectacularly at keeping them out of it. He'd wanted to let them heal and protect their families and instead…

"Wait." Rachel stopped abruptly. "Key and lock. It wouldn't have to be…literal, would it?"

"I mean, we have a key. That's pretty literal."

"Or it's not. It's not about the dream. It's not about the key. It's about Dad. Take me to the cemetery."

"I'm sorry…*what*?"

"The cemetery. Where Mom's buried. It's not far from here. Dad always said… Mom was the key to his lock. Like, always. It was one of his favorite sayings before she died. He doesn't say it much anymore. But he used to. Key and lock."

"Okay," Tucker said gently. "But…"

"Maybe it's nothing. I know it sounds crazy. But Dad

wrote that letter and it says, *Rachel knows the key and the lock*. Well, if he's the lock—she's the key."

Tucker couldn't imagine what might be hiding at the cemetery, let alone at Eva Knight's grave, but it was hard to refuse her request. Even knowing it was beyond a long shot.

"We have to find the car first." He opened the gate and led Rachel through. The Knight ranch was the last turn off on the gravel road. If Tucker had been trying to hide a car, he'd have gone past the gate, then tried to hide the car in a ditch.

They walked down the side, Tucker keeping an eye and ear out for any cars that might be coming.

Just as he'd predicted, he found the car just a ways down, half in a ditch. You'd only see it if you passed the gate and likely their little spy had been counting on no one going that far.

Tucker helped Rachel into the car, then slid into the driver's seat himself, adjusting the seat. It smelled a little too much like cigarettes and cheap cologne, so he rolled down the windows.

Keeping his eye out for a police cruiser, he took the backroads to the cemetery where Eva Knight was buried. The parking lot was empty, which was good. "We can't spend too much time here."

"I know. I just need to… I don't know. If she's the key…"

"I get it." He thought it was too symbolic and metaphorical, but she had to look. Hell, even he had to look or he'd wonder if he'd missed something. He got out of the car, then went over to Rachel's side and helped her out, leading her through the archway of the cemetery entrance.

He didn't have to lead her any farther than that. She'd

clearly been here plenty, since she walked around the other graves with unerring accuracy, before stopping in front of her mother's.

Eva Knight. Loving wife and mother to all her girls. 1970–2006.

She'd been more than that little epitaph. She'd been the only calm, gentle presence across the Knight and Wyatt ranches. Until Rachel had taken on that mantle, and maybe Tucker had tried to be some of that as much as he could.

"I miss her," Rachel said softly.

"Me too." Missed her, and felt suddenly ashamed he'd let Rachel get so involved in this. Eva would have expected him to keep her safe. Keep *all* the girls safe. "She'd want you to be safe. At home."

"No. No, she wouldn't." Rachel smiled at him, and though there were tears in her eyes, they didn't fall. "She wanted everyone to treat me like an equal. Even if it hadn't been for the blindness, I was their only biological daughter and she never wanted the other girls to feel less. She was careful. So careful to treat me like everyone else. To give me the same responsibilities and expectations. Honestly, I think that's why... Well, Dad and Sarah, they kind of treat me like a maid. They don't mean to. It's just, I was always supposed to pull my weight. Mom wanted me on equal footing." She took a deep shaky breath. "I *am* on equal footing. Maybe you have the eyes and the police skills, but I know the key and the lock. What do you see?"

"Just the grave. Just the grass around it. There are some flowers in the holder."

"Fresh?"

"Yeah, they're drooping a bit. Maybe been here a few days, but fresh enough."

"So, Dad's been here recently. Before he left."

"It could have been one of your sisters."

She shook her head. "No. They always tell me if they're going so I can go, too. It had to be Dad. And it was in the last few days. The key *has* to be here."

Tucker didn't remind her that technically they had a key, and they were essentially just searching for a lock. Still, he would do it for her because… Well, his leads were nonexistent. He went around the grave, looking for anything. He even pulled out the flowers and looked into the water holder. He laid his hands over the stone, and it was only as he moved his palm over the side of the grave that he felt something odd under his foot.

Unsure, he stood. "Wait. This is…" Tucker toed the grass with his boot. A whole section of it moved, like a square of sod had been placed down over dirt. Coincidence, no doubt. Still he let go of Rachel and crouched down. He pulled up the square of sod. Underneath was freshly unpacked dirt. Tucker poked his finger into it. Not far beneath the crumbles of dirt was something hard.

"What is it?" Rachel demanded.

He began to dig in earnest. It was just a tiny metal tube, but it had a lid and Tucker screwed it off. He pulled out a slip of paper. It only had numbers on it, but it was clear what they were. "I found a piece of paper buried in the ground. There are numbers on it. It's a combination. Like to a safe."

"The only safe I know of is…"

"Grandma Pauline's," they finished together.

Chapter Sixteen

They drove to Reaves ranch in silence. Rachel felt a little raw as she always did after visiting her mother's grave. She'd only been seven when Mom had died, but she had worked so hard to live up to that memory that it felt like her mom had been around longer.

Which was nice.

It was also strange that Tucker had said Eva would have expected him to keep her safe, and suddenly she understood her place in her family a little better. Mom had done her best to make her an equal for two very different reasons—biology and her blindness—and both had worked. She was an independent, equal individual in her family.

If she'd felt trapped before this all started, or scared her future was never going to change, maybe that was just normal adulthood stuff—not the result of her blindness.

"What are we going to do?" Tucker muttered. "Just barge in and demand Grandma Pauline let us open her safe?"

Rachel didn't think he was actually asking her, but she answered anyway. "She knows something, Tuck. If this leads to *her* safe, Dad certainly didn't hide it there without her knowing."

She could sense his frustration. She wasn't sure exactly what it was toward, so she reached over and rested her hand on his arm. It was tense, and she imagined he was gripping the steering wheel hard enough to break it.

"If Grandma hid something about this, you should be angry with her," he told her.

"I'll save my anger for when I know what actually happened. You're only angry because you're scared."

"Scared?" he demanded.

"Your brothers can take care of themselves, even if they're injured or have kids to protect. You have a certain comfort in knowing they're all law enforcement and know how to deal with these issues. But your grandmother?"

"Raised the six of us, put the fear of God into Ace so he never came after her, and taught us all how to shoot way better than any law enforcement training. I'm not scared for her."

Rachel wasn't so sure. Sometimes you could know someone was strong and good, like her father, and still worry something had changed. Or something had been there that you'd never known.

She sighed as Tucker slowed the car. "How are we going to play this?"

"We're going to go in and tell her we're going to open the safe."

"You've met your grandmother, right? You go in there demanding things, she's going to knock you out with that wooden spoon."

Tucker didn't say anything to that, so she opened the car door and slid out. "You let me handle it," she said decisively. She closed the car door and started striding for the house. Tucker hadn't parked in his normal spot, so once she reached the house she had to feel around for the door.

She didn't knock. She stepped inside, and she could hear Tucker striding quickly behind her as if he meant to beat her to the house and take over.

No. Not on this. "Grandma Pauline?"

"What on earth are you doing here?" Pauline demanded.

Rachel could make out her form over by the sink or oven. "We need to get into the safe."

Tucker closed the door behind her, and she could feel him standing next to her. She couldn't see Grandma Pauline's expression, but she could feel the hesitation in the silence.

Rachel nodded toward Tucker. "We have the combination. Because Dad gave us a clue. He wants us to get into the safe."

Grandma Pauline sighed. "All right, then. Follow me."

"That wasn't exactly asking nicely," Tucker muttered into her ear. He took her arm as if he meant to lead her, and though she didn't need it in this house, she didn't mind her arm in his hand.

"I can say things like that to her. *You* can't," Rachel whispered back as Grandma Pauline led them down into the basement.

Rachel had to trust Grandma Pauline and Tucker to open the safe. To tell her what was inside. She knew from hearing everyone talk about it that it was a giant safe. The boys used to joke it was where Grandma Pauline hid dead bodies.

Rachel shuddered at the thought.

"Bottom shelf there. That's Duke's," Grandma Pauline said in her no-nonsense way.

Tucker let go of her elbow. There was the sound of shuffling and scraping. "It's another safe," Tucker said, sounding wholly baffled. "Not small, either. What on earth is happening here?"

"Is it another combination?"

"No. This one has a lock. I'm assuming that's what the key you found is for."

"Well, open it," she urged. Surely this safe wouldn't lead to yet another. *Surely* this was the last step.

Rachel had to wait more interminable seconds. She could hear Tucker fitting the key into the hole on the lock. The click. A squeak as the safe opened.

Tucker swore. Not angrily but more shock. More... fear. Rachel even heard Grandma Pauline's sharp inhale of surprise.

"What is it?" Rachel demanded when no one spoke.

"Rachel..."

"Tell me," she insisted. "*Now.*"

Tucker sighed. "It looks like... It looks like the knife you described in your dream. And there's...there's old blood on it."

Rachel couldn't even make sense of that. "I don't understand."

"He kept the weapon that injured you. Kept it locked away." There was a ribbon of hurt in Tucker's voice that finally made the words sink in.

Except, how...

"He kept the knife. That hurt me. On purpose."

"You knew," Tucker accused, and Rachel understood he was talking to Grandma Pauline.

"No. Not in the way you think," Grandma Pauline replied. Though she didn't betray any emotion, she didn't speak with her usual verve. "After the accident, Duke was distraught. He needed... Well, he felt alone.

Guilty. Responsible. Now, you've both dealt with the Sons enough to know that it wasn't his fault. It was those awful people's fault."

It was an admonition disguised as fact—Grandma Pauline's specialty. It didn't make Rachel feel any better about anything, though.

"He asked me to hide something for him and not to ask questions. I didn't. He called it insurance. That's all I know about it. Timing-wise, I knew it connected to what happened to Rachel, but not how or what."

"It doesn't make sense. If he had what hurt me, he would have taken it to the police. He would have used it." She turned toward Tucker's form. "Why wouldn't he have used what he could to put them in jail with this when it happened?"

"I don't know, Rach."

He sounded immeasurably sad, which of course made her feel worse. Dad had kept a weapon that had blinded her at the age of three. Locked it up like he was protecting the people who'd hurt her.

"I know it's hard, but let's not jump to conclusions."

"Not jump to conclusions?" Rachel couldn't tell where Grandma Pauline was standing in the dark with her own heart beating so loud in her ears. "I was blinded by a man with that knife when I was *three years old*. I might have been killed. I'll jump to every damn conclusion I want."

And because all she wanted to do was cry, she marched back the way she'd come and up the stairs.

"Well, don't just stand there, boy. Go follow her."

"Grandma…" Tucker couldn't wrap his head around it. He didn't know how this could have gotten so much worse. "This is…"

"You don't know *what* it is. And before you get all high and mighty on me, I don't know what it is, either. I took the safe and put it in my own because a friend asked me to. I didn't ask any questions, because I'd been around enough to understand some things are better left alone."

"He made her believe—and all of us believe—she'd been mauled by an animal."

"Any person who'd use that knife on a child *is* an animal. That's the truth of it. You don't know Duke's truth or what he's done or escaped or how this might have been him protecting her. Don't you think I've done some shady things to protect you and your brothers?"

It was a horrible thought. She'd raised them to do what was right. To uphold the law after watching their father break it, try to destroy it for the entirety of their childhoods. And she was admitting to *shady* things to keep them safe.

"Rachel's hurting. She feels betrayed. Fair enough. But you're protecting her, which means you've got to think beyond her hurt. Duke's a good man. You know it and I know it."

"Maybe he's not as good as we think he is."

"Or maybe, good isn't as simple as you want it to be. Now, go after her."

Tucker did as he was told, in part because it was habit and in part because he was worried what Rachel would do next. *He* knew what it was like to feel like you could never understand or believe in your father, but she never had.

She wasn't in the kitchen and the door was ajar, so he stepped outside. She was pacing the yard. He had a feeling that constant movement was what kept her from losing the battle with tears.

"We need to keep moving. Stay on plan."

She shook her head. "The plan? To save him from those people when he..." She just kept shaking her head as if she could negate the truth. "He shouldn't have that. I can't think of one good reason he'd have it locked up."

"Then let's go find out the reason," Tucker said gently. "We find your father. We have our answers."

"What if the answers are... What if he's..."

She couldn't get the words out, so he supplied them for her. "Not the man you thought he was?"

Her lips trembled, but she gave a sharp nod.

"Nothing he's done changes two very simple facts. One, we know he helped bring down dirty cops. Whatever he's done, he fought for the right thing and probably out of a need to protect his family. Two, he's been a great father and a good man for as long as I've known him. If he made a mistake, it might have been for the right reasons. Or maybe it's forgivable. Or maybe, it wasn't a mistake at all. We don't know until we talk to him." He took her by the shoulders, trying to give her a certainty he didn't fully believe. "He gave you the clue. You figured it out. No matter what...we have to see this through. If only so you can have some answers."

"Answers. What possible answer could make this not awful?"

"I don't know. But that doesn't mean there isn't one."

She leaned into him. They didn't have the time, and yet he couldn't rush her. Not when she was grappling with what he knew too well was... He hated his father. Always had. Yet even with all that hate, it was complicated knowing he was related to someone so awful.

Duke wasn't awful. Grandma had that right. Whatever mistake he might have made, it wouldn't have been done out of cruelty. Tucker had to believe that, and with answers, they'd all be able to move forward.

"Come on. Let's head over to Bonesteel. We'll meet with Cody and come up with a plan to get to Duke. He wanted us to find this, Rach. Maybe it's useful. Important."

"Should we leave it with Grandma Pauline if it's so important?"

"She'll keep it safe. That's why it's here in the first place."

"Tucker..." She pulled away, and tilted her head toward him. Her eyebrows drew together and she opened her mouth but didn't say anything, as if she was struggling to come up with the words.

She needed reassurance, and Tucker didn't feel very sure, but he wanted to give that to her. Wanted her to be able to believe in Duke and trust that they were doing the right thing trying to save him from North Star, the Viannis *and* the Sons. "It'll be okay. I'm not saying it will be easy, but it'll be okay. I know it."

It had to be.

Chapter Seventeen

Tucker had to lead Rachel to Cody and Nina's door. Rachel had been to their house in Bonesteel a few times, but most family get-togethers were at one of the ranches. She didn't know her way around very many other places.

Tucker had explained he was parking around back, so she knew she was being led to the back door, which opened into a kitchen. Since it was the middle of the day, Nina was probably teaching her seven-year-old Brianna and Liza's half sister, the just-turned-five Gigi. Her and Liza traded off homeschool-teaching duties.

The door squeaked open. Immediately Nina went, "Oh," as if she knew exactly what was going on.

Then Rachel was quickly being ushered inside and greeted by her enthusiastic niece.

"Aunt Rachel! I didn't know you were coming over. Are you good at adding?"

"Brianna," Nina said in that warning tone moms always seemed to have. "No having Rachel or Tuck do your math while I go get your father."

"Where's Gigi?" Rachel asked as she heard Nina retreat.

"She's sick. I heard Aunt Liza say she threw up *everywhere*," Brianna said with some glee. "If you had three hundred and twenty-four…um, apples. And then Uncle Tuck brought you fifty-seven more—"

"Brianna!" Nina yelled from somewhere deeper in the house.

Brianna humphed. "Why are you guys visiting in the middle of the day?" Brianna seemed to suddenly realize it was odd timing. "Is there trouble again?"

Poor girl. She was way too intimately acquainted with trouble. Rachel forced a reassuring smile. "Just a little, but it's a problem for Uncle Tuck and me. Nothing for you to worry about."

"You need Daddy's help?"

"Only for a few minutes," Tucker interjected. "He won't even have to leave home."

Brianna sighed with some relief. "So are you guys going to get married then?"

Tucker seemed to choke on his own spit, and Rachel found herself utterly speechless.

"What now?" Tuck finally managed, though his voice sounded croaky at best.

"Well, when Mommy and Daddy were in trouble, they ended up getting married. And same with Aunt Liza and Uncle Jamison. Then Uncle Gage and Aunt Felicity are getting married and having a baby. Uncle Brady and Aunt Cecilia aren't getting married yet, but I heard Mom say that it was *inevitable*. Now you two are in trouble. So…"

"No, sweetheart, that's not…how it works…exactly." Tucker sounded so pained it was almost funny.

There was the sound of footsteps and low murmurs. Then Nina's voice. "Get your math book, Bri. We'll go finish up in the living room."

There was a long suffering sigh and the shuffle of books, papers and feet.

"Say goodbye to your aunt and uncle."

"Aren't they going to stay for dinner? We could order pizza." Nina must have given her a significant mom look because Brianna groaned and stomped away.

Rachel felt Nina's slim hand on her arm. "I'm sure Cody and Tucker can take care of whatever this is."

Rachel slid her arm away. "Don't do that to me. You didn't let Cody and Jamison handle your thing."

"Rach, I'm just saying... You're not a part of this. You could go home and—"

"I *am* a part of this. I'm the only reason we've gotten this far. Isn't that right, Tucker?"

There was a hesitation, like he might refute her so Nina could whisk her away and keep her safe. But there was no safety here. Whether she helped get Dad away from North Star or these other groups or not, Dad had still lied to her—to all of them.

She wanted to believe there was a reason for it. Maybe she had to do this so she could actually...see it. If someone just told her, even Dad, that it was for her own good...

She'd never be able to forgive him.

"Rachel's right," Tucker finally said. "We wouldn't be this far without her. If we're going to get Duke away from North Star—"

"Woah, woah, woah," Cody's voice interrupted Tucker. "What makes you think you're getting *anyone* away from North Star?"

"They tried to kidnap me," Rachel said.

"Rach, if they tried, you'd be kidnapped."

"No, she's right," Tucker told him. "They sent this woman named Shay to take her. They must have been listening in somehow and knew she was getting clues about everything from her dreams. Shay and I fought—"

"No offense, Tuck, but Shay'd take you down in a heartbeat."

"You know her that well?"

There was a pause. "I worked with her quite a bit. She's helped me out of a few jams."

"I have to go help Bri," Nina said softly. "Just...be careful. Both of you." Rachel felt arms wrap around her and squeeze, then heard the sounds of Nina exiting the room.

"I pointed out to Shay that kidnapping an innocent bystander wasn't necessary," Tucker said. "That I wouldn't let anyone put a mission above her life. Eventually, she agreed with me."

"So, she let you go."

"Yeah. Because she knew I was right. She knew that what North Star has been doing isn't what I signed up for."

"What *you* signed up for?"

Tucker huffed out a breath. "What? You don't believe they'd tap me for some help? I'm not North Star material?"

"I didn't say that," Cody said evenly.

Rachel wanted to defend Tucker, but it wouldn't change the fact he felt slighted by his baby brother. Still, she understood a little too well what it was like to be overlooked. Underestimated. To not fully realize it until the crap hit the fan.

I'm sure Cody and Tucker can take care of whatever this is. Nina meant well, because she loved her. Because they were sisters. But it still hurt.

Silence remained. Tucker and Cody were likely having some nonverbal conversation she'd never be privy to.

Rachel could be mad about that, and pout, or she

could take matters into her own hands. "After we ran from Shay, after she let us, Dad sent us a note, through Shay. It led us to the weapon that did this to me." She pointed at her face. "We could hand that over to North Star, but what would they do with it?"

Cody didn't answer for a few seconds. "I couldn't say."

"But you know as well as I do that it wouldn't be used to save my dad or keep me safe. It would be used to take someone down."

"Taking those people down *would* be keeping you safe."

"Would it? Because Ace is in jail. So is Elijah and Andy Jay and all the Sons members who've come after you all this year. They're all in *jail*. Am I safe, Cody? Are you?"

Cody didn't have anything to say to that, either.

"Dad sent me this note in secret. He wanted me to get that evidence without North Star knowing. What does that tell you about what North Star is doing? Shay let us go and she *works* for North Star."

"Look, you avoided getting kidnapped because Shay let you. Maybe you're right and North Star can get a little…people blind. Regardless, you can't get into North Star and get Duke out. You just can't. They're too well organized."

"You know where he's being held?" Tucker asked.

"I have an idea. You wouldn't make it within fifty yards without them picking you up. Then they'd have Rachel like they wanted in the first place. And you're right, mission comes first. It has to or they can't do what they do."

"I don't care what they do, Cody. I care about my father. I care about the fact someone did this to me when

I was *three*, and I won't let them do anything else to my family. Maybe I'm not a detective or a secret operative, but I sure as hell am in the middle of this thing."

"She's right," Tucker said softly. "She remembers things. She knows Duke. North Star wanted to kidnap her. She's smack dab in the middle of this."

"Why are you, Tuck?"

"Because North Star asked me to be. But they've taken a wrong turn, and I won't let that hurt Duke. They asked me to keep his daughters safe—so that's what I'm going to do."

"If I tell you where Duke probably is, like I said, it's not going to go well. I can't tell you how to sneak in. They'll know you're coming a mile away. I can't help you get in there. I'm not part of North Star anymore, and as much as I know, they know I know it. They'd have protections against it if they wanted to keep me—or someone related to me—out."

"You know how to get in touch with Shay."

When Cody spoke, his voice was firm. "I won't get her kicked out."

"She didn't sound like she was in it for the long run," Rachel said. "She got us the note. Surely you can get in touch with her and give her the option of helping us."

"That won't be necessary."

It was a woman's voice, and Rachel could only assume it was Shay herself.

"So, you'll help us?" Rachel demanded.

"Yeah, but you're not going to like how."

TUCKER HAD TO blink to make sure that was indeed Shay entering the room from where Nina and Brianna had disappeared earlier. "How…"

"I figured you'd hit up Cody once you figured out

Duke's note. The weapon that did that, huh?" Shay said, nodding toward Rachel's face.

Tucker glared at Cody. "You didn't tell me she was there," he gritted out.

"He didn't know," Shay said with a grin. "Nina's the one who gave me the heads-up."

"I never should have let you two become friends," Cody muttered. "You'll get kicked out. This would be the last straw."

"I've been saying that for months now. Apparently, Granger loves me. Also, you didn't *let* me become friends with your wife."

"What aren't we going to like?" Tucker demanded, wanting to keep the focus on what needed to be done.

"My brother do that?" Cody asked with some surprise as he noticed Shay's bruised cheek.

Shay shook her head. "He wouldn't hit a woman," she said as if that was a *bad* thing. "Rachel did it."

Cody let out a low whistle. "Nice work, Rach."

"Can we focus?" Tucker demanded.

"So, all you Wyatts are wound that tight, eh?" Shay said to Cody, earning a frown from both Wyatts in question. "Duke's not going to talk to me. Even if I said I was in cahoots with you. Why do you think that letter I smuggled out was in code? We need to get Rachel to him."

"Or we need to get Duke to Rachel."

Shay shook her head. She was still dressed all in black, but no mask or hat. Her blond hair was pulled back in a tight ponytail and she stood there, legs spread, arms folded across her chest like some kind of special ops soldier.

In a way, Tucker supposed she was.

"We're not getting Duke out of there. It's not possible

unless they're distracted by something they need more than Duke's knowledge of the Viannis and the Sons." Shay looked meaningfully at Rachel.

Even though it didn't change what she'd said, Tucker moved in between Shay and Rachel. "No."

"Don't say no," Rachel told him. "Not *for* me. You'll tell me what you mean, and *I'll* say no if I see fit."

"She wants to use you as bait," Tucker said disgustedly.

"And what's wrong with that?" Rachel returned.

He, of course, couldn't answer that. What he thought was wrong with that wouldn't be appreciated.

"How would we do it?" Rachel asked calmly.

Tucker didn't know how she could be calm. Maybe because she hadn't actually seen that knife that had been used to take away her eyesight, sitting there grotesquely in a box. Maybe because she didn't fully grasp what the Sons could do on their own, let alone with another dangerous group of criminals.

Or maybe she was calm because she lived that night over and over again in her dreams and she had no control over that. This...she felt like she could act on.

How could he not support that?

"I take you to headquarters," Shay began. "I'll say I tracked you down and convinced you to ditch Tucker. You'll say you want to help your father in whatever way you can. Which is all true."

"Except it's sending her into the lion's den."

"Only one, and the less dangerous of the three," Shay returned. "While they're focused on getting information from Rachel, it'll give me a chance to slip out and grab Tucker. We'll work together to get Duke out."

"Except Rachel is stuck in there then."

"It might not matter," Rachel said. "Depending on what the full truth is."

"No, it'll matter," Shay corrected. "The whole point of me going against the group I've dedicated six years of my life to is to help keep you and your father from being caught in a crossfire that's got nothing to do with you, and only a little to do with your father. Tucker will take Duke. I'll go back in and get Rachel."

"It'll be your last hurrah. You take people out of North Star custody, no amount of Granger liking you keeps you in North Star," Cody said gravely.

"I'm okay with that. I wasn't at first. But this whole thing… It's been different since you left, Cody. Since Ace has been in jail. It should have made it easier, but we're going at it harder and caring less and less who gets caught in the middle. I won't be party to it any longer."

"All right, what do you need from me?" Cody asked.

Cody and Shay discussed some technical stuff to do with the North Star security systems and Tucker turned to Rachel. She had her chin set stubbornly. It was stupid to try to convince her to back out of this, but…

"You're risking your life. I want you to understand that."

"Duke already risked it," Rachel replied. "Risked Sarah and me, all of us. Didn't he? By going with them."

"North Star brought me in because he wanted you protected. I was there to make sure you weren't brought into the thick of things."

"Maybe, but we're here. In the thick of things. I won't be swept into a corner. Maybe what we found in the safe hurts my feelings. It…hurts. Even if my father has a good reason, to know that's there is painful. But you were the one who told me it doesn't change the fact he's a good man who's always been a good father. He loved my mother. He loved me and my sisters. He raised us when she died, and all the while..." She blew out a breath. "You've all lived with terrible things. Now, I'm living with mine. I won't back down. You wouldn't. None of my sisters would. None of your brothers would, and I know my father wouldn't. So. Why should you expect me to?"

"It's not that I expect you to, Rach. It's that I care about you and I want you to be safe." Which he would have said before kissing her. Of course, he cared about her—about all the Knights. But it felt heavier in his chest, even in this kitchen with his brother and a North Star operative a few feet away.

She reached out and he took her hand. She squeezed it and smiled at him. "We're all doing this because we care about each other."

Which wasn't exactly what he'd meant or felt. He'd meant *her* in a very uncomfortably specific way.

"It's a risk, but it's not like I'm walking into Sons territory. I'm walking into a group who wants to take down two very bad groups of people. It's the lowest risk I could take. You're taking a bigger one trying to get Dad out." Her hand slid up his arm, shoulder, until her palm cupped his cheek. "So, we both have to support each other taking risks to end all this danger. I'd like to have my life back. I'm sorry I ever wanted something different. It was perfectly nice. Well, mostly." Her thumb moved across his jaw, then she dropped her hand as if she remembered there were other people in the room.

"We should move immediately, right?" she asked.

"Right," Shay agreed. She gave Tucker a considering look but crossed to Rachel. "I'm going to give you a panic button of sorts. It's tiny and easy to lose, so I'm going to sew it into the sleeve of your shirt. Okay?"

Rachel nodded and held out her arm to Shay. Shay worked on sewing the tiny button into the inside of Rachel's sleeve, and Tucker was not at all surprised his brother pulled him away from Rachel and into the hallway.

"It's not really going to go down like this."

"What isn't?" Tucker muttered.

"You and Rachel? Don't think I didn't notice that little moment. That's five for five."

Tucker shrugged uncomfortably. "It's not like that... exactly."

"Yeah, *exactly*." Then Cody laughed. Loud and hard. "Jesus. Dev and Sarah."

"Not in a million years," Tucker said, managing a small laugh of his own. "They'd eat each other alive first."

Cody shook his head. "Don't bet against it."

Chapter Eighteen

Rachel did her best not to act nervous. She knew Tucker didn't approve of this plan, but he was going through with it because of her.

So she had to be brave. She had to be sure. Too bad she was wholly terrified.

Shay had sewn a *panic button* into her shirt, instructing her that it had to be pressed three times to send a signal. Which would go to Cody, who would no doubt send the whole Wyatt clan after her.

After *her*, because she was going to be the distraction. The bait. She was going to walk into North Star and demand to see her father.

Shay warned her they wouldn't let that happen. That they'd likely put her in an interrogation room, holding the carrot of seeing her father over her head until she answered all their questions.

She was supposed to refuse. Give them bits and pieces to keep their attention, but mostly be difficult, and lie if necessary. So that all eyes were on her while Shay and Tucker snuck in to get Duke out.

It was a lot of pressure, and while her family treated her as an equal more often than not, no one had actually ever put *pressure* on her. The hardest thing she'd ever done up to this point was demand to teach art classes at the rez. There had been some pressure to succeed so no one pitied her for failing, but not like this.

"Okay, you'll drop us here," Shay instructed Tucker.

The car came to a halt. Rachel was seated in the back. She hadn't realized until this moment she was going to have to trust Shay implicitly, not just to be telling the truth but to guide her through a completely unknown setting.

When the door next to her opened, Rachel had to fight the desire to lean away. To refuse to get out. She stepped into the autumn afternoon instead.

"Don't be afraid to speak up if I'm walking too fast or something. Better to get there in one piece than worry about hurting my feelings or whatever."

The no-nonsense way Shay took her arm and said those words had Rachel's shoulders relaxing. Maybe it was scary, but at least Shay wasn't going to be all weird about her being blind.

"Let me talk to her for a minute," Tucker said briskly.

"All right," Shay said. She let Rachel's arm go and Tuck's hands closed over her shoulders. He gave them a squeeze.

"You be smart. Take care of yourself first. I couldn't..." He let out a ragged breath. "I don't want you hurt, Rach."

"Tuck..." She didn't know what to say. There wasn't time to say anything. So, she could only give him what he'd given her. "I don't want you hurt, either."

"Then we'll stick to the plan, and everything will be okay."

"You don't actually believe that," she said, both because she didn't and because she could hear it in his voice that he didn't, either. "We'll stick to the plan, and hope for the best. And if the best blows up in our face, we'll just have to fight like hell."

He chuckled softly. "Yeah, you got that right."

Then, before she could say anything else, he kissed her. It wasn't sweet or light. It was firm, a little fierce and had her heart beating for an entirely new reason aside from fear. "Stay safe, Rach."

He released her, and she was passed off to Shay. It was disorienting for a lot of reasons, but the whole being shuttled between people in foreign settings certainly undercut the happy buzz of that kiss.

"They all like that?" Shay asked, leading her forward.

"Like what?"

"Like…gentlemen, but not wimps about it. Think of women as equals, and aren't too keen on using them as a punching bag. Kiss like that and then walk away to save your butt—while you're also busy saving your own butt."

Rachel had to smile. "Pretty much."

Shay didn't say anything else to that, just kept leading Rachel forward.

"Can you describe it to me? Give me some kind of idea of where they're going to take me and how to get out?"

"Good idea." Shay explained that it looked like a hunting cabin from the outside. Inside, they had different holding rooms, a medical center and a tech center. She explained the layout, which room Duke was in and what room they'd probably take her into.

"So, if for whatever reason you want to run, they're going to be able to track you until you get off the property. Not much use in it. But, to get out the door, you'd just need to remember how to get to the hallway."

Rachel filed all that away, tried to bring her own picture to her mind. It would help if she found herself needing to escape.

Shay brought her to a stop. "All right. Here we go."

Rachel expected her to knock or buzz in or something, but the sound of the door opening was the first thing she heard once they stopped.

"This is an interesting turn of events," a male voice said. "Where's the guard dog who gave you that shiner?"

"I got to her without Wyatt," Shay returned. She spoke differently to the man. Sharp. All business. Any hint of the woman who'd asked if the Wyatts were all like that was gone.

"How?"

"Everyone has to take a bathroom break now and again, Parker. Now are you going to step aside or what?"

The man grumbled, but Rachel was being led forward so he'd clearly allowed entrance. "Wait here for McMillan."

Rachel listened as the footsteps quieted.

"McMillan is my supervisor," Shay said in a whisper. "He's all bark and mostly no bite. I imagine since he's been handling Duke, he's going to be the one who questions you. If not? Be as difficult as possible until they bring McMillan in."

"All right."

"Shay."

Rachel had assumed Shay was the woman's first name all this time. But the way her superior barked it out, Rachel had to wonder if it was actually her last name.

"Sir. A little late, but better late than never."

"How'd you manage what you failed at earlier?" He

emphasized the word fail as though failure was the absolute worst thing a person could do.

"Followed them. They were on the run, off their home territory. Wyatt let his guard down and I convinced Rachel to talk to us. She's willing, if you let her see her father."

"Dymon!" the man yelled.

More footsteps, a few hushed words, then someone took her other arm. Shay's grip tightened and Rachel felt a bit like she was in the middle of a tug-of-war.

"Who's that?" Shay asked, suspicion threading through her voice.

"Your replacement," McMillan said, his voice so chilly Rachel thought to shiver. "Shay. You're done here."

"Sir, I think a woman should—"

"I said you're done here," McMillan said, and this was no bark or yell. It was cold, a succinct *or-else* order.

Shay slowly released her arm, and Rachel was being led away. The grip on her other arm was unnecessarily rough. She remembered what Shay said about being difficult. "You're hurting me," she said, trying to tug her arm away from the too-tight grasp.

"Oh, you have no idea what's in store for you, little girl," the voice hissed.

Rachel's entire body went cold. She recognized that voice.

It was the voice from her dream.

"Something isn't right."

Tucker whirled, gun in hand. It was only Shay, but she'd snuck up on him soundlessly. Still, he didn't have time to worry about that. "*What* isn't right?"

"New guy. McMillan isn't in the habit of hiring new guys."

"He hired me."

"Not the same. You're not an operative. You're like a...liaison. This guy I've *never seen* is in the South Dakota headquarters of North Star, and I've never heard his name or even heard whispers of a new guy." She rubbed a hand over the back of her neck. "Something isn't right."

"You left Rachel in there? When something wasn't right?"

"Calm down," Shay said sharply. She pulled her phone to her ear. "Wyatt? Yeah, I need you to do some spying for me." She sighed heavily. "Yeah, yeah, yeah, you ask your wife if she thinks you should stay out of it when her sister is in North Star headquarters with a stranger." Another pause. "Yup, that's what I thought. Someone named Dymon. Get me anything you've got on him." She hung up, shoved her phone in her pocket.

"Are you sure they're not tracking you through that?" he asked.

"Do you think I'm dumb? I had your brother take care of all the tracking devices when we were there."

"It never occurred to you that a group that tracked your every move might not be on the up and up?"

"Look. You don't know anything about North Star, or McMillan for that matter," she snapped. "Like that your father was responsible for his wife's death."

Tucker didn't say anything because he hadn't known that. At all.

"Grief does funny things to people. He's not a bad guy, and whatever is going on doesn't make him one. It makes him...human. And, hell, aren't we all?"

Tucker didn't want to think about how human they

all were. Not when being human meant making mistakes, and they couldn't make any with Rachel inside North Star.

"Let's move. The less time she has to be in there, the better."

Shay nodded. "On that, we can agree."

It was Shay's plan since she knew the headquarters—what from the outside looked like an upscale hunting cabin. They bypassed the front, and Shay would occasionally pause to do something on her phone that allegedly moved the cameras or turned off security or whatever else North Star had in place.

"You sure you know all of those?"

"I installed them. I sure as hell should." They finally got to the back door, which was next to a garage of sorts. "I'm going in. I imagine everyone knows I got the boot, but I've got stuff in there. So, I'm going in to collect my stuff. When no one's watching, I'll open this garage and the door inside. You'll head straight for it. If I don't have Duke waiting, you move back into the garage. Check at five-minute intervals. Once he's there, you sneak him out the garage, go in the direct route we came and get to the car. Once you're there, you'll give me fifteen minutes. If I don't show up with Rachel, you get Duke out. I'll contact you or your brother with the next step once I've got Rachel. And whatever you do, don't go all Wyatt on me."

"What does that mean?"

"Don't play the hero. You may hear or see something you don't like, but you focus on Duke. You're going to want to barge back in here and get Rachel, but I've got it handled. You trust me and I trust you."

"That's asking a lot."

"Yeah, it is," she agreed. "For both of us. You up for the challenge?"

He didn't want to be. Trusting someone he barely knew was like tossing a coin with Rachel's life on the line, but hadn't he already done that? Besides, Shay didn't strike him as a stupid woman and she was putting at least some of her safety in *his* hands. It was a risk they both had to take.

"How long do I wait until I open the door?"

"Minute the garage opens you're in. You hear a whistle—I don't mean a sharp whistle, I mean like me whistling a tune—you go back and hide in the garage. We'll keep trying till it's clear."

Tucker nodded. "All right."

Shay nodded in return, then she slid in the back door. Tucker stood in the corner next to the garage, doing his best to hide his body in the way Shay had instructed. When the garage door opened, almost soundlessly, he slipped inside. Then immediately located the door inside and headed for it.

He turned the knob, eased it open and himself inside. He was in a basement that bizarrely looked like any house's basement might. A TV room in a little finished alcove, a laundry area on the opposite side. The hallway was dark.

Tucker remembered what Shay had said and went back to the garage, waited the aforementioned five minutes, then went inside again. He kept his mind blank. Thought of it like detective work—often boring and tedious...until it wasn't.

Fifteen minutes had passed, and finally Duke appeared. Duke studied him there at the end of the hallway and didn't budge. That was when Tucker realized Shay was standing behind him, with a gun to his back, and he only moved forward toward Tuck when she poked it into his back again.

"He's being difficult," she hissed. "Fix it. I've got maybe ten minutes before Parker comes back. Maybe."

Fix Duke Knight's hard head? Yeah, in what world? Still, Tucker moved forward. "We have to get you out."

"Why should I trust you? I trusted Granger and look what happened. Now I've got two North Star operatives trying to sneak me out? That smells like a setup, boy."

"We're trying to help you. It's because of *you*, and what they want to do with your family, that we're turning our back on North Star."

Duke didn't respond to that. "Who's watching the girls?"

Tucker hesitated. "We're all doing what we should be doing," he said carefully, already knowing that wouldn't fly. His hesitation spoke volumes.

Duke narrowed his eyes. "You've always been a crap liar. Where's Rachel?"

"She's…" Tucker couldn't tell Duke under any circumstances. If he knew Rachel was upstairs, he'd charge up there like an angry bull.

"She's upstairs keeping them busy," Shay said.

Tucker nearly groaned, but he had to leap in front of Duke as he charged for the stairs. Though Tucker was taller, Duke was thicker, and he'd been a cowboy for thirty some years so he was no slouch. Still, Tucker had been trained to deal with threats bigger than him.

Tucker managed to shove him a step back. "You don't know what will happen to her or you if you barge in there. Trust that we've got this under control."

"That's my daughter you're risking," Duke said, and though his voice was ruthlessly controlled in volume, his eyes bulged and the tendons in his neck stood out like he was about to explode.

Tucker couldn't blame him if he did.

"She risked herself, buddy. For you. So maybe you make it easy on us so I can get her out without causing a storm where someone gets hurt," Shay said with absolutely *no* finesse.

Which was apparently what Duke needed to hear. He moved forward, though his scowl was still in place. Tucker passed him up to get to the door first. As he did, Duke he full-on sneered.

"I'm holding you personally responsible."

"As if I'm not," Tucker muttered. He glanced back at Shay.

"Take him out, just like we said. I'll go get her."

Tucker nodded. He led Duke into the garage quietly. Then out. Tucker had to hope Shay remembered to close it.

"Shay will bring Rachel to us," Tucker told him, moving in the same direction they'd come. Shay had disabled the cameras, but they could have come back on. Still, he had to trust she'd handle it.

"I can't believe you'd be this stupid," Duke muttered, though he followed behind Tucker.

Tucker looked over his shoulder and raised an eyebrow. "That's really how you want to play this? When we found the weapon that blinded your daughter in Grandma Pauline's safe? I had to beg your daughter to understand that you *must* have had a good reason for that. So—"

Tucker's phone vibrated. He shook his head and kept walking. When it vibrated again, he swore under his breath and pulled the phone out of his pocket. They were finally in some tree cover, but not to the car yet. Tucker saw it was Cody calling and answered.

"Cody—"

"Shay didn't answer, but this is important. I got into North Star's system to look up this Dymon guy. I managed a quick glimpse into the files before they figured out I was hacking in and kicked me right back out. This guy's got connections to Vianni. I suppose he could be a double agent—helping out North Star. Sort of like us."

"Except we never worked for the Sons or our father." Tucker thought about everything Shay had told him. About this whole lead up. "He's working for Vianni. They're so hung up on taking down the Sons, they don't care who they go to bed with."

"Maybe," Cody replied gravely. "Either way? I'd get Rachel out of there ASAP."

Chapter Nineteen

Fear paralyzed Rachel, but all the man from her nightmares had done was drag her deeper into the building and then shove her into a chair. He was almost immediately followed by someone else, and once that person spoke, she knew it was the head guy. What had Shay called him? McMillan?

At least she wasn't alone with her nightmare—but would this man be just as bad?

It didn't matter. As long as she was in this building, she had a chance of survival. Dad was here. Shay was here. Tuck was here. She would survive.

Rachel studied what she could of the room. She reached out and felt the table in front of her. So she was sitting on an uncomfortable chair at a table. The man across from her was McMillan. He had a big dark presence and he appeared to move in such a way that she figured it meant he was sitting down at the table, too. The other man was dressed all in dark colors, too, but not as broad as McMillan. Not as…still.

She remembered that about him from her dream. A need to move. He stood next to McMillan, a vibrating presence. In the vague way she saw things, they appeared to be a unit.

Did McMillan know? Was North Star actually in bed

with Vianni? It was a horrible thought. If they were, she was dead. Shay and Tucker were likely dead, too, and God knew her father was already dead.

Except he wasn't. They'd gone to rescue him. So, surely North Star didn't know.

Unless they needed that knife, and that was the only reason her father was still alive.

Rachel swallowed. "I just want to see my father," she said through a too-tight throat, terror making her feel like lead all the way through. But she couldn't just lie down and die.

She had to figure out a way to fight.

"That's understandable, Ms. Knight. Your father is here under our protection. Just how much do you know about that?"

She didn't let her eyes drift to the man standing. He had to know she knew who he was. Didn't he? Or would he assume because she was blind that she didn't? But he had to have felt how afraid she was. Her reaction to his voice.

He had to know she knew.

"Miss?"

Rachel sucked in an audible breath. McMillan had asked her a question. "I'm sorry. I… I don't know. I know Shay tried to kidnap me at the ranch. She and Tucker fought and Tucker got me away from her. She followed us, I guess. She…" Rachel had never been a good liar, but she let the genuine fear she felt consume her. Her voice shook. She shook. They'd believe it was a result of fear of the situation, not her lies. "She found me later. While Tucker was… Anyway, she said I could see and talk to my father if I came with her. That everything would be explained if I came with her."

"Our operative was sent to retrieve you because of the dream you've been having. Can you tell us about that?"

"I…" Rachel trailed off. They likely knew everything at this point. God knew the man from her nightmare did. If they'd been listening to Tucker before Shay's arrival, they had the full account of how her dream had morphed.

"It was just a nightmare. Just a…memory of what happened to me." She gestured at her face. "I don't see what it has to do with anything."

"You never dream past the moment you were hurt?" McMillan asked.

He made it all sound so clinical, but he couldn't see the nightmare, the reality in his mind like she could. "I was three. A madman slashed my face up and I was saved by a dog. What more would I know than that?"

"What about the knife?" It was the other man's voice. The voice from that dream, and she couldn't help but flinch at it.

"What knife?" she managed to whisper.

"Dymon." It was a warning from the man. "You're not involved in the questioning. If you can't remember that, you can step outside."

She could all but *feel* the tamped-down energy humming off the nightmare man. Still, he didn't say anything else.

But he wanted to know about the knife. The knife in Grandma Pauline's safe. One thing she knew for certain, she couldn't tell them about that.

"I don't know what you're talking about. I told you about my dream, now I want to see my father."

"What do you know about your father's past?"

"None of your business," Rachel snapped. She wouldn't play the cowering victim anymore. Not when she couldn't decide if the man in front of her was good or bad or some mix of the two. But, regardless, she didn't have to be nice to him.

"The group who's after your father has aligned themselves with the Sons. You've got quite a few in-laws who are former Sons members, don't you?"

"If you think being held in that gang as a child against your will is being a *former member*, you're a monster."

The man sighed, like a disappointed teacher or parent.

"Miss, it'd be easier on you if you simply answer our questions. Once you tell us the truth, we'll take you to your father. I understand you're not part of this, but Duke Knight is in a very dangerous situation. He's trying to protect you, but it's not getting us anywhere. It seems this knife might be the answer to some of our... *problems*. I'm sure you want to help him, don't you?"

She thought about what one of her more smart-mouthed sisters might say in this situation. She managed a sneer and did her best impersonation of Liza. "Go to hell."

She thought about laying her cards out on the table. Lifting her chin and saying, *Is that why you've got someone associated with the Viannis in this room with us? To protect him and help him?*

But her father had gone willingly with this group. Shay and Cody, both people who'd helped her and other people, had worked for North Star believing in its mission. Tucker had helped them. Surely, they weren't evil. They couldn't be evil and fool so many good people.

But the Viannis and the Sons *were*. Didn't that mean someone could have infiltrated North Star without them knowing? Maybe North Star was smart, even good at helping people, but they hadn't brought down the Sons fully yet—and how long had it taken them to put Ace in jail?

They'd needed Jamison *and* Cody to do that. So it was plausible, especially by partnering with the Viannis who were more of an unknown, that the Viannis had in turn tricked North Star.

She wanted to believe that—needed to—because the alternative was too bleak to bear.

Rachel hitched in a breath. She had to find a way to tell the man across from her that the man standing beside him had been her would-be kidnapper—the man who'd blinded her. But she couldn't write a note. And she couldn't just come out and *say* it either, because if the man across from her truly didn't know, he'd likely be killed, no matter what kind of operative he was.

"Why don't I go get you some water? Give you some time to think about what direction you want to go in. Dymon here will watch you until you're ready to talk."

It wasn't threatening exactly. Nor was it friendly. A mission. It was all about the mission.

She could hear his chair scrape back as if he was going to get to his feet. As if he was about to leave her with her nightmare. She reached forward in a desperate attempt to grab him. She managed to do just that, both her hands clasping McMillan's arm before he fully stood.

"Please, wait."

Cody had taught her Morse code when they'd been in middle school. She'd been feeling bad about something—she couldn't even remember what it was now. But he'd cheered her up by teaching her Morse code. They'd made a game of it that summer.

She didn't remember it all, and there wasn't time to stumble. Still, she had to try. She *had* to.

"Miss. Let go of my arm," McMillan said, not totally unkindly.

It gave her an awful hope, that glimmer of kindness.

So she tapped what she could think of, in the most succinct terms she could manage.

Danger.

My face.

Him.

He didn't say anything, but he also didn't pull his arm away. He didn't tell her to let go, so she tapped out the code again. The same code. The same words.

He withdrew his arm, but instead of getting up or doing something dismissive, he laid his hand on top of hers and gave it a reassuring pat. "All right," he said, his voice low and controlled. "Dymon, why don't you go get the water? I'll stay here with Ms. Knight."

"I'm sure you've got better things to do, boss."

"You're still new. I wouldn't push your luck," McMillan warned.

"I did pass all your tests. You hired me. You have to trust me to do this stuff when you've got more important things to do."

Rachel held her breath, but the one thing that steadied her the most was McMillan's hand over hers. A reassuring weight that he'd gotten her message, and wasn't going to leave her alone with this man.

"You told me you hadn't had any personal experience with the Knights," McMillan said quietly. "That you were too low on the Vianni totem pole to know more than a few stories about Curtis Washington and his new life in South Dakota."

"That's right," the nightmare man agreed.

"Is that the story you want to stick to right here and right now?"

There was a long tense silence. McMillan's hand was still atop hers, and he began to tap. It took Rachel the second time through to figure it out.

Duck.

And then a gunshot went off.

There was a scuffle, a moan and then Rachel's arm was jerked as she was pulled out from under the table. "Wrong move, little girl."

Her nightmare had her again.

But this time—she would fight.

TUCKER SLID THE phone back into his pocket. He had to remain calm, because Duke was there and Duke wouldn't remain any kind of calm.

They had to head back to the house and get Rachel the hell out of there, even if he had to fight the entirety of North Star to do it.

"How familiar are you with the area?" Tucker asked, careful to keep his voice calm.

"Who was that on the phone?"

"I need you to get to the car. It's parked—"

"Oh, hell no," Duke snarled. "If you're going back in for my daughter, I'm going with you."

"We can't go in guns blazing. We can't—"

"I was a cop before you were born. I know a thing or two about what needs to be done, and I know what I'd do to keep my daughter safe."

At the end of his rope with indecision, Tucker snapped. "Like when a man tried to kidnap her and blinded her in the process?"

"He would have killed her," Duke said flatly. "But she's alive, because of me. She was hurt because of me,

I get it. I don't know how to go back and change my life. I did what I thought was right, always. You perfect?"

No, he couldn't pretend to be that.

"Now, you got another one of those?" Duke asked, nodding at the gun in his hand.

"No." Tucker considered giving it to Duke. Tucker could fight better with his hands than Duke would be able to. It would—

The muffled echo of a *crack* interrupted the picturesque quiet. *Gunshot*. Tucker was off running before he'd even thought it through. He looked back at Duke once. He was running, too, but at a much slower pace.

"Go!" Duke shouted.

Which was all the encouragement Tucker needed to run at full speed back to the house. He'd break down the front door if he had to. He'd—

The explosion was so loud and powerful, it knocked Tucker back. He managed to stay on his feet, but for a horrible second he watched the entire house go up in flames as the sound of glass shattering and debris thundering surrounded him.

Then, after that split second, he ran toward it. What other option was there? People were inside. Rachel. Shay. But as he headed for the door, flames and smoke already enshrouding it, people came pouring out.

Tucker didn't see Shay. He didn't know if that was good or bad. The people were bloody, burned, coughing. He tried to find someone who looked remotely communicative, but they were all in various shapes of injury and couldn't answer his demands as the fire roared around them.

Two figures emerged then, one dragging the other. It was Shay. He couldn't tell whom she was dragging, but it wasn't Rachel. It was a large man. Tucker ran to her.

"Sorry," she rasped. She let go of the man she'd been hauling as people rushed forward to help him.

"He'd been shot," Shay rasped. "I went to the questioning room and he'd been shot. I couldn't find Rachel or the new guy. The Dymon guy. He had to have taken her out the back." She swayed but Tucker managed to catch her before she fell in a heap. "The explosion went off before I managed to do anything. Got emergency services coming," she continued as Tucker helped her into a sitting position on the ground. "But I don't think I'm going to be much help with Rachel."

"Give me your gun," Tucker managed, though terror pounded through him. When she did, he handed it to Duke who huffed up to them. "Shay thinks Rachel got out—or was taken out with someone. I'm going to find the trail. You do the same," he instructed to Duke.

Much as it pained him to leave this misery in his wake, he had to find Rachel before she met a worse fate. He had to make a wide circle around the flames to get to the back. He didn't worry about how close Duke was. He only worried about getting to Rachel.

Debris had flown more back here, which made Tucker think the explosives had been detonated from the back. If whoever had Rachel had detonated the explosives by hand rather than remotely, it made sense. He'd have dragged Rachel out, then set off the bomb before he dragged her away.

Why drag her away and keep her alive, though? Why not let her die in the explosion?

But the guy hadn't. He'd taken her away, and regardless of the reason, Tucker had to believe that's what happened. Believe it and save her from this.

The yard was wooded. Tucker ruthlessly tamped down the panic gripping him. He had to think like a cop. Like the person he'd trained to be. Like his brothers. Calm in the face of crisis. In the face of someone he loved being taken.

He moved to the trees, looking for signs of tracks or struggle. There was nothing, but this was the only way the man could have gone. Tucker scoured the ground. He heard Duke's approach, though they didn't speak. They moved and they looked.

Tucker couldn't let himself think of Rachel being dragged out of that house by some Vianni thug. He couldn't think about the very real possibility that a Sons member was waiting to help—

"Wait." Tucker stopped. The rational thing to do was head for the trees and cover. Unless there was help waiting somewhere else. He tried to orient himself—the house—where it would be in relation to the Sons. The Sons current headquarters was a few hours away, *but* if they were meeting someone with a car, they'd need a road. It wouldn't have been the road Shay had instructed him to use, because that was the main thoroughfare and would be too obvious.

"Go back to the house. Get a car. Anyone you can find," Tucker instructed, already moving north instead of his original west. "Once you've got a car, start driving for Flynn via Route 5. But be careful. The Sons might be involved."

With no time to spare, Tucker took off for Route 5. It meant running through open land, and that was dangerous, but if he could get to Rachel before they got her into a car, he didn't care what they did to him.

Chapter Twenty

Rachel slowly came to. Someone was dragging her, swearing. She could feel the ground beneath her, tell it was still daylight as the sun beat down on her face.

"Stupid plan," the man muttered.

It was like her dream. The fear and his muttering, but she was bigger. She was a woman now. She'd tried to fight him back in that room, but then everything had gone black.

Now, everything hurt, and her head pounded with excruciating pain. He must have knocked her out. She tried to kick out, but her ankles were tied together. So were her hands. She wanted to sob, but she knew instinctively if he didn't know she was awake, she was better off.

She wasn't going to be able to escape him with her hands and feet tied, and she couldn't use the button Shay had sewn into her sleeve. But she was alive. She supposed that was the silver lining. She wasn't dead.

At three years old, she'd survived being cut in the face and losing her sight. She could survive this. She *would* survive this.

The dragging stopped and he dropped her without warning. She couldn't hold back the sharp groan of pain.

"You awake?"

Dymon nudged her with his foot, and she kept her eyes closed. She let her head loll as she made another soft groaning noise, trying to pretend she was still unconscious. Or just coming to.

He muttered something. There was shuffling, the methodical plodding of feet like he was pacing the hard ground beneath them. "I need help. You can't expect me to make it all the way to the road. Yeah, yeah, yeah. Had to shoot McMillan. No, I didn't check. I had to get her out. Yeah, I know no casualties but things went sideways."

Rachel realized he was on the phone, talking to someone about getting her to the road. And if he got her to the road, she'd be put into a car. There'd be more people.

How would anyone find her if she was in a car? Wasn't there something about not ever letting anyone take you to a second location? Better to be killed than make it to that second location.

She swallowed down the fear. Somehow, someway, she had to fight. There was no waiting for Tucker or Shay to find her if there was a car waiting. Once she got in that car, she was as good as dead.

Dymon continued to grumble, and she slowly realized he was done with his phone conversation and was instead just talking to himself. Nothing important or telling, just complaints about being the only one with the balls to do the dirty work.

Rachel continued to pretend as though she were unconscious as she tried to figure out how on earth she was going to get out of this. She couldn't get out of the bonds on her wrists and ankles—they were too tight—but there had to be *something* she could do.

Back in the room, this man had wanted to know

about her dream. About the knife. So…maybe she had to give that to him to keep him occupied, to buy herself time.

Hopefully enough time for Tucker to intercept her before the man got her to the car waiting for him.

She groaned some more, started to move, thrashed a bit against her bonds for effect. She blinked her eyes open.

Dymon grunted. "Thought I knocked you out better than that." He sighed heavily. "Guess I'll have to do a better job this time. Maybe just fix the problem altogether."

He was going to kill her. Here and now. No getting to the road. No second location, just death.

"No. No. Please—please don't." She swallowed at the fear and the bile rising in her throat. She had to be braver than this. "I know where it is," she blurted out. He'd mentioned the knife. She knew which one he was referring to. "I know who you are. I know what you did. And most importantly, I know where the knife you want is."

"So does your father."

"But you have me. Not him."

Dymon made a dismissive noise, and Rachel didn't know if it was agreement or refusal. She had no idea what he planned to do. He was simply a shadowy figure above her and she had no means to fight.

But no matter what was against her, she did not have to die without *trying* to survive. She knew what side of her the man was standing on, and she knew she was on a little bit of an incline. She could roll. And scream. Maybe someone would be able to save her.

If not? At least she'd tried.

She tested the incline, the placement of her own body

and rocked back and forth a little. If he noticed, he didn't say anything. She counted inwardly and then did her best to use momentum to move into a roll—screaming as loud as she could while she started to gain speed down the incline.

Dymon swore at her viciously, and there was the sound of hard footsteps and a stumble and more swearing. Then her rolling was stopped as she knocked into what she was assuming was him.

"You idiot," he yelled.

She had the impression of him getting ready to strike. She could only brace for impact, but instead of pain—a new voice yelled.

"Don't move."

Rachel almost cried out at the sound of Tucker's voice, but the sound caught in her throat as cold steel was pressed to her forehead.

She didn't know where he was, or if he could see her. She only knew there was a gun pressed to her head. She tried to see. Willed her eyes to work.

She could make out Dymon crouched above her, the gun pressed to her forehead. If she kicked out... He might shoot, but he might fall instead. They *were* on a hill. She just needed to place the kick in the right spot. Somehow.

"Rachel," Tucker's voice was very calm, and closer than it had been. "Do you remember what I told you about fighting?"

"She can't fight," the man said disgustedly. "I'm going to put a bullet through her brain. Then yours. Drop the gun."

"She's the only one who knows where it is," Tucker said, his voice so calm and...lethal. She might have shivered in fear if he weren't the only one who could help her survive this. "The evidence you're after. She's the only one."

Rachel thought about what Tucker had said about fighting. He'd told her to always go for the crotch. She just needed to kick the man in the crotch. She could figure out that general area, as long as she could position her body accordingly, she could do it.

"Curtis knows where it's at. I could kill her and—"

"I'm sorry, Rach. I know I promised never to lie to you again. So I won't. Duke died in the explosion."

Rachel jerked. It was a physical pain, even as she worked through what he'd *actually* said. He'd never promised not to lie to her. In fact, he had promised the opposite. So, Tuck was lying now? He had to be. He was supposed to get Dad out. There was no way Dad was dead. No way.

Please, God.

She didn't focus on the words. On what Dymon and Tucker continued to argue about. She focused on the shadowy outline of the man. Where best to kick. Her aim just had to be right.

Or she was dead. And so was Tucker.

Tucker could see Rachel trying to figure out the angle. Slowly, he began to crouch, acting as if he were going to put his gun down. He held one hand up in mock surrender, slowly inching his gun closer and closer to the ground.

He needed Rachel to kick, just one kick even if it wasn't in line would push the guy back. The hill would help with momentum, the gun would go up and Tucker could get a shot off.

All as long as the other guy didn't pull that trigger first.

"That explosion shouldn't have killed anyone," the man finally said after a long tense silence.

Tucker had seen enough of the wreckage to understand where the explosives had detonated. So he had to lie and hope for the best. "Only if everyone was in the front of the house. The basement is another story, and I had a man in there getting Duke out. They're both dead."

He hoped the lies would give Rachel some comfort that Duke wasn't actually dead. That no one was.

Unless McMillan had died of his gunshot wound.

"What's the point of an explosion that doesn't kill anyone, anyway? And you clearly had an in with North Star. Why not take Duke and get what you're after?"

"I could have," the man agreed with a sickening sneer. "But that doesn't finish the job from twenty years ago, does it?"

"This does, though."

All three of them jerked at the sound of Duke's voice, but it didn't last long, since Duke immediately fired a shot that had the man falling to the ground. Lifeless.

"Dad?" Rachel asked tremulously.

Tucker was already halfway to her, but since Duke had come up from the direction of the road, he was closer. He was murmuring to Rachel and untying the bonds on her hands so Tucker took the ones on her feet.

"Dad." They wrapped their arms around each other, so Tucker gave them a moment by making sure the other man was dead.

Tucker couldn't find a pulse, but he still pulled the gun out of his hand and the knife out of his boot. They weren't out of the woods yet, even if they'd managed to end one threat.

"We have to get out of here," Tucker said reluctantly,

since Rachel was still clinging to Duke. "I can't imagine he was working alone."

"He's not. He was talking to someone about dragging me to the car. Is everyone at North Star all right? He shot McMillan. I…" Her hands were shaking, but Duke took them in his. Rachel kept talking. "When Shay took me in, they had this guy. Dymon is his name. He… I recognized his voice, from my dream."

"*He's* the guy?" Tucker looked at Duke for confirmation, and got a slight nod.

Tucker swore. She'd been kidnapped twice by the same man.

"I had to tell McMillan. I didn't think he understood how dangerous he was. So I tapped Morse code into his palm. Then he…this Dymon guy, he shot McMillan. It was so close and McMillan has to be dead, doesn't he?" Rachel asked, trying to wipe at her face, wet with tears. Tucker crouched next to her and used the hem of his shirt to wipe the rest of them away and clean her up a bit. She gave him a small smile.

Tucker could feel Duke's disapproving gaze, but they didn't have time for *that*.

"Shay dragged him out. They were getting him medical attention. He might make it." Probably a bit overly optimistic, but Tucker was willing to give her that in this moment. She'd used Morse code and… God, she was a wonder, but they had to get out of here. "Is there a car down at the road?"

"Yes. Not too far. I didn't see anyone else." Duke helped Rachel to her feet. Tucker flanked her on the other side. The ground was hilly, uneven, and helping Rachel toward the road was no easy task. She stumbled a few times, but they both held her up.

Through the trees, Tucker could begin to make out the road, but it wasn't as deserted as it should have been.

"Get down," Tucker hissed, pulling Rachel to the ground as he ducked for cover behind a swell of earth.

"What is it?" Rachel asked.

"Three men and another car aside from the one Duke drove." Tucker moved so he could get another glimpse. Two men were circling the car Duke had parked in the ditch, and one of them was on his phone. "I need a better look."

Rachel's grip on his arm tightened. "No. You're not going anywhere. Let's just head back to North Star. I know I was unconscious, but it can't be that far."

Tucker didn't want to tell her there wasn't much of North Star left, but more importantly he wanted the opportunity to capture these men who were clearly in on the explosion and kidnapping attempt. The last thing anyone needed was them roaming free—to come after Duke or Rachel again, or whatever else was in their plans.

"Just give me five minutes. Stay put right here." He tugged his arm out of Rachel's grasp and had to trust Duke to keep her there and quiet.

He moved in silence, using trees and rocks and swells of land as cover, until he was close enough to see the three men. Tuck could hear them talking, but couldn't make out what they were saying. He considered getting closer, but with Duke and Rachel not that far away, it wasn't worth the risk.

Knowing he had to get them out of harm's way first, he carefully climbed his way back toward Duke and Rachel.

"Just the three men, but definitely waiting for their guy here to show up with Rachel."

"Vianni," Duke said disgustedly.

"No, they aren't Vianni men. Those are Sons men."

"You recognize them?" Duke asked.

"Got files on all three. The one on the right got off on a rape case because of a technicality. The one in the middle is my suspect on a murder case, but I don't have anything beyond circumstantial evidence and the prosecutor won't issue a warrant. The third has been in and out of jail for dealing drugs, armed robbery, you name it."

"Gotta love the legal system," Duke muttered. "What do we do, then? Pick them off?"

Tucker shook his head. "Too risky. They've got three guys, and three more high-powered weapons than we've got. Even if I use that guy's gun." Tucker glanced at Rachel. She wouldn't agree to this plan, but he didn't feel right trying to make it behind her back either. "Take her back."

"I will not—"

Duke spoke right over her. "What are you going to do?"

"They're accessory to kidnapping, possibly that explosion. I can arrest them."

"On your own, boy? Three against one isn't the best odds."

Tucker pulled out his phone. "I'll even the odds, then."

Duke's expression went even more granite. "And which of your brothers' lives are you willing to risk?"

It was a jab, but somewhere between that explosion and here he'd figured out what he hadn't fully understood until this moment. Yeah, four of his brothers were in love with Duke's foster daughters. Three of them had kids or babies on the way to support and protect.

They had lives, and they shouldn't be taking unnecessary risks.

But they had. Over and over again this summer. Why?

Because nothing was ever going to be truly *good* until the Sons were gone. Truly taken out. The more of them they arrested, the more they had a chance of someone giving that last piece of evidence that brought the entire group to its knees.

"All of them, Duke. All of them."

Chapter Twenty-One

"I will not be carted off while you do something dangerous," Rachel said. She was careful to keep her voice quiet like they were doing, but what she really wanted to do was yell.

Her father's grip was tight on her arm and she wanted to shake it off and rage at him for even *considering* the fact they would go off and leave Tucker to do this, other Wyatt boys or no.

"Give me a second," Tucker said, and then she was being passed off and it was so *infuriating* because she couldn't exactly walk away, could she? Not in this foreign territory she didn't know.

"Listen. I'm not going to do anything stupid. My brothers, law enforcement agents who can also arrest these guys, are going to come and be backup. Maybe get some information that helps us land an even bigger blow to the Sons. I have to do this, and I'm sorry, I can't do it with you here."

Emotion clogged her throat. To get this far and then be relegated to…dead weight. Swept off by her father.

"It isn't right. I didn't *do* anything," she said, feeling raw and cracked open. She *couldn't* do anything. She understood she was a liability in the here and now and it was an awful, awful feeling.

Tucker's hands cupped her cheeks. "Yeah, figuring out where the evidence was, punching Shay in the face, using *Morse* code to tell McMillan his double agent was really a double agent, getting abducted and dragged through the woods but being smart enough to stay alive—nothing at all."

It should have been patronizing, but instead it was soothing. Because Tucker sounded...awestruck. Not in an *oh-poor-little-Rachel-managed-to-do-something* way, but like she was strong and all that stuff had mattered.

And it had. What might have happened if she hadn't gotten the message to McMillan? Yes, he might not have been shot, but Dymon could have gotten away with a lot more, and done a lot more damage.

"The Vianni part of this is over. Now, it's the Sons part. Let your father take you back to North Star. You've contributed, and probably have the concussion to prove it. Now, it's my turn. Okay?"

It wasn't *okay*, but she understood he had to do this. For himself. For his brothers. She moved her hands to his on her face, then slid her palms down the length of his arms, over his shoulders and up to his face.

"Okay," she said, and then pressed her mouth to his. He stiffened, likely because her father was around, but she didn't care. Not when he was going off into danger, and she was letting him.

But he relaxed into it, kissing her back in a way that felt like some kind of promise. He pulled back, taking her hands off his face.

"Be safe, and don't do a thing until your brothers are here." The kiss had felt like a promise, but she needed the words. "Promise me."

There was a pause, and he squeezed her hands in

his. "I promise. Now, let your Dad take you back to North Star. You've got a hell of a bump on your head. I'm completely unscathed."

But he wouldn't stay that way necessarily. Still, there was nothing she could do about that. She'd only be in his way if she tried to convince him to take her along. Rachel knew she'd achieved some important things throughout this whole mess. Now her role was to step back and let him take the next step.

Hadn't she been harping at him to take help from his brothers—no matter what they'd been through and what he wanted to protect them from? Now, she had to take her own advice. Let him get the help he needed.

It didn't make it easy, but it also didn't make her a failure.

"Be safe," she repeated, giving his hands another squeeze before letting him pass her back to her father.

It was hard walking away, but as her father led her, the adrenaline began to fade into something heavier. Her head ached. Her body hurt. She felt nauseous.

"I don't know what you think you're doing kissing that boy," Dad grumbled, once they'd put some distance between them and Tucker. "I hope it doesn't mean what I think it means."

If she'd had any energy, she might have smiled. She was still so relieved he was alive, she couldn't muster any anger toward him. "If all of your daughters end up with a Wyatt, is that really so bad?"

"It is when they have to be dragged through pain and danger to arrive at that conclusion."

She frowned. *Dragged?* "It's your fault I'm even here. That Tucker is even here. This all begins with you."

"If this is all my fault, then the Sons are all those boys' faults."

She opened her mouth to argue, because of course that wasn't true. So, maybe it was true it wasn't her father's fault the Viannis were after him. But... "You had that knife. The one that hurt me. You lied to me, and made me doubt myself."

He was quiet for a few seconds as they walked. She could smell the acrid tinge of smoke on the air and knew they were close to getting to North Star.

"I did what I thought was right at the time. I'm sorry it hurt you, baby. You'll never know... I wanted you all safe. I'd been at the ranch in WITSEC for almost eight years when they found me again. I'd built a life. A better life than the one I'd grown up in, a better life than I'd had on the force. I had your mother, and I had you and the other girls. I could have run, but I wasn't going to give up this life I loved for some lowlife crime group. I needed something stronger than WITSEC, and evidence seemed the best way to keep them gone. An insurance policy."

"So, you let him go?"

"I didn't have him. I had to get you to the hospital. I couldn't go after him. But I could collect what he left behind. I could use it as my own threat. And it worked."

"Until now. Why now?"

"That's why I went to Granger McMillan. When I got a few veiled threats earlier this month, I went to his father. He'd been in charge of WITSEC when they moved me and we'd become friends. He recommended his son's organization to help get to the bottom of it. Because as far as I knew, the Viannis were all dead or in prison. Granger started looking into it, and when he found some connections between the Vianni group and the Sons, he brought me in."

"Of your own volition," she said.

"More or less. I wanted to protect you girls. Getting out of the way seemed the only option. Besides, I had the evidence. I knew I could use it if I needed to, and I thought McMillan could help me get it into the right hands, but I had to be sure I could trust him. I wasn't sure. I'm still not sure."

"He got shot. By this Dymon man. I told him he was the man from my dreams, more or less. He was going to help, but Dymon shot him first."

"Not Dymon. Vianni. The man who blinded you was Vianni's son," Duke explained. "McMillan told me he'd hired a Vianni underling in the hopes he'd be a double agent. He named some low level thug I hadn't ever had contact with, and I didn't recognize him. He must have had plastic surgery, taken on this new identity, because he was supposed to be dead. I was told a hit had taken him out right after your attack. I figured it was because he'd failed. You recognizing his voice is the only reason I put two and two together."

"So, you killed the man who was after you?"

"Appears so. I'm not saying that will end the Vianni group, but the family I put behind bars is mostly dead. It should be over."

"Except Tucker is still out there, trying to take down the Sons."

"He's a Wyatt, Rachel. They can put on a good show, but they can't let it go. Not while the Sons still exist, not while Ace lives, even if he's in prison. You get wrapped up in a Wyatt, that's what you're getting wrapped up in."

He didn't say it like it was some failing, only like it was fact. Which, no doubt, it was.

"You couldn't let injustice go when you saw it. You wouldn't run away when that came back to haunt you."

She inhaled. "I know you love them like sons, and I understand why you'd be protective of your daughters. But you gave us the example. Doesn't it make sense that we'd all see that in you, even if we didn't know the details, and admire it in others?"

Duke was quiet for a long while, though instead of holding her arm he slid his arm around her shoulders and led her that way.

"I want that head of yours checked out," he said, planting a gentle kiss near the place her head hurt the worst.

"Because of Tucker or just in general?"

Duke chuckled. "Both."

Something inside of her eased. She was still scared, worried for Tucker and all the Wyatts. Worried for McMillan and if he'd survived the gunshot wound. But her father was safe and here with her. One arm of this whole complicated thing had been taken care of.

Now Tucker needed to take care of his, and come back to her in one piece.

TUCKER WAS INTENT on keeping his promise. There was just one little problem. The three men on the road weren't staying there. Apparently, they'd grown tired of waiting for the dead man.

Jamison and Cody were close enough that they'd be here in the next ten to twenty minutes, if they rushed, which they likely would. The other three were much farther away, and Brady and Dev were physically compromised in that group.

But Cody had messaged them all.

Tucker wouldn't hide from the men walking up the side of the hill. He'd promised Rachel he wouldn't do anything until his brothers were here, but he could hardly help it when two of the three men were coming for him—one staying behind and poking through the car Duke had left.

Still, Tucker remained still. He kept his gun ready, and he listened.

"These Vianni morons. Soft city idiots. I'm already tired of cleaning up their messes."

"You can't say no to that kind of cash, though. Not with everything falling apart. I've been thinking of heading to Chicago myself."

The other man offered an anatomically impossible alternative and they both chuckled good-naturedly.

Tucker might have been swayed by the fact they sounded like any two men shooting the breeze. But he had files on these guys and he knew what they were capable of. Monsters could walk and talk and laugh, but what they were willing to *do* was what made them monsters.

They were coming up on him. Whatever happened, his brothers were on their way.

"What a lazy SOB. Couldn't even drag her this far?"

"Oh, he got this far," Tucker said companionably.

They whirled on him, one with a gun and the other with a knife. The one Tucker knew from his files as Justin Hollie sneered.

"A Wyatt." He flipped the knife in his hand. "Your free pass is over. We don't have to worry about hurting Ace's kids anymore."

Which wasn't what Tucker had expected anyone to say, let alone so gleefully. "Oh, yeah? Why's that?"

The man snorted. "Guess you're the last to hear. Ace is dead. No need to come after us anymore. He can't do crap." He spread his arms wide. "Now, I'm a reasonable guy. I let you go, you leave us alone."

"Jail isn't dead."

"He died in jail. Crossed the wrong guy." Hollie snapped his fingers. "Boom. Gone. I heard it was even on the news."

Tucker couldn't process that. It couldn't possibly be true. "I don't believe you."

He shrugged. "No skin off my nose. Just telling you there's no beef here anymore."

"Of course, if you want one, we can give you one," the other man said. Travis Clyne, Tucker was pretty sure. The rapist who'd gotten off because the prosecutor hadn't thought the case was tight enough.

Tucker pushed away the thought of his father being dead. It just wasn't possible Ace Wyatt, the black cloud over his entire life, had just been…killed in jail like a common criminal, instead of the evil incarnate that he was.

Because there were two men who'd done plenty of evil right in front of him. "It turns out I've got a beef with kidnapping, explosions, killing people." He turned his gaze from Hollie to Clyne. "Rape."

"Your funeral." Clyne lifted his gun, but before he'd even gotten close to aiming, a shot rang out. It didn't appear to hit anyone, but Cody and Jamison appeared on either side of the Sons members.

The one with the knife whirled out toward Jamison, but Tucker shot, causing Hollie to stumble with a scream of pain. Cody punched Clyne before he could get a shot off at Tucker.

The third man came charging up, likely hearing the commotion. He stopped abruptly when all three Wyatts pointed guns at him. Looking at his friends writhing on the ground, then the guns, the man dropped his own.

"On your knees," Tucker ordered.

"Here. Tie him up." Cody tossed him some zip ties.

"Jeez. Do you always have these on you?" Tucker asked, quickly putting them to use.

"Never leave home without them," Cody returned, using more to tie up the man he'd punched. Jamison was doing the same.

They all stood at the same time.

"Unscathed again," Cody said with the shake of a head. "You've got the touch, Tuck."

Tuck let out a breath, almost a laugh. "Yeah, I felt bad about that for a while. I don't think I do so much anymore."

"I'll call county to pick these guys up. They've already got some guys collecting evidence on the explosives," Jamison said.

"There's also the car down on the road."

Jamison nodded. He quickly called all the information in. When he hung up, Tucker knew he had to broach the topic he didn't really want to understand.

"They said Ace is dead."

Jamison and Cody exchanged a glance. "We heard that too. Gage was getting everything confirmed when you messaged. We told him to stay put, we had this."

"Do you think he actually listened?"

Jamison smiled wryly. "The county guys will pass it along if he started heading this way."

"Do you think it's true?"

Both brothers sobered. Cody shrugged helplessly, and Jamison ran a hand over his neck.

"I don't know what to think," Jamison said. "So, let's focus on the here and now. Waiting for some guys to cart these morons away. Making sure Duke and Rachel are really safe."

Tucker turned to Cody. "North Star is beat up pretty good."

He nodded grimly. "They're all getting transported to the hospital. Liza's got the girls so Nina could drive over and pick up Duke and Rachel."

"She needs a doctor."

"I'm sure Nina will see to it."

Tucker nodded, but the possibility that Ace was dead overshadowed everything. "If he's dead, that means… it's over."

"We're law enforcement, Tuck," Jamison said, ever the cop. "As long as they're out there hurting people, it isn't over."

"No… But he is. Ace existing, linking us to it. The emotional aspect. It's over." He rubbed at his chest. "He can't be the boogeyman if he's dead."

Cody nodded. "So, we'll hope he is. Dead just the way he deserved. Broken and in jail with absolutely no fanfare."

Tucker let that settle through him. It seemed impossible, but it *would* be fitting. No standoff. No showy end. Nothing that could be described as godlike or awe-inspiring to the wrong kind. Ace's worst nightmare. To have a boring death no one remembered.

Tucker smiled at his brothers. Yeah, that's what he'd hope for.

Epilogue

There was fanfare.

No one said they were celebrating Ace Wyatt's death. They were celebrating Duke being okay. They were celebrating Brady healing and Felicity finding out she was having a girl. They were celebrating life and joy.

But Rachel knew that at least some of that joy was in knowing the man who'd caused them such pain and fear was well and truly gone.

Grandma Pauline had made a feast fit for royalty. They'd shoved everyone around the table as they always did. Even Dev was smiling. It was the best dinner in Rachel's memory.

Dad was safe. Everyone was safe. The men Tucker and his brothers had arrested had even agreed to talk, which had led to more arrests and a complete federal raid on the Sons compound. They hadn't been eradicated, but they had been taken down quite a few pegs.

And Ace Wyatt was dead. All the Wyatt men seemed…lighter. A little out of sorts, but lighter. After dinner, no one was quick to leave. Even Dad and Sarah who had ranch chores to see to lingered.

"Why don't you go on out to the porch," Grandma Pauline said quietly into her ear.

Rachel frowned. "Why?"

"Just go on now."

Confused, Rachel did as she was told, stepping out into the quickly cooling off night.

"Rach? You're not headed back on your own are you?"

Tucker. She should have known. He must have snuck out, and Grandma Pauline had sent her to find out why.

"No." She moved toward his voice. "What are you doing out here all by yourself?"

He was quiet for a moment. "I'm not sure. Everyone's so happy. I'm happy. But… It's weird. I don't know how to feel about… I'm happy for all of them. Happy Ace isn't a shadow on our lives anymore, but I always assumed there'd be some big standoff. And now he's just gone. I'm happy, but it's…complicated."

"I think that's fair. I think you get to have whatever feelings on the matter you need to."

"Yeah, I guess so."

His arm came around her shoulders, so she wrapped hers around his waist. She sighed and relaxed into him. A good man, with a good heart. "I'm glad you weren't hurt."

"It seems we all managed to make it through okay. McMillan's going to be released from the hospital tomorrow."

"And Shay didn't lose her job, according to Nina."

"So, all's well that ends well, I guess."

Rachel thought on that. "It's not an ending, though. It's just life. We endured some bad parts. Now, we get to enjoy some good parts."

"Good parts," he echoed. He wound a strand of her hair around her finger. "You know one good part we seemed to have missed? I've never taken you out."

"Taken me out. Like…a date?"

"Yeah, like a date."

She grinned. There hadn't been time to talk much about the things that had transpired between them on a personal level. She'd been nervous to bring it up. Unsure. But he was asking her on a date. "I guess you should probably do that."

"Tomorrow night?"

"I'll see if I can clear my schedule."

They stood in the quiet for a long while. It was a nice moment. A settling moment. He was an honorable man, who'd take her out on a date, and take things slow. But he'd take them seriously, too. She liked to think it was what they both needed after this horrible year.

She turned in his arms, wrapping hers around his neck. "You're a good man, Tucker Wyatt. You're all good men. Whether Ace is dead or alive. That's always been true. Whether you got hurt fighting him or managed to escape unscathed. Who you are doesn't change. I hope you know that."

"I'm getting there. It helps to hear."

"I think you'll find the Knight women are very good at telling you all that."

"I guess it's good I found me one, then."

"Yeah, it is." She moved onto her toes and kissed him. Without fear, without stress. Just the two of them.

His grip tightened, but the kiss remained gentle. Explorative. Because that's exactly what they had ahead of them.

They'd found each other, and somehow ended years of fear. Of worry. Of dark shadows.

Now, they didn't have to worry anymore. They could

get to know each other as something more than friends, find a way to have a life together. With their family.

Happily-ever-after.

* * * * *

FLIRTING WITH THE SOCIALITE DOC

MELANIE MILBURNE

To Alan and Sue Beswick for their continued support of the Heart Foundation in Tasmania.

This one is for you. At last! XX

CHAPTER ONE

EVEN THE DISTANCE of more than seventeen thousand kilometres that Izzy had put between herself and her best friend was not going to stop another Embarrassing Birthday Episode from occurring.

Oh, joy.

'I've got the perfect present winging its way to you,' Hannah crowed over the phone from London. 'You're going to get the biggest surprise. Be prepared. Be very prepared.'

Izzy gave a mental groan. Her closest friend from medical school had a rather annoying habit of choosing the most inappropriate and, on occasion, excruciatingly embarrassing birthday gifts. 'I know you think I'm an uptight prude but do you have to rub my nose in it every year? I'm still blushing from that grotesque sex toy you gave me last year.'

Hannah laughed. 'This is so much better. And it will make you feel a little less lonely. So how are you settling in? What's it like out there?'

'Out there' was Jerringa Ridge and about as far away from Izzy's life back in England as it could be, hot and dry with sunlight that wasn't just bright but violent. Unlike other parts of New South Wales, which had suffered unusually high levels of flooding, it hadn't rained, or at least with any significance, in this district for months.

And it looked like it.

A rust-red dust cloud had followed her into town like a dervish and left a fine layer over her car, her clothes, and had somehow even got into the small cottage she'd been assigned for her four-week locum.

'It's hot. I swear I got sunburnt walking from the car to the front door.' Izzy glanced down at the tiny white circle on her finger where her engagement ring had been for the last four years. *Not sunburnt enough.*

'Have you met any of the locals yet?'

'Just a couple of people so far,' Izzy said. 'The clinic receptionist, Margie Green, seems very nice, very motherly. She made sure the cottage was all set up for me with the basics. There's a general store run by a husband and wife team—Jim and Meg Collis—who are very friendly too. And the guy who owns and operates the local pub—I think his name is Mike something or other—has organised a welcome-drink-cum-party for me for tomorrow night. Apparently the locals grab at any excuse to party so I didn't like to say I'd prefer to lie low and find my feet first.'

'Perfect timing,' Hannah said. 'At least you won't be on your own on your birthday.'

On your own...

Izzy was still getting used to being single. She'd become so used to fitting in with Richard Remington's life—*his meticulously planned life*—that it was taking her a little while to adjust. The irony was she had been the one to end things. Not that he'd been completely devastated or anything. He'd moved on astonishingly quickly and was now living with a girl ten years younger than he was who had been casually employed to hand around drinks at one of his parents' soirees—another irony, as he had been so adamant about not moving in with Izzy while they'd been together.

This four weeks out at Jerringa Ridge—the first of six one-month locums she had organised in Australia—would give her the space to stretch her cramped wings, to finally fly free from the trappings and expectations of her aristocratic background.

Out here she wasn't Lady Isabella Courtney with a pedigree that went back hundreds of years.

She was just another GP, doing her bit for the Outback.

'Have you met the new doctor yet?' Jim Collis asked, as Zach Fletcher came into the general store to pick up some supplies the following day.

'Not yet.' Zach picked up a carton of milk and checked the use-by date. 'What's he like?'

'She.'

He turned from the refrigerated compartment with raised brows. 'No kidding?'

'You got something against women doctors?' Jim asked.

'Of course not. I just thought a guy had taken the post. I'm sure that's what William Sawyer said before he went on leave.'

'Yeah, well, it seems that one fell through,' Jim said. 'Dr Courtney stepped into the breach at the last minute. She's from England. Got an accent like cut glass.'

Zach grunted as he reached for his wallet. 'Hope she knows what she's in for.'

Jim took the money and put it in the till. 'Mike's putting on a welcome do for her tonight at the pub. You coming?'

'I'm on duty.'

'Doesn't mean you can't pop in and say g'day.'

'I'd hate to spoil the party by showing up in uniform,' Zach said.

'I don't know...' Jim gave him a crooked grin. 'Some women really get off on a guy in uniform. You could get lucky, Fletch. Be about time. How long's it been?'

Zach gave him a look as he stuffed his wallet in his back pocket. 'Not interested.'

'You're starting to sound like your old man,' Jim said. 'How is he? You haven't brought him into town for a while.'

'He's doing OK.'

Jim gave him a searching look. 'Sure?'

Zach steeled his gaze. 'Sure.'

'Tell him we're thinking of him.'

'Will do.' Zach turned to leave.

'Her name is Isabella Courtney,' Jim said. 'Got a nice figure on her and pretty too, in a girl-next-door sort of way.'

'Give it a break, Jim.'

'I'm just saying...'

'The tyres on your ute are bald.' Zach gave him another hardened look as he shouldered open the door. 'Change them or I'll book you.'

Zach's father Doug was sitting out on the veranda of Fletcher Downs homestead; the walking frame that had been his constant companion for the last eighteen months by his side. A quad-bike accident had left Doug Fletcher with limited use of his legs. It would have been a disaster for any person, but for a man who only knew how to work and live on the land it was devastating.

Seeing his strong and extremely physically active father struck down in such a way had been bad enough, but the last couple of months his dad had slipped into a funk of depression that made every day a nightmare of anguish for Zach. Every time he drove up the long drive to the homestead his heart rate would escalate in panic in case his dad had done something drastic in his absence, and it wouldn't slow down again until he knew his father had managed to drag himself through another day.

Popeye, the toy poodle, left his father's side to greet Zach with a volley of excited yapping. In spite of everything, he couldn't help smiling at the little mutt. 'Hey, little buddy.' He crouched down and tickled the little dog's soot-black fleecy ears. He'd chosen the dog at a rescue shelter in Sydney when he'd gone to bring his dad home from the rehabilitation centre. Well, really, it had been the other way around. Popeye had chosen him. Zach had intended to get a man's dog, a kelpie or a collie, maybe even a German shepherd like the one he'd worked with in the drug squad, but somehow the little black button eyes had looked at him unblinkingly as if to say, *Pick me!*

'Jim says hello,' Zach said to his father as he stepped into the shade of the veranda.

His father acknowledged the comment with a grunt as he continued to stare out at the parched paddocks, which instead of being lime green with fresh growth were the depressing colour of overripe pears.

'There's a new doctor in town—a woman.' Zach idly kicked a stray pebble off the floorboards of the veranda into the makeshift garden below. It had been a long time since flowers had grown there. Twenty-three years, to be exact. His English born and bred mother had attempted to grow a cottage garden similar to the one she had left behind on her family's country estate in Surrey, but, like her, none of the plants had flourished in the harsh conditions of the Outback.

'You met her?' His father's tone was flat, as if he didn't care one way or the other, but at least he had responded. That meant it was a good day. A better day.

'Not yet,' Zach said. 'I'm on duty this evening. I'm covering for Rob. I thought I'd ask Margie to come over and sit with—'

Doug's mouth flattened. 'How many times do I have to tell you I don't need a bloody babysitter?'

'You hardly see any of your old mates these days. Surely a quiet drink with—'

'I don't want people crying and wringing their hands and feeling sorry for me.' Doug pulled himself to his feet and reached for his walker. 'I'll see people when I can drive into town and walk into the pub on my own.'

Zach watched as his father shuffled back down the other end of the veranda to the French doors that led to his bedroom. The lace curtains billowed out like a ghostly wraith as the hot, dry northerly wind came through, before the doors closed with a rattling snap that made every weatherboard on the old house creak in protest.

These days it seemed every conversation he had with his dad ended in an argument. Moving back home after five years of living in the city had seemed the right idea at the time, but now he wondered if it had made things worse. It had changed their relationship too much. He'd always planned to come back to the country and run Fletcher Downs once his father was ready to retire, but the accident had thrown everything out of order. This far out in the bush it was hard to get carers to visit, let alone move in, and without daily support his father would have no choice but to move off the property that had been in the family for seven generations.

The day Zach's mother had left had broken his father's heart; leaving Fletcher Downs before his time would rip it right out of his chest.

Popeye gave a little whine at Zach's feet. He bent back down and the dog leapt up into his arms and proceeded to anoint his face with a frenzy of enthusiastic licks. He hugged the dog against his chest as he looked at the sunburnt paddocks. 'We'll get him through this, Popeye. I swear to God we will.'

The Drover's Rest was nothing like the pubs at home but the warm welcome Izzy received more than made up for it. Mike Grantham, the proprietor, made sure she had a drink in her hand and then introduced her to everyone who came in the door. She had trouble remembering all of their names, but she was sure it wouldn't be too long before she got to know them, as she was the only doctor serving the area, which encompassed over two hundred and fifty square kilometres.

Once everyone was inside the main room of the pub Mike tapped on a glass to get everyone's attention. 'A little bird told me it's Dr Courtney's birthday today, so let's give her a big Jerringa Ridge welcome.'

The room erupted into applause and a loud and slightly off-key singing of 'Happy Birthday' as two of the local ladies came out with a cake they had made, complete with candles and Izzy's name piped in icing over the top.

'How did you know it was my birthday?' Izzy asked Mike, once she'd blown out the candles.

'I got a call yesterday,' he said. 'A friend of yours from the old country. She gave me the heads up. Said she had a surprise lined up. It should be here any minute now. Why don't you go and wait by the door? Hey, clear a pathway! Let the doc get through.'

Izzy felt her face grow warm as she made her way through the smiling crowd of locals to the front door of the pub. *Why couldn't Hannah send her flowers or chocolate or champagne, like normal people did?*

And then she saw it.

Not it—*him*.

Tall. Muscled. Toned. Buffed. Clean-shaven. A jaw strong and square and determined enough to land a fighter jet on. A don't-mess-with-me air that was like an invisible wall of glass around him. Piercing eyes that dared you to outstare him.

A male stripper.

Dressed as a cop.

I'm going to kill you, Hannah.

Izzy went into damage control. The last thing she wanted was her reputation ruined before she saw her first patient. She could fix this. It would be simple. Just because Hannah had paid the guy—the rather gorgeous hot guy—to come out all this way and strip for her, it didn't mean she had to let him go through with it.

As long as he got his money, right?

'I'm afraid there's been a change of plan,' she said, before the man could put a foot inside the pub. 'I won't be needing your…er…services after all.'

The man—who had rather unusual grey-blue eyes—looked down at her from his far superior height. 'Excuse me?'

Izzy had to speak in a hushed tone as she could feel the crowd starting to gather behind her. 'Please, will you just leave? I don't want you here. It will spoil everything for me.'

One of the man's eyebrows lifted quizzically. 'Let me get this straight…you don't want me to step inside the pub?'

'No. Absolutely not.' Izzy adopted an adamant stance by planting her hands on her hips. 'And I strictly forbid you to remove any of your clothes in my presence. Do you understand?'

Something in those eyes glinted but the rest of his expression was still deadpan. 'How about if I take off my hat?'

She let out a breath and dropped her arms back by her sides, clenching her hands to keep some semblance of control. She *had* to get rid of him. *Now.* 'Are you *listening* to me? I don't want you here.'

'Last time I looked it was a free country.'

Izzy glowered at him. 'Look, I know you get paid to do this sort of stuff, but surely you can do much better? Don't you find this horribly demeaning, strutting around at parties, titillating tipsy women in a leather thong or whatever it is you get down to? Why don't you go out and get a real job?'

'I love my job.' The glint in his eyes made its brief appearance again. 'I've wanted to do it since I was four years old.'

'Then go and do your job someplace else,' she said

from behind gritted teeth. 'If you don't leave right now, I'm going to call the police.'

'He *is* the police,' Mike called out from behind the bar.

CHAPTER TWO

Zach looked down at the pretty heart-shaped face that was now blushing a fire-engine-red. Her rosebud mouth was hanging open and her toffee-brown eyes were as wide as the satellite dish on the roof of the pub outside. He put out a hand, keeping his cop face on. 'Sergeant Zach Fletcher.'

Her slim hand quivered slightly as it slid into the cage of his. 'H-how do you do? I'm Isabella Courtney…the new locum doctor…in case you haven't already guessed.'

He kept hold of her hand a little longer than he needed to. He couldn't seem to get the message through to his brain to release her. The feel of her satin-soft skin against the roughness of his made something in his groin tighten like an over-tuned guitar string. 'Welcome to Jerringa Ridge.'

'Thank you.' She slipped her hand away and used it to tuck an imaginary strand of hair behind her ear. 'I'm sorry. I expect you think I'm a complete fool but my friend told me she'd organised a surprise and I thought—well, I thought you were the surprise.'

'Sorry to disappoint you.'

'I'm relieved, not disappointed.' She blushed again.

'Quite frankly, I hate surprises. Hannah—that's my friend—thinks it's funny to shock me. Every year she comes up with something outrageous to make my birthday memorable.'

'I guess this will be one you won't forget in a hurry.'

'Yes…' She bit her lip with her small but perfectly aligned white teeth.

'Is there a Dr Courtney around here?' A young man dressed in a courier delivery uniform came towards them from the car park, his work boots crunching on the dusty gravel.

'Um, I'm Dr Courtney.' Isabella's blush had spread down to her décolletage by now, taking Zach's eyes with it. She was of slim build but she had all the right girly bits, a fact his hormones acknowledged with what felt like a stampede racing through his blood.

Cool it, mate.

Not your type.

'I have a package for you,' the delivery guy said. 'I need a signature.'

Zach watched as Isabella signed her name on the electronic pad. She gave the delivery guy a tentative smile as she took the package from him. It was about the size of a shoebox and she held it against her chest like a shield.

'Aren't you going to open it?' Zach asked.

Her cheeks bloomed an even deeper shade of pink. 'I think I'll wait until I'm…until later.'

There was a small silence…apart from the sound of forty or so bodies shuffling and jostling behind them to get a better view.

Zach had lived long enough in Jerringa Ridge to know it wouldn't take much to get the local tongues wagging. Ever since his fiancée Naomi had called off their relationship when he'd moved back home to take care of his father, everyone in town had taken it upon themselves to find him a replacement. He only had to look at a woman once and the gossip would run like a scrub fire. But whether he was in the city or the country, he liked to keep his private life off the grapevine. It meant for a pretty dry social life but he had other concerns right now.

'I'd better head back to the station. I hope you enjoy the rest of your birthday.' He gave Isabella Courtney a brisk impersonal nod while his body thrummed with the memory of her touch. 'Goodnight.'

Izzy watched Zach stride out of the reach of the lights of the pub to where his police vehicle was parked beneath a pendulous willow tree. *Argh!* If only she'd checked the car park before she'd launched into her I-don't-want-you-here speech. How embarrassing! She had just made an utter fool of herself, bad enough in front of *him* but practically the whole town had been watching. Would she ever live it down? Would everyone snigger at her now whenever they saw her?

And how would she face him again?

Oh, he might have kept his face as blank as a mask but she knew he was probably laughing his head off at her behind that stony cop face of his. Would he snigger as well with his mates at how she had mistaken him for a— Oh, it was too *awful* to even think about.

Of course he didn't look anything like a stripper, not that she had seen one in person or anything, only pictures of some well-built guys who worked the show circuit in Vegas. One of the girls she'd shared a flat with in London had hung their risqué calendar on the back of the bathroom door.

Idiot.

Fool.

Imbecile.

How could you possibly think he was—?

'So you've met our gorgeous Zach,' Peggy McLeod, one of the older cattleman's wives, said at Izzy's shoulder, with obvious amusement in her voice.

Izzy turned around and pasted a smile on her face. 'Um, yes… He seems very…um…nice.'

'He's single,' Peggy said. 'His ex-fiancée changed her mind about moving to the bush with him. He and his dad run a big property out of town—Fletcher Downs. Good with his hands, that boy. Knows how to do just about anything. Make someone a fine husband one day.'

'That's…um, nice.'

'His mum was English too, did you know?' Peggy went on, clearly not expecting an answer for she continued without pause. 'Olivia married Doug after a whirlwind courtship but she never could settle to life on the land. She left when Zach was about eight or nine…or was it ten? Yes, it was ten, I remember now. He was in the same class as one of my sister's boys.'

Izzy frowned. 'Left?'

Peggy nodded grimly. 'Yep. Never came back, not even to visit. Zach used to fly over to England for holidays occasionally. Took him ages to settle in, though. Eventually he stopped going. I don't think he's seen his mother in years. Mind you, he's kind of stuck here now since the accident.'

'The accident?'

'Doug Fletcher rolled his quad bike about eighteen

months back. Crushed his spinal cord.' Peggy shook her head sadly. 'A strong, fit man like that not able to walk without a frame. It makes you want to cry, doesn't it?'

'That's very sad.'

'Zach looks after him all by himself,' Peggy said. 'How he does it is anyone's guess. Doug won't hear of having help in. Too proud and stubborn for his own good. Mind you, Zach can be a bit that way too.'

'But surely he can't look after his father indefinitely?' Izzy said. 'What about his own life?'

Peggy's shoulders went up and down. 'Doesn't have one, far as I can see.'

Izzy walked back to her cottage a short time later. The party was continuing without her, which suited her just fine. Everyone was having a field day over her mistaking Zach Fletcher for a stripper. There was only so much ribbing she could take in one sitting. Just as well she was only here for a month. It would be a long time before she would be able to think about the events of tonight without blushing to the roots of her hair.

The police station was a few doors up from the clinic at the south end of the main street. She hadn't noticed it earlier but, then, during the day it looked like any other nondescript cottage. Now that it was fully dark the police sign was illuminated and the four-wheel-drive police vehicle Zach had driven earlier was parked in the driveway beside a spindly peppercorn tree.

As she was about to go past, Zach came out of the building. He had a preoccupied look on his face and almost didn't see her until he got to the car. He blinked and pulled up short, as if she had appeared from nowhere. He tipped his hat, his voice a low, deep burr in the silence of the still night air. 'Dr Courtney.'

'Sergeant Fletcher.' If he was going to be so formal then so was she. Weren't country people supposed to be friendly? If so, he was certainly showing no signs of it.

His tight frown put his features into shadow. 'It's late to be out walking.'

'I like walking.'

'It's not safe to do it on your own.'

'But it's so quiet out here.'

'Doesn't make it safe.' His expression was grimly set. 'You'd be wise to take appropriate measures in future.'

Izzy put her chin up pertly. 'I didn't happen to see a taxi rank anywhere.'

'Do you have a car?'

'Of course.'

'Next time use it or get a lift with one of the locals.' He opened the passenger door of the police vehicle. 'Hop in. I'll run you home.'

Izzy bristled at his brusque manner. 'I would prefer to walk, if you don't mind. It's only a block and I—'

His grey-blue eyes hardened. 'I do mind. Get in. That's an order.'

The air seemed to pulse with invisible energy as those strong eyes held hers. She held his gaze for as long as she dared, but in the end she was the first to back down. Her eyes went to his mouth instead and a frisson of awareness scooted up her spine to tingle each strand of her hair on her scalp. Something shifted in her belly...a turning, a rolling-over sensation, like something stirring after a long hibernation.

His mouth was set tightly, as tight and determined as his jaw, which was in need of a fresh shave. His eyes were fringed with dark lashes, his eyebrows the same rich dark brown as his hair. His skin was deeply tanned and it was that stark contrast with his eyes that was so heart-stopping. Smoky grey one minute, ice-blue the next, the outer rims of his irises outlined in dark blue, as if someone had traced their circumference with a fine felt-tip marker.

Eyes that had seen too much and stored the memories away somewhere deep inside for private reflection...or haunting.

'Fine, I'll get in,' Izzy said with bad grace. 'But you really need to work on your kerb-side manner.'

He gave her an unreadable look as he closed the door with a snap. She watched him stride around to the driver's side, his long legs covering the distance in no time at all. He was two or three inches over six feet and broad shouldered and lean hipped. When he joined her in the car she felt the space shrink alarmingly. She drew herself in tightly, crossing her arms and legs to keep any of her limbs from coming into contact with his powerfully muscled ones.

The silence prickled like static electricity.

'Peggy McLeod told me about your father's accident,' Izzy said as he pulled to the kerb outside her cottage half a minute later. She turned in her seat to look at him. 'I'm sorry. That must be tough on both of you.'

Zach's marble-like expression gave nothing away but she noticed his hands had tightened on the steering-wheel. 'Do you make house calls?'

'I...I guess so. Is that what Dr Sawyer did?'

'Once a week.'

'Then I'll do it too. When would you like me to come?'

Some of the tension seemed to leave his shoulders

but he didn't turn to look at her. 'I'll ring Margie and make an appointment.'

'Fine.'

Another silence.

'Look, about that little mix-up back at the pub—' she began.

'Forget it,' he cut her off. 'I'll wait until you get inside. Lock the door, won't you?'

Izzy frowned. 'You know you're really spooking me with this over-vigilance. Don't you know everyone in a town this size by name?'

'We have drive-throughs who cause trouble from time to time. It's best not to take unnecessary risks.'

'Not everyone is a big bad criminal, Sergeant Fletcher.'

He reached past her to open her door. Izzy sucked in a sharp breath as the iron bar of his arm brushed against her breasts, setting every nerve off like a string of fireworks beneath her skin.

For an infinitesimal moment her gaze meshed with his.

He had tiny blue flecks in that unreadable sea of grey and his pupils were inky-black. He smelt of lemons with a hint of lime and lemongrass and something else… something distinctly, arrantly, unapologetically male.

A sensation like the unfurling petals of a flower brushed lightly over the floor of her belly.

Time froze.

The air tightened. Pulsed. Vibrated.

'Sorry.' He pulled back and fixed his stare forward again, his hands gripping the steering-wheel so tightly his tanned knuckles were bone white.

'No problem.' Izzy's voice came out a little rusty. 'Thanks for the lift.'

He didn't drive off until she had closed the door of the cottage. She leant back against the door and let out a breath she hadn't realised she'd been holding, listening as his car growled away into the night.

'So what did your friend actually send you for your birthday?' Margie Green asked as soon as Izzy arrived at the clinic the next morning.

'I haven't opened it yet.' *Because I stupidly left it in Sergeant Fletcher's car last night*.

Margie's eyes were twinkling. 'What on earth made you think our Zach was a male stripper?'

Izzy cringed all over again. Was every person in town going to do this to her? Remind her of what a silly little idiot she had been? If so, four weeks couldn't go fast enough. 'Because it's exactly the sort of thing my friend Hannah would do. As soon as I saw him standing there I went into panic mode. I didn't stop to think that he could be a real cop. I didn't even know if Jerringa Ridge *had* a cop. I didn't have time to do much research on the post because the agency asked me to step in for someone at the last minute.'

'We have two cops...or one and a half really,' Margie said. 'We used to have four but with all the government cutbacks that's no longer the case. Rob Heywood is close to retirement so Zach does the bulk of the work. He's a hard worker is our Zach. You won't find a nicer man out in these parts.'

'I'm not here to find a man.' Why did every woman over fifty—including her own mother—seem to think younger women had no other goal than to get married? 'I'm here to work.'

Margie cocked her head at a thoughtful angle. 'You're here for four weeks. These days that's a long time for a young healthy woman like you to be without a bit of male company.'

Izzy's left thumb automatically went to her empty ring finger. It was a habit she was finding hard to break. It wasn't that she regretted her decision to end things with Richard. It was just strange to feel so...so unattached. She hadn't looked at another man in years. But now she couldn't get Zach Fletcher's eyes or his inadvertent touch out of her head...*or her body*. Even now she could remember the feel of that slight brush of his arm across her breasts—the electric, tingly feel of hard male against soft female...

She gave herself a mental shake as she picked up a patient's file and leafed through it. 'I'm not interested in a relationship. There'd be no point. I'm on a working holiday. I won't be in one place longer than a month.'

'Zach hasn't dated anyone since he broke up with his ex,' Margie said, as if Izzy hadn't just described her plans for the next six months. 'It'd be good for him to move on. He was pretty cut up about Naomi not wanting to come with him to the bush. Not that he's said anything, of course. He's not one for having his heart flapping about on his sleeve. He comes across as a bit arrogant at times but underneath all that he's a big softie. Mind you, you might have your work cut out for you, being an English girl and all.'

Izzy lowered the notes and frowned. 'Because his mother was English?'

'Not only English but an aristocrat.' Margie gave

a little sniff that spoke volumes. 'One of them blue-blooded types. Her father was a baron or a lord of the realm or some such thing. Olivia Hardwick was as posh as anything. Used to having servants dancing around her all her life. No wonder she had so much trouble adjusting to life out here. Love wasn't enough in the end.'

Izzy thought of the veritable army of servants back at Courtney Manor. They were almost part of the furniture, although she tried never to take any of them for granted. But now was probably not a good time to mention her background with its centuries-old pedigree.

Margie sighed as sat back in her chair. 'It broke Doug's heart when she left. He hasn't looked at another woman since…more's the pity. He and I used to hang out a bit in the old days. Just as friends.'

'But you would have liked something more?' Izzy asked.

Margie gave her a wistful smile. 'We can't always have what we want, can we?'

Izzy glanced at the receptionist's left hand. 'You never married?'

'Divorced. A long time ago. Thirty years this May. I shouldn't have married Jeff but I was lonely at the time.'

'I'm sorry.'

Margie shrugged.

'Did you have children?'

'A boy and a girl. They both live in Sydney. And I have three grandchildren who are the joy of my life. I'm hoping to get down to see them at Easter.'

Izzy wondered if Margie's marriage had come about because of Doug Fletcher's involvement with Olivia. How heartbreaking it must have been for her to watch him fall madly in love with someone else, and how sad for Doug to have the love of his life walk out on him and their young son.

Relationships were tricky. She knew that from her own parents, who had a functional marriage but not a particularly happy or fulfilling one. That was one of the reasons she had decided to end things with Richard. She hadn't wanted to end up trapped in an empty marriage that grumbled on just for the sake of appearances.

'Sergeant Fletcher asked me to make a house call on his father,' Izzy said. 'Has he rung to make an appointment yet?'

'Not yet,' Margie said. 'He might drop in on his way to the station. Ah, here he is now. Morning, Zach. We were just talking about you.'

Izzy turned to see Zach Fletcher duck his head slightly to come through the door. Her stomach did a little freefall as his eyes met hers. He looked incredibly commanding in his uniform; tall and composed with an air of untouchable reserve. How on earth she had mistaken him for anything other than a cop made her cheeks fire up all over again. She ran her tongue over her lips before she gave him a polite but distant smile. 'Good morning, Sergeant Fletcher.'

He dipped his head ever so slightly, his eyes running over her in a lazy, unreadable sweep that set her pulse rate tripping. 'Dr Courtney.'

Izzy's smile started to crack around the edges. Did he have to look at her so unwaveringly, as if he knew how much he unsettled her? Was he laughing at her behind that inscrutable cop mask? 'What can I do for you? Would you like to make an appointment for me to come out and see your father today? I could probably work something in for later this afternoon. I'm pretty solidly booked but—'

He handed her the package the delivery guy had delivered the night before, his eyes locking on hers in a way that made the base of her spine shiver and fizz. 'You left this in my car last night.'

Izzy could practically hear Margie's eyes popping out of her head behind the reception counter. 'Oh... right, thanks.' She took the package from him and held it against her chest, where her heart was doing double time.

'Aren't you going to open it?' Margie said.

'Um...not right now.'

Was that a hint of mockery glinting in Zach Fletcher's eyes? 'What time would suit you?' he asked.

'I...I think I'd rather do it when I get home.'

The glint in his eyes was unmistakable this time, so too was the slight curve at one side of his mouth. His version of a smile? It made her hungry to see a real one. Was he capable of stretching that grim mouth that far? 'I meant what time would suit you to see my father.'

Izzy's blush deepened. What was it about this man that made her feel about twelve years old? Well, maybe not twelve years old. Right now she was feeling *incredibly* adult. X-rated adult. Every particle of her flesh was shockingly aware of him. Her skin was tight, her senses alert, her pulse rate rising, her heart fluttering like a butterfly trapped in the narrow neck of a bottle. 'Oh...' She swung back to Margie. 'What time am I free?'

'Your last patient is at four forty-five. It's a twenty-minute drive out to Fletcher Downs so shall we say five-thirty, give or take a few minutes?' Margie said.

'I'll make sure I'm there to let you in,' Zach said.

'My father can be a bit grouchy meeting people for the first time. Don't let him get to you.'

Izzy raised her chin the tiniest fraction. 'I'm used to handling difficult people.'

His eyes measured hers for a pulsing moment. 'Margie will give you a map. If you pass Blake's waterhole, you've gone too far.'

'I'm sure I'll find it without any trouble,' Izzy said. 'I have satellite navigation in my car.'

He gave a brisk nod that encompassed the receptionist as well as Izzy and left the clinic.

'Are you going to tell me how you ended up in his car last night or am I going to have to guess?' Margie asked.

Izzy let out a breath as she turned back around. 'He gave me a lift home.'

Margie's eyes widened with intrigue. 'From the pub? It's like half a block by city standards.'

'Yes, well, apparently Sergeant Fletcher thinks it's terribly unsafe to walk home at night without an escort. Typical cop, they think everyone's a potential criminal. They never see the good in people, only the bad. They have power issues too. You can pick it up a mile off. I'd bet my bottom dollar Zach Fletcher is a total control freak. And a blind man could see he has a chip on his shoulder the size of a boulder.'

Margie smiled a knowing smile. 'You like him.'

'What on earth gives you that idea?' Izzy gave a scornful little laugh but even to her ears it sounded tinny. 'He's not my type.'

And I bet I'm not his either.

CHAPTER THREE

ZACH HAD BEEN at the homestead long enough to change out of his uniform, make his father a cup of tea, and take Popeye for a walk down to the dam and back when he saw Isabella Courtney coming up the driveway.

He waved a fly away from his face as he watched her handle the corrugations of the gravel driveway that was as long as some city streets. A dust cloud plumed out in her wake and a flock of sulphur-crested white cockatoos and salmon-pink corellas flew out of the gum trees that lined the driveway before settling in another copse of trees closer to the dam. The chorus of cicadas was loud in the oven-warm air and in the distance the grey kangaroo he'd rescued as a joey, and who now had a joey of her own, hopped towards a few tufts of grass that had pushed up through the parched ground around the home paddock's water trough.

Popeye gave a whine and looked up at Zach as his body did its little happy dance at the thought of a visitor. 'Cool it, buddy,' Zach said. 'She's not staying long.'

It was hard to ignore the stirring of male hormones in his body as he watched her alight from the car. She had a natural grace about her, lissom and lithe, like a ballerina or yoga enthusiast. She wasn't particularly tall, or at least not compared to him at six feet three in bare feet. She was about five-six or -seven with a waist he could probably span with his hands, and her features were classically beautiful but in a rather understated way. She wore little or no make-up and her mid-length chestnut hair was tied back in a ponytail she had wound around itself in a casual knot, giving her a fresh, youthful look.

But it was her mouth his gaze kept tracking to. It was soft and full and had an upward curve that made it look like she was always on the brink of smiling.

'Oh, what an adorable dog!' Her smile lit up her brown eyes so much that they sparkled as she bent down to greet Popeye. 'Oh, you darling little poppet. Who's a good boy? Hang on a minute—*are* you a boy? Oh, yes, you are, you sweet little thing. Yes, I love you too.' She laughed a tinkling-bell laugh and stood up again, her smile still stunningly bright as she stood and faced Zach. 'Is he yours?'

Zach had to take a moment to gather himself after being on the receiving end of that dazzling smile.

Earth to Zach. Do you read me?

He wondered if he should fob Popeye off as his father's but he had a feeling she wouldn't buy it for a moment. 'Yes.'

She angled her head at him in an appraising manner. 'Funny, I had you picked as a collie or kelpie man, or maybe a German shepherd or Doberman guy.'

He kept his expression blank. 'The station manager has working dogs. Popeye's just a pet.'

She brushed a tendril of hair away from her face that the light breeze had worked loose. 'This is a lovely property. I couldn't believe how many birds I saw coming up the driveway.'

'You're not seeing it at its best. We need rain.'

She scanned the paddocks with one of her hands shading her eyes against the sun. 'It's still beautiful—Oh, there's a kangaroo and it's got a joey! He just popped his head out. How gorgeous!'

'That's Annie,' Zach said.

She swung around to look at him again. 'Is she a pet too?'

'Not really.' He waved another fly away from his face. 'Her mother was killed on the highway. I reared her by hand and released her back into the wild a few years ago, but she hangs about a bit, mostly because of the drought.'

Her eyes widened in surprise. 'You reared her yourself?'

'Yeah.'

Her pretty little nose was wrinkled over the bridge from her small frown. 'Like with a bottle or something?'

'Yep. Six feeds a day.'

'How did you juggle that with work?'

'I took her with me in a pillowcase.'

She blinked a couple of times as if she couldn't quite imagine him playing wet-nurse. 'That's…amazing…' She looked back at the paddock where Annie was grazing. 'It must be wonderful to have all this space to yourself. To be this close to wildlife and to breathe in such fresh air instead of pollution.'

Zach saw her finely shaped nostrils widen to take in the eucalyptus scent of the bush. He picked up a faint trace of her fragrance in the air: a flowery mix that was redolent of gardenias and vanilla. The sun caught the golden highlights in her hair and he found himself wondering what it would feel like to run his fingers through those glossy, silky strands.

Get a grip.

He thrust his hands in his pockets, out of the way of temptation. She was a blow-in and would be gone before the first dust storm hit town. His track record with keeping women around wasn't flash. His mother had whinged and whined and then withdrawn into herself for ten years before she'd finally bolted and never returned. His fiancée hadn't even got as far as the Outback before the call of the city had drawn her back. Why would Isabella Courtney with her high-class upbringing have anything to offer him?

She turned back to look at him and a slight blush bloomed in her cheeks. 'I guess I should get on with why I came here. Is your father inside?'

'Yes. Come this way.'

Izzy stepped into the cool interior of the homestead but it took her eyes a moment to adjust to the dim interior after the assault of the bright sunlight outside. A man who was an older version of Zach sat in an armchair in the sitting room off the long, wide hallway; a walking frame was positioned nearby. He had steel-grey hair at his temples and his skin was weathered by long periods in the sun but he was still a fine-looking man. He had the same aura of self-containment his son possessed, and a strong uncompromising jaw, although his cheeks were hollowed by recent weight loss. His mouth had a downward turn and his blue eyes had damson-coloured shadows beneath them, as if he had trouble sleeping.

'Dad, Dr Courtney is here,' Zach said.

'Hello, Mr Fletcher.' Izzy held out her hand but dropped it back by her side when Doug Fletcher rudely ignored it.

He turned his steely gaze to his son. 'Why didn't you tell me she was a bloody Pom?'

Zach tightened his mouth. 'Because it has nothing to do with her ability as a medical practitioner.'

'I don't want any toffee-nosed Poms darkening my doorstep ever again. Do you hear me? Get her out of here.'

'Mr Fletcher, I—'

'You need to have regular check-ups and Dr Courtney is the only doctor in the region,' Zach said. 'You either see her or you see no one. I'm not driving three hundred kilometres each way to have your blood pressure checked every week.'

'My blood pressure was fine until you brought her here!' Doug snapped.

Izzy put a hand on Zach's arm. 'It's all right, Sergeant Fletcher. I'll come back some other time.'

Doug glared at her. 'You'll be trespassing if you do.'

'Well, at least the cops won't be far away to charge me, will they?' she said.

Doug's expression was as dark as thunder as he shuffled past them to exit the room. Izzy heard Zach release a long breath and turned to look at him. 'I'm sorry. I don't think I handled that very well.'

He raked a hand through his hair, leaving it sticking up at odd angles. 'You'd think after twenty-three years he'd give it a break, wouldn't you?'

'Is that how long it's been since your mother left?'

He gave her a grim look. 'Yeah. I guess you twigged she was English.'

'Peggy McLeod told me.'

He walked over to the open fireplace and kicked a gum nut back into the grate. His back and shoulders were so tense Izzy could see each muscle outlined by his close-fitting T-shirt. He rubbed the back of his neck before he turned back around to face her. 'I'm worried about him.'

'I can see that.'

'I mean *really* worried.'

Izzy saw the haunted shadows in his eyes. 'You think he's depressed?'

'Let's put it this way, I don't leave him alone for long periods. And I've taken all the guns over to a friend's place.'

She felt her heart tighten at the thought of him having to keep a step ahead of his father all the time. The pressure on the loved ones of people struggling with depression was enormous. And Zach seemed to be doing it solo. 'Has his mood dropped recently or has he been feeling low for a while?'

'It's been going down progressively since he came out of rehab.' He let out another breath as he dragged his hand over his face. 'Each day I seem to lose a little bit more of him.'

Izzy could just imagine the toll it was taking on him. He had so many responsibilities to shoulder, running his father's property as well as his career as a cop. 'Would he see someone in Sydney if I set up an appointment? I know it's a long trip but surely it would be worth it to get him the help he needs.'

'He won't go back to the city, not after spending three months in hospital. He won't even go as far as Bourke.'

'Does he have any friends who could spend time

with him?' she asked. 'It might help lift his mood to be more active socially.'

The look he threw her was derisive. 'My father is not the tea-party type.'

'What about Margie Green?'

His brows came together. 'What about her?'

'She's a close friend, isn't she? Or she was in the old days before your parents got together.'

His expression was guarded now; the drawbridge had come up again. 'You seem to have gained a lot of inside information for the short time you've been in town.'

Izzy compressed her lips. 'I can't help it if people tell me stuff. I can assure you I don't go looking for it.'

He curled his lip in a mocking manner. 'I bet you don't.'

She picked up her doctor's bag from the floor with brisk efficiency. 'I think it's time I left. I've clearly outstayed my welcome.'

Izzy had marched to the front door before he caught up with her. 'Dr Courtney.' It was a command, not a request or even an apology. She drew in a tight breath and turned to face him. His expression still had that reserved unreadable quality to it but something about his eyes made her think he was not so much angry at her as at the situation he found himself in.

'Yes?'

He held her gaze for a long moment without speaking. It was as if he was searching through a filing drawer in his brain for the right words.

'*Yes?*' Izzy prompted.

'Don't give up on him.' He did that hair-scrape thing again. 'He needs time.'

'Will four weeks be long enough, do you think?' she asked.

He gave her another measured look before he opened the screen door for her. 'Let's hope so.'

'So, what did you call your new boyfriend I sent you?' Hannah asked when she video-messaged Izzy a couple of nights later.

Izzy looked at the blow-up male doll she had propped up in one of the armchairs in the sitting room. 'I've called him Max. He's surprisingly good company for a man. He doesn't hog the remote control and he doesn't eat all the chocolate biscuits.'

Hannah giggled. 'Have you slept with him?'

Izzy rolled her eyes. 'Ha-ha. I'm enjoying having the bed to myself, thank you very much.'

'So, no hot guys out in the bush?'

She hoped the webcam wasn't picking up the colour of her warm cheeks. She hadn't told Hannah about her case of mistaken identity with Zach Fletcher. She wasn't sure why. Normally she told Hannah everything that was going on in her life…well, maybe not *everything*. She had never been the type of girl to tell all about dates and boyfriends. There were some things she liked to keep private. 'I'm supposed to be using this time to sort myself out in the love department. I don't want to complicate my recovery by diving head first into another relationship.'

'You weren't in love with Richard, Izzy. You know you weren't. You were just doing what your parents expected of you. He filled the hole in your life after Jamie died. I'm glad you saw sense in time. Don't get me wrong—I really like Richard but he's not the one for you.'

Izzy knew what Hannah said was true. She had let things drift along for too long, raising everyone's hopes and expectations in the process. Her parents were still a little touchy on the subject of her split with Richard, whom they saw as the ideal son-in-law. The stand-in son for the one they had lost after a long and agonising battle with sarcoma.

Her decision to come out to the Australian Outback on a working holiday had been part of her strategy to take more control over her life. It was a way to remind her family that she was serious about her career. They still thought she was just dabbling at medicine until it was time to settle down and have a couple of children to carry on the long line of Courtney blood now that her older brother Jamie wasn't around to do it.

But she loved being a doctor. She loved it that she could help people in such a powerful way. Not just healing illnesses but changing lives, even saving them on occasion.

Like Jamie might have been saved if he had been diagnosed earlier...

Thinking about her brother made her heart feel like it had been stabbed. It actually seemed to jerk in her chest every time his name was mentioned, as if it were trying to escape the lunge of the sword of memory.

'Maybe you'll meet some rich cattleman out there and fall madly in love and never come home again, other than for visits,' Hannah said.

'I don't think that's likely.' Izzy couldn't imagine leaving England permanently. Her roots went down too deep. She even loved the capricious weather.

No, this trip out here was timely but not permanent.

Besides, with Jamie gone she was her parents' only child and heir. Not going home to claim her birthright would be unthinkable. She just needed a few months to let them get used to the idea of her living her own life and following her own dreams, instead of living vicariously through theirs.

Izzy's phone buzzed where it was plugged into the charger on the kitchen bench. 'Got to go, Han. I think that's a local call coming through. I'll call you in a day or two. Bye.' She picked up her phone. 'Isabella Courtney.'

'Zach Fletcher here.' Even the way he said his name was sharp and to the point.

'Good evening, Sergeant,' Izzy said, just as crisply. 'What can I do for you?'

'I just got a call about an accident out by the Honeywells' place. It doesn't sound serious but I thought you should come out with me to check on the driver. The volunteer ambos are on their way. I can be at your place in two minutes. It will save you having to find your way out there in the dark.'

'Fine. I'll wait at the front for you.'

Izzy had her doctor's bag at the ready when Zach pulled up outside her cottage. She got into the car and clipped on her seat belt, far more conscious than she wanted to be of him sitting behind the wheel with one of those unreadable expressions on his face.

Would it hurt him to crack a smile?

Say a polite hello?

Make a comment on the weather?

'Do you know who's had the accident?' she asked.

'Damien Redbank.' He gunned the engine once he

turned onto the highway and Izzy's spine slammed back against the seat. 'His father Charles is a big property owner out here. Loads of money, short on common sense, if you get my drift.'

Izzy sent him a glance. 'The son or the father?'

The top edge of his mouth curled upwards but it wasn't anywhere near a smile. 'The kid's all right. Just needs to grow up.'

'How old is he?'

'Eighteen and a train wreck waiting to happen.'

'What about his mother?'

'His parents are divorced. Vanessa Redbank remarried a few years ago.' He waited a beat before adding, 'She has a new family now.'

Izzy glanced at him again. His mouth had tightened into its default position of grim. 'Does Damien see his mother?'

'Occasionally.'

Occasionally probably wasn't good enough, Izzy thought. 'Where does she live?'

'Melbourne.'

'At least it's not the other side of the world.' She bit her lip and wished she hadn't spoken her thoughts out loud. 'I'm sorry...I hope I didn't offend you.'

He gave her a quick glance. 'Offend me how?'

Izzy tried to read his look but the mask was firmly back in place. 'It must have been really tough on you when your mother left. England is a long way away from here. It feels like *everywhere* is a long way away from here. It would've seemed even longer to a young child.'

'I wasn't a young child. I was ten.' His voice was stripped bare of emotion; as if he was reading from a script and not speaking from personal experience. 'Plenty old enough to take care of myself.'

Izzy could imagine him watching as his mother had driven away from the property for the last time. His face blank, his spine and shoulders stoically braced, while no doubt inside him a tsunami of emotion had been roiling. Had his father comforted him or had he been too consumed by his own devastation over the breakdown of his marriage? No wonder Zach had an aura of unreachability about him. It was a circle of deep loneliness that kept him apart from others. He didn't want to need people so he kept well back from them.

Unlike her, who felt totally crushed if everyone didn't take an instant shine to her. Doing and saying the right thing—*people-pleasing*—had been the script she had been handed from the cradle. It was only now that she had stepped off the stage, so to speak, that she could see how terribly lonely and isolated she had felt.

Still felt...

When had she not felt lonely? Being sent to boarding school hadn't helped. She had wanted to go to a day school close to home but her protests had been ignored. All Courtneys went to boarding school. It was a tradition that went back generations. It was what the aristocracy did. But Izzy had been too bookish and too shy to be the most popular girl. Not athletic enough to be chosen first, let alone be appointed the captain of any of the sporting teams. Too keen to please her teachers, which hadn't won her any friends. Too frightened to do the wrong thing in case she was made a spectacle of in front of the whole school. Until she'd met Hannah a couple of years later, her life had been terrifyingly, achingly lonely.

* * *

'When I was ten I still couldn't go to sleep unless all of my Barbie dolls were lined up in bed with me in exactly the right order.' *Why are you telling him this stuff?* 'I've still got them. Not with me, of course.'

Zach's gaze touched hers briefly. It was the first time she had seen a hint of a smile dare to come anywhere near the vicinity of his mouth. But just as soon as it appeared it vanished. He turned his attention back to the grey ribbon of road in front of them where in the distance Izzy could see the shape of a car wedged at a steep angle against the bank running alongside the road. Another car had pulled up alongside, presumably the person who had called for help.

'Damien's father's not going to be too happy about this,' Zach said. 'He's only had that car a couple of weeks.'

'But surely he'll be more concerned about his son?' Izzy said. 'Cars can be replaced. People can't.'

The line of his mouth tilted in a cynical manner as he killed the engine. 'Try telling Damien's mother that.'

CHAPTER FOUR

When Izzy got to the car the young driver was sitting on the roadside, holding his right arm against his chest. 'Damien? Hi, I'm Isabella Courtney, the new locum doctor in town. I'm going to check you over. Is that OK?'

Damien gave her a belligerent look. 'I'm fine. I don't need a doctor. And before you ask—' he sent Zach a glance '—no, I wasn't drinking.'

'I still have to do a breathalyser on you, mate,' Zach said. 'It's regulation when there's been an accident.'

'A stupid wombat was in the middle of the road,' Damien said. 'I had to swerve to miss it.'

'That arm looks pretty uncomfortable,' Izzy said. 'How about I take a look at it and if it's not too bad we can send you home.'

He rolled his eyes in that universal teenage *this sucks* manner, but he co-operated while she examined him. He had some minor abrasions on his forehead and face but the airbag had prevented any major injury. His humerus, however, was angled and swollen, indicative of a broken arm. Izzy took his pulse and found it was very weak and the forearm looked dusky due to the artery being kinked at the fracture site.

'I'm going to have to straighten that arm to restore blood flow,' she said. 'I'll give you something to take the edge off it but it still might hurt a bit.' She took out a Penthrane inhalant, which would deliver rapid analgesia. 'Take a few deep breaths on this…yes, that's right. Good job.'

While Damien was taking deep breaths on the inhalant Izzy put traction on the arm and aligned it. He gave a yowl during the process but the pulse had come back into the wrist and the hand and forearm had pinked up.

'Sorry about that,' she said. 'You did really well. I'm going to put a splint on your arm so we can get you to hospital. You're going to need an orthopaedic surgeon to have a look at that fracture.'

Damien muttered a swear word under his breath. 'My dad is going to kill me.'

'I've just called him,' Zach said. 'He's on his way. The ambos are five minutes away,' he said to Izzy.

'Good,' Izzy said, as she unpacked the inflatable splint. The boy was shivering with shock by now so she gave him an injection of morphine. She was about to ask Zach to pass her the blanket out of the kit when he handed it to her. She gave him a smile. 'Mind-reader.'

He gave a shrug. 'Been at a lot of accidents.'

Izzy hated to think of how terrible some of them might have been. Cops and ambulance personnel were always at the centre of drama and tragedy. The toll it took on them was well documented. But out in the bush, where the officers often personally knew the victims, it was particularly harrowing.

The volunteer ambulance officers were two of the people Izzy had met the other night at the pub, Ken Gordon and Roger Parker. After briefing them on the boy's condition, she supervised them as they loaded Damien onto a stretcher, supporting his arm. And then, once he was loaded, she put in an IV and set some fluids running. The Royal Flying Doctor Service would take over once the ambulance had delivered the boy to the meeting point about eighty kilometres away.

Not long after the ambulance had left, a four-wheel-drive farm vehicle pulled up. A middle-aged man got out from behind the wheel and came over to where Zach was sorting out the towing of the damaged vehicle with the local farmer who had called in the accident.

'Is it a write-off?' Charles Redbank asked.

Izzy paused in the process of stripping off her sterile gloves. Although Zach had called Charles and told him Damien was OK, she still found it strange that he would want to check on the car before he saw his son. What sort of father was he? Was a car really more important to him than his own flesh and blood?

Zach put his pen back in his top pocket as he faced Charles. His mouth looked particularly grim. 'No.'

'Bloody fool,' Charles muttered. 'Was he drinking?'

'No.'

'He's not seriously hurt.' Izzy stepped forward. 'He has a broken arm that will need to be seen by an orthopaedic surgeon. I've arranged for him to be flown to Bourke. If you hurry you can catch up with the ambulance. It's only just left. You probably passed it on the road.'

'I came in on the side road from Turner's Creek,' Charles said. 'And you can think again if you think I'm going to chase after him just because he's got a broken arm. He can deal with it. He's an adult, or he's supposed to be.'

Yes, and he's had a great role model, Izzy thought. 'Damien will need a few things if he stays in hospital for a day or two. A change of clothes, a toothbrush, toiletries—that sort of thing.'

Charles gave her the once-over. 'Are you the new doctor?'

'Yes. Isabella Courtney.'

His eyes ran over her again, lingering a little too long on her breasts. 'Bit young to be a doctor, aren't you?'

Izzy had faced similar comments for most of her medical career. She did her best to not let it get to her. Just because she had a youthful appearance, it didn't mean she wasn't good at her job. 'I can assure you I am quite old enough and have all the necessary qualifications.'

'Your left brake light isn't working,' Zach said to Charles.

Charles rocked back on his heels, his gaze running between Izzy and Zach like a ferret's. 'So that's the way it is, is it? Well, well, well. You're a fast worker. She's only been in town, what, a couple of days?'

Zach's jaw looked like it had been set in place by an invisible clamp. 'I told you three weeks ago to get it fixed.'

Charles's smile was goading. 'She's a bit too upmarket for you, Fletch. And what would your old man say if you brought a posh Pommy girl home, eh? That'd go down a treat, wouldn't it?'

Izzy marvelled at Zach's self-control for even *she* felt like punching Charles Redbank. Zach looked down from his considerable height advantage at the farmer, his strong gaze unwavering. 'I'll give you twenty-four hours to get that light seen to. Ian Cooke is going to tow the car into Joe's workshop. He's gone back to town for the truck now. I'm heading to Bourke for a court appearance tomorrow. If you pack a few things for Damien, I'll swing by and pick them up before I leave in the morning.'

'Wouldn't want to put you to any trouble,' Charles said, with a deliberate absence of sincerity.

'It's no trouble,' Zach said. 'Damien's a good kid. He just needs a little direction.'

Charles's lip curled. 'What? And you think you're the one to give it to him?'

'That's your job,' Zach said, and turned away to leave. 'Coming, Dr Courtney?'

Izzy waited until they were in the car before she said, 'Is there a special section in the police training manual on how to handle jerks?'

He gave her a look as he started the engine. 'He's a prize one, isn't he?'

'You handled that situation so well. I was impressed.' She pulled down her seat belt and clicked it into place. 'Quite frankly, I wanted to punch him.'

'Two wrongs never make a right.'

Izzy studied him for a beat or two. 'Are you really going to Bourke for a court appearance tomorrow?'

He turned the car for town before he answered. 'I have the day off. It'll be an outing for my father if I can convince him to come. Take his mind off his own troubles for a change.'

'He's very lucky to have you.'

'He's a good dad. He's always tried to do his best, even under difficult circumstances.'

The township appeared in the distance, the sprinkling of lights glittering in the warm night air.

'You did a good job out there tonight.' Zach broke the silence that had fallen between them.

Izzy glanced at him again. 'You were expecting me not to, weren't you?'

'Have you worked in a remote region before?'

'I did a short stint in South Africa last year.'

His brows moved upwards. 'So why Outback Australia this year?'

'I've always wanted to come out here,' Izzy said. 'A lot of my friends had come out and told me how amazing it is. I spent a few days in Sydney on my way here. I'm looking forward to seeing a bit more after I finish my six months of locums. Melbourne, Adelaide, Perth, maybe a quick trip up to Broome and the Kimberleys.'

Another silence fell.

Izzy felt as if he was waiting for her to tell him her real reason for coming out here. It was what cops did. They waited. They listened. They observed. She had seen him looking at her ring hand while she'd been strapping up Damien. He'd been a cop too long to miss that sort of detail. 'I also wanted to get away from home for a while. My parents weren't too happy about me breaking off my engagement a couple of months ago.'

'How long were you engaged?'

'Four years.'

'Some people don't stay married that long.'

'True.' She waited a moment before saying, 'Margie told me you'd gone through a break-up a while back.'

'Yeah, well, I can't scratch my nose in this town without everyone hearing about it.' His tone was edgy, annoyed.

Izzy pushed on regardless. 'Were you together long?'

He threw her a hard glance. 'Why are you asking

me? Surely the locals have already given you all the gory details?'

'I'd like to hear it from you.'

He drove for another two kilometres or so before he spoke. 'We'd been seeing each other a year or so. We had only been engaged for a couple of months when my father had his accident.'

'So you came back home.'

'Yeah.'

'She didn't want to pull up stumps and come with you?'

'Nope.'

'I'm sorry.'

'Don't be. I'm not.' He pulled up in front of her cottage and swivelled in his seat to look at her. 'Was your fiancé a doctor?'

'A banker.' She put her hand on the door. 'Um, I should go in. It's getting late.'

'I'll walk you to the door.'

'That's not necessary...' It was too late. He was already out of the car and coming round to her side.

Izzy stepped out of the car but she misjudged the kerb and stumbled forward. Two iron-strong hands shot out and prevented her from falling. She felt every one of his fingers around her upper arms. That wasn't all she felt. Electric heat coursed through her from the top of her head to the balls of her feet. She could smell the scent of his skin, the sweat and dust and healthy male smell that was like a tantalising potion to her overly sanitised city nostrils. Her heart gave a skittish jump as she saw the way his grey-blue gaze tracked to her mouth. The pepper of his stubble was rough along his jaw, the vigorous regrowth a heady reminder of the potent hormones that marked him as a full-blooded man.

'You OK?' His fingers loosened a mere fraction as his eyes came back to hers.

'I—I'm fine…' She felt a blush run up over her skin, the heat coming from the secret core of her body. 'I'm not normally so clumsy.'

He released her and took a step backwards, his expression as unfathomable as ever. 'The ground is pretty rough out here. You need to take extra care until you find your feet.'

'I'll be careful.' Izzy pushed a strand of hair back off her face. 'Um, would you like to come in for a coffee?' *Oh. My. God. You just asked him in for coffee! What are you doing? Are you nuts?*

His brows twitched together. 'Coffee?'

'Don't all cops drink coffee? I have tea if you'd prefer. No doughnuts, I'm afraid. I guess it's kind of a cliché, you know, cops and doughnuts. I bet you don't even eat them.' *Stop talking!*

'Thanks, but no.'

No?

No?

It was hard not to feel slighted. Was she such hideous company that a simple coffee was out of the question? 'Fine.' Izzy forced a smile. 'Some other time, then.' She lifted a hand in a fingertip wave. 'Thanks for the lift. See you around.' She turned and walked quickly and purposefully to the cottage knowing he probably wouldn't drive away until she was safely inside.

'Dr Courtney.'

Izzy turned to see him holding her doctor's bag, which she had left on the back seat of his car. Her cheeks flared all over again. What was it about him that made her brain turn to scrambled mush? 'Oh... right. Might need that.'

He brought her bag to her on the doorstep, his fingers brushing against hers as he handed it over. The shock of his touch thrilled her senses all over again and her heart gave another skip-hop-skip inside her chest. The flecks of blue in his eyes seemed even darker than ever, his pupils black, bottomless inkwells.

'Thanks.' Her voice came out like a mouse squeak.
'You're welcome.'

The crackle of the police radio in the car sounded excessively loud. Jarring.

He gave her one of his curt nods and stepped down off the veranda, walking the short distance to his car, getting behind the wheel and driving off, all within the space of a few seconds.

Izzy slowly released her breath as she watched his taillights disappear into the distance.

Stop that thought.

You did not come all this way to make your life even more complicated.

Zach found his father sitting out on the southern side of the veranda when he got back to the homestead. He let out the tight breath he felt like he'd been holding all day and let his shoulders go down with it. 'Fancy a run out to Bourke tomorrow?'

'What for?'

'Damien Redbank had an accident this evening. He's fine, apart from a broken arm. He'll be in hospital a couple of days. I thought he could do with some company.'

'What's wrong with his father?'

'Good question.' Zach took off his police hat and raked his hands through his sweat-sticky hair.

Doug gave him a probing look. 'You OK?'

Zach tossed his hat onto the nearest cane chair. 'I've never felt more like punching someone's lights out.'

'Understandable. Charles has been pressing your buttons for a while now.'

'He's incompetent as a father,' Zach said. 'He's got no idea how to be a role model for that kid. No wonder the boy is running amok. He's crying out for someone to take notice of him. To show they care about him.'

'The boy hasn't been the same since his mother remarried.'

Zach grunted. 'Yeah, I know.'

The crickets chirruped in the garden below the veranda.

'What time are you thinking of heading out of town?' Doug asked.

'Sixish.'

A stone curlew let out its mournful cry and Popeye lifted his little black head off the faded cushion on the seat beside Zach's father's chair, but seeing Zach's stay signal quickly settled back down again with a little doggy sigh and closed his eyes.

'How'd the new doctor handle things?' Doug asked.

'Better than I thought she would, but it's still early days.'

His father slanted him a glance. 'Watch your step, son.'

'I'm good.'

'Yeah, that's we all say. Next thing you know she'll have your heart in a vice.'

'Not going to happen.' Zach opened and closed his

fingers where the tingling of Izzy's touch had lingered far too long. It had taken a truckload of self-control to decline her offer of coffee. Even if she had just been being polite in asking him in, he hadn't wanted to risk stepping over the boundaries.

His body had other ideas, of course. But he was going to have to tame its urges if he was to get through this next month without giving in to temptation. A fling with her would certainly break the dogged routine he'd slipped into but how would he feel when she packed her bags and drove out of town?

He had to concentrate on his father's health right now.

That was the priority.

Distractions—even ones as delightfully refreshing and dazzling as Izzy Courtney—would have to wait.

CHAPTER FIVE

IZZY REALISED ON her fourth patient the following morning that a rumour had been circulated about her and Zach Fletcher. Ida Jensen, a seventy-five-year-old farmer's wife, had come in to have her blood pressure medication renewed, but before Izzy could put the cuff on her arm to check her current reading, the older woman launched into a tirade.

'In my day a girl wouldn't dream of sleeping with a man before she was married, especially with a man she's only just met.' She pursed her lips in a disapproving manner. 'I don't know what the world's coming to, really I don't. Everyone having casual flings as if love and commitment mean nothing. It's shameful, that's what it is.'

'I guess not everyone shares the same values these days,' Izzy said, hoping to prevent an extended moral lecture.

'I blame the Pill. Girls don't have to worry about falling pregnant so they just do what they want with whoever they want. That boy needs a wife, not a mistress.'

'That…er, boy?'

'Zach Fletcher,' Ida said. 'Don't bother trying to deny it. Everyone knows you've got your eye on him, and him not even over the last one. Mind you, they do say you should get back on the horse, don't they? Never did like that saying. It's a bit coarse, if you ask me. But I think he needs more time. What if his ex changes her mind and comes out here to see you're involved with him?'

'I beg your pardon?'

Ida shifted in her chair like a broody hen settling on a clutch of eggs. 'Not that anyone could really blame you, of course. No one's saying he isn't good looking. Got a nice gentle nature too, when you get to know him.'

Izzy frowned. 'I'm sorry but I'm not sure where you got the idea that I'm involved with Sergeant Fletcher.'

'Don't bother denying it,' Ida said. 'I heard it from a very reliable source. Everyone's talking about it.'

'Then they can stop talking about it because it's not true!' Izzy was fast becoming agitated. 'Have you asked Sergeant Fletcher about this? I suggest you do so you can hear it from him as well that nothing is going on. This is nothing more than scurrilous gossip.' *And I have a feeling I know who started it.*

'Are you sure it's not true?' Ida looked a little uncomfortable.

'I think I would know who I was or wasn't sleeping with, don't you?' Izzy picked up the blood-pressure cuff. 'Now, let's change the subject, otherwise my blood pressure is going to need medication.'

'What? Don't you fancy him?' Ida asked after a moment.

Izzy undid the cuff from the older woman's arm and wrote the figure in her notes. 'I see here you're taking anti-inflammatories for your arthritis. Any trouble with your stomach on that dosage?'

'Not if I take them with food.'

'Is there anything else I can help you with?'

The older woman folded her lips together. 'I hope I haven't upset you.'

'Not at all,' Izzy lied.

'It's just we all love Zach so much. We want him to be happy.'

'I'm sure he appreciates your concern but he's a big boy and can surely take care of himself.'

'That's half the trouble…' Ida let out a heartfelt sigh. 'He's been taking care of himself for too long.'

Izzy stood up to signal the end of the consultation. 'Make another appointment to see me in a week. I'd like to keep an eye on your blood pressure. It was slightly elevated.'

Just like mine.

'Nice work, Fletch,' Jim Collis said, when Zach came in the next morning for the paper.

Zach didn't care for the ear-to-ear grin the storekeeper was wearing. 'What?'

Jim had hooked his thumbs in his belt and tilted backwards on his heels behind the counter. 'Getting it on with the new doctor. Talk about a fast mover. You want me to stock up on condoms?'

Zach kept his expression closed as he picked up a stock magazine his father enjoyed, as well as the paper. He put them both on the counter and took out his wallet. 'You should check your sources before you start spreading rumours like that.'

'You telling me it's not true?'

'Even if it was true, I wouldn't be standing here discussing it.'

'Charles Redbank seemed pretty convinced you two

were getting it on,' Jim said. 'Not that anyone would blame you for making a move on her. Be a good way to get that Naomi chick out of your system once and for all.'

Zach ground his molars together. It got under his skin that the whole town saw him as some sort of broken-hearted dude let down by his fiancée. He was over Naomi. It had been a convenient relationship that had worked well for both of them until he'd made the decision to come back to Jerringa Ridge to help his father. Yes, he was a little pissed off she hadn't wanted to come with him but that was her loss. In time he would find someone to fill her place, but he needed to get his father sorted out first.

'Anyway, way I see it,' Jim went on, 'if you don't hit on Izzy Courtney then you can bet your bottom dollar some other fella soon will.' He cleared his throat as the screen door opened. 'Hi, Dr Courtney, I got that honey and cinnamon yogurt you wanted.'

Zach hitched his hip as he put his wallet in his back pocket before turning to look at her. 'G'day.'

'Hello...' The blush on her cheeks was like the petals of a pink rose. She looked young and fresh, like a model from a fashion magazine. Her simple flowered cotton dress was cinched in at her tiny waist, her legs were bare and her feet in ballet flats. She had a string of pearls around her neck that were a perfect foil for her milk-pure skin. And even with all the other competing smells of the general store he could still pick up her light gardenia scent. It occurred to him to wonder why anyone would wear pearls in the Outback but it was something his mother had done and he knew from experience there was no explaining it.

'So, I'll get those condoms in for you, will I, Fletch?' Jim said with a cheeky grin. 'Extra-large, wasn't it?'

The blush on Izzy Courtney's cheeks intensified. Her eyes slipped out of reach of his and her teeth snagged at her full lower lip. 'Maybe I'll come back later…' She turned and went back out the screen door so quickly it banged loudly on its hinges.

Zach scooped up the paper and the magazine, giving Jim a look that would have cut through steel. 'You're a freaking jerk, you know that?'

Izzy turned at the sound of firm footsteps to find Zach coming towards her. That fluttery sensation she always got when she saw him tickled the floor of her stomach like an ostrich feather held by someone with a tremor. His mouth was tightly set, his expression formidable this time rather than masked. Her earlier blush still hadn't completely died down but as soon as his eyes met hers she felt it heat up another few degrees.

'We need to talk.' He spoke through lips so tight they barely moved.

'We do?' She saw his dark frown and continued, 'Yes, of course we do. Look, it's fine. It's just a rumour. It'll go away when they realise there's no truth in it.'

'I'm sorry but this is what happens in small country towns.'

'I realise that,' Izzy said. 'I've already had a couple of stern lectures from some of the more conservative elders in the community. It seems that out here it's still a sin for a woman to have sex before marriage. Funny, but they didn't mention it being a sin for men. That really annoys me. Why should you men have all the fun?'

His gaze briefly touched her mouth before glancing away to look at something in the distance, his eyes squinting against the brutal sunlight. 'Not all of us are having as much fun as you think.'

Izzy moistened her suddenly dry lips. 'How is your father? Did he go with you to Bourke?'

'Yes.'

'And how was Damien?'

'Feeling a bit sorry for himself.'

'Did his father end up going to see him?' Izzy brushed a wisp of hair away from her face.

He made a sound that sounded somewhere between a grunt and a laugh. 'No.'

'I guess he was too busy spreading rumours back here.'

His brooding frown was a deep V between his brows. 'I should've punched him when I had the chance.'

She studied Zach for a moment. Even without his uniform he still maintained that aura of command and control. She wondered what it would take to get under his skin enough to make him break out of that thick veneer of reserve. There was a quiet intensity about him, as if inside he was bottling up emotions he didn't want anyone to see. 'You don't seem the type of guy to throw the first punch.'

'Yeah, well, I don't get paid to pick fights.' He drew in a breath and released it in a measured way as if he was rebalancing himself. 'I'd better let you get to work. Have a good one.'

Izzy watched as he strode back to where his car was parked outside the general store. She too let out a long breath, but any hope of rebalancing herself was as likely as a person on crutches trying to ice-skate.

Not going to happen.

* * *

Almost a week went past before Izzy saw Zach again other than from a distance. Although they worked within a half a block of each other, he was on different shifts and she spent most days inside the clinic, other than a couple of house calls she had made out of town. But each time she stepped outside the clinic or her cottage or drove out along any of the roads she mentally prepared herself for running into him.

She had seen him coming out of the general store one evening as she'd been leaving work, but he'd been on the phone and had seemed preoccupied, and hadn't noticed her at all. For some reason that rankled. It didn't seem fair that she was suffering heart skips and stomach flips at the mere mention of his name and yet he didn't even sense her looking at him. Neither did he even glance at the clinic just in case she was coming out.

Izzy still had to field the occasional comment from a patient but she decided that was the price of being part of a small community. You couldn't sneeze in a town the size of Jerringa Ridge without everyone saying you had flu.

But on Saturday night, just as she was thinking about going to bed, she got a call from Jim Collis, who was down at the pub. 'Been a bit of trouble down here, Doc,' he said. 'Thought you might want to look in on Zach if you've got a minute. I reckon he might need a couple of stitches.'

'What happened?'

'Couple of the young fellas had too much to drink and got a bit lively. Zach's down at the station, waiting for the parents to show up. I told him to call you but he said it's just a bruise. Don't look like a bruise to me. He's lucky he didn't lose an eye, if you ask me.'

'I'll head down straight away.'

Izzy turned up the station just as a middle-aged couple came out with their son. The smell of alcohol was sour in the air as they walked past to bundle him into the car. The mother looked like she had been crying and the father looked angry enough to throw something. The son looked subdued but it was hard to tell if that was the excess alcohol taking effect or whether he'd faced charges.

When she went inside the building Zach was sitting behind the desk with a folded handkerchief held up to his left eye as he wrote some notes down on a sheet of paper. He glanced up and frowned at her. 'Who called you?'

'Jim Collis.'

He let out a muffled expletive. 'He had no right to do that.' He pushed back from the desk and stood up. 'It's nothing. Just a scratch.'

'Why don't you let me be the judge of that?' She held up her doctor's bag. 'I've come prepared.'

He let out a long breath as if he couldn't be bothered arguing and led the way out to the small kitchen area out the back. 'Make it snappy. I need to get home.'

Izzy pushed one of the two chairs towards him. 'Sit.'

'Can't you do it standing up?'

'I'm not used to doing it standing up…' A hot blush stormed into her cheeks when she saw the one-eyed glinting look he gave her. 'I mean…you're way too tall for me to reach you.' *God, that sounded almost worse!*

He sat in the chair with his long legs almost cutting

the room in half. She had nowhere to stand other than between them to get close enough to inspect his eye. She was acutely aware of the erotic undertones as his muscled legs bracketed her body. They weren't touching her at all but she felt the warmth of his thighs like the bars of a radiator. Her mind went crazy with images of him holding her between those powerful thighs, his body pumping into hers, those muscled arms pinning her against the bed, a wall, or some other surface. Scorching heat flowed through her veins even as she slammed the brakes on her wickedly wanton thoughts.

Doctor face. Doctor face. Mentally chanting it was the only way she could get herself back on track. She gently took the wadded handkerchief off his eye to find it bruised and swollen with a split in the skin above his eyebrow that was still oozing blood. 'You won't need stitches but you'll have a nice shiner by morning.'

He grunted. 'Told you it was nothing.'

Izzy's leg bumped against his as she reached for some antiseptic in her bag. It was like being touched with a laser—the tingles went right to her core. She schooled her features as she turned back to tend to his cut. *Cool and clinical. Cool and clinical.* She could do that. She always did that…well; she did when it was anyone other than Zach Fletcher.

She could hear his breathing; it was slow and even, unlike hers, which was shallow and picking up pace as every second passed.

His scent teased her nostrils, making her think of sun-warmed lemons. He had a decent crop of prickly stubble on his jaw. She felt it catch on the sensitive skin on the underside of her wrist as she dabbed at his wound. 'I'm sorry if this hurts. I'm just cleaning the area before I put on a Steri-strip to hold the edges of the wound together.'

'Can't feel a thing.'

She carefully positioned the Steri-strip over the wound. 'There. Now, all we need is some ice for that eye. Do you have any in the fridge?'

'I'll put some on at home.'

He got to his feet at the same time as she reached to dab at a smear of blood on his cheek. He put his hands on her each of her forearms, presumably to stop her fussing over him, but somehow his fingers slid down to her wrists, wrapping around them like a pair of handcuffs.

Izzy felt her breath screech to a halt as his hooded gaze went to her mouth. The tip of her tongue came out and moistened the sudden dryness of her lips. He was so close she could feel the fronts of his muscle-packed thighs against hers.

He looked at her mouth and her belly did a little somersault as she saw the way his eyes zeroed in on it, as if he was memorising its contours. 'This is a really dumb idea.'

'It is? I mean, yes, *of course* it is,' Izzy said a little breathlessly. 'An absolutely crazy thing to do. What were we thinking? Hey, is that a smile? I didn't think you knew how to.'

'I'm a little out of practice.' He brought her even closer, his warm vanilla- and milk-scented breath skating over the surface of her lips. 'Isn't there some rule about doctors getting involved with their patients?'

'I'm not really your doctor. Not officially. I mean I treated you, but *I* came to see you. You didn't come to see me. It's not the same as if you'd made an appointment and paid me to see you. I just saw you as a one-off. A favour, if you like. It's not even going on the record. All I did was put a Steri-strip on your head. You could have done it yourself.' She took a much-needed breath. 'Um...you're not really going to kiss me, are you?'

His grey-blue eyes smouldered. 'What do you think?'

Izzy couldn't think, or at least not once his mouth came down and covered hers. His mouth was firm and warm and tasted of salt and something unexpectedly sinful. His tongue flickered against the seam of her mouth, a teasing come-play-with-me-if-you-dare gesture that made her insides turn to liquid. She opened her mouth and he entered it with a sexy glide of his tongue that made the hairs on her scalp stand up on tiptoe, one by one. He found her tongue with devastating expertise, toying with it, cajoling it into a dance as old as time.

He put a hand on the small of her back and pressed her closer. The feel of his hot urgent male body against her called to everything that was female in her. She had always struggled with desire in the past. She could talk herself into it eventually, but it had never been an instantaneous reaction.

Now it was like a dam had burst. Desire flowed through her like a flash flood, making her flesh cry out for skin-on-skin contact. Her hands came up to link around his neck, her body pressing even closer against his. Her breasts tingled behind the lace of her bra; she had never been more aware of her body, how it felt, what it craved, how it responded.

He gave a low, deep sound of pleasure and deepened the kiss, his hands going to both of her hips and locking her against him. She felt the hardened ridge of him against her and a wave of want coursed through her so rampantly it took her breath away.

She started on his shirt, pulling it out of his trousers and snapping open the buttons so she could glide her hands over his muscled chest. She could feel his heart beneath her palm. Thud. Thud. Thud. She could feel where his heart had pumped his blood in preparation. It throbbed against her belly with a primal beat that resonated through her body like a deep echo, making her insides quiver and reverberate with longing.

He kept kissing her, deeply and passionately, as his hands ran up under her light cotton shirt. The feel of his broad, warm, work-roughened hands on her skin made her gasp out loud. Her blood felt like it was on fire as it raced through her veins at torpedo speed.

Her inner wild woman had been released. Uncaged. Unrestrained. And the wild man in him was more than up to the task of taming her. She felt it in the way he was kissing her.

This was a kiss that meant business.

This was a kiss that said sex was next.

His hands found her breasts, pushing aside the confines of her bra to cup her skin on skin. She shivered as his thumbs rolled each of her nipples in turn; all while his mouth continued its mind-blowing assault on her senses.

The sound of the door opening at the front had Izzy springing back from him as if someone had fired a gun. She assiduously avoided Zach's gaze as she tidied her clothes with fingers that refused to co-operate.

'You there, Fletch?' Jim Collis called out.

'Yeah. Won't be a tick.' Zach redid the buttons before tucking in his shirt. Izzy envied his cool cop composure as he went out to talk to Jim. Her nerves were in shreds at almost being discovered making out like teenagers in the back room.

'Is the doc still with you?' Jim asked.

There was a moment of telling silence.

'Yes, I'm still here.' Izzy stepped out, carrying her doctor's bag and what she hoped passed for doctor-just-finished-a-consult composure. 'I'm just leaving.'

Jim's eyes twinkled knowingly. 'So you've got him all sorted?'

'Er, yes.' She pasted on a tight smile. 'No serious damage done.'

'I hope you weren't annoyed with me, Fletch, for sending her over to patch you up?' Jim said.

Zach still had his cop face on. 'Not at all. She was very…professional.'

'Did you charge Adam Foster with assault?'

'Not this time. I gave him a warning.'

'You're too soft,' Jim said. 'Don't you think so, Dr Courtney?'

Izzy blushed to the roots of her hair. 'Um, it's late. I have to get home.' She gripped the handle of her bag and swung for the door. 'Goodnight.'

CHAPTER SIX

'WHAT HAPPENED TO your eye?' Doug Fletcher asked the following morning.

'I got in the way of Adam Foster's elbow.' Zach switched on the kettle. The less he talked about last night the better. The less *he thought* about last night the better. He had barely been able to sleep for thinking about Izzy Courtney's hot little mouth clamped to his, not to mention her hot little hands winding around his neck and smoothing over his chest. Even taking into account his eighteen-month sex drought, he couldn't remember ever being so turned on before. He had always prided himself on his self-control. But as soon as his mouth had connected with hers something had short-circuited in his brain.

He gave himself a mental shake and took out a couple of cups from the shelf above the sink. 'You want tea or coffee?'

'What did the doctor say?'

He frowned as he faced his father. 'What makes you think I saw the doctor? It's just a little cut and a black eye, for pity's sake. I don't know what all the fuss is about.'

His father gave him a probing look. 'Is it true?'

'Is what true?'

'The rumour going around town that you're sleeping with her.'

'Where'd you hear that?'

'Bill Davidson dropped in last night while you were at work. Said his wife Jean saw the doctor a couple of days back. She said the doctor blushed every time your name was mentioned.'

'Oh, for God's sake.' Zach wrenched open the fridge door for the milk.

'Find yourself another woman, by all means, but make sure she's a country girl who'll stick around,' his father said.

'Dad, give it a break. I'm not going to lose my head or my heart to Dr Courtney. She's not my type.'

'Your mother wasn't my type either but that didn't stop me falling in love with her, and look how that ended up.'

Zach let out a long breath. 'You really need to let it go. Mum's never coming back. You have to accept it.'

'She hasn't even called, not once. Not even an email or a get-well card.'

'That's because you told her never to contact you again after she forgot my thirtieth birthday, remember?'

His father scowled. 'What sort of mother forgets her own son's birthday?'

A mother who has two other younger sons she loves more, Zach thought. 'What do you want for breakfast?'

'Nothing.'

'Come on. You have to have something.'

'I'm not hungry.'

'Are you in pain?' Zach asked.

His father glowered. 'Stop fussing.'

'You must be getting pretty low on painkillers. You want me to get Dr Courtney to write a prescription for you?'

'I'll manage.'

He threw his father an exasperated look. 'How'd you get to be so stubborn? No wonder Mum walked out on you.'

His father's eyes burned with bitterness. 'That may be why she walked out on me but why'd she leave you?'

It was a question Zach had asked himself a thousand times. And all these years later he still didn't have an answer other than the most obvious.

She hadn't loved him enough to stay.

'So how are you and Zach getting on?' Margie asked on Monday morning.

Izzy worked extra-hard to keep her blush at bay. 'Fine.'

'Jim told me you saw to Zach's eye on Saturday night.'

'Yes.' Izzy kept her voice businesslike and efficient. 'Do you have Mrs Patterson's file there? I have to check on something.'

Margie handed the file across the counter. 'The Shearers' Ball is on the last weekend of your locum. Did Peggy tell you about it? It's to raise money for the community centre. It's not a glamorous shindig, like you'd have in England or anything. Just a bit of a bush dance and a chance to let your hair down. Will I put you down as a yes?'

It sounded like a lot of fun. Would Zach be there? Her insides gave a funny little skip at the thought of those strong arms holding her close to him in a waltz or a barn dance. 'I'll have a think about it.'

'Oh, but you must come!' Margie insisted. 'You'll have heaps of fun. People drive in from all over the district to come to it. We have a raffle and door prizes. It's the social event of the year. Everyone will be so disappointed if you don't show up. It'll be our way of thanking you for stepping in while William Sawyer and his wife were on holiday. They come every year without fail.'

Izzy laughed in defeat. 'All right. Sign me up.'

'Fabulous.' Margie grinned. 'Now I can twist Zach's arm.'

Izzy left the clinic at lunchtime to pick up the sandwich she'd ordered at the corner store. Jim gave her a wink and a cheeky smile as she came in. 'How's the patient?'

She looked at him blankly, even though she knew exactly which patient he meant. 'Which patient?'

'You don't have to be coy with me, Izzy. I know what you two were up to out back the other night. About time Zach got himself back out there. I bet that ex-fiancée of his hasn't spent the last eighteen months pining his absence.'

She kept her features neutral. 'Is my salad sandwich ready?'

'Yep.' He handed it over the counter, his grin still in place. 'Do me a favour?' He passed over another sandwich-sized package in a brown paper bag. 'Drop that in to Zach on your way past.'

Izzy took the package with a forced smile. 'Will do.'

Zach looked up when the door opened. Izzy was standing there framed by the bright sunlight. She was wearing trousers and a cotton top today but she looked no less feminine. Her hair was in one of those up styles that somehow managed to look makeshift and elegant at the same time. There was a hint of gloss on her lips, making them look even more kissable. He wondered what flavour it was today. Strawberry? Or was it raspberry again?

'Jim sent me with your lunch.' She passed it over the counter, her cheeks going a light shade of pink. He'd never known a woman to blush so much. What was going on inside that pretty little head of hers? Was she thinking of that kiss? Had she spent the night feeling restless and edgy while her body had throbbed with unmet needs, like his had?

'Thanks.' He stood up and put the sandwich to one side. 'I was going to call you about my father.'

'Oh?' Her expression flickered with concern. 'Is he unwell?'

'He's running out of prescription painkillers.'

She chewed at her lip. 'I'd have to officially see him before I'd write a script. There can be contraindications with other medications and so on.'

'Of course. I'll see if I can get him to come to the clinic.'

She shifted her weight from foot to foot. 'I could always come out again to the homestead, if you think he'd allow it. I know what it's like to have something unexpected sprung on you. Maybe if you told him ahead of time that I was coming out, he would be more amenable to seeing me.'

'I'll see what I can do.'

The elephant in the room was stealing all the oxygen out of the air.

'What about coming out for dinner tomorrow?' Zach

could hardly believe he had spoken the words until he heard them drop into the ringing silence.

Her eyes widened a fraction. 'Dinner?'

'It won't be anything fancy. I'm not much of a chef but I can rub a couple of ingredients together.'

'What about your dad?'

'He has to eat.'

'I know, but will he agree to eat if I'm there?'

He shrugged, as if he didn't care either way. 'Let's give it a try, shall we?'

Her eyes went to the Steri-strip above his eyebrow. 'Would you like me to check that wound for you?'

Zach wanted her to check every inch of his body, preferably while both of them were naked. He had to blink away the erotic image that flashed through his brain at that thought—her limbs entangled with his, his body plunging into hers. 'It's fine.'

Her gaze narrowed as she peered at him over the bridge of the desk. 'It looks a little red around the edges.'

So do your cheeks, he thought. Her eyes were remarkably steady on his, but he had a feeling she was working hard at keeping them there. 'It's not infected. I'm keeping an eye on it.'

'Right…well, if you think it's not healing properly let me know.'

Zach couldn't figure if it was her in particular or the thought of having sex again that was making him so horny. He had tried his best to avoid thinking about sex for months. But now Izzy Courtney, with her toffee-brown eyes and soft, kissable mouth, was occupying his thoughts and he was in a constant start of arousal. He could feel it now, the pulse of his blood ticking through his veins. His heightened awareness of her sweet, fresh scent, the way his hands wanted to stroke down the length of her arms, to encircle her slim wrists, to tug her up against him so she could feel the weight and throb of his erection before his mouth closed over hers.

Her gaze flicked to his mouth, as if she had read his mind, the point of her tongue sneaking out to moisten her plump, soft lips. 'Um… What time do you want me to come?' Her cheeks went an even darker shade of red. 'Er…tonight. For dinner. To see your dad.'

'Seven or thereabouts?'

'Lovely.' She backed out of the reception area but somehow managed to bump her elbow against the door as she turned on her way out. She stepped out into the bright sunshine and walked briskly down the steps and out of sight.

Zach didn't sit down again until the fragrance of her had finally disappeared.

'What do you mean, you're going out?' Zach asked his father that evening.

His father gave him an offhand glance. 'I'm entitled to a social life, aren't I?'

'Of course.' Zach raked a distracted hand through his hair. 'But tonight of all nights? You haven't been out for months.'

'It's been a while since I caught up with Margie Green. She invited me for dinner.'

'She's been inviting you for dinner for years and you've always declined.'

'Then it's high time I said yes. You're always on about me not socialising enough. I enjoyed that run up to Bourke. It made me realise I need to have a change of scene now and again.'

Zach frowned. 'Isabella Courtney is going to think I've set this up. I asked her to come out to see you, not me.'

'She can think what she likes,' his father said. 'Anyway, I don't want to cramp your style.'

'But what about your painkillers?' Zach asked. 'You know what your rehab specialist said. You have to stay in front of the pain, not chase it.'

Doug chewed that over for a moment. 'I'll think about going to the clinic in a day or two.' A car horn tooted outside. 'That's Margie now.' He shuffled to the door on his frame. 'Don't wait up.'

Within a few minutes of his father leaving with Margie, Izzy arrived. Zach held open the door for her while Popeye danced around her like he had springs on his paws. 'My father's gone out. You probably passed him on the driveway.'

'Yes, Margie waved to me on the way past. I bet she's pleased he finally agreed to have dinner with her.' She picked Popeye up and cuddled him beneath her chin. 'Hello, sweetie pie.'

Zach was suddenly jealous of his dog, who was nestled against the gentle swell of Izzy's breasts. He gave himself a mental kick. He had to stop thinking of that kiss. It was becoming an obsession. 'Why's that?'

'I think she's been in love with him for years,' she said, and Popeye licked her face enthusiastically, as if in agreement.

'She's wasting her time,' Zach said. 'My father is still in love with my mother.'

She put the dog back down on the floor before she faced him. 'Do you really think so?'

He looked into her beautiful brown eyes, so warm

and soft, like melted caramel. The lashes like miniature fans. She seemed totally unaware of how beautiful she was. Unlike his ex, Naomi, who hadn't been able to walk past a mirror or a plate of glass without checking her reflection to check that her hair and make-up were perfect.

Another mental kick.

Harder this time.

'He's never looked at anyone else since.'

'Doesn't mean he still loves her. Some men have a lot of trouble with letting go of bitterness after a break-up.'

Zach coughed out a disparaging laugh. 'How long does he need? Isn't a couple of decades long enough?'

She gave a little lip-shrug. 'I guess some men are more stubborn than others.'

He wondered if she was having a little dig at his own stubbornness. He knew he should have found someone else by now. Most men would have done. It wasn't that he wasn't ready… He just hadn't met anyone who made him feel like…well, like Izzy did. Hot. Bothered. Hungry.

At this rate he was going to knock himself unconscious with all those mental kicks. 'What would you like to drink? I have white wine, red wine or beer…or something soft?'

'A small glass of white wine would be lovely.' She handed him a small container she was carrying. 'Um…I made these. I thought your father might enjoy them.'

He opened the plastic container to find home-baked chocolate-chip cookies inside. The smell of sugar and chocolate was like ambrosia. 'His favourite.' *And mine.* He met her gaze again. 'How'd you guess?'

She gave him a wry smile. 'I don't know too many men who would turn their nose up at home baking.'

'The way to a man's heart and all that.'

She looked taken aback. 'I wasn't trying to—'

'He'll love you for it. Eventually.'

After he'd put the cookies aside he handed her a glass of wine. 'Have you had the hard word put on you about the Shearers' Ball yet?'

'Margie twisted my arm yesterday to sign up. You?'

'I swear every year I'm not going to go and somehow someone always manages to convince me to show up if I'm in town. I try to keep a low profile. I'm seen as the fun police even when I'm not in uniform.'

'I've never been to a bush dance before. Is it very hard to learn the steps?'

'No, there's a caller. That's usually Bill Davidson. He's been doing it for years. His father did it before him. You'll soon get the hang of it.'

'I hope so…'

He couldn't stop looking at her mouth, how softly curved it was, how it had felt beneath the firm pressure of his. Desire was already pumping through his body. Just looking at her was enough to set him off. She was dressed in one of her simple dresses, black, sleeveless and just over the knee, with nothing but the flash of a small diamond pendant around her neck. There were diamond studs in her ears and her hair was in a high ponytail that swished from side to side when she walked. She had put on the merest touch of make-up: a neutral shade of eyeshadow with a fine line of kohl pencilled on her eyelids and beneath her eyes, emphasising the dark thickness of her lashes.

Zach cleared his throat. It was time to get the elephant on its way. 'Look, about the other night when I—'

'It's fine.' She gave him another little twisted smile. 'Really. It was just a kiss.'

'I wouldn't want you to get the wrong idea about me.' He pushed a hand through his hair. 'Contrary to what you might think, I'm not the sort of guy to feel up a woman as soon as he gets her alone.'

Her gaze slipped away from his. 'It was probably my fault.'

He frowned down at her. 'How was it *your* fault? I made the first move.'

'I kissed you back.' She bit her lower lip momentarily. 'Rather enthusiastically, if I recall.'

He *did* recall.

He could recall every thrilling moment of that kiss.

The trouble was he wanted to repeat it. But a relationship with Izzy would be distracting, to say the least. He had to concentrate on getting his dad as independent as he could before he spared a thought to what *he* wanted. He hadn't been that good at balancing the demands of a relationship and work in the past. It would be even worse now with his dad's needs front and centre. He couldn't spread himself any thinner than he was already doing.

His ex had always been on at him to give more of himself but he hadn't felt comfortable with that level of emotional intimacy. He had loved Naomi…or at least he thought he had. Sometimes he wondered if he'd just loved being part of a couple. That was a large part of the reason he'd agreed to her moving in with him. Having someone there to share the sofa with while he zoned out the harrowing demands of the day in front of the television or over a meal he hadn't had to cook.

He sounded like a chauvinist, but after living alone with his dad for all those years he'd snapped up Naomi's willingness to take over the kitchen. Asking her to marry him had been the logical next step. Her refusal to move to the country with him after his father's accident had been not so much devastating as disappointing. He was disappointed in himself. Why had he thought she would follow him wherever life took him? She had her own career. It was unfair of him to demand her to drop everything and come with him. And living in the dry, dusty Outback on a sheep property with a partially disabled and disgruntled father-in-law was a big ask.

Zach blinked himself out of the past. 'Do you want to eat outside? There's a nice breeze coming in from the south. Dad and I often eat out there when a southerly is due.'

'Lovely. Can I help bring anything out?'

He handed her a pair of salad servers and a bottle of dressing.

Her fingers brushed against his as she took the bottle from him and a lightning-fast sensation went straight to his groin. He felt the stirring of his blood; the movement of primal instinctive flesh that wanted something he had denied it for too long.

Her eyes met his, wide, doe-like, the pupils enlarged. Her tongue—*the tongue he had intimately stroked and sucked and teased*—darted out over her lips in a nervous sweeping action. He caught a whiff of her fragrance, wisteria this time instead of gardenias, but just as alluring.

But then the moment passed.

She seemed to mentally gather herself, and with another one of those short on-off smiles she turned in the direction of the veranda, her ponytail swinging behind her.

Zach looked down at Popeye, who was looking up at him with a quizzical expression in those black button eyes. 'Easy for you. You've had the chop. I have to suffer the hard way. No pun intended.'

CHAPTER SEVEN

IZZY PUT THE salad servers and the dressing on the glass-topped white cane table then turned and looked at the view from the veranda. The paddocks stretched far into the distance where she could see a line of trees where the creek snaked in a sinuous curve along the boundary of the property. The air was warm with that hint of eucalyptus she was coming to love. It was such a distinctive smell, sharp and cleansing. The setting sun had painted the sky a dusky pink, signalling another fine day for tomorrow, and a flock of kookaburras sounded in the trees by the creek, their raucous call fracturing the still evening air like the laughter of a gang of madmen.

She turned when she heard the firm tread of Zach's footsteps on the floorboards of the veranda. Popeye was following faithfully, his bright little eyes twinkling in the twilight. Zach looked utterly gorgeous dressed casually in blue denim jeans and a light blue cotton shirt that was rolled up to his forearms. The colour of his shirt intensified the blue rim in his grey eyes and the deep tan of his skin.

Her stomach gave a little flutter when he sent her a quick smile. He was so devastatingly attractive when he lost that grim look. The line of his jaw was still firm, he was too masculine for it ever to be described as anything but determined, but his mouth was sensual and sensitive rather than severe, as she had earlier thought.

Her mouth tingled in memory of how those lips had felt against hers. She remembered every moment of that heart-stopping kiss. It was imprinted on her memory like an indelible brand. She wondered if she would spend the rest of her life recalling it, measuring any subsequent kisses by its standard.

He had deftly changed the subject when she had stumblingly tried to explain her actions of the other night. He had given an apology of sorts for kissing her, but he hadn't said he wasn't going to do it again. She was not by any means a vain person but she was woman enough to know when a man showed an interest in her. He might be able to keep his expression masked and his emotions under lock and key but she had still sensed it.

She had *felt* it in his touch.

She had *tasted* it in his kiss.

She sensed it now as he handed her the glass of wine she had left behind. His eyes held hers for a little longer than they needed to, something passing in the exchange that was unspoken but no less real. She tried to avoid touching his fingers this time. It was increasingly difficult to disguise the way she reacted to him. Would any other man stir her senses quite the way he did? Her body seemed to have a mind of its own when he came near. It was like stepping inside the pull of a powerful magnet. She felt the tug in her flesh, the entire surface of her skin stretching, swelling to get closer to him.

'Thanks.' She took a careful sip of wine. 'Mmm... lovely. Is that a local one?'

He showed her the label. 'It's from a boutique vineyard a couple of hundred kilometres away. I went to boarding school with the guy who owns it.'

'How old were you when you went to boarding school?'

'Eleven.' He swirled the wine in his glass, watching as it splashed around the sides with an almost fierce concentration. 'It was the year after my mother left.' He raised the glass and took a mouthful, the strong column of his throat moving as he swallowed deeply.

'Were you dreadfully homesick?'

He glanced at her briefly before looking back out over the paddocks that were bathed in a pinkish hue instead of their tired brown. 'Not for long.'

Izzy suspected he had taught himself not to feel anything rather than suffer the pain of separation. Homesickness—like love—would be another emotion he had barred from his repertoire. His iron-strong reserve had come about the hard way—a lifetime of suppressing feelings he didn't want to own. She pictured him as an eleven-year-old, probably tall for his age, broad shouldered, whipcord lean and tanned, and yet inside just a little boy who had desperately missed his mother.

She pushed herself away from the veranda rail where she had been leaning her hip. 'I went to boarding school when I was eight. I cried buckets.'

'Eight is very young.' His voice had a gravelly sound to it and his gaze looked serious and concerned, as if he too was picturing her as a child—that small, inconsolable little pigtailed girl with her collection of Barbie dolls in a little pink suitcase.

'Yes…but somehow I got through it. I haven't got any sisters so the company of the other girls was a bonus.' *Or it was when I met Hannah.*

'Any brothers?'

Izzy felt that painful stab to her heart again. It didn't matter how many years went past, it was always the same. She found the question so confronting. It was like asking a first-time mother who had just lost her baby if she was still a mother. 'Not any more…' She swallowed to clear the lump in her throat. 'My brother Jamie died five years ago of sarcoma. He was diagnosed when he was fourteen. He was in remission for twelve years and then it came back.'

'I'm sorry.' The deep gravitas in his voice was strangely soothing.

'He wasn't diagnosed early enough.' She gripped the rails of the veranda so tightly the wood creaked beneath her hands. 'He would've had a better chance if he'd gone to a doctor earlier but he was at boarding school and didn't tell anyone about his symptoms until he came home for the holidays.' She loosened her grip and turned back to look at him. 'I think that's what tortures me most. The thought that he might've been saved.'

His eyes held hers in a silent hold that communicated a depth of understanding she hadn't thought him capable of on first meeting him. His quiet calm was a counterpoint to her inner rage at the cruel punch the fist of fate had given to her family and from which they had never recovered.

'Are your parents still together?'

'Yes, but they probably shouldn't be.' Izzy saw the slight questioning lift of his brow and continued. 'My father's had numerous affairs over the years. Even before Jamie's death. In fact, I think it started soon after Jamie was diagnosed. Mum's always clung to her comfortable life and would never do or say anything to jeopardise it, which is probably why she doesn't understand why I ended things with Richard.'

'Why *did* you break it off with him?'

Izzy looked into his blue-rimmed eyes and wondered if he was one of that increasingly rare breed of men who would take his marriage vows seriously, remaining faithful, loyal and devoted over a lifetime. 'I know this probably sounds ridiculously idealistic, romantic even, but I've always wanted to feel the sort of love that stops you in your tracks. The sort that won't go stale or become boring. The sort of love you just know is your one and only chance at happiness. The sort of love you would give everything up for. I didn't feel that for Richard. It wasn't fair to him to go on any longer pretending I did.'

His top lip lifted in a cynical manner. 'So in amongst all those medical textbooks and journals you've managed to sneak in a few romance novels, have you?'

Izzy could have chosen to be offended by his mockery but instead she gave a guilty laugh. 'One or two.' She toyed with the stem of her glass. 'My friend Hannah thinks I'm a bit of a romance tragic.'

'What did she send you in that package? A stack of sentimental books?'

'If only.' She laughed again to cover her embarrassment. Just as well it was dark enough for him not to see her blush.

'What, then?'

'*Please* don't make me tell you.'

'Come on.' His smile was back and it was just as spine-melting as before. 'You've really got my attention now.'

And you've got mine. 'Promise not to laugh?'

'Promise.'

She let out a breath in a rush. 'A blow-up doll. A male one. I've called him Max.'

He threw his head back and laughed. He had a nice-sounding laugh, rich and deep and genuine, not booming and raucous like Richard's when he'd had one too many red wines.

Izzy gave him a mock glare. 'You promised not to laugh!'

'Sorry.' He didn't look sorry. His lips were still twitching and his eyes twinkled with amusement.

'Hannah thought a stand-in boyfriend would stop me from being lonely. I think I already told you she has a weird sense of humour.'

'Are you going to take him with you when you move on?'

'I'm not sure the Sawyers will appreciate him as part of the furniture.'

'Where do you head after here?' The question was casual. Polite interest. Nothing more.

'Brisbane,' Izzy said. 'I've got a job lined up in a busy GP clinic. After that I have a stint in Darwin. The locum agency is pretty flexible. There's always somewhere needing a doctor, especially out in the bush. That's why I took this post. The guy they had lined up had to pull out at the last minute due to a family crisis. I was happy to step in. I'm enjoying it. Everyone's been lovely.'

Zach absently rubbed the toe of his booted foot against one of the uneven floorboards. 'Everyone, apart from my father.'

'I haven't given up on him.'

The silence hummed as their gazes meshed again.

Izzy's breath hitched on something, like a silk sleeve catching on a prickly bush. She moistened her lips as his gaze lowered to her mouth, her stomach feeling as if a tiny fist had reached through her clothes and clutched at her insides.

Male to female attraction was almost palpable in the air. She could feel it moving through the atmosphere like sonic waves. It spoke to her flesh, calling all the pores of her skin to lift up in a soft carpet of goosebumps, each hair on her head to stand up and tingle at the roots. A hot wire fizzed in her core, sparking a wave of restless energy unlike anything she had ever felt before. It moved through her body, making her as aware of her erogenous zones as if he had reached out and kissed and caressed each one in turn. Her neck, just below her ears, her décolletage, her breasts, the base of her spine, the backs of her knees, her inner thighs…

His eyes moved from her gaze to her mouth and back again. He seemed to be fighting an internal battle. She could see it being played out on his tightly composed features. Temptation and common sense were waging a war and it seemed he hadn't yet decided whose team he was going to side with.

'Are you still in love with your ex?' It was a question Izzy couldn't stop herself asking. Was a little shocked she had.

The night orchestra beyond the veranda filled the silence for several bars. The percussion section of insects. A chorus of frogs. A lonely solo from a stone curlew.

Izzy found herself holding her breath, hoping he wasn't still in love with his ex-fiancée. Why? She couldn't answer. Didn't want to answer. Wasn't ready to answer.

'No.' The word was final. Decisive. It was as if a line had been drawn in his head and he wasn't going back over it.

'But you were hurt when she ended things?'

He gave her a look she couldn't quite read. 'How did your ex take it when you broke things off?'

'Remarkably well.'

One of his brows lifted. 'Oh?'

'He found a replacement within a matter of days.' Izzy looked at the contents of her glass rather than meet his gaze. 'Don't get me wrong...I didn't want him to be inconsolable or anything, but it was a slap in the face when he found someone so completely the opposite of me and so quickly.'

'Why did you accept his proposal in the first place?' Was that a hint of censure in his tone?

Izzy thought back to the elaborate proposal Richard had set up. A very public proposal that had made her feel hemmed in and claustrophobic. She hadn't had the courage to turn him down and make him lose face in front of all of her friends and colleagues. The banner across the front of the hospital with *Will You Marry Me, Izzy?* emblazoned on it had come has a complete and utter shock to her on arriving at work. She could still see Richard down on bended knee, with the Remington heirloom engagement ring taken out of his family's bank vault especially for the occasion, his face beaming with pride and enthusiasm.

No had been on her tongue but hadn't made it past her embarrassed smile. She'd told herself it was the right thing to do. They'd known each other for years. They'd drifted into casual dating and then into a physical relationship. He had been one of Jamie's close friends and had stuck by him during every gruelling bout of chemo. Her parents adored him. He was part of the family. It was her way of staying connected with her lost brother. 'Lots of reasons.'

'But not love.'

'No.' Izzy let out a breath that felt like she had been holding it inside her chest for years. 'That's why I came out here, as far away from home as possible. I want to know who I am without Richard or my parents telling me what to do and how and when I should do it. My parents have expectations for me. I guess all parents do, but I've got my own life to live. They thought I was wasting my time going to medical school when I have enough money behind me to never have to work. But I want to make a difference in people's lives. I want to be the one who saves someone's brother for them, you know?'

Zach's gaze was steady on hers, his voice low and husky. 'I do know.'

Izzy bit her lip. Had she told him too much? Revealed too much? She put her glass down. 'Sorry. Two sips of wine and I'm spilling all my secret desires.' She gave a mental cringe at her choice of words. 'Maybe I should just leave before I embarrass you as well as myself.'

Zach blocked her escape by placing a hand on her arm. 'What do you think would happen if we followed through on this?'

Her skin sizzled where his hand lay on her arm. She could feel the graze of the rough callus on his fingers, reminding her he was a man in every sense of the word. 'Um…I'm not sure what you mean. Follow through on what?'

His eyes searched hers for a lengthy moment. 'So that's the way you're going to play it. Ignore it. Pretend it's not there.' He gave a little laugh that sounded very deep and very sexy. 'That could work.'

Izzy pressed her lips together, trying to summon up some willpower. Where had it gone? Had she left it behind in England? It certainly wasn't here with her now. 'I think it's for the best, don't you?'

'You reckon you've got what it takes to unlock this banged-up cynical heart of mine, Dr Courtney?' He was mocking her again. She could see it in the way the corner of his mouth was tilted and his eyes glinted at her in the darkness.

She gave him a pert look to disguise how tempted she was to take him on. 'I'm guessing I'd need a lot more than a month, that is if I could be bothered, which I can't.'

He brushed an idle fingertip underneath the base of her upraised chin. 'I would like nothing better right now than to take you inside and show you a good time.'

Izzy suppressed the shiver of longing his light touch evoked. 'What makes you think I'd be interested?'

His gaze moved between each of her eyes. 'Have you slept with anyone since your fiancé?'

'No, but I hardly see how that's got anything to do with anything.'

His fingertip moved like a feather over her lower lip. 'Might explain the fireworks the other night.'

'Just because I got a little excited about a kiss doesn't mean I'm going to jump into bed with you any time soon.' She knew she sounded a little schoolmarmish but she desperately wanted to hide how attracted she was to him. She had never felt such an intensely physical reaction to a man before. His very presence made every nerve in her body pull tight with anticipation.

His tall, firm body was not quite touching hers but was close enough for her to feel the warmth that emanated from him. He planted a hand on the veranda post just above the left side of her head. 'Thing is…' his eyes went to her mouth again '…everyone already thinks I'm doing you.'

A wave of heat coursed through her lower body as his eyes came back to burn into hers. The thought of him 'doing' her made her insides contort with lust. She could picture it in her mind, his body so much bigger and more powerfully made than her ex-fiancé's. Somehow she knew there would be nothing predictable or formulaic about any such encounter. She wouldn't be staring at the ceiling, counting the whorls on the ceiling rose to pass the time. It would be mind-blowing pleasure from start to finish.

'It's just gossip… I'm sure it'll go away once they see there's no truth in it…' If only she could get her voice to sound firm and full of conviction instead of that breathy, phone-sex voice that seemed to be coming out.

'Maybe.'

She saw his nostrils flare as he took in the fragrance of her perfume. She could smell his lemon-based aftershave and his own warm, male smell that was equally intoxicating. She could see the shadow of stubble that peppered his jaw and around his nose and mouth and remembered with another clench of lust how it had felt so sexily abrasive against her skin when he'd kissed her.

A wick of something dangerous lit his gaze. 'Ever had a one-night stand before?'

'No.' She swept her tongue over her lips. 'You?'

'Couple of times.'

'Before or after your fiancée?'

'Before.'

Izzy couldn't drag her gaze away from his mouth. She remembered how it had tasted. How it had felt. The way his firm lips had softened and hardened in turn. The way his tongue had seduced hers. Bewitching her. Giving her a hint of the thorough possession he would take of her if she allowed him. 'So...no one since?' She couldn't believe she was asking such personal questions. It was so unlike her.

'No.' He took a wisp of her hair and curled it around one of his fingers, triggering a sensual tug in her inner core. 'We could do it and get it over with. Defuse the bomb, so to speak.'

She moistened her lips again. She could feel herself wavering on a threshold she had never encountered before. Temptation lured her like a moth towards a light that would surely scorch and destroy. 'You're very confident of yourself, aren't you?'

His gaze had a satirical light as it tussled with hers. 'I recognise lust when I see it.'

Izzy felt the lust she was trying to hide crawl all over her skin, leaving it hot and flushed. She took an uneven breath, shocked at how much she wanted him. It was an ache that throbbed in her womb, prickling and swelling the flesh of her breasts until they felt twice their normal size. 'I'm not the sort of girl who jumps into bed with virtual strangers.' *Even if he was the most attractive and intriguing man she had ever met.*

His eyes held hers for a semitone of silence. 'You know my name. Where I live. What I do for a living. You've even met my father. That hardly makes me a stranger.'

'I don't know your values.'

His mouth kicked up wryly in one corner. 'I'm a cop. Can't get more value-driven than that.'

Izzy gave him an arch look. 'I've met some pretty nasty wolves in cops' clothing in my time.'

His hand was still pressed against the post of the veranda, his strongly muscled arm close enough for her cheek to feel its warmth. His warm breath with its hint of summer wine caressed her face as he spoke in that low, deep, gravel-rough voice. 'I only bat for the good guys.'

Izzy could feel herself melting. Her muscles softened, her ligaments loosened, her hands somehow came up to rest against the hard wall of his chest. His pectoral muscles flinched under the soft press of her palms as if he found her as electrifying as she found him. His eyes were locked on hers, a question burning in their grey-blue depths. An invitation. 'I don't normally do this sort of thing…' Her voice was not her own. It was barely a whisper of sound, and yet it was full of unspoken longing.

His eyes lowered to gaze at her mouth. 'Kiss men you hardly know?'

She looked at his mouth, her belly shifting like a foot stepping on a floating plank. He had a beautiful mouth, sensual and neatly sculpted, the lips neither too thick nor too thin. 'Is that all we're doing? Kissing?'

His gaze became sexily hooded. 'Let's start with that and see where it takes us.'

CHAPTER EIGHT

His mouth came down and covered hers in a kiss that tasted of wine and carefully controlled need. It was a slow kiss, with none of the hot urgency of the other night. This one was more languid, leisurely, a slow but thorough exploration of her mouth that made her pulse skyrocket all the same.

Her heart beat like a drum against her ribcage, her hands moving up his chest to link around his neck. He was much taller than her, so that she had to lift up on her toes, bringing her pelvis into intimate contact with his. The pressure of his kiss intensified, his tongue driving through the seam of her mouth in a commanding search of hers. She felt its sexy rasp, the erotic glide and thrusts that so brazenly imitated the act of human mating. Carnal needs surged like a wild beast in her blood; she felt them do the same in his. The throbbing pulse of his erection pounded against her belly; so thick, so strong, so arrantly male it made her desire race out of her control like a rabid dog slipping its leash.

She pressed herself closer, loving the feel of his chest against her breasts, the way the cotton of his shirt smelt, so clean and laundry fresh with that sexy understory of male body heat.

His tongue played with hers, light and teasing and playful at first, determined and purposeful the next. He drew her closer with a firm, warm hand in the small of her back, the other hand skimming over her right breast, the touch light but devastatingly arousing. Izzy liked it that he hadn't made a grab for her, squeezing too tightly or baring her flesh too quickly. His fainéant touch caused a sensual riot in her body, making her ache to feel his calloused palm on her soft skin. She made a murmur of assent against his mouth, reaching for his hand and bringing it back to the swell of her breast. He cupped her through her clothes; his large palm should have made her feel inadequately small but never had she felt more feminine.

His mouth moved down from hers, along the line of her jaw, lingering at the base of her ear where every sensitive nerve shrieked in delight as his tongue laved her flesh. 'You like that?' His voice came from deep within him, throaty, husky.

She sighed with pleasure. 'Hate it.'

He gave a little rumble of laughter as his lips moved to her collarbone. 'Let's see how much you hate this, then.' His hand released the zipper on the back of her dress just enough to uncover one of her shoulders. The feel of his lips and tongue on the cap of her shoulder made her spine soften like candlewax. For a man who hadn't had sex in a while he certainly hadn't lost his touch. Izzy had never been subjected to such a potent assault on her senses. Her body was a tingling matrix of over stimulated nerves, each one screaming out for assuagement.

He moved from her shoulder to the upper curve of her breast showing above her lowered dress. His lips left a quicksilver trail of fire over her flesh, causing her to whimper as the need tightened and pulled inside her.

He tugged her dress a little lower, not bothering to unclip her bra; he simply moved it out of his way and closed his mouth over her tightly budded nipple. The moist warmth of his mouth, the graze of his teeth and the salve of his tongue as he nipped and licked and sucked her in turn made her shudder with pleasure.

Izzy splayed her fingers through the thickness of his hair, holding him to her, prolonging the delicious sensations for as long as she could. His hand on the small of her back moved around her body to possess her hip. It was a strong alpha type of hold that thrilled her senses into overload. Her inner core moistened as he brought her hard against him.

He left her breast to lick the scaffold of her collarbone in one sexy sweep of his tongue. 'We should stop.'

'W-we should?' Izzy had to remind her good girl to get back inside her head and her body. 'Yes. Right. Of course we should.' She pulled her dress back up over her shoulder but she couldn't quite manage the zip with her fumbling fingers.

He turned her so her back was towards him, his fingers an electric shock against her skin as he dragged the zipper back up. His body brushed hers from behind, his hands coming to rest on the tops of her shoulders as if he couldn't quite bring himself to release her just yet. The temptation to lean back against his arousal, to feel him probe her in that sinfully erotic fashion was overwhelming. Just the thought of him there, so close, so thick and turgid with want, was enough to make her flesh hot all over.

'Um…you can let me go now.' Her voice was still that whisper-soft thread of sound.

His hands tightened for the briefest of moments before they fell away. He stepped back, the floorboards of the veranda creaking in protest as if they too felt her disappointment. 'You want a top-up of your drink before dinner?'

Izzy couldn't believe how even his tone was, so cool and calm and collected as if his senses hadn't been subjected to the biggest shake-up of all time. 'I'd better not. What I've had so far seems to have gone straight to my head.'

Even though most of his face was in shadow she caught a glimpse of a half-smile before he turned and went back to the kitchen to see to their meal.

Izzy looked at Popeye, who was looking up at her with bright button eyes. 'Don't look at me like that. I wasn't going to do it. I'm not a one-night stand sort of girl.'

Popeye barked and then jumped off the cane chair and trotted after his master.

Zach planted his hands on the kitchen bench and drew in a long, slow breath to steady himself. It had been a long time since he had let hot-blooded passion overrule common sense. That was the stuff of teenage hormones, not of a thirty-three-year-old man who had responsibilities and priorities.

But, damn it, Izzy Courtney was tempting. His body was thrumming with need, his mouth still savouring the sweetness of hers. Was he asking for trouble to indulge in a fling with her while she was here? It wasn't as if either of them would be making any promises.

She had an end point in sight. She had plans. Commitments elsewhere. He had responsibilities he couldn't leave. Wouldn't leave.

The trouble was he liked her. Not just sexual attraction. He actually *liked* her. She was intelligent, hard-working, committed to serving the community. Everyone was talking about how well she was fitting in. He hadn't heard a bad said word about her.

Zach heard the sound of a mobile phone ringing. He glanced at his phone lying on the bench but the screen was dark. He wasn't on duty tonight, Rob Heywood was.

Izzy came in from the veranda with an apologetic look on her face. 'I'm sorry, Zach. I have to leave. Caitlin Graham's little girl Skylar has fallen off a bed while playing with her older brothers and cut her forehead. It might not be much but with little kids you can never be sure. I'm going to meet them at the clinic.'

Zach snatched up his keys. 'I'll drive down with you.'

'But I've only had a couple of sips of wine.'

'It's not that. We can take both cars.' He turned off the oven on his way past. 'Caitlyn's new boyfriend, Wayne Brody, is a bit of a hot head, especially if he's been drinking.'

Izzy's eyes widened. 'Are you saying Skylar might not have fallen out of bed?'

Zach kept his expression cop neutral. 'Best we take a look at the evidence first.'

Zach and Izzy arrived at the clinic just as a young woman in her early to mid-twenties was getting out of a car that looked like it could do with a makeover. But then, Caitlyn Graham looked the same. Her skin was weathered by a combination of harsh sun and years of smoking, the tell-tale stain of nicotine on her fingers mirroring the rust on her car, her mouth downturned at the edges as if there wasn't much in her life to smile about. There was no sign of the boyfriend Zach had mentioned, which made Izzy wonder if what he had alluded to had any grounds in truth. Caitlyn carried a whimpering two-year-old girl in her arms and two little boys of about five and seven trailed in her wake, the younger one sucking his thumb, the older one carrying a toy dinosaur.

'I'm sorry to drag you out but I think she needs stitches,' Caitlin said, hitching her daughter to her other bony hip as she took the five-year-old's hand. The little girl buried her head against her mother's thin chest and gave another mewling cry.

'Let's go inside and take a look.' Izzy smiled at the boys. 'Hi, guys. Wow, that's a nice triceratops.'

The seven-year-old gave her a scornful look from beneath long spider leg eyelashes. 'It's a stegosaurus.'

'Oh, right. My mistake.' Izzy caught Zach's glinting glance as she led the way into the clinic.

On examination little Skylar had a gash on her forehead that had stopped bleeding due to the compress her mother had placed on it but still needed a couple of stitches to ensure it healed neatly. There were no other injuries that she could see and the child otherwise seemed in good health.

'I'll put some anaesthetic cream on her forehead before I inject some local,' Izzy said to Caitlyn. 'It'll still sting a bit but hopefully not too much.'

Once the stitches were in place, Izzy handed the little tot a choice of the lollipops she kept in a jar on her desk. 'What a brave little girl you've been.'

The little girl chose a red one and silently handed it to her mother to take the cellophane wrapping off.

'Can I have one too?' the five-year-old, called Eli, asked around his thumb.

'Of course. Here you go.' Izzy then passed the jar to the seven-year-old with the stegosaurus. The boy hesitated before finally burying his hand in the jar and taking out two lollipops.

'Only one, Jobe,' Caitlyn said.

The boy gave his mother a defiant look. 'I'm taking one for Dad.'

Caitlyn's lips tightened. 'It'll be stale before you see him again.'

Izzy watched as Jobe's dark eyes hardened. It was a little shocking to see such a young child exhibiting such depth of emotion. Not childlike emotion but emotion well beyond his years. 'I'd like to see Skylar in a couple of days to check those stitches,' she said to defuse the tense atmosphere. 'If it's tricky getting into town, I can always make a house call.'

'I can get here no trouble.'

Was it her imagination or had Caitlin been a little bit too insistent? Izzy shook off the thought. Zach's comments earlier had made her unnecessarily biased. Not every stepfather was a child abuser. Jobe was a tense child but that was probably because he missed his biological father, who apparently was no longer on the scene. 'Let's make an appointment now.' She reached for the computer mouse to bring up the clinic's electronic diary.

'I'll call Margie tomorrow,' Caitlin said. 'I'd better get back. My partner will wonder what's happened.'

'You can use the phone here if you like.'

Caitlyn was already at the door. 'Come on, boys. It's way past your bedtime.'

Jobe was looking at Zach with an intense look on his face. 'Do you always carry a gun?'

'Not always,' Zach said. 'Only when I'm on duty.'

'Are you on duty now?'

'No. Sergeant Heywood is.'

'What if a bad guy came to your house? Would you be allowed to shoot him if you're not on duty?'

Caitlyn came back over and grabbed Jobe by the back of his T-shirt. 'Come on. Sergeant Fletcher's got better things to do than answer your dumb questions.'

The little boy shrugged off his mother's hand and scowled. 'They're not dumb.'

'Don't answer back or I'll give you a clip across the ear.'

Zach crouched down to Jobe's level. 'Maybe you and your brother could drop into the station one day and have a look around. I can show you how the radio works and other cool stuff.' He glanced up at Caitlyn. 'That all right with you?'

Caitlyn's mouth was so tight her lips were white. 'Sure. Whatever.'

Izzy chewed at her lower lip as she began to tidy up the treatment area. Zach came back in from seeing the young family out to the car. She turned and looked at him. 'Cute kids.'

He was frowning in a distracted manner. 'Yeah.'

'You think she would hit Jobe or the other two?'

'A lot of parents do. It's called discipline.'

'There are much better ways to discipline a child than to hit them,' Izzy said. 'How can you teach a child not to hit others if you're hitting them yourself?'

'You're preaching to the choir,' he said. 'I don't agree with it either but some parents insist it's their right to use corporal punishment.'

'I didn't notice any bruises or marks on the little one but Jobe seems a very tense little boy. He doesn't seem to have a close relationship with his mother, does he?'

'He misses his dad.'

'Where is he?'

He shrugged. 'Who knows? Probably shacked up with some other woman with another brood of kids by now.'

Izzy washed her hands at the sink and then tore off a paper towel to dry them. 'Beats me why some people have kids if they're just going to abandon them when the going gets tough.'

'Tell me about it.'

She looked at him again. 'Did your mother remarry?'

'Yes. Got a couple of sons. They take up a lot of her time.'

'I'm sorry…I shouldn't have asked.'

'It was a long time ago.'

She put the used paper towel in the pedal bin. 'Do you want kids?' *Where on earth had that question come from?* 'Sorry.' She bit her lip again. 'None of my business.'

'I do, actually.' He picked up a drug company's promotional paperweight off her desk and smoothed his right thumb over its surface. 'Not right now, though.

Maybe in a couple of years or so. I have to get a few things straightened out first.'

'Your father?'

He put the paperweight down and met her gaze. 'It's a good sign he went out tonight.'

'Yes, I agree. Social isolation isn't good for someone suffering depression.'

There was a little silence.

'What about you?' he asked. 'Do you want kids or is your career your top priority?'

'I would hate to miss out on having a family. I love my career but I really want to be a mum one day.'

It was hard to tell if her answer met with his approval or not. He had his cop face on again. 'Caitlyn Graham had Jobe when she was fifteen. She was a kid with a kid.'

'It looks like she's had it tough,' Izzy said. 'Do all three kids have the same father?'

'No, Eli and Skylar are another guy's. A drifter who came into town for a couple of years before moving on again.'

'Does Caitlyn have any extended family to support her?'

'Her mother comes to visit from Nyngan now and again but she never stays long.' His mouth took on a cynical line. 'Just long enough to have a fight with Caitlyn's new boyfriend.'

'He doesn't sound like a good role model for the boys,' Izzy said.

He gave her a grim look. 'He's not. He's been inside for assault and possession and supply of illegal drugs. He's only just come off parole. Reckon it won't be long before he ends up back behind bars.'

'Once a criminal, always a criminal?'

'In my experience, most of the leopards I've met like to hang onto their spots.'

'Don't you think people can change if they're given some direction and support?' Izzy asked.

'Maybe some.'

She picked up her bag and hitched it over her shoulder. 'Were you always this cynical or has your job made you that way?'

He held the door open for her. 'I'll tell you over dinner.'

'You still want me to—?'

His look was unreadable. 'You're still hungry, aren't you?'

Izzy had a feeling he wasn't just talking about food. 'It's getting late. Maybe I should just head home. Your dad will be back soon in any case.'

'If that's what you want.' He sounded as if he didn't care either way.

It wasn't what she wanted but she wasn't quite ready to admit it. She wasn't sure how to handle someone as deep and complicated as Zach Fletcher. He was strong and principled, almost to the point of being conservative, which, funnily enough, resonated with her own homespun values. But she was only here for another three weeks. It wouldn't be fair to start something she had no intention of finishing. 'Thanks for coming down with me to see to little Skylar.'

'You'd better get Margie to give Caitlyn a call tomorrow. She's not good at following through on stuff.'

'Yes, I gathered that.'

Once she had locked the clinic and set the alarm, Zach walked her to her car. He waited until she was inside the car with her seat belt pulled down and clipped into place.

'Thanks again.'

He tapped the roof of her car with his hand. 'Drive safely.'

'Zach?'

He stopped and turned back to look at her. 'Yes?'

'Maybe I could cook dinner for you some time…to make up for tonight?'

He gave her the briefest of smiles. 'I'll get working on my appetite.'

CHAPTER NINE

'How did your evening go with Doug Fletcher?' Izzy asked Margie the next morning at the clinic.

'I was about to ask you the same question about yours with Zach.'

'It got cut short. I got called out to Caitlyn Graham's little daughter, who'd cut her forehead,' Izzy said. 'Can you call her to make a follow-up appointment? I'd like to see Skylar on Thursday. And can you check to see whether all three kids are up to date on their vaccinations?'

'Will do. Did Caitlyn's boyfriend come with her?'

'No, but Zach warned me about him. He came with me to the clinic.'

Margie's brows lifted. 'Did he, now?'

Izzy felt a blush creep over her cheeks. 'He's a bit of a stickler for safety.'

'Wayne Brody is a ticking time bomb,' Margie said. 'Wouldn't take much to set him off. Zach's got a good nose for sensing trouble.'

'Why would Caitlyn hook up with someone so unsavoury? There must be some other much nicer young man out here.'

Margie shrugged. 'Some girls would rather be with

anybody rather than nobody. Her mother's the same. Hooked up with one deadbeat after the other. I don't think Caitlyn has ever met her biological father. I'm not sure her mother even knows who it is. Caitlyn had one stepfather after the other. Now she's doing the same to her kids. It's a cycle that goes on one generation after another. It's a case of monkey see, monkey do.'

'Are there any playgroups or activities for young mums like her around here?' Izzy asked.

'Peggy McLeod tried to set one up a few years back but her arthritis set in and she had to give it up. No one's bothered to do anything since.'

'The community centre…do you think I could book it for one morning this week?' Izzy asked. 'I could re-arrange my clinic hours. I could get some toys donated or buy them myself if I have to. It'd be a place for the mums and kids to hang out and chat and play.'

'Sounds good, but who's going to take over when your time with us is up?'

'I could get one of the mums to take charge,' Izzy said. 'It might be a chance to get Caitlyn engaged in something that would build her self-esteem.'

Margie gave a snort. 'There's nothing wrong with that girl's self-esteem. It's her taste in men that's the problem.'

'But that's exactly my point,' Izzy said. 'She thinks so badly of herself that she settles for the first person who shows an interest in her. There's a saying I heard once. You get the partner in life you think you deserve.'

Margie gave her a twinkling look. 'And who do you think you deserve?'

Izzy felt that betraying blush sneak back into her

cheeks. 'Did you manage to convince Doug to book in for a check-up?'

Margie's twinkle dulled like a cloud passing over the sun. 'I'm working on it.'

'Are you going to see him again?'

'I'm working on that too,' Margie said. 'I mentioned the Shearers' Ball but he was pretty adamant he wasn't going to go.'

'I guess it's pretty hard to dance when you're on a walking frame.'

'It's not about the dancing.' Margie's eyes suddenly watered up. 'I couldn't give a toss about the dancing. I just want to be with him. I've waited so long for him but he's got this stupid idea in his head that no one could ever want him the way he is now.'

Izzy gave Margie's shoulder a gentle squeeze. 'I hope it works out for you and him. I really do.'

Margie popped a tissue out of the box on the reception counter and blew her nose. She tossed the tissue in the bin under the desk and assembled her features back into brisk receptionist mode. 'Silly fool. A woman of my age fancying herself in love. Phhfft. Ridiculous.'

'It's not ridiculous,' Izzy said. 'Falling in love isn't something you can control. It just happens—' she caught Margie's look '—or so I'm told,' she added quickly. She took the file for her first patient of the day from the counter as the front door of the clinic opened. 'Mrs Honeywell? Come this way.'

Zach was leaving the station a couple of days later when he saw Izzy coming out of the clinic and walking towards her car. It had been a brute of a day, hot and dry with a northerly wind that was gritty and relentless.

He could think of nothing better than a cool beer and a swim out at Blake's waterhole… Actually, he could think of something way better than that. Izzy Courtney lying naked underneath him while he—

She suddenly turned and looked at him as if she had felt his gaze on her. Or read his X-rated thoughts. 'Oh…hello.' She gave him a smile that looked beaten up around the edges.

'You look like you've had a tough day.'

Her mouth twisted as she scraped a few tendrils of sticky hair back behind her ear. 'Caitlyn didn't show up for Skylar's check-up. Margie confirmed it with her but she didn't come. I called her on the phone to offer to go out there but there was no answer.' She blew out a little breath of frustration. 'I can't force her to bring the child in. And I don't want to turn up at her house as if I'm suspicious of her.'

'I've got a couple of things for Jobe and Eli,' Zach said. 'Stuff I had when I was a kid. I found them in a cupboard in one of the spare rooms at home. We can drop them round now just to see if everything's OK. Better take your car, though. Might not get such a warm welcome, turning up in mine.'

Her caramel-brown eyes brightened. 'That was thoughtful of you. What sort of things? Toys?'

Zach found himself trying to disguise a sheepish look. 'I went through a dinosaur stage when I was about seven or eight. Got a bit obsessive there for a bit.'

She gave him a smile that loosened some of the tight barbed wire wrapped around his heart. 'So you can tell a stegosaurus from a triceratops?'

'Any fool can do that.'

She pursed her lips and then must have realised he

was teasing her for her sunny smile broke free again. 'You're a nice man, Sergeant Fletcher. I think I'm starting to like you after all.'

The house Caitlyn Graham was living in was on the outskirts of Jerringa Ridge. It was a stockman's cottage from the old days that looked like it hadn't had much done to it since. The rusty gate was hanging on one hinge and the once white but now grey picket fence had so many gaps it looked like a rotten-toothed smile. A dog of mixed breeding was chained near the tank stand and let out a volley of ferocious barking as Izzy pulled her car up in front of the house. 'Can he get off, do you think?' she asked, casting Zach a worried glance.

'I'll keep an eye on him.'

'Poor dog tied up like that in this heat.' She turned off the engine and unclipped her belt. 'Is anyone around? There's no car about that I can see.'

'Stay in the car and I'll have a mosey around.' Zach got out and closed the door with a snick. The dog put its ears back and brought its body low to the ground as it snarled and bared its teeth.

Izzy watched as Zach ignored the dog as he walked up the two steps of the bull-nosed veranda, opening the screen door to knock on the cracked paint of the front door. The dog was still doing its scary impersonation of an alien beast from a horror movie but Zach didn't seem the least put off by it. He left the bag of toys near the door and came back down the veranda steps. Apart from the dinosaurs, Izzy had spotted a set of toy cars and a doll that looked suspiciously new. She had seen one just like it in the corner store yesterday but it hadn't been there when she'd picked up her sandwich today at lunchtime.

Zach made a clicking sound with his tongue and the dog stopped growling and slunk down in a submissive pose. Zach picked up the dog's water dish, took it over to the tap on the base of the tank, rinsed the rusty water out of it and filled it with fresh, setting it down in a patch of shade next to the dog's kennel. The dog drank thirstily, so thirstily Zach had to refill the dish a couple of times.

He came back to the car after doing another round of the house. 'No one home.'

Izzy started the engine. 'You certainly have a way with wild animals.'

'He's not wild.' He leaned his arm along the back of her seat as she backed the car to turn around. 'He's scared. Probably had the boot kicked into his ribs a few too many times.'

Izzy could see the tightness around his jaw. That grim look was back. The look that was like a screen behind which the horrors and cruelty and brutal inhumanity he'd seen first hand were barricaded. 'How do you cope with it? The stuff you see, I mean. The bad stuff.'

'Reckon you've seen your share of bad stuff too.'

'Yes, but I'm not usually out on the coalface. Most of the stuff I see is in the controlled environment of a clinic or hospital. And mostly it's stuff I can fix.'

He didn't speak until Izzy had driven back to the road leading to town. 'It doesn't get any easier, that's for sure. Rocking up to someone's place to tell them their only kid is lying in the morgue after a high-speed accident is the kind of stuff that gets to even the toughest cops.' He paused for a beat. 'Anything to do with kids gets me. Abuse. Neglect. Murder. It's not something you can file away like the investigation report. It stays with you. For years.' He released a jagged breath. 'For ever.'

Izzy glanced at him. 'Did you think it would be as bad as it is when you first joined the force?'

He gave her a twisted smile that had nothing to do with humour. 'Most cops fresh out of the academy think they're going to be the one that changes the world. We all think we're going to make a difference. To help people. Trouble is, some people don't want to be helped.'

'I've been talking to Margie about setting up a playgroup in town,' Izzy said, 'for mums like Caitlyn and their kids. A place to hang out and chat and swap recipes and stuff. Do you think it's a good idea?'

'Who's going to run it?'

'I will, to start with.'

He flashed her an unreadable look. 'And who's going to take over when you drive off into the sunset in search of your next big adventure?'

Izzy pressed her lips together. Was he mocking her or was he thinking of the locals getting all excited about something only to have it fall flat once she left? A little flag of hope climbed up the flagpole of her heart. Was he thinking of how *he* would feel when she left? 'I'm going to be here long enough to get it up and running. After that it's up to the locals to keep things going, if that's what they want.'

He gave a noncommittal grunt, his eyes trained on the road ahead.

Izzy let a silence pass before she added, 'So what's wrong with looking for adventure?'

'Nothing, as long as you don't hurt others going in search of it.'

'I'm not planning on hurting anyone.' She found her fingers tightening on the steering-wheel and had to force herself to relax them. 'I suppose this attitude of yours is because of your mother leaving the way she did.'

She felt the razor-sharp blade of his gaze. 'You really think you've got what it takes to make a difference out here in a month? You haven't got a hope, sweetheart.'

'Don't patronise me by calling me sweetheart.'

He gave a sound midway between a laugh and a cynical snort. 'You flounce into town, sprinkling your fairy dust around, hoping some of it will stick, but you haven't got a clue. The country out here is tough and it needs tough people to work in it and survive. It's not the place for some pretty little blow-in who's looking for something to laugh about over a latte with her friends when she gets back from her big adventure with the rednecks in the antipodes.'

Izzy tried to rein in her anger but it was like trying to control a scrub fire with an eyedropper. The one thing she hated the most was people not taking her seriously. Thinking she was too much of a flake to get the job done. A silly little socialite playing at doctors and nurses. 'Thanks for the charming summation of my motives and character,' she said through tight lips.

'Pleasure.'

She pulled up outside the police station a few bristling minutes later. 'Have a nice evening, Sergeant,' she said, her voice dripping with sarcasm.

He didn't even bother replying, or at least not verbally. He shut the car door with a sharp click that could just as easily be substituted for an imprecation.

***

'What's got under your skin?' Doug asked Zach over dinner later that evening. 'You've been stabbing at that steak as if it's a mortal enemy.'

Zach pushed his plate away. 'It's too hot to eat.'

'Tell me about it.' Doug wiped the back of his hand over his forehead. 'Must be something wrong with the air-con. I'm sweating like a pig.'

Zach frowned as he saw his father's sickly colour. 'You all right?'

'Will be in a minute…' Doug gripped the arms of the standard chair. 'Just a funny turn. Had one earlier… just before you got home.'

'When was the last time you took a painkiller?'

'Ran out last night.'

Zach swore under his breath. 'You're not supposed to stop them cold turkey. You're supposed to wean yourself off them. You're probably having withdrawal symptoms. It can be dangerous to suddenly stop taking them.'

Doug winced as he pushed back from the table. 'Maybe you should call the doctor for me. Pain's pretty bad…' He sucked in a breath. 'Getting worse by the minute.'

Zach mentally rolled his eyes as he reached for his phone. The one time he wanted some distance from Izzy Courtney and his father springs a turnaround on him. He considered waiting it out to see if his father recovered without intervention but he knew he would never forgive himself if things took a turn for the worse. His father's health hadn't been checked since William Sawyer had left on holidays. He was supposed to be monitored weekly for his blood pressure. Severe pain could trigger heart attacks in some patients and the last thing Zach wanted was to be responsible for inaction just because of a silly little tiff with the locum doctor.

He was annoyed with himself for reacting the way he had. He didn't want Izzy thinking she had any hold over him. So what if she wanted to get a playgroup going before she left? It was a good idea—a *great* idea. It was exactly what the town needed. She was doing all she could in the short time she was here to make a difference. Once she was done waving her magic wand around he would wave her off without a flicker of emotion showing on his face.

That was one lesson he had learned and learned well.

Izzy arrived twenty-five minutes later, carrying her doctor's bag and a coolly distant manner Zach knew he probably deserved. 'He's in the bedroom, lying down,' he said.

'How long has he been feeling unwell?'

'Since before I got home. He's run out of pain meds. It's probably withdrawal.'

'Is he happy to see me?'

He inched up the corner of his mouth in a sardonic curl. 'You think I would've called you otherwise?'

Her brown eyes flashed a little arc of lightning at him. 'Lead the way.'

Zach knew he was acting like a prize jerk. He couldn't seem to help it. It was the only way to keep his distance. He was worried about complicating his life with a dalliance with her even though he could think of nothing he wanted more than to lose himself in a bit of mindless sex. He didn't have her pegged as the sort of girl who would settle for a fling. She'd been engaged to the same man for four years. That didn't sound like a girl who was eager to put out to the first guy who showed an interest in her.

And Zach was more than interested in her.

He couldn't stop thinking about her. How she'd felt in his arms, the way her mouth had met the passion of his, the softness of her breast in his mouth, the hard little pebble of her nipple against his tongue, the taste of the skin of her neck, that sweet, flowery scent of her that reminded him of an English cottage garden in spring.

'Hello, Mr Fletcher.' Izzy's voice broke through Zach's erotic reverie. 'Zach told me you're not feeling so good this evening.'

'Pain...' Doug gestured to his abdomen and his back; his breathing was ragged now, his brow sticky with sweat. 'Bad pain...'

Zach watched as she examined his father's chest and abdomen and then his back with gentle hands. He couldn't help feeling a little jealous. He would have liked those soft little hands running over his chest and abdomen and lower. His groin swelled at the thought and he had to think of something unpleasant to get control again.

She took his father's blood pressure, her forehead puckered in concentration as she listened to his account of how he had been feeling over the last few hours.

'Any history of renal colic?' she asked. 'Kidney stones?'

'A few years back,' his father said. 'Six or seven years ago, I think. Didn't need to go to hospital or anything. I passed them eventually. Hurt like the devil. None since.'

'I'll give you a shot of morphine for the pain but I think we should organise an IVP tomorrow if the pain doesn't go away overnight,' Izzy said. 'When was the last time you passed urine?'

'Not for a while, three hours ago maybe.'

'Any pain or difficulty?'

'A bit.'

'Do you think you could give me a urine sample if I leave you with a specimen bottle?' she asked as she administered the injection.

'I'll give it a try.'

'I'll wait in the kitchen to give you some privacy.' She clipped shut her bag and walked past Zach, her body brushing his in the doorway making him go hard all over again.

'Might need a hand getting to the bathroom, Zach,' his father said.

Zach blinked a couple of times to reorient himself. 'Right. Sure.'

CHAPTER TEN

Izzy was sitting on one of the kitchen chairs with Popeye on her lap when Zach came back in, carrying a urine sample bottle inside the press-lock plastic bag she'd provided. She put the dog on the floor and stood, taking the sample from him and giving it a quick check for blood or cloudiness that would suggest infection, before putting it next to her bag on the floor.

She straightened and kept her doctor face in place, trying to ignore the way her body was so acutely aware of the proximity of Zach's. 'Your father should be feeling a little better in the next half-hour or so. Make sure he drinks plenty of clear fluids over the next twenty-four hours. If he has any trouble passing urine, don't hesitate to call. If the bladder blocks I can insert a catheter to drain it until we can get him to hospital. But I don't think it will come to that. It seems a pretty standard case of renal colic. Being less active, he probably doesn't feel as thirsty as much as he used to. Older men often fail to keep an adequate intake of fluids.' She knew she was talking like a medical textbook but she couldn't seem to stop it. 'That's about it. I'll be on my way. Goodbye.'

'Izzy.' His hand was firm and warm on the bare skin of her arm. It sent a current of electricity to the secret heart of her.

Izzy met his gaze. It wasn't hard and cold with anger now but tired, as if he had grown weary of screening his inner turmoil from view. Her heart stepped off its high horse and nestled back down in her chest with a soft little sign. 'Are you OK?'

His mouth softened its grim line. 'Sorry about this afternoon. I was acting like a jerk.' His thumb started stroking the skin of her arm, a back-and-forth motion that was drugging her senses.

'You've got a lot on your mind right now with your dad and everything.'

'Don't make excuses for me.' His thumb moved to the back of her hand, absently moving over the tendons in a circular motion. 'I was out of line, snapping your head off like that.'

Izzy gave him a mock reproachful arch of her brow. 'Fairy dust?'

His thumb stalled on her hand and he looked down at it as if he'd only just realised he'd been stroking it. He released her and took a step backwards, using the same hand to score a crooked pathway through his hair. 'Thanks for coming out. I appreciate it. I think you've won my dad over.'

What about you? Have I won you over? Izzy studied his now closed-off expression. 'I hope he has a settled night. Call me if you're worried. I'll keep my phone on.'

He walked her out to the car but he hardly said a word. Izzy got the impression he couldn't wait for her to leave. It made her spirits plummet. She'd thought for a moment back there he'd been going to kiss her, maybe even take it a step further.

She hadn't realised how much she wanted him to until he hadn't.

Caitlyn Graham turned up at the clinic the following day with Skylar. 'Sorry about missing our appointment,' she said. 'I took the kids for a drive to see a friend of mine on a property out of town. I forgot to phone and cancel. There's no signal out there so I couldn't call even when I remembered.'

'No problem,' Izzy said. 'Just as long as Skylar's OK.' She inspected the little tot's forehead and asked casually, 'How are the boys?'

'They're at school,' Caitlyn said. 'Jobe made a fuss about going. He hates it. He has a tantrum about going just about every morning.'

'Is he being bullied?'

'What, at school? Nah, don't think so. Wayne would have a fit if he heard Jobe couldn't stand up for himself.'

'Did you get the bag of toys Zach dropped in for the kids?' Izzy asked.

Caitlyn's expression flickered with something before she got it under control. 'Wayne wasn't too happy about that. He doesn't think it's right to spoil kids, especially if they're not behaving themselves.'

'Does Wayne get on well with the kids?'

'All right, I guess.' Caitlyn brushed her daughter's fluffy blonde hair down into some semblance of order. 'They're not his. None of my kids are.'

'Do you have any contact with Jobe's father?' Izzy asked.

'No, and I don't want to.' Caitlyn's expression tightened like a fist. 'Jobe's got it in his head Connor is some sort of hero but he's just another loser. Connor caused a lot of trouble between Brad and me—that's Eli and Skylar's dad. It's what broke us up, actually.'

'What sort of trouble?'

'Picking fights. Saying things about Brad that weren't true. Punch-ups on the street. Making me look like trailer trash. I took a restraining order out on him. He can't come anywhere near me or Jobe.'

'What about Brad? Does he have contact with Eli and Skylar?'

'Now and again but Wayne's not keen on it. Thinks I might be tempted to go back to him or something. As if.' She rolled her eyes at the thought. 'Wayne's no prize but at least he brings in a bit of money.'

'What does he do?'

'He's a truck driver. He does four runs a week, sometimes more. He's the first man I've had who's held down a regular job.'

'It must get lonely out here for you with him away a lot,' Izzy said.

'It's no picnic with three kids, but, as my mum keeps saying, I made my bed so I have to lie in it.'

Izzy brought up the subject of a playgroup at the community centre. Caitlyn shrugged as if the thought held little appeal but Izzy knew apathy was a common trait amongst young women who felt the world was against them. 'I'll let you know once we get things sorted,' she said as Caitlyn left the consulting room. 'Skylar will enjoy it and we might even be able to do an after-school one if things go well so the boys can come too.'

'I'll think about it. See what Wayne says. I like to fit in with him. Causes less trouble that way.'

Izzy closed the door once Caitlyn had left. It was a shock to realise she had no right to criticise Caitlyn for accommodating her partner's unreasonable demands.

Hadn't she done more or less the same with Richard for the last four years?

Margie put the reception phone down just as Izzy came out of her room. 'That was Doug Fletcher. He passed a couple of kidney stones last night. He's feeling much better.'

'I'm glad to hear it.'

'Not only that,' Margie continued with a beaming smile, 'he asked me to go over there tonight. I'm going to make him dinner.'

'That's lovely. I'm pleased for you.'

'I have a favour to ask.'

'You want to leave early?' Izzy asked. 'Sure. I can do the filing and lock up.'

'No, not that.' Margie gave her a beseeching look. 'Would you be a honey and invite Zach to dinner at your place tonight?'

'Um…'

'Go on. He'll feel like a gooseberry hanging around with us oldies,' Margie said. 'A night out at your place will be good for him. It'll give him a break from always having to keep an eye on his dad.'

'I don't know…'

'Or ask him to join you for a counter meal at the pub if you're not much of a cook.'

'I can cook.'

'Then what's the problem?'

Izzy schooled her features into what she hoped

passed for mild enthusiasm. 'I'll give him a call. See what he's up to. He might be on duty.'

'He's not. I already checked.'

Zach was typing a follow-up email to his commander in Bourke when Izzy came into the station. He pressed 'Send' and got to his feet. 'I was going to call you. My dad's feeling a lot better.'

'Yes, Margie told me. He called the clinic earlier this morning.'

'You were spot on with your diagnosis.'

'I may not know a triceratops from a stegosaurus but I'm a whizz at picking up renal colic.'

Zach felt a smile tug at his mouth. 'You doing anything tonight?'

She gave him a wry look. 'Apparently I'm cooking dinner for you.'

'Yeah, so I heard. You OK with that?'

'Have I got a choice?'

Zach found it cute the way she arched her left eyebrow in that haughty manner. 'I wouldn't want to put you to any trouble. I can pick up a bite to eat at the pub. Mike hates it when I do, though. He says it puts his regulars off.'

'You don't have to go in uniform.'

'Wouldn't make a bit of difference if I went in stark naked.'

Her cheeks lit up like twin fires. 'Um…dinner's at seven.'

'I'll look forward to it.' She was at the door when he asked, 'Hey, will your stand-in boyfriend Max be joining us?'

She gave him a slitted look over her shoulder and then flounced out.

* * *

Izzy had cooked for numerous dinner parties for her friends when living in London and she'd never felt the slightest hint of nerves. She was an accomplished cook; she'd made it her business to learn as she'd grown up with cooks at Courtney Manor and wasn't content to sit back and watch, like her parents, while someone else did all the work. From a young age she had taken an interest in preparing food, getting to know the kitchen staff and talking to the gardeners about growing fresh vegetables and herbs.

But preparing a meal for Zach in an Outback town that had only one shop with limited fresh supplies was a challenge, so too was trying not to think about the fact she was sure that food was not the only thing they would be sharing tonight.

She put the last touches to the table, thinking wistfully of the fragrant roses of Courtney Manor as she placed an odd-looking banksia on the table in a jam jar, the only thing she could in the cottage that was close to a vase.

Izzy looked at Max sitting at the end of the table. It had taken her half an hour to blow him up manually as she didn't have a bicycle pump. He was leaning to one side, his ventriloquist dummy-like eyes staring into space. 'I hope you're going to behave yourself, Max.' *Why are you talking to a blow-up doll?* 'No talking with your mouth full or elbows on the table, OK?'

The doorbell sounded and Izzy quickly smoothed her already smooth hair as she went to answer it. Zach was standing on the porch, wearing an open-necked white shirt with tan-coloured chinos. His hair was still damp from a shower; she could see the grooves where his comb or brush had passed through it. Her first 'Hi…' came out croakily so she cleared her throat and tried again. 'Hi. Come on in.'

'Thanks.'

She could smell the clean fresh scent of fabric softener on his shirt as he came through the door, that and the hint of lemon and spice and Outback maleness that never failed to get her senses spinning.

'I brought wine.' He handed her a bottle, his eyes moving over her in a lazy sweep that made her insides feel hollow. 'Something smells good.'

Izzy took the wine, getting a little shock from his fingers as they brushed against hers. 'I hope you're hungry.'

'Ravenous.'

She swallowed and briskly turned to get the glasses, somehow managing to half fill two without spilling a drop in spite of hands that weren't too steady. 'Max decided to join us after all.' She handed Zach a glass of the white wine he had brought. 'I hope you don't mind.'

A hint of a smile played at the corners of his mouth. 'Aren't you going to introduce us?'

Izzy felt her own smile tug at her lips. 'He's not one for small talk.'

'I'm known to be a bit on the taciturn side myself.' The smile had travelled up to his eyes with a twinkle that was devastatingly attractive.

She led the way to the small eating area off the kitchen. 'Max, this is Sergeant Zach Fletcher.' She turned to Zach. 'Zach, this is Max.'

Zach rubbed at his chin thoughtfully. 'Mmm, I guess a handshake is out of the question?'

A laugh bubbled out of Izzy's mouth. 'This is ridiculous. I'm going to kill Hannah. I swear to God I will. Would you like some nibbles?' she asked as she thrust a plate of dips and crackers towards him. 'I have to check on the entrée.'

His eyes were still smiling but they had taken on a smouldering heat that made the backs of her knees feel tingly. 'Do you think Max would get jealous if I kissed you?'

Izzy's stomach hollowed out again. 'I don't know. I've never kissed anyone in front of him before.'

He put a hand to the side of her face, a gentle cupping of her cheek, the dry warmth and slight roughness of his palm making her inner core quiver like an unset jelly. 'I wouldn't want to cut in on him but I've been dying to do this since last night.' His mouth came down towards hers, his minty breath dancing over the surface of her lips in that tantalising prelude to take-off.

Izzy let out a soft sigh of delight as his mouth connected with hers, a velvet brush of dry male lips on moist, lip-gloss-coated female ones. The moment of contact made shivers flow like a river down her spine, the first electrifying sweep of his tongue over her lips parted them, inviting her to take him in. She opened to the commanding glide of his tongue, shuddering with need as he made contact with hers in a sexy tangle that drove every other thought out of her mind other than what she was feeling in her body. The stirring of her blood, the way her feminine folds pulsed and ached to be parted and filled, just like he was doing with her mouth. The way her breasts tingled and tightened, the nipples erect in arousal.

His hands grasped her by the hips, pulling her against his own arousal, the hard heat of him probing her intimately, reminding her of everything that was different between them and yet so powerfully, irresistibly attractive.

Izzy snaked her arms around his neck, stepping up on her toes so she could keep that magical connection with his mouth on hers. She kissed him with the passion that had been lying dormant inside her body, just waiting for someone like him to awaken it. She had never felt the full force of it before. She'd felt paltry imitations of it, but nothing like this.

This was fiery.

This was unstoppable.

This was inevitable.

'I want you.' Izzy couldn't believe she had said the words out loud, but even if she hadn't done so her body was saying them for her. The way she was clinging to him, draping her body over him like a second layer of skin, was surely leaving him in no doubt of her need for him. She pressed three hot little kisses, one after the other, on his mouth and repeated the words she had never said to anyone else and meant them quite the way she meant them now. 'I want you to make love to me.'

Zach brought his hands back up to cup her face. 'Sure?'

Izzy gazed into his beautiful haunted eyes. 'Don't you recognise consent when you see it?'

His thumbs stroked her cheeks, his eyes focused on her mouth as if it were the most fascinating thing he had ever seen. 'It's been a while for me.'

'I'm sure you still know the moves.'

One of his thumbs brushed over her lower lip in a caress that made the base of her spine shiver. 'Are we having a one-night stand or is this something else?'

'What do you want it to be?'

He took a while to answer, his gaze still homed in on her mouth, the pads of his thumbs doing that mesmerising stroking, one across her cheek, the other on her lower lip. 'You're only here for another couple of weeks. Neither of us is in the position to make promises.'

'I'm not asking for promises,' Izzy said. 'I had promises and they sucked.'

His mouth kicked up at the corner. 'Yeah, me too.'

She placed her fingertip on his bottom lip, caressing it the way he had done to hers. 'I've never had a fling with someone before.'

Something in his gaze smouldered. Simmered. Burned. 'Flings can be fun as long as both parties are clear on the rules.'

Izzy shivered as he took her finger in his mouth, his teeth biting down just firmly enough for her insides to flutter in anticipatory excitement. 'You're mighty big on rules, aren't you, Sergeant? I guess that's because of that gun you're wearing.'

His hands encircled her wrists like handcuffs, his pelvis carnally suggestive against hers. 'I'm not wearing my gun.'

Her brow arched in a sultry fashion. 'Could've fooled me.'

He scooped her up in his arms in an effortless lift, calling out over his shoulder as he carried her towards the bedroom, 'Start without us, Max. We've got some business to see to.'

Izzy quaked with pleasure when Zach slid her down the length of his body once he had her in the bedroom. And there was a *lot* of his body compared to hers. So tall, so lean and yet so powerfully muscled she barely came up to his shoulder once she'd kicked off her heels. His hands cupped her bottom and pulled her against him, letting her feel the weight and heft of his erection. Even through the barrier of their clothes it was the most erotic feeling to have him pulse and pound against her. He kissed her lingeringly, deeply, taking his time to build her need of him until she was whimpering, gasping, clawing at him to get him naked.

'What's the hurry?' he said against the side of her neck.

Izzy kissed his mouth, his chin, and then flicked the tip of her tongue into the dish below his Adam's apple. 'I've heard things go at a much slower pace in the Outback but I didn't realise that included sex.'

He gave a little rumble of laughter and pulled the zipper down the back of her dress in a single lightning-fast movement. 'You want speed, sweetheart?' He unclipped her bra and tossed it to the floor. 'Then let's see if we can pick up the pace a bit, shall we?'

Izzy whooshed out a breath as she landed on her back on the mattress with a little bounce. As quickly as he had removed her clothes, he got rid of his own, coming down over her, gloriously, deliciously naked.

The sexy entanglement of limbs, of long and hard and toned and tanned and hair-roughened muscles entwining with softer, smoother, shorter ones made everything that was feminine in her roll over in delight. His hands, those gorgeously manly hands, sexily grazed the soft skin of her breasts. That sizzling-hot male mouth with its surrounding stubble suckled on each one in turn, the right one first and then the left, the suction just right, the pressure and tug of his teeth perfect, the roll and sweep of his tongue mind-blowing.

Izzy had never been all that vocal during sex in the past. The occasional sigh or murmur perhaps—sometimes just to feed Richard's ego rather than from feeling anything spectacular herself—but nothing like the gasps and whimpers that were coming out of her now. It wasn't just Zach's mouth that was wreaking such havoc on her senses but the feel and shape of his body as it pinned hers to the bed. Not too heavy, not awkward or clumsy, but potent and powerful, determined and yet respectful.

He moved down from her breasts to sear a scorching pathway to her bellybutton and beyond. She automatically tensed when he came to the seam of her body, but immediately sensing her hesitation he placed his palm over her lower abdomen to calm her. 'Trust me, Izzy. I can make it good for you.'

Should she tell him she had never experienced such intimacy before? She didn't want to make Richard sound like a prude, but the truth was he had made it clear early on in their relationship that he found oral sex distasteful. In spite of her knowledge as a doctor to the contrary, his attitude had made her feel as if her body was unpleasant, unattractive and somehow defective. 'Um…I've never done it before… I mean no one's done it to me…'

He looked at her quizzically. 'Your ex didn't?'

She knew she was blushing. But rather than hide it she decided to be honest with him. 'It wasn't Richard's thing.'

He was still frowning. 'But it's one of the best ways for a woman to have an orgasm.'

Izzy was silent for just a second or two too long.

He cocked an eyebrow at her questioningly. 'You have had an orgasm, right?'

'Of course...' Majorly fiery blush this time. 'Plenty of times.'

'Izzy.' The way Zach said her name was like a parent catching a child out for lying.

'It was hard for me to get there...I always took too long to get in the mood and then Richard would pressure me and I...' Izzy gave him a helpless look '...I usually faked it.'

His frown had made a pleat between his grey eyes. 'Usually?'

'Mostly.' She bit her lip at his look. 'It was easier that way. I didn't want to hurt Richard's feelings or make him feel inadequate. Seems to me some men have such fragile egos when it comes to their sexual prowess.'

He stroked her face with his fingers. 'Being able to satisfy a partner is one of the most enjoyable aspects of sex. I want you to enjoy it, Izzy. Don't pretend with me. Be honest. Take all the time you need.'

Izzy pressed her lips against his. 'If we take too long Max might wonder what we're doing.'

He smiled against her mouth. 'I reckon he's got a pretty fair idea.' And then he kissed her.

CHAPTER ELEVEN

'Thank you so much for stepping in last night,' Margie said when Izzy arrived at work the next morning. 'Doug and I had the most wonderful time. It was as if the last twenty-three years hadn't happened. We talked for hours and hours. Just as well Zach didn't get back till midnight.' Her eyes twinkled meaningfully. 'Must have been a pretty decent dinner you cooked for him. He looked very satisfied.'

Izzy had all but given up on trying to disguise her blush. Her whole body was still glowing from the passionate lovemaking she had experienced in Zach's arms last night. He had been both tender and demanding, insisting on a level of physical honesty from her that was way outside her experience. But she had loved every earth-shattering second of it.

The things she had discovered about her body had amazed her. It was capable of intense and repeated orgasms. Zach had taught her how to relax enough to embrace the powerful sensations, to let her inhibitions go, to stop over-thinking and worrying she wasn't doing things according to a schedule. He had let her choose her own timetable and his pleasure when it had come had been just as intense as hers. That the pleasure had been mutual had given their sensual encounter a depth, an almost sacred aspect she'd found strangely moving.

The only niggling worry she had was how was she going to move on after their fling was over? Falling in love with him or anyone was not part of her plan for her six months away from home. She had only just extricated herself from a long-term relationship. The last thing she wanted was to tie herself up in another one, even if Zach was the most intriguing and attractive man she had met in a long time. Strike that—had *ever* met.

'Yes, well, there's certainly nothing wrong with his appetite,' Izzy said as she popped her bag into the cupboard next to the patients' filing shelves.

'Are you going to see him again?'

'I see him practically every day.' Izzy straightened her skirt as she turned round. 'In a town this size everyone sees everyone every day.'

Margie pursed her lips in a you-can't-fool-me manner. 'You know what I mean. Are you officially a couple? I know the gossip started the moment you showed up in town but that was Charles Redbank's doing. He just wanted to make trouble. He's never forgiven Zach for booking him for speeding a couple of months back.'

'We're not officially anything.' Izzy resented even having to say that much. She wasn't used to discussing her private life with anyone other than Hannah and even then there were some things she wasn't prepared to reveal. Even to herself.

'It'd be lovely if you stayed on a bit longer,' Margie said. 'Everyone loves you. Even that old sourpuss Ida Jensen thinks you're an angel now that you've sorted out her blood-pressure medication. And Peggy McLeod's thrilled you suggested she help start up the playgroup again. She's already got a heap of toys and play equipment donated from the locals. She even got Caitlyn Graham's boyfriend, Wayne Brody, to donate some. He dropped by a bag of stuff yesterday, most of it brand new. Wasn't that nice of him?'

Izzy kept her features schooled, even though inside she was fuming. 'Unbelievably nice of him.'

Margie glanced at the diary. 'Your first patient isn't until nine-thirty. You've got time for a coffee. Want me to make you one here or shall I run up to the general store and get you a latte from Jim's new machine?'

'I'll go,' Izzy said. 'There's something I want to see Sergeant Fletcher about on the way past.'

Zach was typing up an incident report on the computer at the station when he heard the sound of footsteps coming up the path. He knew it was Izzy even before he looked up to check. His skin started to tingle; it hadn't stopped tingling since last night, but it went up a gear when he caught a whiff of summer flowers. He had gone home last night with her fragrance lingering on his skin. He had even considered skipping a shower this morning to keep it there. The way she had come apart in his arms had not only thrilled him, it had made him feel something he hadn't expected to feel.

Didn't want to feel.

He stood as she came in. 'Morning.' He knew he sounded a bit formal but he was having trouble getting that feeling he didn't want to feel back in the box where he had stashed it last night.

His manner obviously annoyed her for her brow puckered in a frown and her lips pulled tight. 'Sorry to disturb you while you're busy, but I forgot to tell you something last night.'

Would this be the bit about how she didn't want to continue their fling? He mentally prepared himself, keeping his face as blank as possible. 'Fire away.'

Her hands were balled into tight little fists by her sides, her cheeks like two bright red apples, and her toffee-brown eyes flashing. 'The toys you left for Caitlyn's kids?' She didn't give him time to say anything in response but continued; 'Wayne wouldn't let her give them to the kids.'

Zach was so relieved her tirade wasn't about ending their affair it took him a moment to respond. 'There's not much I can do about that. They were a gift and if Caitlyn didn't want to accept—'

'You're not listening to me,' she said with a little stamp of her foot. 'Caitlyn would've loved them for the kids, I know she would, she's too frightened to stand up to Wayne. But even worse than that, he passed them off as his own donation to Peggy McLeod for the community centre playgroup. He's passing off *your* gift as his own largesse. It makes my blood boil so much I want to explode!'

He came round from behind the desk and took her trembling-with-rage shoulders in his hands. 'Hey, it's not worth getting upset about it. At least the kids will have a chance to play with the toys when they go to the centre.'

Her pretty little face was scrunched up in a furious scowl. 'If that control freak lets them go. He'll probably put a stop to that too. Can't you do something? Like arrest him for making a false declaration of generosity or something?'

Zach fought back a smile as he rubbed his hands up and down her silky arms. 'My experience with guys like him is that the more you show how much they get under your skin the more they enjoy it. Best thing you can do is support Caitlyn and the kids. Helping to build up her confidence as a parent is a great start.'

She let out a sign that released her tense shoulders. 'I guess you're right…'

He tipped up her chin and meshed his gaze with her still troubled one. 'Do you have any plans for tonight?'

Her eyes lost their dullness and began to sparkle. 'I don't know. I'll have to check what Max has got planned. He might want to hang out. Watch a movie or something. He gets lonely if he's left on his own too long.'

Zach had no hope of suppressing his smile. 'Then why don't we take him on a picnic out to Blake's waterhole? I'll bring the food. I'll pick you up at six-thirty so we can catch the sunset.'

She scrunched up her face again but her eyes were dancing. 'I'm not sure Max has a pair of bathers.'

Zach gave her a glinting smile as he brought his mouth down to hers. 'Tell him he won't need them.'

Izzy spread the picnic blanket down over a patch of sunburned grass near the waterhole while Zach brought the picnic basket and their towels from the car. The sun was still high and hot enough to crisp and crackle the air with the sound of cicadas. But down by the water's edge the smell of the dusty earth was relieved by the earthy scent of cool, deep water shadowed by the overhanging craggy-armed gums. Long gold fingers of sunlight were poking between the branches to gild the water, along with a light breeze that was playfully tickling the surface.

Zach put the picnic basket down on the blanket. 'Swim first or would you like a cold drink?'

Izzy looked at him, dressed in faded blue denim jeans with their one tattered knee, his light grey body-hugging T-shirt showcasing every toned muscle of his chest and shoulders and abdomen. He looked strong and fit and capable, the sort of man you would go to in a crisis. The sort of man you could depend on, a man who was not only strong on the outside but had an inner reserve of calm deliberation. He was the sort of man who wasn't daunted by hard work or a challenging task. The way he had moved back to the bush to help his father even though it had cost him his relationship with his fiancée confirmed it. He was a man of principles, conviction. Loyalty.

It made her think of Richard, who within a couple of days of her ending their relationship had found a replacement.

Zach, on the other hand, had spent the last eighteen months quietly grieving the loss of his relationship and the future he had planned for himself, devoting his time to his father and the community. Doing whatever it took, no matter how difficult, to help his father come to terms with the limitations that had been placed on him. He didn't complain. He didn't grouse or whinge about it. He just got on with it.

Zach must have mistaken her silence for something else. 'There are no nasties in the water, if that's what's putting you off. An eel or two, a few tadpoles and frogs but nothing to be too worried about.'

A shiver of unease slithered down her spine. 'Snakes?'

'They're definitely about but more will see you than you see them.' He gave her a quick grin. 'I'll go in first and scare them away, OK?'

'Big, brave man.'

He tugged his T-shirt over his head and tossed it onto one of the sun-warmed rocks nearby. 'Yeah, well, that's more than I can say about that roommate of yours squibbing at the last minute.'

Izzy feasted her eyes on his washboard stomach and then her heart gave a little flip as he reached for the zipper on his jeans. She disguised her reaction behind humour but was sure he wasn't fooled for a second. 'It wasn't that he was scared or anything. He's got very sensitive skin. He was worried about mosquitoes. One prick and he might never recover.'

Zach's smile made her skin lift up in goose-bumps as big as the gravel they had driven over earlier. He came and stood right in front of her, dressed in nothing but his shape-hugging black underwear. He flicked the collar of her lightweight cotton blouse with two of his fingers. 'Need some help getting your gear off?'

Izzy found it hard to breathe with him so deliciously close. The smell of him, the citrus and physically active man smell of him made her insides squirm with longing. His grey-blue eyes were glinting, his mouth slanted in a sexy smile that never failed to make her feminine core contract and release in want. Her body remembered every stroke and glide and powerful thrust of his inside hers last night. Her feminine muscles tightened in feverish anticipation, the musky, silky moisture of her body automatically activated in response to his intimate proximity. 'Are you offering to do a strip search, Sergeant Fletcher?' she asked with a flirty smile.

His eyes gleamed with sensual promise as his fingers went to the buttons on her shirt. 'Let's see what you've got hidden under here, shall we?'

One by one he undid each button, somehow making it into a game of intense eroticism. His fingers scorched her skin each time he released another button from its tiny buttonhole, the action triggering yet another pulse of primal longing deep in her flesh. He peeled the shirt off her shoulders, and then tracked his finger down between her breasts, still encased in her bra. 'Beautiful.'

How one word uttered in that deep, husky tone could make her feel like a supermodel was beyond her. It wasn't just a line, a throw-away comment to get what he wanted. She knew he meant it. She could feel it in his touch, the gentle way he had of cupping her breasts once he'd released her bra, the way his thumbs stroked over her nipples with a touch that was both achingly tender and yet tantalisingly arousing.

Her cotton summer skirt was next to go, the zip going down, the little hoop of fabric circling her ankles before he took her hand and helped her step away from it like stepping out of a puddle. He put a warm, work-roughened hand to the curve of her hip just above the line of her knickers, holding her close enough to the potent heat of his body for her to feel his reaction to her closeness.

He was powerfully erect. She could feel the thrum of his blood through the lace of her knickers, the hot, urgent pressure of him stirring her senses into frantic overload.

He touched her then, a single stroke down the lace-covered seam of her body, a teasing taste of the intimate invasion to come. She whimpered as he slid her knickers aside, waiting a heart-stopping beat before he touched her again, skin on skin.

Izzy tugged his underwear down so she could do the same to him, taking him in her hands, stroking him, caressing the silky steel of him until he was breathing as raggedly as she was.

He slipped a finger inside her, swallowing her gasp as his mouth came down on hers. His kiss was passionate, thorough, and intensely erotic as his tongue tangled with hers in a cat-and-mouse caper.

Izzy's caressing of him became bolder, squeezing and releasing, smoothing up and down his length, running her fingertip over the ooze of his essence, breathing in the musky scent of mutual arousal.

There was something wildly, deeply primitive about being naked with a man in the bush. No sounds other than their hectic breathing and those of nature. The distant warble of magpies, the throaty arck-arck of a crow flying overhead, the whisper of the breeze moving through the gum leaves, sounding like thousands of finger-length strips of tinsel paper being jostled together.

Zach pressed her down on the tartan blanket, pushing the picnic things out of the way with his elbow, quickly sourcing a condom before entering her with a thrust that made her cry out with bone-deep pleasure. He set a fast rhythm that was as primal as their surroundings, the intensity of it thrilling her senses in a way she had never thought possible just a few short weeks ago. Her life in England had never felt more distant. It was like having another completely different identity that belonged back there.

Over there she was a buttoned-up girl who had spent

years of her life pretending to be happy, pleasing others rather than pleasing herself.

Out here she was a wild and wanton woman, having smoking-hot sex with a man she hadn't known a fortnight ago.

And now...now she was rocking in his arms as if her world began and ended with him. The physicality of their relationship was shocking, the blunt, almost brutal honesty of the needs of their bodies as they strove for completion was as carnal as two wild animals mating. Even the sound of her cries as she came were those of a woman she didn't know, had never encountered before. Wild, shrieking cries that spoke of a depth of passion that had never been tapped into or expressed before.

Zach's release was not as vocal but Izzy felt the power of it as he tensed, pumped and then flowed.

He didn't move for a long moment. His body rested on hers in the aftermath, his breathing slowly returning to normal as she stroked her hands up and down his back and shoulders, their bodies still intimately joined.

'I think there's a pebble sticking into my butt,' Izzy finally said.

He rolled her over so she was lying on top of him, his eyes heavily lidded, sleepy with satiation. 'Better?'

'Much.'

He circled her right breast with a lazy finger. 'Ever skinny dipped before?'

'Not with a man present.' Izzy gave him a wry smile. 'I did it with Hannah and a couple of other girlfriends when we were thirteen at my birthday party. It was a dare.'

His finger made a slow, nerve-tingling circuit of her

other breast. 'Is that how the crazy birthday stuff with her started?'

Izzy sent her own fingers on an exploration of his flat brown nipple nestled amongst his springy chest hair. 'Come to think of it, yes. She was always on about me being too worried about what other people thought. She made it her mission in life to shock me out of my "aristocratic mediocrity", as she calls it.'

He stroked his hand over the flank of her thigh. 'Somehow mediocre isn't the first word that comes to mind when I think of you.'

Izzy angled her head at him. 'So what word does?'

He gave her a slow smile that crinkled up the corners of his eyes in a devastatingly attractive manner. 'Cute. Funny. Sexy.'

She traced the outline of his smile with her fingertip. 'I never felt sexy before. Not the way I do with you.' She bit down on her lip, wondering if she'd been too honest, revealed too much.

He brushed her lower lip with his thumb. 'You do that a lot.'

'What?'

'Bite your lip.'

Izzy had to stop her teeth from doing it again. 'It's a nervous habit. Half the time I'm not even aware I'm doing it.'

His thumb caressed her lip as if soothing it from the assault of her teeth. 'Why don't you come down here and bite mine instead?'

Izzy leaned down and started nibbling at his lower lip, using her teeth to tug and tease. She used her tongue to sweep over where her teeth had been, before starting the process all over again. Nip. Tug. Nip. Tug.

He gave little grunts of approval, one of his hands splayed in her hair as he held her head close to his. 'Harder,' he commanded.

A shudder of pleasure shimmied down her spine as his hand fisted in her hair. She pulled at his lip with her teeth, stroked it with her tongue and then pushed her tongue into his mouth to meet his. Zach murmured his pleasure and took control of the kiss, his masterful tongue darting and diving around hers.

It was an exhilarating kiss, wild and abandoned and yet still with an element of tenderness that ambushed her emotionally.

She wasn't supposed to be feeling anything but lust for this man.

This was a fling.

A casual hook-up like all her girlfriends experienced from time to time. It was a chance to own her sexuality, to express it without the confining and formal bounds of a relationship.

She was only here for another couple of weeks. She was moving on to new sights and experiences, filling her six months away from home with adventure and memories to look back on in the years to come.

Falling in love would be a crazy…a totally disastrous thing to do…

Izzy eased off Zach while he dealt with the condom. She gathered her tousled hair and tied it into a makeshift knot, using the tresses as an anchor. Her body tingled with the memory of his touch as she got to her feet, tiny aftershocks of pleasure rippling through her.

She was dazed by sensational sex, that's all it was.

It wasn't love. How could it be?

Maybe it was time to cool off.

'Are you sure it's safe to swim here?'

'Not for diving but it's fine for a dip.' He took her hand and led her down to the water. 'Not quite St Barts, is it?'

Izzy glanced at him. 'You've been there?'

'Once.' He looked out over the water as if he was seeing the exclusive Caribbean holiday destination in his mind's eye, his mouth curled up in a cynical arc. 'With my mother and her new family when I was fourteen. Cost her husband a packet. I'm sure he only took us all there to make a point of how good her life was with him instead of my father. I didn't go on holidays with them after that. I got tired of having all that wealth thrust in my face.'

Izzy moved her fingers against his. 'I hated most of my family holidays. I'm sure we only went to most of the places we went to because that's where my parents thought people expected to see us. Skiing at exclusive lodges in Aspen. Sailing around the Mediterranean on yachts that cost more than most people ever see in a lifetime. I would've loved to go camping under the stars in the wilderness but, no, it was butlers and chauffeurs and five stars all the way.'

He looked at her with a wry smile tilting his mouth. 'Funny, isn't it, that you always want what you don't have?'

I have what I want right now. Izzy quickly filed away the thought. She looked down at the mud that was squelching between her toes. The water was refreshingly cool against her heated skin. She went in a little further, holding Zach's hand for balance until she was waist deep. 'Mmm, that's lovely.' She went in a bit deeper but something cold and slimy brushed against her leg and she yelped and sprang back and clung to Zach like a limpet. 'Eeek! What was that?'

He held her against him, laughing softly. 'It was just a bit of weed. Nothing to worry about. You're safe with me.'

Her arms were locked around his neck, her legs wrapped around his waist and her mouth within touching distance of his. She watched as his gaze went to her mouth, the way his lashes lowered in that sleepily hooded way a man did when he was thinking about sex. A new wave of desire rolled through her as his mouth came down and fused with hers.

You're safe with me.

Izzy wasn't safe. Not the way she wanted to be. Not the way she needed to be.

She was in very great danger indeed.

CHAPTER TWELVE

As Zach packed the picnic things back in the car Izzy looked up at the brilliant night sky with its scattering of stars like handfuls of diamonds flung across a bolt of dark blue velvet. The air was still warm and the night orchestra's chorus had recruited two extra voices: a tawny frogmouth owl and a vixen fox, looking for a mate.

That distinctive bark was a sound from home, making Izzy feel a sudden pang of homesickness. She wondered if sounds like those of a lonely feral fox had caused Zach's mother to grieve for the life she had left behind. Had the years fighting drought and dust and flies or floods and failed crops and flyblown sheep finally broken her spirit? Or had she simply fallen out of love with her husband? Leaving a husband one no longer loved was understandable, but leaving a child to travel to the other side of the world was something else again. Leaving Zach behind must have been a very difficult decision.

Izzy couldn't imagine a mother choosing her freedom over her child, but she recognised that not all mothers found the experience as satisfying and fulfilling as others.

Leaving Zach behind...

The words reverberated inside her head. That was what she would have to do in a matter of a fortnight. She would never see him again. He would move on with his life, no doubt in a year or two find a good, sensible, no-nonsense country girl to settle down with, raise a family and work the land as his father and grandfather and forebears had done before him. She imagined him sitting at the scrubbed pine kitchen table at Fletcher Downs homestead surrounded by his wife and children. He would make a wonderful father. She had seen him with Caitlyn's children, generous, gentle and calm.

Izzy heard his footfall on the gravel as he came to join her. 'Have you found the Southern Cross?' he asked.

'I think so.' She pointed to a constellation of stars in the south. 'Is that it there?'

He followed the line of her arm and nodded. 'Yep, that's it. Good work. You must've done your research.'

Izzy turned and looked at him, something in her heart contracting as if a hand had grabbed at it and squeezed. 'Would you ever consider living somewhere else?' she asked.

A frown flickered over his brow. 'You mean like back in the city?'

Izzy wasn't sure what she meant. She wasn't sure why she had even asked. 'Will you quit your work as a cop and take over Fletcher Downs once your father officially retires?'

He looked back at the dark overturned bowl of the sky, his gaze going all the way to the horizon, where a thin lip of light lingered just before the sun dipped to wake the other side of the world. 'I love my work as a cop…well, most of the time. But the land is in my blood. The Fletcher name goes back a long way in these parts, all the way back to the first European settlers. I'm my dad's only heir. I can't afford to pay a manager for ever. The property would have to be sold if I didn't take it on full time.'

'But is that what *you* want?'

He continued to focus on the distant horizon with a grim set to his features. 'What I want is my dad to get back to full health and mobility but that doesn't look like it's going to happen any time soon.'

'But at least he's becoming more socially active,' Izzy said. 'That's a great step forward. Margie's determined to get him out more. It would be so nice if they got together, don't you think?'

He looked back at her with that same grave look. 'My father will never get married again. He's been burned once. He would never go back for a second dose.'

'But that's crazy,' Izzy said. 'Margie loves him. She's loved him since she was a girl. They belong together. Anyone can see that.'

His lip curled upwards but it wasn't so much mocking as wry. 'Stick to your medical journals, Izzy. Those romance novels you read are messing with your head.'

It's not my head they're messing with, Izzy thought as she followed him back to the car.

It was her heart.

Zach brought a beer out to his father on the veranda a couple of days later. 'Here you go. But only the one. Remember what the doctor said about drinking plenty of clear fluids.'

'Thanks.' Doug took a long sip, and then let a silence slip past before asking, 'You seeing her tonight?'

Zach reached down to tickle Popeye's ears. 'Not tonight.'

'Wise of you.'

'What's that supposed to mean?'

Doug took another sip of his beer before answering. 'Better not get too used to having her around. She's going to be packing up and leaving before you know it.'

Zach tried to ignore the savage twist of his insides at the thought of Izzy driving out of town once her locum was up. He'd heard a whisper the locals were going to use the Shearers' Ball as a send-off for her. William Sawyer and his wife would be back from their trip soon and life would return to normal in Jerringa Ridge.

Normal.

What a weird word to describe his life. When had it ever been normal? Growing up since the age of ten without a mother. Years of putting up with his father's ongoing bitterness over his marriage break-up. For years he hadn't even been able to mention his mother without his father flinching as if he had landed a punch on him.

Dealing with the conflicted emotions of visiting his mother in her gracious home in Surrey, where he didn't fit in with the formal furniture or her even more formal ridiculously wealthy new husband who never seemed to wear anything but a suit and a silk cravat, even on St Barts. Those gut-wrenching where-do-I-belong feelings intensifying once her new sons Jules and Oliver had been born. Coming back home and feeling just as conflicted trying to settle back in to life at Fletcher Downs or at boarding school.

Always feeling the outsider.

'I know what I'm doing, Dad.'

His father glanced at him briefly before turning to look at the light fading over the paddocks. It was a full minute, maybe longer before he spoke. 'I'm not going to get any better than this, am I? No point pretending I am.'

Zach found the sudden shift in conversation disorienting. 'Sure you are. You're doing fine.' He was doing it again. It was his fall-back position. A pattern of the last twenty-three years he couldn't seem to get out of—playing Pollyanna to his father's woe-is-me moods. He could recall all the pep-talk phrases he'd used in the past: *Time heals everything. You'll find someone else. Take it one day at a time. Baby steps. Everything happens for a reason.*

Doug's hand tightened on his can of beer until the aluminium crackled. 'I should've married Margie. I should've done it years ago. Now it's too late.'

It's never too late was on the tip of Zach's tongue but he refrained from voicing it. 'Is that what Margie wants? Marriage?'

'It's what most women want, isn't it?' His father gave his beer can another crunch. 'A husband, a family, a home they can be proud of. Security.'

'Margie's already got a family and a house and her job is secure,' Zach said. 'Seems to me what she wants is companionship.'

His father's top lip curled in a manner so like his own it was disquieting to witness. 'And what sort of companion am I? I can't even get on a stepladder and change a bloody light bulb.'

'There's more to a relationship than who puts out the garbage or takes the dog for a walk,' Zach said.

His father didn't seem to be listening. He was still looking out over the paddocks with a frown between his eyes. 'I didn't see it at the time...all those years ago I didn't see Margie for who she was. She was always just one of the local girls, fun to be around but didn't stand out. Then I met your mother.' He made a self-deprecating sound. 'What a fool I was to think I could make someone like her happy. I tried for ten years to keep her. Ten years of living with the dread she would one day pack up and leave. And then she did.' He clicked his fingers. *Snap.* 'She was gone.'

Zach remembered it all too well. He could still remember exactly where he had been standing on the veranda as he'd watched his mother drive away. He had gripped the veranda rail so tightly his hands had ached for days. He had watched with his heart feeling as heavy as a headstone in his chest. His mouth had been as dry as the red dust his mother's car had stirred up as she'd wheeled away.

For weeks, months, even years every time he heard a car come up the long driveway he would feel his heart leap in hope that she was coming back.

She never did.

Doug looked at Zach. 'It wasn't her fault. Not all of it. I was fighting to keep this place going after your grandfather died and then your grandmother so soon after. I didn't give her the attention she needed. You can't take an orchid out of an English conservatory and expect it to survive in the Outback. You have to nurture it, protect it.'

'Do you still love her?'

Doug's mouth twisted. 'There's a part of me that will always love your mother. Maybe not the same way

I did. It's like keeping that old pair of work boots near the back door. I'm not quite ready to part with them yet.'

'I'm not sure Mum would appreciate being compared to a pair of your old smelly work boots,' Zach said wryly, thinking of his mother's penchant for cashmere and pearls and designer shoes.

A small sad smile skirted around the edges of Doug's mouth. 'No...probably not.'

A silence passed.

'Why's it too late for you and Margie?' Zach asked. 'You're only fifty-eight. She's, what? Fifty-two or -three? You could have a good thirty or forty years together.'

'Look at me, Zach.' His father's eyes glittered with tightly held-back emotion. 'Take a good look. I'm like this now, shuffling about like a man in his eighties. What am I going to be like in five or even ten years' time? You heard what the specialist said. I was lucky to get this far. I can't do it to Margie. I can't turn her into a carer instead of a wife and lover. It'd make her hate me.' His chin quivered as he fought to keep his voice under control. 'I couldn't bear to have another woman I love end up hating me.'

'I think you're underestimating Margie,' Zach said. 'She's not like Mum. She's strong and dependable and loyal.'

'And you're such a big expert on women, aren't you, Zach? You've got one broken engagement on the leader board already. How soon before there's another?'

'There's not going to be another.'

'Why?' His father's lip was still up in that nasty little curl. 'Because you won't risk asking her, will you?'

Zach could barely get the words out through his clenched teeth. 'Ask who?'

His father pushed himself to his feet, nailing Zach with his gaze. 'That toffee-nosed little doctor you spend every spare moment of your time with.'

'I'm not in love with Isabella Courtney.'

'No, of course you're not.' Doug gave a scornful grunt of laughter. 'Keep on telling yourself that, son. If nothing else, it'll make the day she leaves a little easier on you.'

Izzy knew it was cowardly of her to pretend to be busy with catching up on emails and work-related stuff two nights in a row but spending all her spare time with Zach was making it increasingly difficult for her to keep her emotions separate from the physical side of their relationship. No wonder sex was called making love. Every look, every touch, every kiss, every spine-tingling orgasm seemed to up the ante until she wasn't sure what she felt any more. Was it love or was it lust?

Had it been a mistake to indulge in an affair with him? She had spent four years making love—*having sex*—with Richard and had never felt anything like the depth of feeling she did with Zach, and she had only known him three weeks.

And there was only one to go.

Margie looked very downcast when Izzy got to the clinic the next morning. She was sitting behind the reception desk with red-rimmed eyes and her shoulders slumped. 'Don't ask.'

'Doug?'

Margie reached for a tissue from the box on her desk. 'He said it's best if we don't see each other any more, only as friends. I've been friends with him for most of my life but it's not enough. I want more.'

'Oh, Margie, I'm so sorry. I thought things were going so well.'

Margie dabbed at her eyes. 'It's my fault for thinking I could change his mind. I should have left well alone. Now he knows how I feel about him it makes me feel so stupid. Like a lovesick schoolgirl or something.'

'Is there anything I can do?'

'Not unless you can make him fall out of love with his ex-wife.'

Izzy frowned. 'Do you really think that's what it's about?'

'What else could it be? Olivia was his grand passion.' Margie plucked another tissue out of the box and blew her nose.

'What if it's more to do with his limitations? He's a proud man. Having to rely on others for help must be really tough on someone like him.'

'But I love him. I don't care if he can't get around the way he used to. Why can't he just accept that I love him no matter what?'

Izzy gave her a sympathetic look. 'Maybe he needs more time. From what I've read of his notes, his injuries were pretty severe. And this latest bout of renal colic has probably freaked him out a bit. It's very common for every ache or pain in someone who's suffered a major illness or trauma to get magnified in their head.'

Margie gave a sound of agreement. 'Well, enough about me and my troubles. How are you and Zach getting on?'

'Fine.'

'Just fine?'

Izzy picked off a yellowed leaf from the pot plant on

the counter. 'There's nothing serious going on between us. We both know and understand that.'

'Would you like it to be more?'

'I'm leaving at the end of next week.'

'That's not the answer I was looking for,' Margie said.

'It's the only one I'm prepared to give.'

Margie looked at her thoughtfully for a lengthy moment. 'Don't make the same mistake I made, Izzy. I should've told Doug years ago what I felt for him. Now it's too late.'

'I spent four years with a man and then realised I didn't love him enough to marry him,' Izzy said. 'What makes you think I would be so confident about my feelings after less than four weeks?'

Margie gave her a sage look. 'Because when you know you just know.'

CHAPTER THIRTEEN

Izzy walked down to the community centre during her lunch break. She had arranged to meet Peggy McLeod there as well as Caitlyn Graham, who had finally agreed to work with Peggy in a mentor and mentee role. Peggy as a mother and grandmother with years of wisdom and experience working in the community was just what Caitlyn needed as a role model. Peggy had even offered to babysit Skylar occasionally when the boys were at school so Caitlyn could get a bit of a break. But when Izzy arrived at the centre Peggy was on her own.

'Where's Caitlyn?'

Peggy gave Izzy a miffed look over her shoulder as she placed a box of building blocks on the shelves one of the local farmers had made specially. 'Decided she had better things to do.'

'But I confirmed it with her yesterday,' Izzy said. 'She said she was looking forward to it. It was the first time I'd ever seen her excited about something.'

'Yes, well, she called me not five minutes ago and told me she's changed her mind.'

Changed her mind or had it changed for her? Izzy wondered. 'I think I'd better go and check on her. Maybe one of the kids is sick or something.'

'The boys are at school,' Peggy said. 'I waved to them in the playground when I drove past.'

'Maybe Skylar's sick.'

'Then why didn't she just say so?'

Izzy frowned. 'What *did* she say?'

Peggy pursed her lips. 'Just that she'd changed her mind. Told me she didn't want me babysitting for her either. I've brought up five kids and I'm a grandmother twelve times over. What does she think I am? An axe murderer or something?'

'Don't take it personally,' Izzy said. 'She's not used to having anyone step in and help her. I'll duck out there now and see if I can get her to change her mind.'

Izzy thought about calling Zach to come with her but changed her mind at the last minute. His car wasn't at the station in any case and she didn't want to make a big issue out of what could just be a case of Caitlyn's lack of self-esteem kicking in. She'd tried calling her a couple of times but the phone had gone to message bank.

Caitlyn's old car was parked near the house but apart from the frenzied barking of the dog near the tank stand there was no sign of life. Izzy walked tentatively to the front door, saying, 'Nice doggy, good doggy,' with as much sincerity as she could muster. She put her hand up to knock but the door suddenly opened and she found herself face to face with a thick-set man in his late twenties, who was even scarier than the dog lunging on its chain to her left.

'What do you want?' the man snarled.

'Um... Hello, is Caitlyn home? I'm Isabella Courtney, the locum filling in for—'

'Did she call you?'

'No, I just thought I'd drop past and—'

'She don't need no doctor so you can get back in your fancy car and get the hell out of here.'

The sound of Skylar crying piteously in one of the back rooms of the house made Izzy's heart lurch. 'Is Skylar OK? She sounds terribly upset. Is she—?'

'You want me to let the dog off?' His cold eyes glared at her through the tattered mesh of the screen door.

Izzy garnered what was left of her courage. She straightened her shoulders and looked him in the eye with what she hoped looked like steely determination. 'I'd like to talk to Caitlyn before I leave.'

Wayne suddenly shoved the screen door wide open, which forced her to take a couple of rapid steps backwards that sent her backwards off the veranda to land in an ungainly heap on her bottom in the dust. 'I said clear off,' he said.

Izzy scrambled to her feet, feeling a fool and a coward and so angry and utterly powerless she wanted to scream. But she knew the best thing to do was to leave and call Zach as soon as she was out of danger. She dusted off the back of her skirt and walked back to her car with as much dignity as she could muster. Her hand trembled uncontrollably as she tried to get her car key in the ignition slot to start the engine. It took her five tries to do it. Her heart was hammering in her chest and terrified sobs were choking out of her throat as she drove out of the driveway.

Zach was on the road when he got a distressed call from Izzy. 'Hey, slow down, sweetheart. I can't understand a word you're saying.'

She was crying and gasping, her breathing so erratic

it sounded like she was choking. 'I think Wayne's hurt Caitlyn. She didn't turn up at the playgroup. I heard Skylar screaming in the background. I think he'd been drinking. I could smell it. You have to do something. You have to hurry.'

'Where are you?'

'I—I'm on the road just past the t-turnoff.'

'Stop driving. Pull over. Do it right now.' He didn't let out his breath until he heard her do as he'd commanded. 'Good girl. Now wait for me. I'm only a few minutes away. I'll call Rob for back-up. Just stay put, OK?'

'OK…'

Zach called his colleague and quickly filled him in. He drove as fast as he could to where Izzy was parked on the side of the road. She was as white as a stick of chalk and tumbled out of the car even before he had pulled to a halt.

He gathered her close, reassuring himself she was all right before he put her from him. 'I'm going to check things out. I've called the volunteer ambulance and put them on standby. I want you to stay here until I see what the go is. I'll call you if we need you. It might not be as serious as you think.'

Her eyes looked as big as a Shetland pony's. 'You won't get hurt, will you?'

'Course not.' He quickly kissed her on the forehead. 'I've got a gun, remember?'

Izzy took a steadying breath as she waited for Zach to contact her. It seemed like ten hours but it was only ten minutes before he called her to inform her Caitlyn and Skylar were fine. 'Brody was his usual charming self,' he said. 'But Caitlyn insisted he hadn't hurt her or the child. She didn't appear to have any marks or bruises and the child seemed settled enough. She was sound asleep when I looked in on her. Apparently Brody was insisting she take a nap and wouldn't let Caitlyn go in to comfort her.'

'And you believed him?'

'I can't arrest him without evidence and Caitlyn swears he didn't do anything.'

Izzy blew out a breath of frustration. 'If he didn't hurt her today he will do sooner or later. I just know it.'

'Welcome to the world of tricky relationships.'

They can't get any trickier than the one I'm in, Izzy thought. 'Can I see you after work?'

'Not too busy with emails and video calls to your friends?'

'Not tonight.'

'Good,' he said. 'I happen to be free too.'

Izzy got back to the clinic in time to see her list of afternoon patients but just as she was about to finish for the day Margie popped her head into her consulting room. 'You got a minute?'

'Sure.' Izzy put down the pen she had been using to write up her last patient's details, mentally preparing herself for another emotional outpouring of Margie's unrequited love story. It wasn't that she didn't want to listen or support her. It was just too close to what she was feeling about Zach. How could it be possible to fall in love with someone so quickly? Did that sort of thing really happen or was that just in Hollywood movies? Was she imagining how she felt? Was it just this crazy lust fest she had going on with him that was colouring her judgement?

Margie rolled her lips together, looking awkward and embarrassed as she came into the room. 'It's not about Doug or anything like that… It's a personal thing. A health thing.'

'What's the problem?'

'I found a lump.'

'In your breast?'

Margie nodded, and then gave her lower lip a little chew. 'I've been a bit slack about doing my own checks but when you ordered that mammogram for Kathleen Fisher earlier today it got me thinking. I went to the bathroom just then. I found a lump.'

Izzy got up from her chair and came from behind the desk. 'Hop on the examination table and I'll have a feel of it for you. Try not to worry too much. Breast tissue can go through lots of changes for any number of reasons.'

Margie lay back on the table and unbuttoned her blouse and unclipped her bra. 'I can't believe I've been so stupid not to check my own breasts. I haven't done it for months, maybe even a couple of years.'

Izzy palpated Margie's left breast where, high in the upper part, there was a definite firm nodule, about the size of a walnut. 'You're right, there is a lump there. Is it tender at all?'

'No, it's not sore at all. It's cancer, isn't it?'

'Hang on, Margie. It could be any of several things. It could be a cyst, some hormonal thickening, maybe a benign tumour. It could possibly be cancer, but we have to do some tests in Bourke to tell what it is.'

'What do we do now?' Margie's expression was stricken. 'I'm worried. What am I going to tell the kids?'

'We'll do what we always do—we'll go step by step, figure out what the lump is and then fix it,' Izzy said. 'First we get a mammogram and ultrasound. Then, at the same time, we'll get the mammogram people to take a needle sample of the lump. That should give us the diagnosis. If it's a cyst, we just aspirate the fluid with a needle and that's usually the end of it. If the biopsy shows cancer cells, we get a surgeon to deal with it.'

'If it's cancer, will I have to have a mastectomy?'

'Mastectomies are very uncommon these days. Usually just the lump plus one lymph gland is removed, and then the breast gets some radiotherapy. If the lymph node was positive, possibly some more surgery to the armpit and maybe some chemo or hormonal therapies.'

Margie swung her legs off the examination table, her expression contorted with anguish as her fingers fumbled with the buttons on her blouse. 'I don't want to die. I have so much I want to do. I want to see my grandkids grow up. I want Doug to—' She suddenly looked at Izzy. 'Oh, God, what am I going to say to Doug? He'll never want me now, not if I've got cancer.'

Izzy took Margie's hand and gave it a comforting squeeze. 'No one's talking about dying. These days breast cancer is a very treatable disease when it's caught early. Let's take this one step at a time.'

'But who will run the clinic while I go to Bourke for the biopsy?'

'I'm sure I'll manage for a day without you,' Izzy said. 'I can divert the phone to mine, or maybe I could ask Peggy to sit by the phone. I'm sure she wouldn't mind.'

Margie sank her teeth into her lip. 'You know...the scary thing is if you hadn't been here filling in for William Sawyer I might not have bothered asking him to check me. I've known him so long it's kind of embarrassing, you know?'

'A lot of women feel the same way you do about seeing a male doctor for anything gynaecological or for breast issues, but all doctors, male or female, are trained to assess both male and female conditions.' Izzy wrote out the biopsy order form and a referral letter. 'I'll phone the surgeon and see if I can get you in this week. The sooner we know what we're dealing with the better.'

'Thanks, Izzy.' Margie clutched the letter to her chest. 'I don't mind if you tell Zach about this. I think Doug would want to know.'

'Why don't you call Doug yourself?'

Margie's eyes watered up. 'Because I'll just howl and blubber like a baby. I think it's better if he hears it from Zach. Will you be seeing him tonight?'

'He's dropping in after work.'

Margie's hand stalled on the doorknob as she looked back at Izzy over her shoulder. 'William is going to retire in a year or so. Maybe if you stayed you could job-share or something.'

'I can't stay. My home is in England.' She said it like a mantra. Like a creed. 'It's where I belong.'

'Is that where your heart is?'

'Of course.' Izzy kept her expression under such tight control it was painful. 'Where else would it be?'

Izzy opened the door to Zach a couple of hours later. 'Hi.'

He ran a finger down the length of her cheek in a touch as light as a brushstroke. 'You OK?'

She blew out a long exhausted-sounding breath. 'What a day.'

He closed the door behind him and reached for her, cupping her face in his hands and kissing her gently on the mouth. A soft, comforting kiss that was somehow far more meaningful and moving than if he'd let loose with a storm of passion. It was his sensitivity that made her heart contract. It wasn't because she was in love with him. That thought was off limits. Her brain was barricaded like a crime scene. Cordoned off. *Do Not Enter.*

He pulled back to look at her, still holding her hands in his. 'I've got some good news.'

Izzy gave him a weary look. 'I could certainly do with some. What is it?'

'Caitlyn Graham filed a domestic assault complaint an hour ago. That's why I'm late. Rob's taking Wayne Brody to Bourke to formally charge him.'

Izzy clutched at his hands. 'Is she all right? Should I go and see her?'

'She's gone to Peggy McLeod's place with the kids. I thought you'd had enough drama for one day.'

'What happened? I thought you were certain he hadn't hurt her when you went out there?'

'He hadn't at that stage,' Zach said. 'He'd verbally threatened her. Refused to let her leave the house, that sort of thing. But a couple of hours after we left, when the boys got home from school on the bus he started trying to lay into her. Apparently he's done it before but never in front of the boys. Jobe called triple zero.'

'Are you sure Caitlyn's not hurt? Are the kids OK?'

'Brody was too tanked to do much after the first swing, which Caitlyn luckily managed to dodge. She barricaded herself and the kids in the bathroom and waited for Rob and me to arrive.'

Izzy shuddered at the thought of the terror Caitlyn and the kids must have felt. 'I'm so glad she's finally out of danger. I felt sure it would only be a matter of time before he did something to her or one of the kids. He was so threatening to me. I thought he was going to assault me for sure.'

'If he had, he would've had me to answer to.' A quiver went through her at the implacability in his tone and his grey-blue eyes had a hard, self-satisfied glitter to them as he added, 'As it was, I already had a little score to settle with him.'

Izzy ran a gentle fingertip over the angry graze marks on the backs of the knuckles on his right hand. 'You wouldn't do anything outside the law, would you, Sergeant?' she asked.

He gave her an inscrutable smile. 'I'm one of the good guys, remember?'

She stepped up on tiptoe and pressed a kiss to his lips. 'I didn't realise they still made men like you any more.'

He threaded his fingers through her hair, gently massaging her scalp. 'You sure you're OK?'

Sensitive. Thoughtful. Gallant. What's not to love?

Izzy stepped back behind the yellow and black tape in her head. 'Margie has a lump in her breast.'

His brows snapped together in shock. 'Cancer?'

'I don't know yet. She has to have a mammogram and ultrasound and possibly a fine needle biopsy. I've managed to get her an appointment the day after tomorrow.' Izzy let out a breath. 'She wanted me to tell you so you could tell your dad.'

'Why doesn't she want to tell him herself?'

'I asked her the same thing but she's worried about getting too upset.'

He dropped his hands from her head and raked one through his own hair. 'Poor Margie. This town would be lost without her. My dad would be lost without her.'

'What a pity he hasn't told her that,' Izzy said on another sigh.

He gave her a thoughtful look. 'He will when he realises it.'

CHAPTER FOURTEEN

'Cancer?' Doug's face blanched. 'Why on earth didn't she tell me herself?'

Zach mentally rolled his eyes. 'You're the one who blew her off because she was getting too close.'

His father looked the colour of grey chalk. 'Is it serious? Is she going to die?'

'I don't know the answer to that. No one does yet. Izzy's organised a biopsy for her in Bourke. We'll know more after the results of that come through.'

'I need to see her. Will you drive me there now? I just want to see her to make sure she's all right.'

'What, *now?*'

'Why not now?' Doug said. 'She shouldn't be on her own at a time like this. Better still, I'll pack a bag and stay with her. I'll go with her to the appointment. She'll want someone with her. Might as well be me.'

Zach felt a warm spill of hope spread through his chest. 'You sure about this? You haven't stayed anywhere overnight other than hospital or rehab since the accident.'

Doug gave him a glowering look. 'I'm not a complete invalid, you know. I might not be able to do some of the things I used to do but I can still support a friend when they need me. Margie was the first person other than you to come to see me after the accident. She sat for days by my bedside. It's only right that I support her through this.'

Three days later Izzy opened the letter from the surgeon with trembling hands. Margie and Doug were sitting together in her consulting room, holding hands like teenagers on their first date.

'I want you to know I'm going to marry Margie, no matter what that letter says,' Doug said. 'I've already talked to Reverend Taylor.'

Izzy acknowledged that with a smile. Zach had already told her the good news. Now it was time for the bad news. She looked at the typed words on the single sheet of paper with the pathology report attached. She breathed out a sigh of relief. Not such bad news after all. 'It's not as bad as it could be. It's a DCIS—'

'What's that?' Doug asked, before Izzy could explain.

'DCIS is duct cancer in situ. It's not cancer but a step before you to get to cancer. It's like catching the horse just before it bolts.'

'So I don't have cancer? But you said duct cancer. I don't understand. Do I have it or not?' Margie asked.

'I'll try and explain it the best I can,' Izzy said. 'Think of it like this. Our body is made up of trillions of cells. Each cell has a computer program in it, telling it what to do. The computer program becomes damaged in some cell and the cell doesn't do what it's supposed to do. The worst-case scenario is when a whole lot of damage occurs, the cell goes out of control, starts multiplying too many copies of itself and won't stop. The copies spread throughout the body. That's cancer. But DCIS is where only a little bit of damage has occurred so far—the cell is a bit iffy when it comes to taking orders, but isn't yet out of control. If the lump is fully removed the problem has been cured.'

'Cured? Just by removing the lump? You mean surgery will fix this?' Doug asked.

'Yes, but the surgeon is still recommending radiotherapy afterwards because although the palpable lump of DCIS will be removed, there could be other unstable cells in the breast about to do the same thing. You'll need regular follow-up but it's certainly a lot better news than it could have been.'

Doug hugged Margie so tightly it looked like he was going to snap her in two. 'I can't believe what a fool I've been for all these years. We'll get married as soon as it can be arranged and go on a fancy cruise for our honeymoon once you've got the all-clear.'

Margie laughed and hugged him back. 'I feel like I've won the lottery. I'm not going to die and I've got the man of my dreams wanting to marry me.' She turned to Izzy. 'How can I thank you?'

'Nothing to thank me for,' Izzy said. 'I'm just doing my job.'

Which will end in two days' time.

Zach had been dreading the Shearers' Ball. Not just because too many of the locals had too much to drink and he had to be the fun police, but because it was the last night Izzy was going to be in town. Neither of them had mentioned that fact over the last couple of days. The drama with Margie and then the relief of his father finally getting his act together had pushed the elephant out of the room.

Now it was back...but Zach was painfully aware its bags were packed.

As soon as Zach arrived at the community centre where the country-style ball was being held he saw Izzy. She was wearing a fifties-style dress with a circle skirt in a bright shade of red that made her look like a poppy in a field of dandelions. He had never seen her look more beautiful. He had never seen *anyone* look more beautiful. Her hair was up in that half casual, half formal style, her creamy skin was highlighted with the lightest touch of make-up and those gorgeous kissable lips shimmered with lip-gloss.

The locals surrounded her, each one wanting to have their share of her. Caitlyn Graham was there with the kids, looking relaxed and happy for the first time in years. Peggy McLeod was cuddling Skylar and smiling at something Caitlyn had said to Izzy.

Jim Collis wandered over with a beer in his hand. 'She's something else, isn't she?'

Zach kept his expression masked. 'I see you got your tyres fixed.'

'Cost me a fortune.' Jim took another swig of his beer. 'Hey, good news about Margie and your old man. About bloody time. Look at them over there. Anyone would think they were sixteen again.'

Zach looked towards the back of the community hall where his father was seated next to Margie on a hay bale, their hands joined, his father's walking frame proving a rather useful receptacle for Margie's handbag as well as a place to put their drinks and a plate of the delicious food Peggy and her team had organised. 'Yeah. I'm happy for him. For both of them.'

'So...' Jim gave Zach a nudge with his elbow. 'What about you and the doc?'

'She's leaving tomorrow.' Zach said it as if the words weren't gnawing a giant hole in his chest. 'Got a new locum position in Brisbane. Starting on Monday.'

'Brisbane's not so far away. Maybe you could—'

'What would be the point?' Zach said. 'She's going back to England in July. It's where she belongs. Excuse me.' He gave Jim a dismissive look. 'I'm going to get something to drink.'

Izzy saw Zach standing to the left of the entrance of the community centre with a can of lemonade in his hand. He had his cop face on, acknowledging the locals who greeted him with a stiff movement of his lips as if it physically pained him to crack a full smile. She knew events like these were often quite stressful for country police officers. There were always a couple of locals who liked to drink a little too much and things could turn from a fun-loving party into an out of control mêlée in less time than it took to shake a cocktail. Friends could become enemies in a matter of minutes and the cop on duty had to be ready to control things and keep order.

Izzy had spent a few hours last night with Zach but the topic of her leaving had been carefully skirted around. She'd told him she was looking forward to the Brisbane locum but even as she'd said the words she'd felt a sinkhole of sadness open up inside her. It was like her mouth was saying one thing while her heart was saying another. *Feeling* another. But it wasn't like she could tell him how she felt. What woman in her right mind would tell a man she had only known a month that she loved him? He'd think she was mad.

It was a fling. A casual hook-up that had suited both of them. They had both needed to get over their broken engagements. Their short-term relationship had been a healing process, an exercise in closure so now they were both free to move on with their lives.

The trouble was it didn't feel like a fling. It had never felt like a fling.

Izzy went over to him with a plate of savoury nibbles Peggy had thrust in her hand on her way past. 'Having fun over here all by yourself?'

He gave her a dry look. 'You know that word "wallflower"? I'm more of a wall tree.'

She smiled. 'I'm pretty good on a city nightclub dance floor but out here among the hay bales I'm not sure what might happen.'

'Are you asking me to dance with you?'

Izzy was asking much more than that and wondered if he could see it in her eyes. His expression, however, was much harder to read. He had that invisible wall around him but whether it was because he was on duty or because he was holding back from her for other reasons she couldn't quite tell. 'Not if you don't want to.'

He put his can of lemonade on a nearby trestle table. 'Come on.' He took her hand as the music started. 'One dance then I'm back on duty.'

As soon as his arms went around her Izzy felt as if everyone else in the community centre had faded into the background. It was just Zach and her on the hay-strewn dance floor, their bodies moving as one in a waltz to a poignant country music ballad.

Zach's breath stirred her hair as he turned her round in a manoeuvre that would have got a ten out of ten on a reality dance show. 'You know what happens if you play country music backwards?'

Izzy looked up at him with a quizzical smile. 'No, what?'

'You get your job back, your dead dog comes back to life and your girlfriend stops sleeping with your best mate.'

It was a funny joke and it should have made her laugh out loud but instead she felt like crying. She blinked a couple of times and forced a smile. 'I'm really going to miss Popeye. Do you think I could—?' She looked at his shirt collar instead. 'No, maybe not. I'm not very good at goodbyes.'

'What time do you leave?' The question was as casual as *What do you think of the weather?*

'Early. It's a long drive.' Izzy was still focusing her gaze on his collar but it had become blurry. 'I don't want to rush it.'

'Izzy…' His throat moved up and down as if he had taken a bigger than normal swallow.

She looked into his grey-blue eyes, her heart feeling like it had moved out of her chest and was now beating in her oesophagus. 'Yes?'

His eyes moved back and forth between each of hers as if he was searching for something hidden there. 'Thank you for what you did for my father.'

Izzy wondered if that was what he had really intended to say. There was something about his tone and his manner that didn't seem quite right. 'I didn't do anything.'

He stopped dancing and stood with his arms still

around her, his eyes locked on hers. It was as if he had completely forgotten they were in the middle of the community centre dance floor, with the whole town watching on the sidelines. 'You didn't give up on him.'

Izzy gave him another wry smile. 'I like to give everyone a decent chance.'

He looked about to say something else but the jostling of the other dancers seemed to jolt him back into the present. A shutter came down on his face and he spoke in a flat monotone. 'We're holding up traffic.' He dropped his hands from her and stepped back. 'I'll let you mingle. I'll catch you later.'

'Zach…?' Izzy's voice was so husky it didn't stand a chance over the loud floor-stomping music Bill Davidson had exchanged for the ballad. She watched as Zach walked out of the community centre without even acknowledging Damien Redbank, who spoke to him on the way past.

It was another hour before Izzy could get anywhere near Zach again. She got caught up in a progressive barn dance and then a vigorous Scottish dance that left one of the older locals a little short of breath. She had to make sure the man was not having a cardiac arrest before she could go in search of Zach. She found him talking on his mobile out by the tank stand. He acknowledged her with a brief flicker of his lips as he slipped his phone away. 'All danced out?'

Izzy grimaced as she tucked a damp strand of hair behind her ear. 'I've been swung about so energetically I think both my shoulders have popped out of their sockets.'

'The Gay Gordons not your thing, then?' It was difficult to tell if he was smiling or not as his face was now in shadow.

'I loved it. It's the best workout I've had since...well, since last night.'

He stepped out of the cloaking shadow of the community centre but didn't look at her; instead, he was looking out into the sprawling endless darkness beyond town. 'That was my mother on the phone.'

'Does she call you often?'

'Not often.' Izzy heard him scrape the gravel with the toe of his boot. 'That's probably as much my fault as hers.'

'Would you ever consider going over to see her again some time?'

He lifted a shoulder and then let it drop. 'Maybe.'

'Maybe you could look me up if you do.' As soon as she'd said the words she wished she hadn't. They made her sound as if she was content to be nothing more than a booty call. She wanted more. *So much more.*

'What would be the point?'

Izzy rolled her lips together. 'It would be nice to catch up.'

'To do what?' His eyes looked as hard as diamond chips now. 'To pick up where we left off?'

She let out a slow, measured breath. 'I just thought—'

'What did you think, Izzy?' His tone hardened, along with his gaze. 'That I'd ask you to hang around so we could pretend a little longer this is going to last for ever? This was never about for ever. We've had our fun. Now it's time for you to leave as planned.'

Izzy swallowed a knot of pain. 'Is that what you want?'

His expression went back to its fall-back position. Distant. Aloof. Closed off. 'Of course it is.'

'I don't believe you.' She held his strong gaze with indomitable force. 'You're lying. You want me to stay. I know you do. You *want* me, Zach. I feel it in every fibre of my being. How can you stand there and pretend you don't?'

His mouth flattened. 'Don't make this ugly, Izzy.'

'You're the one making it ugly,' she said. 'You're making out that what we've shared has been nothing more than some tawdry little affair. How can you do that?'

A pulse beat like a hammer in his jaw. 'It was good sex. But I can have that with anyone. So can you.'

Izzy looked at him in wounded shock. This was not how things were supposed to be. The flag of hope in her chest was slipping back down the flagpole in despair. It was strangling her. Choking her. He was supposed to tell her he wanted more time with her. That he wanted her to stay. That he loved her. Not tell her she was replaceable.

Somehow she garnered her pride. 'Fine. Let's do it your way, then.' She stuck out her hand. 'Goodbye, Zach.'

He ignored her hand. He stood looking down at her with a stony expression on his face as if everything inside him had turned to marble. He didn't even speak. Not one word. Even the ticking pulse in his jaw had stopped.

Izzy returned her hand to her side. She would not let him see how much she was hurting. She straightened her shoulders and put one foot in front of the other as she walked back to the lights and music of the community centre.

When she got to the door and glanced back he was nowhere to be seen.

'All packed?' Margie asked, her smile sad and her eyes watery, as Izzy was about to head off the next morning.

'All packed.' Izzy had covered the track marks of her tears with the clever use of make-up but she wasn't sure the camouflage was going to last too long. Fresh tears were pricking like needles at the backs of her eyes and her heart felt like it was cracking into pieces. She'd lain awake most of the night, hoping Zach would come to her and tell her he'd made a terrible mistake, that he wanted her to stay, that he loved her with a for-ever love. But he hadn't turned up. He hadn't even sent a text. But that was his way. She had only known him four weeks but she knew that much about him. Once his mind was made up that was it. Over and out. No going back.

Doug shuffled forward to envelop her in a hug. 'Thanks.'

Izzy knew how much emotion was in that one simple word. She felt it vibrating in his body as she hugged him back as if he too was trying not to cry. 'Take care of yourself.'

'Where's Zach?' Margie asked Doug. 'I thought he'd be here to say goodbye.'

Doug's expression showed his frustration. 'I haven't seen him since daylight. Didn't say a word to me other than grunting something about taking Popeye for a walk. Haven't seen him since.'

'But I thought—' Margie began.

'He said all that needed to be said last night,' Izzy said, keeping her expression masked.

'Should've been here to see you off,' Doug said, frowning. 'What's got into him?'

Margie gave him a cautioning look before reaching to hug Izzy. 'I'm going to miss you *so* much.'

'I'll miss you too.'

With one last hug apiece Izzy got into her car and drove out of town. She had to blink to clear her vision as an overwhelming tide of emotion welled up inside her; it felt like she was leaving a part of herself behind.

She was.

Her heart.

Zach skimmed a stone across the surface of Blake's waterhole, watching as it skipped across the water six times before sinking. His record was fourteen skips but he wasn't getting anywhere near that today. He had been out here since dawn, trying to make sense of his feelings after his decision last night to end things with Izzy.

He kept reminding himself it was better this way. A clean cut healed faster than a festering sore.

But it didn't feel better. It felt worse. It hurt to think of Izzy driving away to her next post, finding some other guy to spend the rest of her life with while he tried to get on with his life out here.

He had never been a big believer in love at first sight. He had shied away from it because of what had happened between his parents. They'd married after a whirlwind courtship and his mother had spent the next decade being miserable and taking it out on everyone around her.

He didn't want to do that to Izzy. She hadn't had

enough time to get to know herself outside a relationship. He had no right to ask her to stay. What if she ended up hating him for it after a few weeks, months or years down the track?

He skimmed another stone but it only managed four skips before sinking. It felt like his heart, plummeting to the depths where it would never find the light of day again.

He thought of Izzy's smile, the way it lit up her face, the way it had beamed upon the dark sadness he had buried inside himself all those years ago. Would anyone else make him feel that spreading warmth inside his chest? Would anyone else make him feel alive and hopeful in spite of all the sickness and depravity of humanity he had to deal with in his work?

Izzy was not just a ray of sunshine.

She was *his* light.

He'd wanted to tell her last night. He'd *ached* to tell her. The words had been there but he'd kept swallowing them back down with common sense.

She was young and idealistic, full of romantic notions that didn't always play out in the real world. He was cynical and older in years, not to mention experience.

How could they make it work? How did any relationship work? *Could* they make theirs work?

How could he let her leave without telling her what he felt about her? If she didn't feel the same, he would have to bear that. At least he would be honest with her. He owed her that.

He owed himself that.

Zach drove out to the highway with Popeye on the seat beside him. 'I can't believe I'm doing this.' Popeye gave an excited yap. 'I mean it's crazy. I never do things like this. We've only known each other a month. It's not like she said she loved me. Not outright. What if I've got this wrong? What if she says no?' His fingers gripped the steering-wheel so tightly he was reminded of his grip on the veranda rail all those years ago.

What would have happened if he'd called out to his mother that day? Would it have changed anything? If nothing else, at least it would have assured his mother he loved her, even if she'd still felt the need to leave. He had never told his mother he loved her. Not since he was a little kid. That was something he would have to fix.

But not right now.

Miraculously, he suddenly saw Izzy's car ahead. He forced himself to slow down and watched her for a while, mentally rehearsing what he was going to say. He wasn't good at expressing emotion. He had spent his childhood locking away what he'd felt. His job had reinforced that pattern, demanding he kept his emotions under control at all times and in all places. What if he couldn't say what he wanted to say? Should he just blurt it out or lead in to it? His stomach was in knots. His heart felt as if it was in danger of splitting right down the middle.

He loved her.

He *really* loved her.

Not the pedestrian feelings he'd felt for Naomi.

His love for Izzy was a once-in-a-lifetime love. An all-or-nothing love.

A grand passion.

A for-ever love.

He suddenly realised her car was gathering speed. He checked his radar monitor. She was going twenty kilometres per hour over the limit! Acting on autopilot, he reached for his siren and lights switch, all the bells and whistles blaring as he put his foot down on the throttle.

Izzy was reaching for another tissue when she heard a police siren behind her. She glanced in the rear-view mirror, her heart flipping like a pancake flung by a master chef when she saw Zach behind the wheel, bearing down on her. She put her foot on the brake and pulled over to the gravel verge, trying to wipe the smeared mascara away from beneath her eyes. If he wanted a cold, clean break then that's what she would give him. Cold and clinical.

His tall, commanding figure appeared at her driver's window. The rim of his police hat shadowed his eyes and his voice was all business. 'Want to tell me why you were going twenty over the limit?'

She pressed her lips together. So that was going to be his parting gift, was it? *A speeding ticket!* 'I'm sorry, Officer, but I was reaching for a tissue.'

'Why are you crying?'

'I'm *not* crying.'

'Get out of the car.'

Izzy glowered at him. 'What *is* this?'

'I said get out of the car.'

She blew her cheeks out on a breath and stepped out, throwing him a defiant look. 'See? I'm not crying.'

His gaze held hers with his inscrutable one. 'Either you've been crying or you put your make-up on in the dark.'

Izzy put her hands on her hips and stared him down. 'Is it a crime to feel a little sad about leaving a town

I've grown to love? Is it, Sergeant show-no-emotion Fletcher? If so, go ahead and book me.'

A tiny glint came into his eyes. 'You love Jerringa Ridge?'

She folded her arms across her chest, still keeping her defiant glare in place. 'Yes.'

'What do you love about it?'

She was starting to feel a flutter of hope inside her chest, like a butterfly coming out of a chrysalis. 'I love the way it made me feel like I was the most beautiful person in the world. I love the way it made me feel passion I've never felt before. I love the way it opened its arms to me and held me close and made me feel safe.'

'That all?'

'That about covers it.'

He gave a slow nod. 'So...Brisbane, huh?'

She kept her chin up. 'Yes.'

He took off his hat and put it on the roof of her car, his movements slow, measured. 'You looking forward to that?'

'Not particularly.'

'Why not?'

Izzy looked into his now twinkling eyes. 'Because I'd much rather be here with you.'

He put his arms around her then, holding her so tightly against him she felt every button on his shirt pressing into her skin. 'I love you,' he said. 'I should've told you last night. I almost did...but I didn't want to put any pressure on you to stay. A public proposal seemed... I don't know...kind of tacky. Kind of manipulative.'

She looked up into his face with a wide-eyed look. 'A proposal?'

His expression was suddenly serious again. 'Izzy,

darling, I know we've only known each other a month. I know you have a life back in England, family and friends and roots that go deep. I would never ask you to give any of that up. All I'm asking is for you to give us a chance. We can make our home wherever you want to be. I can employ a manager for Fletcher Downs. Dad and Margie will be able to keep an eye on things. We can have the best of both worlds.' He cupped her face in his hands. '*You* are my world, darling girl. Marry me?'

Izzy smiled the widest smile she had ever smiled. 'Yes.'

He looked shocked. Taken aback. '*Yes?*'

'Yes, Zach.' She gave a little laugh at his expression. 'I will marry you. Why are you looking so surprised?'

'Because I didn't think it was possible to find someone like you.' He stroked her hair back from her face, his expression tender. 'Someone who would make me feel like this. I didn't know it could happen so fast and so completely. I want to spend the rest of my life with you. I think a part of me realised that the first time we kissed. It scared the hell out of me, to tell you the truth.'

'I felt that way too,' Izzy said. 'I was so miserable last night. I couldn't believe you were just going to leave it at that after all we'd shared. Our relationship was supposed to be a fling but nothing about it felt like a fling to me.'

He hugged her tightly again. 'I was trying to do the right thing by you by letting you go. But I couldn't believe how the right thing felt so incredibly painful. I decided I had to tell you how I felt, otherwise I'd spend the rest of my life regretting it.'

Her eyes twinkled as she looked up to hold his gaze. 'Promise me something?'

'Anything.'

'No five-star destinations for our honeymoon, OK?'

His eyes glinted again. 'You want to go camping?'

'Yes, and I want to swim naked and make love under the stars.' She hugged him close. 'I don't even mind if Max comes along as long as he has his own tent.'

'No way, baby girl,' Zach said. 'Max will have to find another place to stay while we're on our honeymoon. I'm not sharing you with anyone. Where is he, by the way?'

She gave him a sheepish look. 'He's in the boot. He wasn't too happy about being stashed in there but your dad and Margie came to say goodbye and I didn't have time to let him down properly.'

Zach grinned at her and pulled her close again. 'Maybe if I kiss you right now I won't think I'm dreaming this is happening. What do you reckon?'

She smiled as his mouth came down towards hers. 'I think that's an excellent idea.'

* * * * *

TANGLED WITH A TEXAN

YVONNE LINDSAY

To my fellow Texas Cattleman's Club: Houston authors, always a pleasure working with you, ladies!

One

As if it wasn't enough she'd had to hand over her additional casework to the rest of her already overloaded team, now she was headed all the way out to Royal, Texas. Zoe Warren was a city detective, hell, city girl, through and through. She already could start to feel her skin itch at the thought of cattle and cowboys and all that open pasture. Mind you, driving the three hundred or so miles to Royal had presented as a far more attractive option than facing yet another blind date set up by one of her four older brothers or her parents, who seemed to think she needed help settling down. And who said she wanted to settle down, anyway? She'd worked long and hard for her place on Houston P.D.'s detective squad, and her career trajectory was heading straight up. You weren't a third generation cop without some dreams and goals ahead of you—and at only thirty years old, she had plenty of dreams and goals to fulfill while quite happily still single.

Sure, one day it might be nice to get married, throw a couple more Warren genes into the pool of rapidly growing family her brothers and cousins were constantly adding to. But not right now. And not on her ever-loving family's timetable, either.

The open country that surrounded her had a raw beauty to it that even her citified eyes couldn't help but appreciate. But always, in the back of her mind, she was working. As lead detective on the homicide case that was sending her on this journey, she was beginning to feel like the more they uncovered about the deceased, Vincent Hamm, the less they actually knew about him, and for her, following down each and every rabbit hole in Hamm's life had become an obsession. The good thing about having this time on her own as she drove west toward Maverick County was that it gave her the opportunity for some thinking time. Time without the constant pressures that came with the responsibilities of her job.

Everything about this case was off. First, the vic had disappeared into thin air, then he'd never shown back up for work, and after the floodwaters had receded at the site of the new Texas Cattleman's Club being built in Houston, he was eventually found dead with his face destroyed. Whoever killed him had taken great pains to ensure he couldn't be visually identified—although the floodwaters had taken their toll, too.

Zoe took a swig of her water bottle and grunted in annoyance when she found it empty. Still, not long now and she'd be in Royal—she could stock up at a convenience store there. But first, a quick swing by the sheriff's office was in order to make a courtesy visit and let them know that she'd arrived in the county. Nathan Battle, the sheriff, had made a personal visit to Houston to lend his support to the case. Her vic was the son of a friend of his and she'd expected Battle to be loudmouthed at the very least, and difficult at worst. Instead, she'd been quietly surprised by his demeanor. Oh, there was no mistaking the determination behind his promise to Hamm's family to get to the root of who murdered their son, but he was a by-the-rules guy and his help here in Royal could prove invaluable to her investigation. She'd gone to great lengths to ensure she was doing everything in her power to bring the murderer to justice, and she was confident she'd earned the older man's trust. She liked the guy. Not pushy, just determined. She respected that.

About ten minutes later, guided by the GPS on her phone—without which she'd be totally lost anywhere, not having inherited the direction gene her brothers took for granted—Zoe pulled up outside the Royal sheriff's office. Three minutes after that she was back in her car. Turned out the good sheriff was out on a call, but she'd left a message for him to phone her when he got back.

She reprogrammed the GPS and found the midrange motel she'd booked just on the other side of town. It didn't take more than ten minutes to check in and unpack. She called for updates from her colleagues back in Houston and let them know she'd arrived safely, then decided to take a short walk around town to stretch her legs and familiarize herself.

Royal struck her as a prosperous town with a decent-sized population scurrying about their daily business. Being late afternoon, there were all kinds of people out and about. Business people, moms and kids, a handful of idlers loitering here and there, but overall the place had a good feel about it. She turned and headed back to the motel, her mind still churning over the facts of the case. Just as she reached her unit, her phone buzzed in her pocket. She slipped it out and looked at the screen. Nathan Battle.

"Sheriff, thanks for calling," Zoe answered.

"Thanks for coming by and letting me know you're in town. Did you want to meet?"

"How about tomorrow afternoon?" she suggested, mentally reviewing her plans for tomorrow morning, which included following up on the lead that had brought her to Royal in the first place.

She heard the flick of paper, followed by a grunt of assent. "Yup, works for me. I'll meet you at the Royal Diner for coffee and a slice of pie, say, three o'clock?"

Zoe's stomach growled in response to the mention of food. "Sounds like a plan. See you then."

That would give her plenty of time to make the drive out to the Stevens ranch in the morning and ask a few questions. Hopefully more than a few. That cryptic message left on Hamm's answering machine saying no more than "Thanks for nothing, Hamm" had spoken volumes when taking into account the tone of the speaker and the fact that Vincent Hamm had gone missing around the same time. They'd been able to trace the message to a local rancher, Jesse Stevens. Research had shown Stevens and Hamm had been friends at one time, but what had happened to drive them apart? Had it been enough to make Jesse Stevens want to kill his former friend?

Stevens was quite a force here in Royal. The wealthy rancher was very involved in the politics of the local Texas Cattleman's Club, and while Zoe may be grasping at straws, the fact that her vic had been found in the building currently being developed into a new Cattleman's Club might not be such a coincidence after all. Right now, she had to look at everything. Pressure from the chief of police and Houston's mayor was constant, and so far her team had little to show for their investigation. Her captain had pulled her aside just yesterday and asked her if she was getting stale. The question had made her bristle. Stale? When all she did lately was live, eat, sleep and breathe this case? Not likely. But he'd made it clear—he needed to see results or she might be stood down.

Thinking about it, Zoe reached a decision. She didn't want to wait until morning to go face-to-face with Stevens. She could drive out to his ranch right now. October sunset wasn't until around seven, which gave her three hours of daylight. Plus, the element of surprise would be in her favor if she just rolled up without an appointment. She opened her map app on her phone and pulled up the address she'd saved for Stevens's ranch before leaving Houston. The ranch was outside Royal and isolated. Nothing but pasture and cattle. Zoe ignored the itch between her shoulder blades and got into her car, set her phone in the hands-free holder and hit Start on the journey planner.

The drive took longer than she expected, but as she pulled through the gates of Stevens's ranch she felt a sense of triumphant relief that she had made it. People could tease her all they liked about her reliance on modern technology to get anywhere, but it got the job done, she thought with a small smile.

She was still smiling when she went up the front stairs of the impressive ranch house and knocked on the front door. But her smile slipped when no one came to answer. She knocked again and waited a couple of minutes before walking along the front porch to one of the side windows. She looked in. No movement, nothing. Zoe blew out a huff of frustration. Maybe a phone call would have been a better idea after all. Still, she had a list of his known associates here in Royal and she knew one of them was his neighbor. She walked back to the car and reprogrammed her app to the next address on her list.

This time she struck gold when she knocked at the door

of the neighboring ranch, which was no less impressive in size and structure than the Stevens property. She'd always known ranching was a prosperous undertaking when done right, but the two properties she'd been on so far were something else. She plastered a smile on her face and flicked her short dark hair back off her forehead as the steady sound of footsteps coming to the door echoed from the other side.

The words she was about to say dried on the tip of her tongue as the door opened, revealing a tall, imposing presence. While the guy wasn't heavily muscled, there was no doubting the latent strength in the shoulders that bunched beneath the checkered shirt he wore over a crisp white T-shirt. Zoe's gaze flicked up—something she wasn't always used to doing when wearing boots that, combined with her natural height, put her at around six feet. Instantly, her attention was captured by the man's eyes. Light brown and shot with gold, they were incredibly mesmerizing and were set in a face that was all sharp lines and angles softened by a generous dusting of five o'clock shadow that wrapped his jaw. There was an almost wolflike look to him—as if he were assessing her as prey.

Rather than getting put on the defensive, Zoe found herself reacting on a far more visceral level—each facet of her mind sharpening, while every cell in her body responded with pure feminine interest. A wave of physical need pulled from deep within her, robbing her of breath and making her nipples harden against the lacy cups of her bra. She drew her full lower lip between her teeth to stop herself from making the involuntary sound—something like a moan—that threatened to spill from her.

The man's hair was wet, as if he'd recently stepped from a shower and just slicked it back—its wet ends kissed the edge of his collar and left a damp trail. She drew in a sharp breath, only to discover how intoxicating the scent of him was. She was shocked at how deeply and suddenly he had affected her. She had trained herself from day one at the police academy not to show her emotions. Good things, bad things—it made no difference. She had learned to remain impassive, detached. But right now, she was anything but detached. In fact, right now, every instinct was screaming at her oversensitized body to plaster itself against his length and take his mouth in a possessive kiss that would leave him in no doubt of how much she wanted him. For a nanosecond she allowed herself the luxury of imagining where that might lead. To their two bodies, glistening with perspiration, tangled in tumbled sheets, gliding together, perhaps? She blinked hard and forced herself under control. This was utter madness. She couldn't even remember the last time she'd reacted to a guy this intensely.

Those intriguing eyes narrowed as he looked at her, and she realized that neither of them had spoken.

"Miss? Can I help you?"

His voice poured over her. Deep and strong and sexy as hell. This guy could recite a list of traffic infringements and make her knees turn to water.

"Detective," she corrected him, showing him her badge. "Zoe Warren, Houston P.D."

"You're a little out of your jurisdiction, aren't you?"

She wasn't mistaken. The warmth and pure male interest she'd seen reflected in his eyes had dimmed, his gaze sharpening warily.

"The boundaries of our investigation have stretched a little," she said carefully. "I'd like to ask you a few questions, Mister…?"

"Cord Galicia," he answered abruptly and thrust out his hand.

Zoe debated taking it. If her reaction to him on a purely

visual basis had been so extreme, how on earth would she react when she actually touched him? There was only one way to find out. She drew in a sharp breath, took the proffered hand and clasped it. A slow sizzle of awareness tracked along her skin. His hand was larger than hers, the palm firm, and she could feel the calluses that spoke of the hard work he did. The title of rancher wasn't simply some token. This man clearly worked, and worked hard. Did he apply himself to everything else he did with as much vigor? she wondered before giving his hand a quick shake and releasing it.

"May I come in?" she asked.

To her surprise, her voice remained steady. Quite a feat when her insides were jangling about as hard as they had in junior high when she'd been asked to prom by the captain of the soccer team. She was already head and shoulders taller than him but it hadn't bothered her—until she found out the whole thing had been a joke designed by the rest of the team. But that initial response, the delicious sense of anticipation and excitement, she'd never forget. She just never expected to feel it here on the outskirts of Royal, Texas, while working a homicide investigation.

For a moment it looked as if he'd refuse, but then he stepped back from the doorway and gestured for her to move inside. He closed the door decisively behind her, but Zoe didn't let it rattle her. She'd dealt with people with far fewer social graces than Cord Galicia.

"Can I get you anything to drink?" he asked as he led the way into a large open-plan living room.

"Water would be great, thanks."

"Take a seat," he said gruffly before heading through a doorway toward what was, presumably, the kitchen.

Zoe sank into a large leather sofa. In a smaller room the piece of furniture would have dominated, but not here. She looked around, taking in the high raftered ceiling—must be a bitch to keep clean, she pondered—and the tall windows that led to a paved courtyard outside. Large round ceramic pots in a jumble of bright colors, some with mosaics, were filled with flowers, and beyond that Zoe caught a glimpse of the sparkle of late-afternoon sunlight on water. A pool or an ornamental pond? she wondered.

"Here you are."

Cord Galicia stood before her holding a sweating tall glass of water in one hand. She reached up to take it.

"Thank you."

The man moved with the stealth of a wild animal, she realized. There weren't many who could sneak up on her like that.

"You said you had questions," he said as he settled onto the other end of the sofa.

"Yes, I do. Your neighbor, Jesse Stevens—are you well acquainted?"

She knew the men were best friends, but she was curious to see how Galicia reacted to being questioned. She kept her eyes focused on her host and didn't miss the way his body stiffened.

"What do you want with Jesse?"

"Please, Mr. Galicia, just answer the question."

"He's my neighbor, of course we're acquainted," Cord said begrudgingly. "But I don't see what he has to do with some investigation in Houston."

"That's my job," Zoe said with a grim smile. "Tell me, what's Mr. Stevens like as a man?"

"What do you mean?"

"Is he quick to anger? The type to follow up on a grudge?"

"I don't like where you're heading with this. Jesse is a decent man and an upstanding member of our community. If you're looking at him, you're looking in the wrong direction."

Zoe decided to take a different tack. "Do you remember Vincent Hamm?"

"Yeah, he grew up around here. We all did."

"Were he and Mr. Stevens particularly close?"

Cord shook his head. "No, I wouldn't say that. Jesse knew him, sure. But we all did. Is that who this is about? Hamm? Look, we were sorry to hear he'd passed, but it's not like we'll miss him. Seriously, we haven't moved in the same circles for years. Like I said, if you're after Jesse, you're after the wrong person. He's the most law-abiding and stand-up person I know."

"You'll forgive me if I don't immediately jump to believe you. That's pretty much what everyone says when asked about the people they think they know."

Two

"*Think* they know?" Cord didn't bother to keep the irritation out of his voice. "Since I've known the man most of my life, I can safely say I know Jesse Stevens pretty damn well, Ms. Warren."

"Zoe, please."

Oh, so she was attempting to play nice now? He let his gaze drift over her. He wouldn't have minded playing nice with her, if she'd been anything but a cop. She was exactly his type. Long and lean with sweet curves in just the right places. Even her short-cropped dark hair was sexy, and he bet it looked even sexier mussed up against a crisp white cotton-covered pillow. He shifted slightly in his seat as his body reacted in ways his mind was determined not to.

"The fact remains, I know my friend, *Zoe*," he said with emphasis. "And you're barking up the wrong tree."

She dragged in a deep breath, and he couldn't help but notice how her fitted shirt strained against the buttons across her chest. Oh yes, sweet curves all right. But off-limits, as was any woman serving in the police force. Cord let his gaze drift to the photo frame sitting on the antique sideboard across the room. Britney. God. Seeing her graduation picture from the police academy every day was a reminder of everything he'd lost. Her death two years ago, while on her first shift of active duty, had been soul destroying, and it was Jesse who'd kept him sane through that awful, dark time.

No, Jesse was not the kind of man to commit murder, and Cord would do whatever he could to ensure Detective Warren knew that. And, he reminded himself as he flicked his gaze back to the woman in front of him, if he ever embarked on a long-term relationship again, it wouldn't be with a woman who wore a badge and a gun and hunted down bad guys for a living. No matter how much his libido told him otherwise.

"Sometimes we're not always honest with the people we're closest to," she said in an obvious attempt to placate him. "Do you know when would be a good time for me to catch Mr. Stevens at home? I called on him earlier and no one was in."

"He runs a working ranch, so I guess it's safe to say there's never a good time. We have to make the most of the daylight hours available to us," Cord said, hedging, unwilling to give the woman more information than was absolutely necessary.

"Well, I caught you at home, didn't I? Mr. Galicia, are you being deliberately obstructive or is this just your charming way of treating all strangers?"

"Obstructive?" Cord felt a trickle of irritation at her insinuation. He wasn't being obstructive; he was being careful. They were two very different things.

"That's the usual terminology when someone deliberately withholds information."

He watched as she picked up her water glass and drained it. Her throat was long and slender, the muscles working delicately as she swallowed her drink. Damn if the sight of that pale column of skin didn't give him a hard-on. She snapped the glass back onto the table in front of her and rose on those enticingly long legs, then reached into her back pocket for a business card. She handed it to him as he hastened to stand.

"Call me if you suddenly remember how I can best reach Mr. Stevens," she said with a slight curl of her lip. "I'll be staying in Royal for a few days."

"Does the sheriff know you're in town?"

He could see she wanted to tell him that was none of his business, but instead she gave him a brusque nod.

"Of course," she said. "He's assisting in my inquiries."

Cord nodded. That made sense. The sheriff and the Hamm family went way back. "Maybe he can tell you how to get ahold of Jesse, since he's assisting you and all."

He couldn't resist goading her just a little. It rankled that she'd come out here without any notice on some jumped-up idea that Jesse was involved in Vincent Hamm's murder. The very thought was ridiculous. Jesse was the kind of guy to always bend over backward to help others, and Cord knew he'd gone the extra mile with Hamm on several occasions. And then the one time Jesse had to ask Hamm for a favor...

A frisson of warning prickled at the back of his mind. Was that what this was about? Had this woman unearthed something about Jesse asking Hamm a favor? A favor Hamm had refused to act on. Was that her angle? That Jesse had somehow been mad enough to exact revenge?

"I'm sure he will. Next time I talk to him, I'll be certain to get the lowdown on you, too."

"Me? Hey, you want to know about me, feel free to ask me anything." Cord spread his arms wide and quirked one corner of his lips up in a smile. "I'm an open book."

She sniffed. "Thank you for the water. No doubt I'll be speaking to you again."

The thought of seeing her again had its merits, but he doubted she meant what he was thinking.

"I'll look forward to it," he replied, imbuing into that handful of words enough innuendo to make Ms. Warren stiffen and give him a hard look.

"We'll see about that."

He led the way to the front door and watched her as she stepped onto the porch. There was a determined set to her shoulders, and he knew she wouldn't be deterred by him. One way or another she'd track Jesse down, and Cord didn't want it to be today. Jesse had enough on his plate with his sister's emergency surgery today. It had started out as routine to remove an inflamed appendix, but the dang thing had already ruptured, spilling infection through Janet's body. While she was receiving the best care possible, Jesse was beside himself with worry. Last thing Jesse needed was this detective visiting him in the hospital.

Maybe Cord could appeal to her good will, he thought. Just as the woman reached her grime-covered car, he called out.

"Jesse is at the hospital—that's why he's not at home right now. His sister had an operation today. There were complications. He's been there all day. A decent person would leave him be."

"Mr. Galicia, are you suggesting I'm not a decent person?" She cocked one brow as she raised the question.

"Well, that remains to be seen, doesn't it?" he challenged. "Give him a couple of days at least."

"And what do you suggest I do in the meantime? Paint my nails?"

He had to hand it to her. She didn't back down, not one bit. He probably shouldn't have told her about Jesse being at the hospital, but he'd hoped he could appeal to her sense of compassion. Surely she had one in there somewhere behind that blue-eyed deadpan stare of hers?

"Maybe we could have a drink or a meal somewhere?"

"Are you asking me on a date?"

The incredulity on her face would have been funny if it hadn't been so insulting.

"Sure, why not?"

For a second or two she looked totally at a loss for words. As a distraction tactic, asking her out clearly had merit, he thought with a quiet twinge of satisfaction. At least it appeared to have stopped her in her stride.

"What about it?" he pressed. "Tonight, just a drink. You can ask me anything you want."

"I can ask you anything I want anytime I want. I have a badge, remember?"

"What? Are you afraid of spending time with me?"

She snorted. "I'm not afraid of anything, Mr. Galicia. Especially not you. Sure, fine. What time and where?"

"Why don't I pick you up? Where're you staying?"

She named the motel.

"How about seven?" he asked, beginning to wonder what in hell he was letting himself in for.

"Seven is good."

Then, without another word, she got into her car and swung it around the circular driveway and back toward the main road. Cord watched until she went out of sight, then slowly closed the door to his house. His grandmother would have said he'd gone totally loco. Even he didn't understand fully what had prompted him to make the offer to Detective Warren, aside from the need to protect his best friend from her questioning. He flicked a look at his watch. Jesse said he'd be at the hospital until the nurses kicked him out. It would take the detective about forty minutes to get to town from here, then no doubt she'd want to fluff a bit like women did. She wouldn't have time to go to the hospital and bother Jesse, but just in case, Cord dragged his cell phone from his back pocket and thumbed a text to his friend.

How's Janet doing?

She's holding her own. They're talking about removing the breathing tube later tonight.

Cord felt a pang for his friend. Janet was the only family he had left, and to say he was protective of his younger sibling was an understatement. This hiccup with what should have been a routine procedure today had surely devastated him.

Good to hear. BTW, Houston detective in town asking questions about Hamm. I'm taking her out for a drink so she doesn't bother you.

Jesse's reply was swift.

LOL, taking one for the team? Such hardship. Is she pretty?

Trust his friend to ask the hard questions.

Yeah.

But she's a cop.

Yeah.

Do you know what you're doing?

Keeping her away from you, remember.

There was a pause, and Cord began to wonder if that was an end to their conversation, but then his phone pinged again.

Are you sure that's all?

You know my rules.

Okay. Don't do anything dumb.

As if. Hey, give Janet my love.

Will do. And let me know how your date goes.

It's not a date.

She's pretty. It's a date.

Cord rolled his eyes before texting his reply.

She's a cop. It's not a date. End of story.

He pocketed his phone and went to his room to get ready to head into town. But even as he changed into a good pair of jeans and a fitted shirt and splashed on a little cologne, he couldn't help but wonder why he was going to so much effort for the woman. Was it because he was trying to keep her distracted and away from Jesse, or was there something more? He snagged his car keys in one hand and headed toward the garage. There was only one way to find out.

Three

Zoe paced the confines of her motel room, wondering why the hell she'd agreed to this—whatever this was—with Cord Galicia. The man exuded pheromones like body odor. Both were equally unwelcome in her book. Galicia had been far too cagey about Stevens, and her own experience had shown that people don't generally hide something that doesn't need to be hidden. And even though he had said she could ask him anything she wanted, she doubted that would extend to more information about his neighbor.

She flicked a glance at the digital clock next to the bed. He'd be here any minute. As if she'd conjured him up merely by thinking about him, there was a firm knock at her door. She swung around and checked the peephole. Yup, just as sexy as the first time, she thought. She forced herself to take a deep, steadying breath before unlatching the chain and opening the door.

Even with the distance of a couple of hours, he still

packed the same punch. She'd never met a man before who had made her feel so darn feminine. She wanted to say she didn't like it, but there was something about the way the blood in her veins fizzed when he was around that she had to admit wasn't entirely unpleasant.

"Good evening," Galicia said, then bowed with a flourish. "Your chariot awaits."

"We're not walking?" she asked, stepping through the door and carefully locking it behind her.

"Nah, the place I'm taking you is on the other side of town."

"If you'd have said, I'd have met you there."

"What's the matter, Detective? Don't you trust me?"

She snorted. "I can handle you."

He gave her a sharp look that made her draw in a hasty breath. It was clear his mind had gone straight below the waist. Come to think of it, so had hers. Instead of giving in to the sudden roar of heat that flamed from deep inside her, she narrowed her gaze at him.

"Well, where's this chariot?"

He laughed, the sound a deep rumble that hit straight to her solar plexus. A delicious, lazy sound better suited to a bedroom than a parking lot beside a B-grade motel.

"Over here."

He gestured toward a classic F-150, and as they drew nearer, he opened the passenger door for her. She eyed the antique surface of the truck. Clearly left to go to rack and ruin at some point, the vehicle had been restored, but the paintwork remained aged and patchy—almost as if the rust was a badge of honor.

"Ranching not going so well?" she asked, casting an obvious eye over the multicolored hood.

"Let's just say I appreciate the patina of time. It's been

treated and clear coated. A testament to the age and longevity of the beast."

Zoe cast him a sideways glance. A somewhat romantic statement from a man who made his living from the land and the animals upon it. Eschewing further comment, she climbed up onto the front seat and waited while he closed her door and stepped around to the driver's side. The cab had seemed so spacious until he swung up beside her. Then his shoulders were suddenly too close to hers and the cologne he wore wove around her on subtle waves of body heat. She turned her head to the window, but it was no good. Her senses were powerfully attuned to him. She didn't need to see him to know that his leather jacket was so soft and worn that it fitted his shoulders like a second skin, or that the crisp denim of his jeans pulled across his hips when he sat at the wheel.

She also knew that no matter where she was, she'd never again smell that scent and not think of him. Of the raw masculinity he exuded in his simple stance, or the latent power in his hands, the teasing in his eyes, the sardonic curl of his lip. She gave herself a mental shake. What the hell was she doing, thinking of him in these terms? Right now, he was someone of interest in her inquiries. Someone to question, not drool over. She was not that weak nor that vulnerable.

But it had been a while since she'd been intimate with anyone, and, she reminded herself bluntly, a woman had needs. Needs, it seemed, that were hell-bent on distracting her from her job. Well, she owed it to her victim to get to the bottom of who was behind his murder—and to bring them to justice.

They hadn't driven long before Galicia pulled up the truck outside a small hotel.

"This is us," he said, getting out of the truck and walking around to her side.

To preempt him opening her door, she did it herself and dropped down onto the pavement. She'd keep her distance from him, get whatever information she needed and then she'd be on her way. She didn't want to stay here in Royal any longer than necessary. It might be a thriving town, it might even be civilized, but it wasn't her city. These weren't her people. Especially not the tall, commanding figure walking beside her as they entered the hotel and headed toward the bar.

If she wasn't mistaken, there was a brief flare of approval in his eyes. Not that she cared. She wasn't here to impress him. He gave her a brief nod and put a hand at the small of her back, guiding her toward the bar. As they entered, he gestured to one side of the room.

"We'll sit over there."

She noted he made it a gentle order, not a suggestion. Okay, so he thought he was in charge. It was his turf. She'd play his game. For now.

"What's your poison?" Galicia asked as they reached their seats. "No, wait, let me guess."

She played along, watching as he stroked his chin and eyed her thoughtfully.

"Something frilly to counteract the tough-cop act."

"I assure you, it's no act—and you'd be wrong. I'll have a beer."

She couldn't help but notice the attention paid to him by the waitress who hurried over to take their order, but aside from a polite "thanks," he paid the woman no heed. Instead, he kept his searing focus very firmly on Zoe. The waitress was back in a moment, two chilled glasses and two ice-cold longneck lagers on her tray. She set the drinks onto the table in front of them.

"So, Cord, did you want these on your tab or—" the waitress started.

"I'll take care of them," Zoe said, flicking some bills from her pocket and dropping them onto the woman's tray. "Keep the change."

The waitress looked from Cord to Zoe and back again, Obviously she wasn't used to Cord's dates picking up the tab. She left as Cord picked up a beer, poured it into Zoe's glass and did the same for himself.

"You're quick," Cord said with a quirk of his lips. "I appreciate it. Thank you."

"I pay my way."

"Gender equality and all that?"

"You drove, I bought the first round. Gender equality has nothing to do with it." She arched a brow at him as he chuckled softly. "Are you deliberately trying to irritate me? Because if so, you'll find I'm hard to put off."

"I'm definitely not trying to put you off."

He smiled again, the movement of his lips sending a sucker punch to her gut. How did he manage to have such a strong effect on her? This was crazy. She'd been out with plenty of men, had relationships with a few, but she'd never felt this intense, visceral response before. It made her feel vulnerable, as if she were cast slightly adrift, and she didn't like it one bit. Determined to maintain the upper hand, she took charge of the conversation.

"So, how long have you lived around Royal?" she asked.

"Ah, the inquisition continues," he drawled. He sat back in his chair, hooking one arm over the back, and gazed at her through narrowed eyes.

"Inquisition?"

"Yeah, it's what you do, isn't it? Grill people?"

"Like dressed in black leather with torture implements and stuff like that?"

His lips quirked again, sending a spiral of sensation curling through her lower body. Oh, that mouth. How would it feel against hers? How would he taste?

"I could see you in that getup."

She snorted a laugh. "In your dreams, buster. So, back to my question. How long have you lived here?"

His nostrils flared on an indrawn breath. "Am I wet off the back of the truck, do you mean?"

She rolled her eyes. He was needling her, twisting her words to sound like a veiled insult. That might be the angle some of her colleagues would have taken, given there was no mistaking Galicia's Mexican heritage. But she was not that kind of person. In fact, none of her family was.

"Look, I asked you a simple question. You're being deliberately evasive again." She lifted her glass and took a long sip of her beer, relishing the bite of hoppy flavor as it rolled over her tongue and down her throat. "I'm not sure what you call conversation in this neck of Texas, but where I come from, when we meet a person, we chat, ask questions. Y'know, get to know one another."

He nodded slowly. "We have similar customs here."

She fought back a laugh. "I wouldn't have guessed it. Maybe it'd help if I went first? I'm Houston born and raised. Youngest of five. Third-generation cop. Your turn."

"Royal born and raised. Only child. My grandparents came here, bought land, ranched it, expanded the ranch. My father took over, did more of the same."

She nodded. "And you? Still expanding?"

He shrugged. "Not in land, more in better ways to use it."

She sat back in her chair and felt herself relax as he began to open up and discuss a little of how he planned to diversify his business operations. She let his voice roll over her, enjoying the timbre and the slow, measured way in which he spoke. She gestured to the waitress for two more beers.

"Let me get those," he said.

"If you insist," she acceded.

Once the drinks were on their table, she decided to turn the conversation back to her investigation.

"So, you and Jesse Stevens. You guys grew up together?"

"Yeah. And he's not the man you're looking for."

Ha, so much for softening him up and then pouncing with a question, Zoe admitted to herself with a measure of reluctance. Cord Galicia may have relaxed with her, but it didn't mean his mind wasn't as alert as a fox's.

"Why are you protecting him?"

"Protecting him?" Cord laughed. "Nope, I'm just saving you time."

"You realize I have to question him."

"Why? Is my word not good enough?" Galicia challenged her.

She saw the latent anger that simmered beneath the surface. Was it because she wanted to question his friend, or because she was impugning his honor by not accepting his word?

"I'm sure your word is just fine." She sighed. "But that's not how we conduct an investigation."

Silence stretched between them, and for a moment Zoe thought the evening was over. She felt a pang of regret. If she'd met this man under any other circumstances, then maybe they could have explored this simmering attraction that burned between them. She watched Galicia's face carefully, but he gave nothing away. Eventually, he leaned forward and put his hand out.

"How about a truce, then?" he suggested.

"A truce? I didn't know we were at war."

"Oh, we're at something, but I'm not quite sure what it is yet. How about, while we find out, we agree that you won't ask me anything about Jesse and then I won't need to stonewall you?"

She hesitated a moment before taking his hand. If she did this, she was opening herself up for a whole lot of trouble. She could feel it in her gut. But then again, what was life if it meant not taking risks? She reached out her hand and felt a surge of awareness the moment their palms touched. He felt it, too; she could see it in his eyes. He wasn't smiling now; in fact, he looked serious—serious about her.

Her inner muscles clenched on a wave of pure lust. Right now, she wanted to do nothing more than lean across their table, sweep their drinks aside and reach for him, then drag his face to hers and plant her lips on his mouth in a deep, drugging kiss that would hopefully assuage some of this crazy pent-up tension he manifested in her.

Instead, she jerked her hand free and reached for her beer, downing half of it. When she looked back at Galicia, amusement reflected back at her in his gaze and she knew, in that instant, he was dangerous. Maybe not in the criminal sense of the word, but certainly in terms of her equilibrium.

She was a long, tall streak of trouble. He knew that as surely as he knew the head count of his herd. But he couldn't leave her alone. Even now, after that stupid handshake, he wanted to touch her again—and not just her hand. He wanted to see if those pert breasts he could see pushing against the fabric of her shirt would fit neatly into the palms of his hands. He wanted to trace the cord of her throat with his lips and his tongue, to taste her and inhale the very essence of her.

Damn, but she did things to him that twisted his gut in knots without even trying. Which meant he had to be doubly careful. He was breaking every single one of his own rules by taking her out tonight. Still, it wasn't as if he was going to marry her or anything dumb like that, he told himself. He was distracting her. Keeping her away from Jesse. She had no business with his friend, and the sooner she realized that and returned to Houston, the sooner he could get back to his normal life. Thank goodness things were a little quieter on the ranch right now. The calves had been dried out and had regained condition. His pastures were under control and his hands were onto the usual maintenance required before winter set in. He had time to spare and he'd make sure he used it well.

"Say, you want to grab a burger or something?" Cord asked before finishing off his beer.

"I could eat a burger," Zoe admitted.

"C'mon, the Royal Diner makes the best burgers in the state."

"That's quite a claim," she said, rising from her seat.

"It's no claim. It's a fact," he boasted.

Putting his hand at the small of her back again, he guided her to the door. He liked the way she moved, all smooth and lithe, her gait a match for his own. His mind flashed in an instant to how they would move together— on a dance floor, between the sheets of his extra wide bed. Damn if he didn't get a hard-on. He reminded himself that this wasn't just about him. This was about keeping Zoe Warren away from his best friend.

Cord knew Jesse had been in touch with Hamm before Hamm's tragic death. He also knew Jesse had been fired up about the guy. If Zoe figured that out, she'd likely put two and two together and make whatever the hell she wanted out of it. There was no way Jesse had killed Hamm. He might have been mad at the guy, but violence had never been Jesse's style, not even when truly provoked.

They reached the truck, and he held her door for her. She brushed by so close he could smell the scent of her shampoo or whatever it was she'd used in her hair. It made him want to lean in and inhale more deeply. To touch her short black hair and see if he could tangle his fingers in it as he brought her face to his. He must have made a sound, because Zoe stopped midway getting into the truck.

"You okay?" she asked.

"Never better."

"Hmm."

She swung up, giving him an all-too-brief glimpse of her sweet butt showcased in dark denim. He closed the door firmly and went around to his side, all the while wondering what on earth he'd let himself in for.

Four

The woman had an appetite, Cord observed admiringly as she tucked into a double beef burger with all the trimmings. He'd ordered the same for himself. He nodded at a few of the people he knew as they went by, but mostly his attention was on the woman seated opposite him in the booth.

"Nice place, even better food," Zoe said when she finished her first bite.

"It's a staple here in Royal. You're always guaranteed a good meal."

"I like it. Thanks for bringing me here."

The simple compliment with her thanks made him feel ridiculously proud.

"So, tell me more about yourself," he said. "You mentioned you're the youngest of five? Is that right?"

"Yeah. I like to tell everyone that my mom and dad tried five times before they got the mixture right. My brothers would disagree. If they ever listened to me, that is."

Cord smiled. "Wow, four brothers. I can't even begin to imagine what that was like growing up."

As an only child whose future running the family spread was clearly outlined from birth, he had often wondered what it would have been like to share the load with one or more siblings. But from what he'd seen with a lot of his peers, siblings were overrated. Zoe spent the rest of their meal regaling him with stories of the things her brothers got up to while trying to keep her in line. Emphasis on the word *trying*. Seems she'd been a handful as a kid, and Cord wouldn't mind betting she hadn't changed much.

They were lingering over coffee when he saw her fight back a yawn. It made him realize the time—nearly ten. While that wasn't late, when you'd done a five-hour drive, like she had, or in his case, been up since before the crack of dawn, it was definitely time to bring the evening to an end.

"It's getting late. I'd best get you to your bed."

His choice of words had color flaming in her cheeks. He felt an answering wave of heat pulse through his body, too. To distract them both, he signaled for the check and paid, without demur from his guest this time, and they went out to the truck. When they reached her motel, he got down from the truck and walked her to her door.

"Thank you for dinner," Zoe said after opening her motel room and flicking on the light. "I enjoyed the company. It can get lonely on trips like this."

"Happy to help you pass the time," he drawled in response.

Even though he'd chosen his words to tease, oddly, he meant it. He'd engineered tonight to keep her away from Jesse but found himself enjoying her company. Hell, if he was totally honest, enjoying her. The air grew thick and heavy between them as she looked up into his eyes. Without thinking, Cord raised one hand and slid it around the back of her neck as he lowered his face to hers and gave in to the impulse to see if she tasted as good as he'd been imagining all evening.

He felt the shock that rippled through her body as his fingers touched the bare skin at her nape. Felt the sense of hesitation before her lips parted and she kissed him back. He'd been wrong. She tasted far better than he could ever have imagined, and somewhere along the line their kiss went from a questing beginning to something hot and hard and hungry. It was as if they were combustible elements, drawn together into a conflagration that took them both by surprise.

Zoe made a sound, like a deep hum, and he was lost. He wanted her—all of her. Forget she was a cop, forget she was investigating his best friend and most likely him, as well. Forget everything but the sweet, spicy flavor of her mouth, the softness of her lips and the urgency that pulled them together.

He snaked one arm around her waist, hauling her to him. Being tall, she lined up against his body perfectly, her hips against his, her mound pressing on his erection. She rolled her hips, and he groaned involuntarily. The subtle pressure of her body against his was driving him to the brink of his control. If this was what she could do to him clothed, imagine what they could do to each other naked.

Her hands slid over his shoulders; her fingers clenched on the leather of his jacket as he deepened the kiss. When his tongue tasted hers, she shuddered from head to foot. He did it again. Ah yes, there was that little hum from deep in her throat. She wasn't a passive woman. She gave back as good as he'd given. Her tongue was now dueling with his. And then she was pulling him through the doorway. Together they shuffled over the threshold. He kicked the motel room door closed behind them and spun her to push her up against the door.

Lacing his fingers with hers, he lifted her hands up so they were against the door on either side of her head. Then he bent and kissed a hot trail of wet sucking kisses from her lips to her finely boned jawline and down the sweet cords of her neck. Beneath his touch he felt her heated skin jump as sensation transferred from his touch to her. He let go of one of her hands and cupped her breast through her shirt, groaning in frustration as he felt the pebbled nipple against his palm.

This wasn't enough. He needed to touch her properly, without the barrier of clothing. His hand was at her buttons before he knew he'd even formed the thought clearly. In his haste he realized he'd torn one button loose from her shirt entirely when he heard the faint sound as it hit the carpet at their feet. But even that couldn't stop him in his pursuit of the need to see her naked. The front of her shirt fell open and he tugged the tails from her waistband and shoved the fabric aside.

He sucked in a sharp breath. She wore a black lace bra under that almost-masculine shirt of hers. The woman was a total contradiction. Touch-me-not plain clothing and lingerie made for sin beneath it.

"What do you think you're doing?" she asked, her breathing ragged.

"What does it look like I'm doing, Detective? I'm undertaking an investigation of my own," he growled.

He reached to cup one of her breasts in his large hand. Yeah, she fit like she was made for him. Rubbing his thumb across her distended nipple, he leaned in and buried his face against her skin and inhaled deeply.

"You smell so good. I could lose myself in you, Zoe Warren. Fair warning."

The hand he'd freed stroked down the front of his body until she cupped his erection through his jeans. "Looks like I have something to scrutinize here, myself."

He flexed against her, enjoying her boldness. "You gotta do what you gotta do, right?" he chuckled.

The sound strangled in his throat as she tightened her grip on him. She wasn't shy, but then neither was he. He gently tugged down the lacy cup of her bra, exposing her breast to his mouth. Taking her nipple carefully between his teeth, he rolled the nub with his tongue. Zoe's head fell back against the door and she moaned. Letting her other hand go, he reached behind her back to loosen the hooks of her bra. He was still impeded by the straps remaining over her shoulders, but at least now he could shove the enticing garment up, exposing both her breasts to his starving gaze.

Her nipples were a dark raspberry pink, topping luscious creamy skin. He kissed one, then the other, his hands cupping her from underneath as he divided his attention between them. Zoe had let go of him, her fingers now knotted in his hair, holding him to her as if she never wanted to let go. That was fine by him, he decided as he let one hand drop to the fastening of her jeans. He swiftly undid the button and pushed down her zipper before reaching inside.

He felt the heat of her before he even reached the damp lace at the juncture of her thighs. It was a tight fit, his large hand inside her jeans, but it was worth the discomfort to feel how hot she was for him, how ready. His own arousal grew to painful proportions as he touched her through the lace, pressed on that spot that made her cry out in pleasure.

He took her mouth again in a deep, intoxicating kiss, his tongue probing her mouth in time to the pressure of his fingers on her down below. She pressed into him, as if she couldn't get close enough, and then, in a sudden rush of heat, he felt her climax against his hand.

It took every ounce of control not to come in his jeans as she shuddered beneath his touch. Instead, he used his caresses to gentle her, as he would one of his horses, with slow sweeps of his hands—drawing out her pleasure, prolonging his own torture. He knew it would take only a moment to unfasten his jeans, sheath himself and drive into her heat right here against the motel room door. But when he made love to her properly—and he knew he would sometime, hopefully very soon—it would be in a large comfortable bed where he could truly explore what they could achieve together.

Cord straightened her clothing and kissed her again.

"I'd better go."

"Go?"

For the first time since he'd met her, she sounded unsure.

"Yeah, I'll be seeing you soon."

With that, he moved her bodily away from the door and opened it. He strode straight to his truck and got immediately inside, no mean feat when he had a hard-on that made his jeans uncomfortably tight as he settled himself into the drive home. He hazarded just one look at the motel room door before he backed out of the parking space. She stood there, holding the front of her shirt together with a bemused expression on her face.

Good, let her be bemused. While he might be in agony and his balls might be blue, he'd left with the upper hand. Let her think on that for a while.

Zoe rose the next morning still mad. She should never have let him kiss her, let alone touch her like that. And she'd climaxed, right there against the motel room door, she thought, staring balefully at the unassuming slab of wood. She never came like that—so quick, so intense.

Even now, thinking about it, she felt a tingle of anticipation all over again. Damn Cord Galicia for being so clever with his hands. *And don't forget his lips and tongue*, her subconscious oh-so-helpfully supplied.

This was hopeless. She needed to get out of here and do something, anything, to replace the memories Cord had instilled in her last night. She wondered how he'd felt as he'd left—whether he'd taken care of himself later once he'd gotten home. Perhaps in the shower, with hot water coursing over his body like a lover's caress. It was all too easy to picture in her mind and all too distracting, again.

She strode angrily to the bathroom. It was basic but, like the rest of the motel room, clean and functional. Besides, with how uptight she was feeling right now, there was no way she was going for comfort. Setting the shower to as cold as she could bear, she got under the spray and pulled the curtain across to encapsulate herself in the small space. She lathered up quickly and rinsed off, skimming her body with her hands and determinedly pushing back the memories of another set of hands on her pale skin. Of broad suntanned fingers touching and teasing her body, of those same fingers coaxing responses from her that had left her limp and sated and hungry for more at the same time.

It angered her that she'd been that easy. She'd come to Royal to further her investigation, not to have meltingly hot sex against a motel room door. And what was with that? Where had all her good sense gone? She'd been the one to drag him across the threshold and into her room. And when he kissed her, she kissed him back, as if she'd been starving for that level of attention. Okay, so maybe that bit was true, she admitted ruefully as she snapped off the shower and reached for her towel. It had been a while, and she'd never been the type to enjoy casual encounters. Her work made maintaining a relationship difficult at the best of times. She worked long hours, dedicated to both her team and to the victims whose stories she had to uncover. And that was what she was here for, she reminded herself sternly as she wiped her still-tingling body dry. Work, not play.

By the time she was dressed, she realized she was starving. She'd spied a coffee shop when she'd driven into town yesterday. It might be a good place for her to formulate her plan of attack for today. She still needed to get ahold of Jesse Stevens and actually talk to the man. She got into her car and, using the hands-free kit, called the number she had for the Stevens ranch. This time she got a staff member, but she still wasn't able to speak to Jesse. Frustrated, Zoe drove to the coffee shop.

She got a parking space right out front and walked up to the café, laughing under her breath at the name, the Daily Grind. Her nostrils were assailed with the delicious aroma of freshly roasted coffee beans the moment she entered. She ordered her coffee and a Danish and took a seat looking out the front window. Royal was a busy place, she realized, as people headed on their daily commute to work and school. The Daily Grind was no less busy as people stopped in for their morning coffee on their way to work, or settled in for a quick breakfast. When her coffee and Danish came, she took her time enjoying the flavors and skimmed the news on her phone. It looked like the Houston papers were still bemoaning the lack of progress in the Hamm murder.

She knew it wasn't personal—they had little to go on, but even so it irked her intensely that they hadn't been able to discover more by now. A heading regarding the Texas Cattleman's Club caught her eye. It looked like the official opening would be going ahead next month. No doubt that would be a glittering affair with all of Houston's who's who of anything important in attendance. She wondered about the guy who'd featured as an early suspect in the Hamm case—Sterling Perry. A leading contender for the presidency of the new club, he was an arrogant piece of work who wore his family's wealth like a second skin. She would have loved to have seen his ass nailed when her colleagues had arrested him on suspicion of operating a Ponzi scheme, but he'd been cleared of that. Even when he'd been suspected of being involved in Hamm's murder there'd been nothing to support the initial leads—the guy was like Teflon. Nothing stuck.

And then there was the other guy vying for the presidential role, Ryder Currin. Younger than Sterling Perry, Currin was far more charismatic and her research had shown he'd come into most of his money through sheer, hard work. Even now, despite his millions, the guy dressed as if he'd just stepped off the ranch. Zoe had wondered if the rivalry between the men had anything to do with Hamm's murder, but Ryder Currin had an airtight alibi for the window of time when Hamm was murdered. He'd been stranded at a local shelter when the storm hit and Angela Perry, Sterling Perry's daughter, had been there, too, and had vouched for him.

Zoe consumed her Danish and knocked back her coffee before leaving a tip and returning to her car. Maybe she'd have better luck tracking Stevens down at the hospital. Cord had told her his sister was there.

The Royal Memorial Hospital was easy to find, and visitor parking was relatively empty at this early hour. No doubt because visiting hours weren't until later in the day, she realized. She clipped her badge onto her waistband and went inside, knowing that the badge might give her access she would otherwise not get.

Sure enough, she was shown through to a ward where

Janet Stevens was recovering. The young woman was in a room on her own—apparently having been moved there not long before, after a brief stint in ICU post surgery. That was obviously why Cord had been so protective of his friend, knowing the other man must have been worried about his sibling. Galicia's protectiveness was, at its heart, an admirable trait, except for the part where he'd attempted to stall her investigation.

It made her wonder anew if that incident between them last night hadn't just been a distraction tactic. Something to blur her mind and keep her off Stevens's trail. Maybe he'd thought the little woman would be so blown away by what he'd done to her that she'd even hightail it back home.

Zoe discarded the thought almost as quickly as it bloomed in her mind. She'd been the one to pull him into her room, not the other way around. If anything, she was to blame for what had happened between them. And he'd been the one to walk away, unfulfilled. What did that say about the man? She shook her head. He was a conundrum, that was for sure. One she wouldn't have minded exploring further, if the circumstances had been different. But they weren't, and she had a job to do.

Zoe presented her badge to the duty nurse and asked if she could have a few words with Janet Stevens. The nurse was cagey, but after a quick call to Janet's doctor she said that Zoe was allowed five minutes, no more. Grateful for that, Zoe entered the younger woman's room.

Janet Stevens was pale but breathing without assistance. Walking farther into the room, Zoe watched the other woman as she opened her eyes.

"Good morning, Ms. Stevens. How are you feeling today?"

"Okay, I guess."

Janet's voice was groggy, as if she was still on some heavy-duty pain relief.

"I won't take much of your time," Zoe said quickly and introduced herself, explaining why she was there. "I'm sorry to bother you, but I can't seem to get ahold of your brother. I need to ask him a few questions."

"About Vincent? Whatever for? I know Jesse was mad at him, but he would never have hurt him," Janet protested.

"Can you tell me why your brother was mad at Mr. Hamm?" Zoe pressed, feeling a surge of excitement that she might finally be getting closer to finding some of the answers she needed.

"It's all my fault," Janet said weakly. "Jesse asked Vincent if he could return a favor and find me an internship at Perry Holdings. I've completed my MBA and Jesse thought Vincent would be decent about helping me. Turns out that while he was happy to accept Jesse's help plenty of times, he wasn't so keen to return the favor."

Would that have been enough to make Jesse Stevens commit murder? People killed over less. And it depended on the level of help Stevens had extended to Hamm in the past and what he thought the dead man owed him. She needed to meet the man to gauge for herself. A sound at the door had her looking up. Seemed she'd be meeting Jesse Stevens sooner rather than later, judging by the thunderous appearance on the face of the man entering the room.

"Who the hell are you and what are you doing in my sister's room?" he growled.

He was tall, blond like the girl in the bed beside her and he had piercing green eyes that looked as if they could cut through steel. His sister lifted a hand.

"Jesse, please," she implored gently.

"Detective Zoe Warren, Houston P.D.," Zoe said, gesturing to her badge on her waistband. "And you are?"

Even though she knew exactly who he was, it was important to her to establish who was in control.

"Jesse Stevens."

He answered bluntly, without offering his hand. It seemed she was persona non grata. A tiny smile curled her lips. Good, she liked knowing she'd riled him from the outset. Holding the upper hand was always her chosen starting point.

"Ah, Mr. Stevens. I've been trying to get ahold of you. Didn't you get my messages?"

A faint flush of color marked his cheeks. "I did."

She maintained her silence while raising one brow at him. His flush deepened. Just then, the nurse who'd directed Zoe to Janet's room appeared in the door and gave Zoe a stern look.

"Ms. Stevens needs to rest," she said pointedly.

"Thank you, I'm just leaving. Mr. Stevens, can I have a word with you outside?" Zoe asked.

"One minute, that's all."

Well, we'll see about that, Zoe thought to herself as she preceded him into the hallway outside his sister's room.

"Is there somewhere we could speak privately?" Zoe asked the nurse.

The woman gestured to a small sitting room down the hallway.

"C'mon," Zoe said to Stevens. "The sooner we get started, the sooner you can get back to your sister."

Realizing he had no reason to object, he fell into step behind her. Once they were in the room, Zoe closed the door behind him.

"What do you want?" Jesse asked, his voice and stance both belligerent.

"Just need to ask you a few questions."

"Ever heard of email?"

Zoe snorted lightly. "It's a strange thing," she said slowly. "We cops prefer to do things face-to-face. You can learn a lot about a person that way. So, tell me, why have you been avoiding me? Got something to hide?"

Anger flashed in his eyes for a moment before he visibly dragged himself under control.

"I have nothing to hide. What's this about?"

"Vincent Hamm." She threw the name into the conversation as if it were a gauntlet thrown in challenge.

"I knew him. What about it?"

"Been in touch with him lately?" she probed.

His gaze grew flat and cold. "Not for a few months. Why?"

"And when was the last time you spoke with him?"

"To be honest with you, I haven't spoken to him in a long time." Stevens huffed out a breath and rubbed his cheeks with one long-fingered hand.

Zoe grabbed her notebook out of her jacket pocket and flipped through a few pages before citing a date from a couple of months ago.

"Does that date sound familiar?"

"No more than any other date," Stevens replied.

"What about this—*Thanks for nothing, Hamm.* Do you remember saying that?"

"That's what this is about? A phone message?"

"Answer the question, please."

"Yeah, I remember saying that."

"You sounded pretty pissed off."

"Look, it isn't what you're thinking."

"And what am I thinking, Mr. Stevens?"

"How the hell would I know? You're a cop. It's bound to be bad, right?"

"Mr. Hamm is dead. I want to know how he came to be that way."

Stevens, to his credit, looked stunned. "You think I did it?"

"I'm not sure what to think right now," Zoe said honestly. "But you're not helping your case by being evasive with me. Let me warn you, Mr. Stevens. I am very good at my job, and I will get to the bottom of this."

"Look, it wasn't me. I wasn't anywhere near Houston when he was killed."

"So, you know exactly when he was killed?" she asked pointedly.

"Of course I don't. Look, whatever happened to him, I had no part of it. In fact, I was at a stock auction, buying cattle. I've even got receipts to prove it."

"Perhaps you would like to inform me what part you do have in my investigation during a formal interview to which you can bring those receipts."

Stevens rubbed his face again. "Sure, when?"

"Let me talk to Sheriff Battle. I'll work something out with him and I'll be in touch. And this time…?"

"Yeah?"

"Answer your damn phone."

Five

Cord's phone chimed to signal an incoming message. It was from Jesse.

Met your new girlfriend today.

Cord tapped the icon that would ring Jesse's phone. Texting was all well and good but sometimes you just needed to talk. This was definitely one of those times. His friend answered on the second ring.

"Is Janet doing okay now?" Cord asked.

No matter how mad he was right now, certain things needed to be taken care of first.

"Yeah, surprisingly well, considering how sick she was straight after surgery. They moved her onto the ward this morning before I got there. Gave me a heart attack to get up to ICU and find she wasn't there."

"I bet."

After Jesse and Janet's parents died, the two of them became even closer, since all they had left was each other. Cord could only imagine how Jesse must have felt to find Janet missing from the room where she'd been taken after surgery.

"I was surprised to see your girlfriend had beaten me there, though."

"I don't have a girlfriend," he enunciated carefully.

Even so, he knew exactly who Jesse was talking about, and the slow burn of fury rose from deep within. She hadn't listened to a word he'd said. Not only had she not stayed away from Jesse, she'd gone to the hospital and bothered Janet while she was at it. He rode the wave of anger for a few long seconds. Jesse was talking, but the buzz in Cord's ears made him sound like he was some distance away. Eventually Jesse's words sank in.

"She's a mighty fine-looking woman, even if she is a pain in the ass. Had some questions for me and wouldn't leave until she'd asked them."

"She questioned you? There at the hospital?"

She had nerve, he'd give her that.

"Yup, and I've agreed to an interview at the sheriff's office, too."

"You don't need to do that." Cord bristled. "And if you do, make sure you take your lawyer."

"I don't need my lawyer, Cord. No matter how much I wanted to wring the guy's neck, I did not kill Vincent Hamm."

"I know you didn't. Aside from the fact you're not that kind of guy, weren't you away around that time?"

Jesse made a sound of assent. "I've got nothing to hide, and the sooner your girlfriend realizes that, the better."

"Like I said, she's not my girlfriend."

Jesse chuckled. "But there's something going on, isn't there?"

The man was too damn astute. Yeah, there was something, but even he couldn't define the way Zoe Warren had crawled under his skin.

"She's a cop. Trust me, there's nothing going on," Cord said firmly.

"If you say so."

Their conversation drifted to ranching matters, and they eventually finished their call. Cord pocketed his phone and felt tension coil within his body. He wanted nothing more right now than to take his horse to the open pastures and go for a blistering ride. Anything to expend this pent-up energy that resided in a red-hot knot in the center of his gut.

He still couldn't believe the nerve of Detective Warren. The idea that the woman he'd left trembling last night had calmly gotten up this morning and gone straight to the hospital made him so mad he needed to do something to work it off. Preferably something to do with her. The random thought struck him square in the solar plexus, robbing him of breath. He strode through the house and out to the stables, the ride he'd been thinking of at the forefront of his mind. But then halfway through saddling up his favorite gelding, he hesitated and pulled his cell phone from his pocket.

Since he'd left Zoe Warren last night, he'd all but talked himself into staying away from her, but it seemed that would have to take a back seat. He needed to talk to the woman and set her straight about a few things. Clearly she hadn't been listening yesterday. He needed to ensure she listened to him today.

Zoe spent much of the middle part of the day back in her motel room working on her computer and going over all the information she had to date. No matter which way she looked at things, the answers she sought remained very firmly out of reach. She put in a call to her boss and apprised him of where she was so far. His response had not been heartening. Zoe's stomach grumbled, bemoaning the fact she hadn't picked up anything for lunch, when her reminder pinged to say it was time to meet the sheriff at the diner.

Her mouth watered the minute she set foot in the place. A wave from a booth near the front windows drew her attention, and she walked over to the sheriff and stuck out her hand.

"Sheriff Battle, good to see you again."

The sheriff stood and took her hand. "Call me Nate."

His grip was firm and dry, and unlike a lot of men she met in the line of duty, he didn't seem to feel the need to exert pressure and dominance over her by crushing the bones in her hands with the introductory gesture.

"Something sure smells good here," Zoe commented as she slid into the seat opposite him.

"I can recommend the pie. Of course, I am biased. This is my wife's business." He patted his firm stomach. "Hell of a job staying fit with that temptation in my life."

Zoe laughed. A waitress came over and poured her a coffee. She smiled her thanks and ordered a slice of pie to go with it. So what if it wasn't exactly healthy to eat pie for lunch this late in the day? A woman deserved a treat every now and then, right?

When the pie was delivered, she quickly sampled a bite and closed her eyes and made a blissful sound deep in her throat.

"Told you it was good," the sheriff said laconically as he leaned back against the red faux-leather booth.

"You weren't lying," Zoe agreed, quickly scooping up

another bite before putting her fork down and dabbing at her mouth with a paper napkin. It was time she got to the point. "What can you tell me about Jesse Stevens?"

"Jesse?" Nate Battle looked puzzled for all of two seconds. "I thought you were after Sterling Perry?"

"He's been cleared. So, Stevens?"

"You think he's got something to do with Vincent's murder?"

His tone was cautious, as if he was sounding her out, even though he clearly didn't believe she was on the right track. She explained about the voice mail message Stevens had left, then played the sound file from her phone.

"He sure sounds annoyed," the sheriff said mildly. "But that doesn't mean he did anything."

"You don't think he's capable of murder?" Zoe challenged.

"I didn't say that."

"But?" She knew he was leaving more unsaid.

"I just can't see it. The man's a hard worker, keeps to himself when necessary, steps up for the community through the Texas Cattleman's Club on a regular basis. But murder? No. Jesse's not the kind of guy to hold a grudge."

"Well, we'll see about that when I interview him."

Between her and the sheriff they arranged a suitable day and time. She wasn't worried that Jesse would run out of town. His devotion to his sister had been more than clear. He wouldn't be leaving her while she was in the hospital, and judging by how frail the young woman was, she'd probably need some continued care at home, too. There was no way Jesse was leaving anytime soon.

Thinking about Jesse led her thoughts to his neighbor. The guy had been defensive on his friend's behalf yesterday—and very distracting last night every time she'd tried to draw the conversation toward her investigation. Thinking about it this morning, once her mind had cleared from the unaccustomed haze of sensual fog he'd wrapped her in, she'd begun to wonder if his attention to her wasn't part of some greater scheme to distract her from her purpose.

"What do you know about Cord Galicia?" she blurted.

Battle gave her a strange look. Maybe because the instant she'd asked the question she felt heat begin to rise from her chest and up her throat. If she wasn't mistaken, she'd be breaking out in the nervous blotches of color that used to be her curse when she was a teenager facing a stressful situation.

"Cord? Well, he's Jesse's neighbor. They grew up together. Help one another out when necessary. They even learned to fly together back when they were in their late teens."

"But what about the man himself?"

The waitress came and poured the sheriff another coffee, and he took his time doctoring it how he liked it before he responded.

"He's a decent guy. You don't think he did it, do you? He and Jesse are tight, but Cord wouldn't commit murder for him."

"I don't know. Galicia was very protective of Stevens when I questioned him yesterday."

"You questioned him yesterday?" He blew out a breath. "You sure didn't waste any time upsetting the locals, did you? I thought we'd agreed to talk before you started questioning people."

She heard the note of censure in his voice. "I just wanted to get a feel for where people were situated on this thing. You can appreciate that my goal is to find whoever is guilty of Hamm's murder and charge them accordingly. I'm not here on vacation."

"I get that, but don't go off like a steer at a gate. Upset

folks and they'll close ranks and you'll get nothing out of them."

Zoe closed her eyes and breathed in deeply before opening them again. "I'm just doing my job. I've been living and breathing this case for months now. I want it solved."

"If it can be solved."

She didn't want to admit it, but he was right. "Yeah, there's that, too. The longer this takes, the harder it's going to be to find the evidence we need. Everything was compromised in the flood."

The sheriff's phone buzzed on the table in front of him and he glanced at the screen.

"I'm sorry, I'm going to have to take that."

"Go ahead."

She watched as he answered the call and got up to pace the sidewalk outside the diner. After a few minutes he shoved the phone into his pocket and came back inside.

"I have to go. Get in touch with my office to arrange a time to use the interview room. They'll make sure you have all the equipment you need."

"Thanks, Sheriff. I appreciate it."

"And call me before you go questioning my people, okay? You may actually get a better result if I come along with you."

"Noted, thanks."

She finished her pie and lingered over another coffee before heading to the sheriff's department, where she arranged to interview Jesse using their equipment. Apparently it would take a day or two to set up, because their camera and recording equipment were glitchy. While the news was frustrating, there was nothing she could do about it other than wait. There were probably worse places to cool her heels for a few days. The problem was she couldn't think of any right now.

* * *

Cord felt a whole ton better after a hard ride, but the irritation he'd felt over Zoe confronting Jesse at the hospital still prickled under his skin. He grabbed his phone and scrolled through his saved numbers, then punched the one he was looking for with a determined index finger. It rang three times before going to voice mail. Ha, she was avoiding him, was she? He contemplated hanging up without leaving a message, but where was the fun in that? Instead, he forced himself to smile as he spoke.

"I couldn't sleep last night for thinking about you. Call me."

Hopefully his message would rile her enough for her to call him. If not, well, he'd be paying her a visit. He was contemplating adding a hard swim in his pool to the ride he'd just had, when his phone buzzed in his pocket. A quick glance at the display brought a smile curling around his lips.

"Missing me?" he answered.

"Not at all," Zoe said breezily. "Did you want me for something?"

He hesitated, letting the silence play between them before speaking. "Now there's a leading question."

"Quit fooling, Galicia. Why did you call?"

"Come to the ranch for barbecued ribs tonight. Seven o'clock."

"What if I'm busy?"

"You gotta eat."

He could feel her indecision over the phone and chose his next words very carefully. "What are you afraid of, Zoe?"

"Not you," she answered swiftly.

He chuckled. "See you at seven."

He severed the call before she could respond. A smile

wreathed his face as he imagined her irritation at not having had the last word. It was kind of fun to keep her off-kilter just that little bit. To get where she was in her line of work, she had to be some kind of dogged control freak—turning over metaphorical stones and looking for clues every day. He'd bet she wasn't used to someone making decisions for her, and he really liked that, in this instance, it was him doing it.

She'd turn up tonight—he'd bet his newly weaned calves on it.

The entire drive to the Galicia spread, Zoe cursed under her breath. The arrogance of the man, ordering her around like that. *But you're going there, aren't you?* a voice in the back of her mind taunted. *You want to see him again.*

"Shut up!" she said aloud.

Or maybe you just want him?

The question rattled around in her mind as she rolled through the gates and up the long driveway to his house. He'd gotten her off so damn fast last night that he'd left her reeling. She hadn't even known she could feel so much so quickly. For her, lovemaking had always been a long, slow buildup, not always followed by release. But with him? It had been mere minutes. And every sensation he'd wrought from her had made her want more.

So, yeah, she was prepared to admit she wanted him. She couldn't continue to fool herself that she was coming out here to question him about Jesse Stevens, especially when Stevens himself had said he'd turn up for the recorded interview in a couple of days.

Zoe stopped her car and got out, staring at the house for the second time in as many days and admiring the stone exterior. The place looked solid, durable and reliable. *A reflection of its master?* she wondered. There was movement at the door, and Cord Galicia strode out, his presence commanding her eye from the second he came through the doorway.

Yes, *master* was the right term for him. Master of all he surveyed? *He might like to think so.* She smiled inwardly. But he was no master to her. She'd come here because she wanted to, not because he'd all but ordered her presence.

"I'm glad you came," he said as she approached the front entrance.

"Ribs are my weakness," she answered with as much insouciance as she could muster.

He showed her inside and then led her through the house and outside to a loggia. The scent of hickory smoke hung in the air and, combined with the aroma of barbecuing meat, made Zoe's mouth water in anticipation.

"What can I get you to drink? Wine?"

"No wine for me, not when I have to drive back to town," Zoe protested.

"You could always stay."

Her inner muscles tightened on a swell of desire at the simplicity of his words. She shouldn't have been surprised. She'd been half expecting it, hadn't she? Half *wanting* it, too?

"We'll see," she answered, keeping her words deliberately evasive.

"Wine it is, then."

She didn't argue when he poured two glasses of red wine and passed one to her.

"Thanks. The ribs smell good."

"They are good."

"Oh, you're so confident of your ability?"

"Abuelita's secret recipe," he said with a sly wink.

"Not so secret if you know it," Zoe felt compelled to point out.

"True, but she spent a lot of time showing me how to look after myself. She also told me that to win the heart of a good woman, a man needs to know how to do more than reheat a can of beans."

Zoe laughed. "Is that what you're doing? Trying to win my heart?"

As soon as she said the words, she realized they'd have been better left unsaid. A shadow passed over Cord's face and his light mood changed.

"Just offering some Royal hospitality while you're here," he said before taking a sip of wine. "What do you think of the wine?"

She took a sip, too. "Mmm, it's good, like velvet. I like how it doesn't leave a dry aftertaste on your tongue."

"It'll taste even better with the ribs."

He gestured for her to take a seat on the large outdoor rattan sofa, and she sank comfortably against the overstuffed pillows. He lowered himself in the seat opposite.

"A girl could fall asleep here if she wasn't careful," she commented.

"Didn't sleep so good last night?"

A flush stained her cheeks. "Look, about last night."

"Hmm?"

He looked at her over the rim of his glass, and at the heat in his gaze Zoe felt her toes curl in her sensible low-heeled shoes.

She shook her head. "Never mind. Least said, soonest mended."

He laughed. "Is that something your grandmother used to say?"

She smiled a little. "Yeah."

"Zoe," he said as he leaned forward, his gaze intense. "Last night was merely an appetizer."

Six

Cord wasn't sure what devil of impulse had driven him to say that to her, but it was satisfying to watch the play of raw emotion that danced across her features. He could pinpoint the exact moment she decided to take control.

"Is that so?" she asked, arching a dark brow at him. "We'll see about that."

"Yes." He nodded. "We will."

Again he had the satisfaction of seeing her lose her tenuous grip on the conversation, and he decided to turn things to more general matters. He didn't want to alienate her entirely. It was enough, for now, that she was here.

"What do you do in your spare time?" he asked, reaching for the bottle and topping off her glass.

"Spare time?" She laughed. "What's that?"

"You're a workaholic?"

"Aren't you? You can't run a spread as big as this one without long hours, right?"

He tipped his head in acknowledgment. "But I have people I delegate to. An experienced foreman, ranch hands. Are you telling me your work is your life?"

"My work is a very important part of my life. I want to be the best."

"Better than your dad."

"Better than everyone in my family."

He looked at her a little closer. Being the youngest in a testosterone-heavy family had obviously left its scars. Zoe Warren felt she had something to prove to the males in her family, and it had to be proven on their battleground.

"What would you have done if you hadn't been a cop?"

"I never wanted to be anything else, much to my mom's great disappointment. After four boys she thought she could raise a kindred spirit. Someone who might enjoy shopping with her, attending high teas or getting pampered at the beauty shop. But that's not me. It doesn't mean she's given up on me, though," Zoe finished saying with a deep chuckle.

"Sounds like an intrepid woman."

"She is. I admire her, a lot. It can't be easy to see every person you love step out the door every day and have to wonder whether or not they'll come home safely."

Cord felt that unwelcome clench around his heart that he always got when reminded of Britney. He knew exactly what Zoe was talking about, and he knew just how much it hurt when that loved one didn't come home again. He put his glass onto the wooden table between them and got up to check on the ribs, anything to put a little distance between him and the reminder that while he may be powerfully attracted to Zoe Warren, she was first, last and always a police officer. He wouldn't go through that again.

The ribs were almost done. His grandmother would have been proud.

"I'm just going to grab the salad and corn bread. Be back in a minute," he said in Zoe's direction.

"Can I help?"

"Nope. You just stay right there," he said firmly.

As large as his kitchen was, he didn't want to be moving around it with her behind him. After last night he was struggling to keep his hands and his mouth to himself, and it had taken some effort to play the considerate host. To pass her a glass of wine without touching her fingers. To watch her sample the beverage without leaning forward to kiss the residue from her lips.

Damn, he was getting hard just thinking about it. To distract himself he went to the large double fridge and pulled out the bowl of salad he'd prepared shortly before her arrival. Setting it on a tray, he then grabbed the basket of corn bread he'd put in the oven to warm. He already had utensils and plates in an old painted wooden sideboard out in the loggia.

"You look very domesticated," Zoe commented as he quickly set the outdoor table and lit a bunch of squat candles in the center of the table.

"I'm a man of many talents. Come, take a seat," he suggested. "I'll get the ribs off the grill."

He plated up the ribs and brought the platter to the table.

"You mentioned your grandmother. Did she raise you?" Zoe asked as he settled into his place.

"Both my grandparents were still here with us when my father took over the ranch. My grandfather died five years ago but Abuelita is still fighting fit. She lives with my parents. When Dad retired, he decided he wanted to get away from ranching. Told me that if he lived here, or near here, he'd always be interfering in my way of doing things and he didn't think that was fair. They bought a condo in Palm Springs, but to be honest, I don't think he's happy there. Oh, he puts on a good face and all, but he's a farm boy at heart. Rounds of golf and cocktails at five?" Cord shook his head. "That's not his lifestyle."

"I guess he made his choice, though, right?"

"It worries me that he's unhappy. His pride won't let him admit he's made a mistake. I would welcome him back. His knowledge is invaluable, and God knows the house is big enough for us all to continue living here without tripping over one another. It worked for him and his parents. I don't see why it wouldn't have worked for us." He shrugged. "Whatever, it is what it is."

"I couldn't wait to move out of home and get a place of my own. Even though my brothers are all married, I just felt suffocated by my family's expectations of me."

"Their expectations?" Cord probed.

"I'm a girl. They want me to settle down and have babies."

"And quit your career?"

Her laugh was scornful. "They don't see this as my career. It's a placeholder to them, until I do the right thing and find a good man and settle down and let him support me. My family is fiercely traditional."

"Well, there's traditional and there's dark ages," Cord commiserated.

He picked up the wine bottle and held it above her glass without pouring, just waiting for her assent or refusal. There was no way she'd be legal to drive if she had another glass of wine. They both knew it. If she accepted the drink, she was staying. It wasn't until he allowed the thought to form again in his mind that he realized just how much he wanted her to stay. How much he wanted to explore her again. The moment Zoe's fingers lightly grasped the slender stem of the wineglass and lifted it toward the bottle, every particle in his body stirred.

Her blue eyes met his and locked. He saw the faint remnants of indecision fade and be replaced by something else. Heat. Need. Desire. He slowly tipped the bottle and poured.

"Thank you," she said, lifting the glass to her lips and taking a sip.

"No, thank you," Cord said, his voice no more than a rumble.

He dragged his focus back to their meal, to the succulent meat that, with a gentle bite, simply twisted off the ribs, then melted on the tongue in a burst of flavors. But right now his taste buds were flooded with the memory of Zoe's skin from last night, and the longing to repeat the experience—and more.

He couldn't say how he got through the rest of the meal or what they discussed. All he could think about was the fact that Zoe Warren was staying the night. Sure, she might yet take him up on the guest-room idea, but he had a feeling that she'd be sleeping with him. Actually, sleeping was the furthest thing from his mind. The anticipation of how the rest of their night would unfold settled around him, filling him with a sizzling buzz of excitement. Yeah, this was going to be a good night. He would put aside the reasons she'd come here and what she did for a living, and he'd make damn sure she forgot them, too.

Zoe felt herself relax in increments. It had to be the wine she'd unwisely drunk, she told herself. It would have nothing to do with the man sitting opposite her. The man who'd put together a meal that was worthy of any five-star restaurant, because even in its simplicity, it had been imbued with a myriad of flavors that varied in intensity but each of which created both craving and satisfaction. A bit like the man himself.

And just like that she didn't feel quite so relaxed anymore. She'd made a conscious decision here tonight. The moment she'd accepted his offer of wine, she knew she'd be staying—and forget about any guest room. The hum of her body had heightened to a persistent buzz of need, and the idea of taking care of that need on her own held little appeal when there was a warm and willing partner right here in front of her. She allowed herself to revel in the air of expectancy that built between herself and Cord Galicia.

When they finished their food, Cord began to clear their things away. Zoe swiftly rose to assist him.

"You don't need to help. You're my guest here tonight," Cord protested.

"Of course I'm helping you," she answered firmly, stacking plates and cutlery.

She followed him through to the kitchen, where she rinsed dishes while he stacked the state-of-the-art dishwasher. Clearly ranching was a profitable business for this family, not that money impressed her necessarily, but she liked seeing people enjoy the fruits of their hard labor—even if it was something as simple as a dishwasher. She made a passing comment, complimenting Cord on his choice in kitchenware. He laughed.

"You think I had anything to do with any of this?" He flung out his arms to encapsulate the entire room. "No way. When Dad declared his retirement, my mom and Abuelita took it as a chance to ensure that I didn't have to lift more than a finger without a woman here to look after me. Everything was changed. You just about need a software degree to operate the oven, let alone the microwave."

Zoe laughed along with him, but inside she felt something pull tight and close up like a clamshell. Clearly there was an expectation in this family that the women took care of their men. Not that looking after a household and all the multiple things that fell under that umbrella was in any way less important than what she did, but to Zoe her career was everything. She wouldn't give it up for anyone.

And no one is asking you to, that voice in the back of her mind reminded her tersely. *Basically you're here to satisfy an urge. Don't expect any more than that, nor any less.*

With that voice ringing clearly in her mind, Zoe cocked her head and watched Cord as he completed the cleanup. There was something very satisfying about watching a strong and capable man busy in the pursuit of domestic duties. Sexy even. Yeah, definitely sexy. Cord had big, strong hands with long, deft fingers. He kept his nails short and clean, but there was no denying those hands had calluses earned through hard work and determination. And yet they could be gentle, too, she thought on a shiver of memory.

"Everything okay?" Cord said as he turned to face her.

"Oh yes," she replied. "Just thinking about dessert."

"Dessert?"

"Yeah. You said last night was the appetizer. You've just fed me dinner. Which kind of leaves…" She let her voice trail away suggestively.

"Dessert."

He took a step closer, and Zoe felt the heat in the room skip up a few notches. When he reached out a hand to stroke her face with his fingertips, it was all she could do not to throw herself into his arms. Instead, she stood there, her eyes locked with his, her body all but visibly shaking as she waited to see what he would do next. She didn't have to wait long.

Cord moved fast, his arms going around her and one hand cupping the back of her head as he lowered his face to hers and took her lips in a searing kiss that all but turned her legs to water. Hot, steaming water, but boneless nonetheless. She reveled in the feel of his firm body as he hauled her against him, plastering her soft curves against his harder frame. And she lost herself in the taste of him—hot, sinful, spicy and sweet all at once.

Suddenly he was moving away from her, his hand clasping one of hers firmly as he tugged her after him.

"We're not doing this here," he said in a gravelly tone.

"As impressed as I am by your appliances, I concur with your decision," she teased in return.

He threw her a grin over his shoulder and headed for the staircase. She followed close behind as he continued down a carpeted hallway to the end, where he threw open a door and yanked her inside.

"I want you naked," he said in a voice that brooked no argument.

"How convenient. I want the same of you," she said bluntly and began to peel her clothing from her body.

Opposite her, Cord undressed just as quickly. She could barely keep her eyes off him. The sinewy strength of his arms showed in the way his muscles bunched and released as he dragged off his shirt with little respect for the buttons that tore free and bounced onto the carpet beneath their feet. He kicked off his boots and shucked his jeans and socks in a smooth movement, which left him standing there in front of her in only his boxer briefs. Clad in only her bra and panties, red lace this time, she eyed his very obvious erection constrained behind the cotton knit of his briefs. She sucked in her bottom lip and bit down hard to hold back the moan of delight that threatened to break free.

Cord, too, was taking a moment to feast his eyes on her body.

"Red lace? Ah, Detective, you slay me," he groaned as he moved forward to take her into his arms.

The shock of their skin touching made her draw in a sharp breath, which in turn made her breasts swell. The heat of his chest poured through her lacy bra, and she wished she'd been faster to disrobe so she could feel him more closely, without any barriers between them. She shifted, reaching her arms behind her only to feel him trap them in his hands.

"Not so fast, Detective. I think I want to enjoy the sight of you just a little longer."

He carefully walked her backward until she felt the softness of bed linen behind her knees.

"On the bed," he ordered.

"Are you always this bossy in the bedroom?" she asked.

But even as she said the words, she did as he'd commanded because she was eager to feel him against her again. Eager to feel him everywhere.

"Well, we'd have to do this more than once for you to have a basis for comparison, wouldn't we?" he responded.

She laughed. "Bossy and confident. What a combination."

"You forgot something else," he said as he hooked his thumbs into the waistband of his briefs. "I'm also very, very good at what I do."

Her mouth dried and her voice was little more than a croak when she spoke. "Ah yes, I'd forgotten. Perhaps you could refresh my memory."

His smile was feral and made every cell in her body clench on a wave of anticipation. Had she provoked the beast? It would seem so. He slid his briefs off his hips, freeing his straining erection to her hungry gaze.

"Mmm, dessert," she managed before he moved onto the bed.

"I'm not sure if you've earned your dessert yet," he murmured against her ear.

"Oh? Tell me what I've done wrong."

"Well, let's see. There's the matter of you pestering Jesse and his sister today."

"Not to have done so would be in dereliction of my duty."

"I'd asked you not to," he said, taking an earlobe between his teeth and biting gently.

Zoe squirmed as sensation shot through her.

"Actually," she said, breathless now, "you ordered me not to."

"You admit you were disobedient?"

He nipped a trail down her neck, while one hand brushed against her bra, rasping against her budded nipple before his fingers closed around the aching peak and squeezed just right. It felt like he already knew every intimate secret about her erogenous zones because he managed to zero in immediately on every one.

"I admit nothing," she gasped as he squeezed her nipple more firmly. "Besides, I have to wait until the sheriff's office equipment is repaired before I can interview him properly."

A spear of pleasure shot straight to the apex of her thighs and she squirmed again. She could feel her panties getting wet as her need for him increased in rapidly expanding increments.

"Equipment?" he asked, nuzzling against her skin, his hot breath making her feel even hotter.

"Yeah, video camera and recording equipment. Have to do things by the letter. But why are we talking about this? Haven't you got something more important to attend to?"

"More important?" He lifted his head and looked at her with a teasing glow in his eyes.

"Yeah—me."

He laughed. "Bossy, Detective. I see I'm going to have

to continue my investigation a little more carefully, just to remind you who's in charge here," he promised, his voice deadly serious.

His wet, hot mouth replaced his fingers at her breast.

"Cord, please," she begged, without even knowing exactly what she was begging for.

"Please—now that sounds nice. Please what? Please bite you?"

She groaned but nodded her assent.

"Your wish is my command," he said, his voice getting rougher with each touch he bestowed on her.

She felt his erection against her as he lowered himself and bit her gently through her bra.

"Naked, please. I want to be naked. This isn't fair."

"Fair? The detective wants fair?"

She felt his fingers at the clasp of her bra, felt her breasts spill free as the fabric mercifully fell away. Then there was nothing but sensation as he kissed and licked her heated flesh. She arched beneath him, desperate for her skin to meet with his, desperate for his touch lower down her body, where she ached with a hunger that was all consuming.

"Don't rush, Zoe. Some delights are best savored slowly," he teased as he spent more time first on one tautly beaded nipple and then the other. "Ah, you taste divine. I could do this all night long."

"Surely not all night... I may melt apart in your arms before that."

"Well, maybe not all night, then," he conceded with a chuckle. "Are you always so pedantic?"

"Details are my thing," she admitted on a rushed breath as he began to trail that wicked mouth of his down the center of her rib cage and lower to her belly button.

"I'm finding I like pretty much everything there is about you, Detective," Cord drawled.

"I have to admit I'm enjoying your journey of discovery."

He laughed again, and Zoe thrilled on the sound of it. Sex had been infrequent but good, but even so, she'd never enjoyed this level of fun in the process. Nor this level of aching demand that throbbed through her. If he kept this up, he'd have only to breathe on her clit and she'd be transported to the stratosphere. She could feel her body pulse as Cord continued his voyage lower, and lower still—but not quite low enough or fast enough for her satisfaction.

"I like what you've done here," he said, pulling back a little and stroking her neatly groomed body hair. "Intriguing. Hard to maintain?"

"Seriously, you're asking me about my personal grooming?"

"Why not? It hasn't distracted me from your punishment."

He pressed a kiss on her mound. Close, but still too far from her aching bud for her liking.

"Laser hair removal, and a regular trim." She ground out the words.

He kissed her again, a tiny bit closer to her clit, to her release. She shivered and pressed her head back into the pillow as he traced his fingertips up the inside of her thigh. Shivers rippled through her.

"Consider me punished," she begged. "Just please, touch me."

"Like this?" he asked, slowly pressing one finger into her wet core.

He stroked her, dragging a sound from her that spoke volumes to her level of need.

"More."

"And still the lady thinks she's in control." He sighed and withdrew his finger.

At her moan of distress he pressed two fingers inside

her and stroked her again, and then, at last, he closed his mouth around the aching, pulsing bead of flesh that had been his goal all along.

"Mmm, dessert," Cord said against her heated skin.

Zoe began to laugh, but then he changed the pressure of his tongue, moved his fingers, and all humor was suspended as he sent her soaring on a pounding wave of pleasure so intense she lost all sense of who and where she was. All she knew was the man who had delivered this pleasure was virtually a stranger to her, and right now she didn't care.

It was some time later before Zoe felt herself come back to any kind of awareness. Cord was lying on his side next to her, one arm bent under his head, his free hand softly stroking her belly.

"You're not going to leave me now, are you?" she asked, lifting a hand to trace the strong lines of his face.

"Nope," he said simply. "Not this time. Besides, we're at my place and I'm not letting you go anywhere."

"Good," she replied. "Because I want you inside me."

"Making demands of me now?"

"Yeah, got a problem with that?"

He flashed her a smile. "Not at all."

"But first…"

"First?"

"*My* dessert."

Zoe moved quickly to sit astride him. Beneath her bottom she could feel his erection, but that would have to wait awhile. First, she wanted to bestow on him a little of the same punishment he'd dealt to her. Cord's hands moved to grasp her hips but she shook her head.

"Uh-uh," she cautioned. "No touching. Not yet. Hold on to the headboard until I say you can move."

"Are you planning to frisk me, Detective?"

"I've told you, I'm conducting an investigation," she said with a playful curl of her lips. "A very important investigation."

She trailed her fingertips along the underside of his upper arms. His skin was softer there—deliciously so. As she traced around his armpits to the top of his rib cage, she felt his skin grow goose bumps at her touch.

"Do you like that?" she whispered.

"Oh yeah."

He shifted a little beneath her, and she lifted one finger to caution him.

"Don't make me get my cuffs."

"You brought cuffs to dinner?"

"And my gun. They're in my handbag along with my badge. I never leave home without them."

"Duly noted," Cord said with a slight frown.

Zoe hesitated in her movements, leaning back a little to study his face. His eyes still glittered with desire but his expression had become more closed, less playful.

"Does it worry you I carry a gun everywhere?"

She began to stroke his smooth chest, her fingertips tingling at the sensation of her skin on his.

"Not my place to worry about you."

"That's right, it's not. Enough talking. Now, just feel."

And she made sure he did. She smoothed her hands flat and skimmed the muscles of his chest, learning the dips and curves that made up the appealing shapes of his body, from his broad shoulders to his narrow waist. She bent down and kissed him before transferring her mouth from his lips to the flat discs of his nipples. They drew into small peaks against her tongue as she pinched and played with him. His hips shifted again and she clamped her thighs tight around him, halting his movement. Let him suffer the way he'd made her suffer—although it had been a delectable torment that he'd made her endure before bringing her to completion, and she had every intention of ensuring he experienced the same level of satisfaction.

And if he didn't? Well, she'd have to go back to square one and start over again. Her mouth curved into another smile at the thought, and she applied her attention to making him squirm beneath her as she tasted, licked and sucked at his skin. He wore a subtle cologne, but it was his own special scent that she'd quickly become addicted to. It made her want to nuzzle against him and draw in deep breath after deep breath. Never before had she felt this visceral level of attraction to another person, and it was intoxicating.

She rose up slightly and shifted her legs lower as she explored his torso, delighting in the way his skin jumped beneath her tongue as she followed the light trail of hair from his belly button down to his groin. His erection left her in no doubt as to his readiness, but she wanted to prolong this as much as possible. She let her tongue drift along the shadowed line of his inner hip—down, then up again. The hitch in his breathing told her that she was tormenting him, but to his credit he kept his hands firmly attached to the headboard, even though the muscles of his arms were bunched with tension.

Maybe it was time to take pity on him, she thought, and she turned her attention to his swollen shaft. She nuzzled at the base, breathing in the hot, musky scent of his skin, then trailed her tongue from base to tip. Cord groaned out loud at her actions, his hands suddenly letting go of the headboard and coming to cup her head, his fingers tangling in her short hair. She licked him again before taking the hot, silky head into her mouth and playing her tongue against the smoothness. His fingers tightened, and she felt his entire body clench as he fought against the urge to thrust deeper into her mouth.

Suddenly it became important to her to make him lose control, and she used every trick she'd ever read about as she licked, sucked and stroked him to a wild, shaking climax. When he was spent, she shifted until she was lying beside him, her head nestled against his chest, her arm across his waist. His heart beat like a herd of stampeding cattle in his chest and his body glistened with a light sheen of perspiration.

She'd done that to him, she thought with a touch of pride. She'd reduced this man—who had at first appeared to be fierce and determined, but who could cook like a dream, who could bring her to orgasm with a deftness she'd never known before—to one who'd put all sense of responsibility and control aside to revel in pure gratification. It was empowering to know she'd done that for him, liberating to realize that she could meet him on an even playing field where there were no specific roles based on gender. Only sensation, and pleasure and, she smiled anew, fun. Her time in Royal was shaping up to be very interesting indeed.

Seven

Cord waited some time until he could trust himself to speak again.

"That wasn't how I envisaged this evening happening," he stated bluntly.

Zoe continued tracing tiny shapes with her fingertips at his waist.

"Oh, disappointed?" she teased.

He felt something swell in his chest. Happiness? It had been so long since he'd felt anything like it, let alone trusted anyone with his body the way he'd trusted Zoe, that he found it hard to define.

"Definitely not disappointed," he growled. Cord rolled over so Zoe lay beneath him, his face directly over hers. "But I feel like we could do better."

She laughed—a deep-seated chuckle that made her whole body shake.

"By all means let's try it. You can never have too much dessert, after all."

She was a woman after his own heart, it seemed, and this time, when they made love, he made certain that, despite several delightful detours, they joined as one, thanking his lucky stars that the condoms in his drawer hadn't expired. He knew, because he'd checked before she arrived tonight, and while he hadn't wanted to assume this night would end with them both in his bed, he was so very glad it had.

Her long, supple legs hooked around his waist when he entered her, her heat and inner muscles drawing him in deep. Cord locked his gaze with hers, watched as her eyes became glassy as they rocked together in a dance as old as time. He felt her entire body clench on the first wave of orgasm as it hit her, and he allowed himself free rein, until they reached the summit together and hung there suspended in mutual bliss, before descending back to reality.

Morning came all too soon. In the distance, Cord could hear the sounds of his hands out on the ranch moving cattle, the lowing beasts voicing their thoughts on being brought in to a new pasture. He should be out there, working alongside them, but a certain tall, dark-haired detective was still entangled in his sheets. Not that he was complaining. She felt good—too good. Too easy to get used to and that sure wouldn't be a good thing. Not only did she live in Houston, she was a cop. A dedicated one at that. She wasn't in her career for a few years to pass time. No, this was a lifetime choice for her.

He hadn't been intimate with anyone since Britney, which probably explained why this thing with Zoe had flared up so quickly. There was no way it could be long-term. Fires that burned this brightly extinguished just as swiftly.

He thought about her bag downstairs, about the gun

she'd admitted was secreted in there. Even on a social visit, she was armed. It was part and parcel of who she was, and the danger that was associated with the kind of people she tracked down was equally a part of her every day.

He'd thought he could handle it with Britney. He'd supported her in her dream to become a cop, told her he'd be there for her 100 percent. But his support didn't equate to squat when she faced down a liquor-store robber only a few hours into her first shift. And being there as they pulled life support in ICU days after she'd been shot—well, that had been unarguably the darkest day of his life. He would not go down that road again. He simply could not.

Rebuilding himself had been hard, but his parents had put off their planned early retirement to see him back on his feet. His *abuelita* had been a strong, silent presence at his back, feeding his body and feeding his soul whenever he would let her. He'd resumed a life, of sorts. He'd dated once or twice, but things had never gotten to the stage they had with Zoe. Hell, he didn't even understand how things had moved this fast with her.

She was everything he never again wanted in a woman. Career focused, a detective and undoubtedly fiercely independent. She'd have had to fight her way into her position—past the expectations of her family that she fit into a more traditional mold, and past the obstacles that she no doubt had to overcome to be recognized in her working world. He'd always told himself that if he ever took the risk of another relationship again, it would be with a woman without career-focused ambition. One who shared the same dreams and goals as he had and who would partner with him in everything to do with life on the ranch. One who wanted stability, security and who had a desire to continue to build a legacy for future generations of Galicia children.

There was a sharp stab in his chest at the thought of

kids. He'd always taken for granted that he'd be a father one day, but now he wasn't so sure. That took a level of commitment he wasn't certain he was capable of anymore—not only to the children themselves, but to their mother, too. One thing was for certain, though—a woman like Zoe Warren was not on the same life path as he was. The whole city-versus-country thing would never work between them. He loved life on the ranch. He'd been born and bred into it as much as she'd been born and bred into her life in Houston. They were chalk and cheese, oil and water—and yet he couldn't seem to get enough of her.

Zoe stirred and stretched, untangling her limbs from his and rolling onto her back. Cord let his gaze slide over the lean lines of her body and then back to the surprising fullness of her breasts. Now that he knew how sensitive they were, he dreamed of ways he could tease them into the taut peaks that spoke evocatively of her depth of desire.

"Good morning," he said, his voice still a little gruff with sleep.

"How good is yet to be determined. On the meal basis we've covered appetizers, main courses and dessert. What's breakfast like around here?"

Never one to back down from a challenge, he showed her, and it was a full half hour later before he chased her into the bathroom, where they showered together. He would have taken her there again if he hadn't run out of condoms, but he had to satisfy himself with soaping her up and washing her hair and helping her rinse off. When she exited the shower stall, he switched the water to cold, determined to get his body under some semblance of control, but one look at her as she wiped her body dry with one of his thick, fluffy towels and he knew it was an exercise in hopelessness. The only way he'd return to any kind of normal was when she'd gone, and oddly, he didn't want her to leave.

She was dressed when he came into the bedroom with a towel wrapped firmly around his waist.

"I have to go," she said with obvious reluctance. "Thanks for dinner and…everything."

"Anytime," he drawled in response. "In fact, how about dinner tonight? We can go to the Texas Cattleman's Club."

"I've heard about it. Isn't the dress code pretty strict in the restaurant there?"

"I could lend you a suit," he offered only half tongue in cheek. In fact, the more he thought about her in one of his suits wearing that sinfully seductive lingerie underneath, the more he liked the idea.

"I'll sort something out. What time?"

"I'll pick you up at seven thirty."

"I'll be ready."

The second he heard her car start and head down the driveway, he grabbed his cell phone and dialed the number of an old school friend.

"Frank, you working on the sheriff's recording and video equipment?"

"Yeah, but how'd you know that?"

Cord's hand tightened on his phone. "That's not important. Tell me, how long do you think it'll take to get it all up and running again?"

Frank hemmed and hawed a little before speaking. "Should be done by the end of the day."

He started to get into some of the technical jargon that made Cord's eyes cross, so Cord interrupted him the moment Frank drew in a breath.

"Look, you remember how I bailed you out with Sissy when she thought you were having an affair. Gave you an alibi?"

"Yeah?" There was a note of caution in Frank's voice that hadn't been there before.

"You owe me one, right?"

"Sure do," Frank agreed.

Cord closed his eyes briefly. He hated having to do this. He knew Frank hadn't been unfaithful to his wife. Sissy had been feeling insecure when she was pregnant, and it was easier for Cord to say he'd been with Frank than for Frank's biggest secret—the fact that he was learning to read as an adult, so he could read to his newborn child—to come out to all and sundry.

"Could you take a little longer over that repair?" Cord eventually asked.

"Like a day or two more?"

"How about a week, maybe two?"

"And then we'd be even?"

"More than even."

"I could do that," Frank agreed.

"Thanks, Frank, appreciate it."

"You gonna tell me why you want me to delay on this?"

"No."

"Okay, then. Sounds like I'll be struggling to source a vital thingymabobwotsit."

"Darn hard things to track down," Cord agreed with a smile before ending the call.

Ryder Currin rode the elevator to Sterling Perry's floor determined to put this old rivalry to bed once and for all. The pain and damage it was causing had gone on long enough.

"Mr. Currin!" the receptionist gasped, recognizing him instantly as he swept out of the elevator and past the main reception area. "You can't—"

"Don't bother announcing me. I'll announce myself," he said over his shoulder as he strode toward Perry's office.

He heard the scuffle of activity behind him, but no one was going to stop him now. He'd had enough. The roll-on effect of Perry's bitterness, fed by years of lies and innuendo from everyone around them, had taken a toll far greater than either man could ever have anticipated. And, as far as Ryder was concerned, it stopped now. It was one thing for Perry to hold a grudge because of Ryder's close friendship with Perry's late wife, Tamara, but quite another for him to stand in the way of his daughter Angela's happiness. Ryder's relationship with Angela had been fragile from the get-go, but despite that they'd found a way to make it work—until the old rumors of Ryder's relationship with her mom had resurfaced. Ryder and Tamara Perry had never been more than friends back when he'd worked as a hand on the York ranch—close friends, sure, but nothing more than that. He'd been her shoulder to cry on when things got tough and when he'd questioned her happiness in her marriage to Sterling, she'd made it clear her loyalty to her husband was unswerving and she would always remain with him, no matter what.

In the face of the vicious claims that had begun to circulate Ryder knew there'd be a wedge driven between him and Angela or Angela and her father, and she'd have to choose between them. Out of respect for both Tamara's memory and for her daughter, who he loved more than life itself, he'd walked away from Angela and his promise to marry her because there was no way he was forcing her to make that choice. He'd regretted his actions every second of every day since. He couldn't work things out with Angela until he'd worked things out with Perry.

Perry's manipulation of those around him had done a lot of damage, but the older man's meddling had resulted in an unexpected bonus and thanking him would be Ryder's starting point. Thanks to Perry's anonymous labor complaint—one that unfortunately had a strong basis in fact and that Ryder had known nothing about until the complaint had been brought to his attention—he'd been able to institute worker reforms. Firing Willem Inwood had been unpleasant, but regrettably necessary. No one got away with treating his staff badly, especially not someone in a position of privilege and respect such as Inwood had held.

Just the thought of the man was enough to get Ryder's dander up, and he forced himself to shove his anger down deep before it could potentially damage the impromptu meeting he was about to have with Sterling Perry. Like he always told his kids—Xander, Annabel and Maya—never approach anything or anyone important in anger. He stopped in his tracks, squared his shoulders and took a steadying breath. At his destination, Ryder knocked twice, then pushed open the door to Perry's office. The older man was just putting down his phone.

"You'd better be quick," Sterling said with a sardonic curl of his lip. "I'm informed security is on their way."

"Tell them to stand down. I'm not here to fight with you."

"Really? Forgive me if I don't believe you," he taunted.

"Well, you can believe it. In fact, I'm here to thank you."

"Oh?" Perry's brows rose in genuine surprise.

"Yeah. Thanks to your anonymous—" Ryder made air quotes with his fingers "—complaint, I was able to cut the rot from my business and institute reforms to ensure such abuses never happen again. We'll be stronger than ever now, and it's all thanks to you."

He watched the play of emotions across Perry's face. It wasn't often the man let his facade down, and it was enlightening to see the short burst of confusion followed by reluctant acceptance.

"I see," Perry replied, leaning back in his chair. "You'd better take a seat."

Ryder sat in the chair nearest to him, just as security arrived in the room.

"Mr. Perry, we'll deal with your unexpected visitor right away."

"No need. It appears that Mr. Currin and I have some business to discuss. Please leave us." Perry waved a hand toward the door.

"You want us to wait outside?"

"That won't be necessary, thank you."

Ryder waited until Perry's muscle left the room. Had he really wanted to hurt the older man, there was no way his security detail had been here quick enough. Ryder made a comment to that effect, eliciting a burst of unexpected laughter from the man who'd become his nemesis.

"You're giving me advice now? What's going on? Has the world turned upside down?" Perry commented with his signature brand of cynicism.

"Not upside down, not yet, anyway. But we need to talk. Settle things once and for all."

"I have nothing to settle with you. As far as I'm concerned, you're nothing more than a burr under my saddle. Now that you and Angela are no longer engaged, I can rest happy in the knowledge that, aside from today, I need never face you again."

Ryder let the man's words roll over him. The bitterness in the other man's tone was deep-seated and went back twenty-five long and often unhappy years. Ryder didn't want the next twenty-five to be the same. Somehow they had to reach a reconciliation of sorts. If they couldn't, he'd never be able to go back to Angela and beg her forgiveness for walking away on their love, their life, their future together. That knowledge forced him to remain calm in the face of Perry's veiled insults.

He drew in a deep breath. "Look, I know you hate my guts—"

"That would require effort I wouldn't even bother expending," Sterling said as if the conversation bored him.

"You still resent my friendship with your late wife."

"Your relationship with Tamara was inappropriate," Sterling replied, biting back. "But she chose me. She always chose me."

"I know, but I want you to know that I never had an affair with her. I'll swear it on a stack of Bibles if it will help you to believe me, but as much as I admired and respected her, I never touched her. Not that way. We were friends, that's all."

Sterling shook his head. "Why should I believe you? You've not long come from my daughter's bed. What kind of man are you, anyway? First the mother? Then my daughter? That's just sick."

Disgust dripped from his every word.

"It would be sick if it were true. But I did not sleep with Tamara, ever. And my relationship with Angela is completely different. I loved Tamara, sure, as a friend, as a mentor in many ways, and I certainly didn't think you deserved her. Still don't, to be honest. But like you said, she remained with you and she remained true to her vows to you until her death, as well. For better or worse, Perry, she loved you and only you."

There must have been something in his words that started to sink in, because the hardened set to Perry's face began to soften. Not a lot, but enough for Ryder to begin to hope that maybe they could get past this at long last.

"So what if what you're telling me is the truth? It doesn't

change the things you've done since. The land you inherited from Tamara's father—the land that was so rich it oil it made your damn fortune—should always have been ours, not yours."

"You want it back in your family's hands?"

"Damn straight I do."

"Then give me your blessing to marry Angela."

The air between them crackled with barely restrained energy.

"Impossible. You broke off your engagement. She won't have you back."

"She will if she knows she doesn't have to choose between us. Angela loves me and I love her. We deserve to be happy. We deserve to be together."

"Why? You couldn't win her mother from me, so now you're settling for my daughter?"

"If I weren't a decent man I'd punch you in the mouth for that remark," Ryder growled through gritted teeth. "How dare you speak of your daughter so disparagingly. She deserves way better than that."

"I could argue that she deserves way better than you," Sterling spat back in return.

Ryder clenched his hands tight and then forced himself to relax his fingers. He had no doubt that Sterling was deliberately baiting him, seeking any excuse to call security back into this office and to see him escorted out of the building. He would not give the man the satisfaction.

"Luckily for you, I'm not the piece of crap you think I am. Look, we both love Angela. We both want her to be happy. I know that, as her husband, I can make her happy. I want to devote the rest of my life to her."

"And why should I believe you?"

"Because you can see it's true. I'm here, aren't I? I'm extending an olive branch. Deep down, you know Angela loves me, too. Despite everything you've ever done to try to turn her away from me. But I won't stand between the two of you, not the way you're standing between her and me. I loved her enough to let her go, but not having her in my life isn't fair to either of us. Now I'm telling you I love her enough to make a deal with you. If you agree to stand aside and stop trying to influence Angela against me, I will deed the land that her grandfather willed to me to her on our marriage."

There, he'd laid his trump card on the table.

"Obviously," he continued, "I would have preferred you to bestow your blessing on our relationship without what some may see as a bribe, but I prefer to look at it as an act of good faith. And Angela, well, she can make of it what she may. I'm sure you would rather your daughter see you through eyes that aren't clouded by the thought that you only gave us your blessing because it meant, in the long run, your family would get their hands back on land you've always considered should have been yours and Tamara's.

"Look, I love your daughter with all my heart. I will be a good husband to her and a fine father to any children we might be lucky enough to have. That land will eventually become theirs. Isn't that what you want in the long run?"

Sterling leaned back in his executive chair and pressed his fingertips together, studying Ryder carefully over their steepled peaks.

"Let me think about it," he finally said.

Ryder felt himself begin to relax. As progress went, that was a start. Certainly a better position than where they'd been before he walked into Perry's office today. Perry might have conceded to think about it, but Ryder could see that his stony visage had softened. By sweetening the pot with the land he'd inherited from Tamara's father, he knew he stood a far greater chance of winning the man's support.

"Which brings me to the Texas Cattleman's Club," Ryder started.

"I wondered when you'd bring that up. Don't push me, Currin. I might consider supporting your marriage to my daughter, but I will not relinquish my pitch for control of the TCC here in Houston."

"I'm not asking you to. But I do think we need to declare a truce and actually start to work together to find the killer. On opposite sides of the boardroom table we're formidable, but think how much stronger we could be if we worked together. Both for Angela's sake and for the reputation of the Houston club."

Again, silence stretched between the two men. After a couple of minutes Sterling Perry stood and came around to where Ryder had also risen from his seat. Was this where he ejected him from his office? Ryder wondered. He didn't know who was the more surprised when Perry stuck out his hand. Ryder didn't waste a second. He took it and shook it firmly.

"Truce," Perry said.

"Truce," Ryder agreed.

Eight

Zoe paced her motel room in irritation. Still no confirmation from the sheriff's office of a day when she'd be able to interview Jesse Stevens. Royal wasn't that antiquated. Someone was stalling; they had to be. In the meantime, she had an investigation to complete. She'd spent much of the day visiting places around town, asking random questions about Mr. Stevens and how the people around here saw him. So far all she'd heard were his praises sung from the rooftops. It was starting to get on her last nerve. No one was that perfect.

She'd begun to think she'd be better off hauling him back to Houston and questioning him there, but she knew if she did that, she'd likely get offside with Sheriff Battle, and she'd been at this long enough to know that you needed all the friends and solid contacts you could get. You never knew when you might need to call in a favor. So that left her cooling her heels, wondering what the heck to do next.

Take up horse riding? A course in cattle branding, perhaps? Both ideas made her skin crawl.

Zoe reached for her laptop and fired it up, scrolling again through the case notes she had on Vincent Hamm. It had all been so convincing, the way he'd left work after bitching about his job for weeks and vocally dreaming of a life in the Caribbean, spending his days surfing, then virtually disappearing into thin air before sending a text from the British Virgin Islands. But she knew he couldn't possibly have sent that text. Then who'd done it?

For a guy who had no enemies, he still managed to end up dead. Instinct told her it had to be connected to the building where he was found—the proposed Texas Cattleman's Club in Houston. But then there was this message from Jesse Stevens on Hamm's phone. As far as she knew, Stevens had nothing to do with the new club, but maybe there was a link she was missing here. Someone had tracked Hamm to the building. Was it Stevens? The crime-scene pictures were useless. After the flooding there'd been little chance of retrieving what could have been vital evidence. The forensic examination of his body by the medical examiner had also yielded very little, besides a grossly bloated body with its face gone.

"Argh!" she groaned out loud and closed her computer.

Maybe a run would clear her head. She glanced at her watch and decided she had time before getting ready for tonight. Across the room the garment bag hanging on the door of the cupboard that passed as a wardrobe in this place caught her eye. She'd splashed out on the new dress specifically with Cord's reaction to it very firmly in her mind. Together with the skinny-heeled black patent leather pumps, the emerald green cocktail dress with its plunging neckline was bound to excite him. Heck, it had excited her just trying it on in the store. And teamed with the green-

and-white crystal necklace she'd bought to go with it, and the white crystal studs the sales girl had told her were the perfect accompaniment to the outfit, she knew she'd knock his eyes out.

She thought for a second of how much she'd spent. Almost a month's salary. And for a guy? Someone she'd known, what, two days? She had to be mad. But that ever-present tingle that took over her body every time she thought of him reasserted itself, reminding her that this wasn't just about pleasing him or seeking his approval. It was about pleasing herself, too. She wanted to look good. So what if it wasn't the kind of outfit she'd wear to a family barbecue, which was pretty much the sum total of her social life. There'd be other men, other dates.

As soon as she thought of it, she pushed the idea out of her head. She didn't have time for dating. Not now. Not when a murderer still roamed free. But a dalliance with a handsome rancher? Yeah, she thought, smiling to herself as she subconsciously reached out to stroke the garment bag, she could squeeze that in.

Feeling as though she'd fooled herself into total justification for her shopping spree, Zoe changed into her running gear and slipped out of the motel, locking the door firmly behind her. An hour ought to do it, and maybe it'd help wear off the edge of sexual hunger that constantly badgered her every time she thought about Cord Galicia.

She was wrong. Two hours wouldn't have even been enough. Even though she'd pushed herself hard in the early evening heat, after returning to her room she still had that crazy itchy feeling that she knew only Cord Galicia could scratch. She was losing her grip. Normally at this stage of a case she'd be 100 percent focused on the job—no distractions. And yet with this one—and very possibly because there was so little to go on—she was all too easily distracted.

Maybe she ought to call Cord and cancel their arrangements for tonight. She even got as far as pulling his number up on her phone, but as her finger hovered over the call command, she backed out of the app and put her phone back down again. She groaned out loud and stomped one foot in frustration. She couldn't do it. She wanted to see him tonight. There, she admitted it.

Groaning again at her weakness for a man she should never have hooked up with, Zoe went through to the cramped bathroom and stripped off her running gear before stepping under the cool spray. She sucked in a sharp breath as the water hit her overheated body and goose bumps rose on her skin. It took a couple of minutes before the water came up to temperature, and it gave her time to get her thoughts in order and her raging libido under control.

Normally she'd be fine at this stage of a relationship. She snorted as she squirted some shampoo into her hand and massaged the liquid through her short, thick hair. Relationship? No way this was anything approaching that kind of serious. Besides, she didn't do serious. Didn't want to. Not yet, anyway. She had several more notches she wanted to achieve on the metaphorical belt that was her career with Houston P.D. She'd made it this far without distraction; she didn't plan on derailing her momentum any time soon.

Zoe rinsed out the shampoo and applied conditioner before using shower gel to wash herself clean of the grime she'd picked up during her run. Half an hour in one direction and she'd been out of town in open space. Sure, there'd been signs of civilization, like fences and the occasional car, but overall, there'd been a sense of openness and calm that she'd never felt before. Running in her neighborhood in Houston was always risky. Whether it was traffic or other sidewalk users, she always had to have her wits about her. She came home satisfied with the physical outlet but less mentally fulfilled than she felt today. Maybe the country had something to recommend it after all. Not that she'd ever live here, not with her work in Houston. But visit from time to time? Yeah, she could do that.

As she dried herself off and blew out her hair, tousling it with her fingers, she thought about her family. They'd hooted with laughter when she'd told them where she was heading, knowing how citified she was. And her sisters-in-law had chuckled alongside her brothers in total agreement. While Zoe loved the fact that her brothers had met their perfect matches, and that her parents were still incredibly happy together, she did wonder sometimes if she'd find that level of contentment herself.

When she thought about her future, contentment never really factored in, anyway. It was all about drive and progress and promotion. At a certain point, though, she'd have to stop, unless she wanted to find herself chief of police one day. She smirked at her reflection as she smoothed on some tinted moisturizer and dusted it with a light coating of powder. Her? Chief of police? She'd never handle the politics or the glad-handing required. But she wouldn't mind, one day, finding the balance between work and play and settling down with that special someone.

Her parents had fallen in love in high school and married the day after graduation. Her brothers had waited until they were a little older, but each had met his future wife and known what he wanted almost immediately. None of them had wasted time on long courtships or engagements. It seemed the Warren family were all about knowing what they wanted and going for it.

She'd never found that one person that made her feel certain that he was the one. Except for Cord.

She froze, her hand midway to her eyes and the mascara wand dangling uselessly in her fingers. Where the hell was she going with this? She wasn't ready to be married. She wasn't ready to settle down. Cord had made it clear, even if he hadn't used the exact words, that he was the kind of guy that wanted a woman who was all about home and hearth and family. She was definitely not that person. She was driven by her career. By the need to bring the bad guys to justice, by the determination to see that her victims wouldn't remain victimized for the rest of their lives. That they'd have closure.

Geez, she didn't even know why she was letting her mind flow down this track. That was the trouble with having to leave the city. It left you too much damn time to think and let your mind wander down ridiculous paths that under normal circumstances you wouldn't consider at all.

Giving herself a sharp mental shake, Zoe finished applying her makeup and stepped through to the main room to take the cocktail dress from the hanger. It was nothing to look at just hanging there; in fact, she'd been very ho-hum about it when the shop assistant had suggested it to her. But when she'd put it on, it was transformed—and it transformed her right along with it. Not just her appearance, but how she felt. In this dress she felt all woman. A woman with wiles.

The deep V of the neckline made wearing a bra impossible, and due to the silkiness of the fabric Zoe had accepted the suggestion she wear nipple covers with the outfit. Given her company for the night, and the way he made her feel, she thought she'd spare the rest of the restaurant the evidence of her perpetual desire for Cord Galicia. She chuckled as she put the things on, then slipped on a skin-toned thong before putting on the dress.

She smoothed it over her hips, then reached for the jewelry she'd bought to go with it. Finally she slid her feet into her shoes and picked up the small evening bag she'd bought to complete the ensemble. She went back into the bathroom to check her reflection in the floor-length mirror behind the door and barely recognized the creature who stared back at her.

A knock at her motel room door made her move away from the mirror and the stranger she'd seen there. Was this what seeing someone like Cord was doing to her? Changing her into someone she no longer identified with? But it was still her beneath the figure-hugging emerald green dress and the hair and makeup. Just a different her. And there was no reason why this version of herself couldn't have free rein right now, was there?

She swung the door open and felt her heart skitter in her chest at the sight of the man standing there waiting for her. Dressed all in black, from his boots to his shirt and jacket, and wearing a stunning silver-and-turquoise bolo tie, Cord looked about as dark and mysterious as a man could get. Until he smiled and her new lover shone through under his frank appreciation as his eyes skimmed her from head to foot and back again.

"Wow. You look amazing."

"Thank you. You look very nice, too," she answered and stepped through the door, making sure it was locked behind her.

"Nice? I'll have you know I went to a great deal of effort for you tonight."

His tone sounded wounded, but there was no doubt he was teasing her. It was another of the things she enjoyed about being with him. Nothing was too serious. Even when making love they could joke with each other.

"And I appreciate that," she said, patting him on the chest before fingering the bolo. "I especially like this."

"It was my grandfather's. I think he'd have liked you. He enjoyed the company of strong women."

Zoe felt a sense of accomplishment at the compliment. Sure, she knew that Cord found her sexually attractive, but underneath all that she'd sensed a reserve—as if she wasn't quite the kind of woman he wanted but, for the same reasons that drew her to him, he simply couldn't resist her.

"C'mon," he said, taking her by the hand. "Let's go."

The warmth of his skin permeated her own, sending that intriguing buzz of electrical current through her as they walked to his car. She took a step back.

"This is yours?"

She gestured to the sleek and shiny low-slung black Maserati that graced the parking lot next to her own dusty vehicle.

"Like it?" he asked before opening the passenger door and holding it for her.

"It's beautiful. I had no idea you had something like this. I was expecting the truck."

Cord smiled in response. "A beautiful woman deserves a beautiful form of transport."

He closed the door and went around to his side of the car. They completed the journey out to the Texas Cattleman's Club mostly in silence, but it didn't feel awkward. Cord had reached across and taken her hand, resting it beneath his own on his thigh as he drove. She enjoyed the intimacy of the action about as much as she enjoyed the man sitting beside her.

"So, the food is good here?" she commented as they

arrived out front of the club and pulled up next to the car valet who'd stepped forward. "It looks popular."

"*Popular* is an understatement. This place is a part of the fabric of Royal."

He put a hand to the small of her back and guided her through the front door.

Cord couldn't believe his self-restraint. Seeing Zoe framed in the doorway of her motel room dressed like she'd stepped off the cover of some glossy European fashion magazine had forced him to call on every ounce of gentlemanlike behavior to prevent himself from walking her straight back into the room and closing the door behind them. All he'd wanted to do in that instant was lose himself in her, and the truth of that frightened him. Sure, he'd started this in an attempt to keep her distracted and away from Jesse while he tended to Janet. But right now Cord couldn't say his motives were entirely philanthropic. In fact, they were the complete opposite.

Even now, with his hand against the small of her back as they entered the club, he was fighting with the base urge to turn her right around and back out to the car and take her home again. He wasn't in the mood for polite company and the conversation that he knew being seen with a woman here tonight would engender. What the hell had he been thinking?

"Mr. Galicia, good to see you this evening. Your table is ready. Please, come with me," the maître d' said as they entered the restaurant.

Cord let his hand drop from Zoe's back and gestured for her to follow the maître d' while he kept a circumspect two paces behind her. All the better to see the delicious curves of her butt in that dress, his alter ego reminded him. He clamped down on the thought but not before he felt the ripple of arousal the view before him wrought. The food tonight was going to have to be spectacular to distract him from what seeing her in that dress did to him. And the shoes... He felt another ripple shudder through him. Those heels were seriously sexy. He wondered, briefly, if she'd keep them on later for him, if he asked real nice.

You're not doing yourself any favors, he growled at himself. He watched as Zoe was seated at the table and felt a somewhat feral burst of protectiveness as the maître d's gaze lingered a second too long on Zoe's exposed cleavage as he shook out her napkin and laid it across her lap. Forcing himself to uncurl the fingers that had instinctively formed into fists, he took his seat and listened with half an ear as the man told them he'd send their waiter along shortly.

"Nice place," Zoe said, looking around.

"I'm sure you've seen similar in Houston," he said a little flatly.

Somehow seeing the way that guy had stared at Zoe had taken a little of the shine off the evening for him. In fact, he was beginning to question what he'd been thinking inviting her here. Showing off? Letting the city girl know he could give her as good as she was used to? *Idiot*, he told himself. They weren't even a couple in the true sense of the word. He had no right to feel possessive about her, no matter how intimately he knew her body.

"Not quite as sumptuous as this," she said with a smile and took a sip from her water glass.

The wine waiter came across and took their orders, shortly followed by the waiter bringing menus and letting them know the specials. Cord was grateful for the respite when they took their time selecting their appetizers and mains, and a little surprised, too, when he discovered they'd each chosen the same.

"Great minds think alike, hmm?" Zoe said with a warm smile that sent a wave of lust straight to his groin.

"Fools seldom differ," he countered, still a little surly.

Zoe reached across the table and took his hand. "Is everything okay? Would you rather we left?"

He shook his head. Of course she'd notice his change in mood. She was trained to observe these sorts of things. To study the human condition and ascertain the difference between the truth and the lies. Was that what she was doing with him all the time? Did she realize that while he'd started using sex as a distraction tactic, it had quickly become something else that he didn't want to define? He realized she was waiting for an answer and gave her fingers a squeeze.

"No, it's nothing. It's been a while since I've dined here is all."

In fact, the last time he'd eaten here was when he proposed to Britney, just before she left for training. The memory made his heart ache. Just two short years ago and yet it felt like a lifetime. And here he was, overlaying a new memory. He didn't know whether to be annoyed with himself or pleased that he was finally letting go. One thing was for sure, though—this thing with Zoe wouldn't go any further than the time she was here in Royal. He'd make sure of it. He couldn't handle the constant fear of living with a woman who carried a gun for a living again. His worst nightmare had already been realized once; there was no way he was tempting fate again.

The food, when it came, was sublime, and there was something inherently sensuous about the way Zoe enjoyed her food. He found he took pleasure in watching her, listening to the cadence of her voice as they talked, simply enjoying her presence. The last of his bad mood brushed away, and they were lingering over coffee and sharing a truly delicate serving of crème brûlée when he became aware of someone stopping beside their table.

"Cord, darling, how are you? We haven't seen you here in ages."

Cord rose to his feet, identifying one of his mother's Women's Institute cronies and her long-suffering husband hovering right behind her.

"Mrs. Radison, good to see you looking so well."

"Oh, you charmer, you. I received an email from your mom the other day. Seems like they're enjoying Palm Springs. And who is this?"

Just like that, the woman dispensed with the niceties and got straight to the point that he knew had led her to stop at his table. He had no doubt that the fact he'd been out with a new woman would be all around the gossips in town within five minutes of Olive Radison leaving the building. She put the word *social* in capital letters when it came to social media.

"Zoe Warren, please meet Olive Radison and her husband, Bert," Cord said, hoping this encounter would be over soon.

"Pleased to meet you, dear," Olive Radison purred. "So lovely to see Cord moving on. After all, it's been a while now, hasn't it, dear?" She patted Cord gently on the cheek, oblivious to the way his body had stiffened as if set in concrete. "Come along, Bert. We mustn't keep these young people from enjoying one another's company any longer."

And then she was gone, leaving behind a generous waft of her floral fragrance and a sense of discomfort settling on Cord's shoulders like a leaden cloak.

"Sorry about that. One of my mom's friends."

"No problem. She seemed friendly," Zoe commented lightly.

But there was something there in her gaze now that

wasn't there before. Questions that remained unasked and, on his part, unanswered. Suddenly he couldn't wait to get out of here.

"You done?" he asked abruptly.

Zoe's eyes flicked to his, and she stared at him a moment before giving him a quick nod. "Sure," she answered, gathering up her bag and rising from her chair. "I'll just go to the bathroom. Be back in a minute."

The dessert sat on the table, still unfinished, just like so many other things between them, he thought as he gestured for the bill. He'd settled the account by the time she returned to the dining room, and he rose to meet her halfway across the room. Together they went out to wait for the valet to bring his car around. The trip back to her motel felt a whole lot longer than the journey out. It was only as they neared the motel that they saw the flash of red lights and saw the fire engines and hoses lining the street.

"What the hell?" Zoe cried out as it became apparent it was the motel that had been on fire.

Cord pulled over and together they approached the area where the motel manager had assembled with a few of the occupants.

"What's going on?" Zoe asked when the woman turned to her to give her attention.

"I'm sorry, hon. But it seems someone's phone charger started a fire in the end unit. Once it took hold in the roof it spread quickly. There are fire walls between the units, but even so, there is a lot of smoke and water damage. I'm not sure they'll be allowing anyone back in to stay tonight. We'll have to reassess in the morning."

"Our things? Can we retrieve them?"

"I'll speak to the fire chief when he's free, okay, hon? Have you got somewhere else you can stay tonight?"

"She's staying with me," Cord said firmly.

"Thank goodness," the manager said with obvious relief. "The other motel near here is closed for renovations, and the hotel in town is able to put up a few people, but they're almost at capacity themselves, so we're short of beds."

Cord felt Zoe shiver as the manager moved away to where it looked like a command center had been established. He identified the fire chief there, and Nate Battle, too.

"My weapon is in there and my computer. I have to be able to clear my things from my room safe," Zoe said firmly. "I should go and speak to the sheriff."

That cold slice of reality cut through him again. Every time he let himself relax a little, forget a little, that one piece of hell-no-don't-go-there would come back and smack him clean in the face.

"Let's wait a bit. You're a registered guest. They know you're here. They'll come to us when they can," he said. "Are you warm enough?"

Before she could answer, he shrugged off his jacket and laid it around her shoulders. He could see she was at the point of protesting but thankfully she didn't. The night air was cooler than it had been, and she sure wasn't dressed for the climate.

It was another hour before the fire crew deemed it safe for those in units farthest from the burned-out room to enter their rooms and retrieve their belongings. Zoe didn't waste a second. Cord went with her, packing her toiletries in the bathroom as she grabbed her small case and her gun and laptop.

"This it?" he asked as he came through from the bathroom.

She gave him a brusque nod.

"You sure pack light."

"I wasn't planning on staying long."

Cord felt a twinge of guilt at her comment. She would be staying a whole lot longer now, thanks to him and his little discussion with Frank.

"Hey, don't worry about it. At least you know you can stay at my place."

"Your ranch is hardly the hub of activity here in Royal. What if I get bored?"

She gave him a challenging look.

"Then it will be up to me, as your host, to ensure you don't get bored, won't it? C'mon, let's go. The stink of this place is getting right up my nose."

Zoe followed the Maserati out to the ranch. She didn't want to be stranded when the call came to say she could conduct the interview with Stevens, and she couldn't see Cord letting her use the Maserati, although the idea had merit.

She pulled her car up outside Cord's house, swinging it off to one side of the driveway as he turned toward the multibay garage to the side of the property. He met her at the steps to the front door.

"You could have parked in the garage," he suggested.

"I prefer to be parked for a quick getaway," she said, only half joking.

He snorted, and she could see he wasn't entirely pleased with her response. *Well, so what*, she thought. This evening had gone from a very promising beginning to crash and, quite literally, burn in a very short space of time. And, she noticed as they entered the house, she had managed to get soot on her new dress into the bargain. There'd better be a decent dry cleaner in town.

She fought back a yawn. With last night's lack of sleep and the drama this evening, she felt exhausted.

"You want your own room this time?" Cord asked as they went up the stairs.

"Sure," she said, annoyed that he'd offered.

Something had crawled under his skin tonight, but she was too tired and irritated to try to figure it out. He showed her into a large room that, come morning, would be bathed in sunshine. The white bed linens reminded her of her somewhat-grimy state. Despite the fact the fire hadn't reached her unit, the soot and smoke had managed to permeate everything she'd touched or brushed against.

"Thanks," she said abruptly as Cord showed her the door to the connecting bathroom. "I can manage from here."

He stopped directly in front of her. "Are you sure about that? You look done in, and—" he paused to sniff "—your stuff smells of smoke."

She groaned in frustration. "I'd better put my stuff through the wash before bed."

"Don't worry about it. Leave it with me. Go." He tugged the bag from her hands and pushed her gently in the direction of the bathroom. "Shower. I'll leave something for you to sleep in on the bed."

He was gone before she could protest. All he'd left her with was her laptop case and her toiletries bag. Her gun was tucked into the side of the computer bag, and she'd seen his gaze flick past it. It was obvious he had some aversion to her carrying a weapon. Odd, when Texas was an open carry state. It wasn't unusual to see any adult carrying a gun. But, she'd noticed, he didn't carry one himself. She shrugged, putting the thought aside for now.

The shower was everything she longed for. She let the hot water sluice over her body and wash away the tension of the evening. What had that all been about, anyway? Something from Cord's past, obviously. And, just as obviously, something he hadn't wanted to discuss. Maybe she could probe a little more about that tomorrow, but for now, she needed rest.

She toweled off and padded through to the bedroom on bare feet. Cord had been back in here, she noticed. The drapes had been drawn and a deliciously soft T-shirt had been laid on the bed. She picked up the garment and held it to her face, inhaling the faint scent of his cologne. It felt sinfully wicked letting the wash-worn cotton skim over her body, almost like a lover's caress. And just like that, weariness fled from her body and a sensual tug of longing infused her instead.

He'd turned down her bed while she'd been showering, and she eyed the crisp white sheets with a mix of longing and aversion. It would take only a moment to head down the hallway to his room. She shook her head and yanked the sheets back a little farther. No, she was being strong. He'd clouded her mind quite enough for the very short time she'd known him. She needed to take charge of herself again.

She slid into bed and tugged the comforter up to her chin and lay there as stiff as a board, staring at the ceiling. It wasn't more than a half hour when she heard a soft knock at her bedroom door. It was so soft that if she'd been asleep, she probably wouldn't have heard it.

"Yeah," she called out.

The door opened a crack. From the soft light of the hallway she saw Cord standing there, his torso naked and a pair of pajama pants barely clinging to his hips.

"Everything okay?" he asked.

"I can't get to sleep," she admitted.

"Need some company?"

"Sure."

He was crossing the room before the word was fully

spoken, and she felt him get into the bed beside her. A few seconds later and his strong arms had pulled her against him, her back to his front. She felt him kiss the top of her shoulder where his T-shirt had fallen away to expose her skin.

"Go to sleep now," he said softly.

And, to her surprise, she did.

Nine

Zoe woke the next morning feeling like she'd had the best rest in a very long time. She rolled over to greet Cord, but he was already gone, and his side of the bed was cold, too, alerting her to the fact he'd been up for some time. Well, this was a working ranch, she reminded herself as she headed to the bathroom. When she came out, she was at a loss for what to wear and ended up staying in the T-shirt of Cord's that she'd slept in.

She made her way back downstairs and went to the kitchen, drawn by the aroma of freshly made coffee. Her mouth was quite literally watering by the time she found a mug in the cupboard and poured a cup from the carafe on the warmer.

"Good morning."

A voice from behind her made her spin around.

"Good morning to you, too. Good coffee, thanks," she answered, holding her mug up to Cord in a toast. "You're a man of surprising talents."

He smiled, the action sending a punch of heat straight through her body and making her all too aware that she stood here before him dressed in nothing but an oversize T-shirt. For all that it covered her butt and skimmed her thighs, she knew her nipples had to be prominent against the well-washed white cotton. She hazarded a glance downward. Yup, there they were. Perky as all get-out and happy as hell to see him.

And he was a sight this morning. Dressed in blue jeans, worn in all the right places, and a loose-fitting chambray shirt that was open a few buttons at the neck, he was a visual feast. Zoe took a sip of her coffee, sucking down the hot brew as if it wasn't burning the roof of her mouth and scalding her throat. Anything to distract herself from taking those few short steps across the kitchen and jumping up into Cord's arms and hooking her legs around his waist.

"Speaking of talents," he said as he grabbed a mug and poured himself a coffee, too. "Your clothes are dry and ready for you when you want to get dressed."

He made it sound as though getting dressed was optional, and for a moment she considered tormenting him by just hanging out in his T-shirt all day long. But she knew she would be the one to suffer. Already she felt as though she was at a disadvantage.

"Thanks, I'll grab them now."

"Would you like to look around the ranch with me today? I need to check some fences in the outer pastures."

"On horseback?" she asked, barely suppressing a shudder.

Sure, she could see the value of horses in this environment, but nothing and no one said she'd ever have to ride one. As far as she could tell, one end bit and the other kicked. She wasn't interested in what came in between.

"Not keen?"

"Not on horses, no. Got bikes?"

"I'm sure you'll enjoy what I'm planning. Why don't you get dressed, then we can have breakfast and get going."

"Yes, sir," she said with a mock salute. "Question."

"Yeah?"

"Where's the laundry room?"

He chuckled and pointed down a hallway off the kitchen she hadn't been down before. "Down there. You'll find it."

"Thanks."

She grabbed her things and went up to her room to dress. In no time she was back in the kitchen. She moaned out loud at the scent of breakfast cooking.

"Are those huevos rancheros?"

"Yup," Cord said, sliding eggs onto the plated tortillas topped with fried beans.

He spooned fresh salsa over the eggs and then crumbled feta cheese over the top and garnished it all with chopped cilantro. He took their plates over to the large wooden kitchen table and set them down.

"Eat," he said simply and gestured for her to take a seat.

Zoe didn't waste another second. She sampled the breakfast and moaned again.

"This is amazing. I think you must have missed your calling. Ranching? Forget it. You should have been a chef."

Cord smiled in return. "I did think about learning to cook professionally, but I was born to this ranch and its way of life. From the day I was old enough to walk, I was out there with my dad learning the ropes from the ground up, the way he learned from his dad."

"And the way you'll teach your children one day, too?"

He stiffened, his fork halfway to his mouth. "Maybe," he admitted before letting his fork clatter down onto his plate. "What about you? Planning to have kids one day?"

She shrugged, not entirely comfortable with the conversation being turned back to her. "Maybe," she replied, mimicking his answer. "But the cooking? This is seriously good. If you ever decide to give up ranching, you could make a killing with your food."

Cord helped himself to a little more salsa from the bowl he'd put on the table.

"They're my grandmother's recipes. I'll be sure to tell her you're impressed."

"Please do. This is feta cheese, right?"

Cord nodded.

"I've never been a fan of it before, but this tastes divine," Zoe enthused.

"I make it myself. I keep a few goats and like to dabble in new ideas. Who knows, maybe one day I can expand my herd some more and turn the goats and the cheese into a more commercial operation."

"Seems I learn something new about you every day," Zoe commented as she cleaned up her plate with the last scrap of a tortilla.

Cord shrugged. "I'm not complicated. If you want to know anything about me, just ask."

Zoe leaned back in her chair and looked at him. "What went wrong last night?"

"With the fire?"

"No." She pushed. "Before that. You were all good until we got to the club, and then when that woman stopped by, it was like you had been frozen in ice."

"Old memories."

Zoe waited for him to expand on that, but it seemed he felt that was quite enough on the subject because he abruptly rose from the table and cleared their plates away. Zoe rose to help him but he shooed her off.

"Go do whatever it is you women do before going out.

We'll be leaving in about fifteen minutes. Meet me by the garage."

Accepting she'd been summarily dismissed after touching on what was obviously a very raw subject for him, she did as he suggested and went back up to her room. After a quick trip to the bathroom she folded her clothes and stacked them in one of the empty drawers. They didn't take up a lot of room. Satisfied she'd killed enough time, she went downstairs and out to the garage. Cord was waiting by his truck. She could see he'd loaded some tools and a roll of fencing wire in the back of the truck.

As they headed down the drive Zoe asked, "Where are we going?"

"You'll see," Cord responded cryptically.

She fought back the urge to press him for more information, but they hadn't traveled more than five minutes before he turned off the road and drove toward what looked like a hangar. A wind sock hung limply at the end of what she worked out was a runway.

"You have an airport?"

"A private strip. Jesse and I share it, as it borders both our properties. We learned to fly together. He prefers to stick with fixed-wing and I prefer choppers."

"Choppers."

"Don't tell me you'd rather go horse riding?" he laughed.

"Actually, no, I wouldn't," she responded firmly. "Choppers are fine."

"So glad you approve," he teased. "Here, come and give me a hand with these."

He gave her his toolbox to carry while he grabbed the roll of fencing wire, then led the way into the hangar.

"We're going up in that?" Zoe asked, eyeing the small chopper settled on one side of the hangar.

"What, cold feet, Detective?"

"It's smaller than I'm used to, that's all."

"The Robinson R44 is perfect for around the ranch. We use it to monitor stock, find strays and check the fence lines. All sorts of things. It's highly maneuverable, so it's perfect for the kind of work we do."

"Sounds versatile."

"Oh, it is. You'll see for yourself in a few minutes."

"Where do you want this?" she asked, gesturing to the toolbox she'd set at her feet.

"I'll take it," he said, stepping toward her and picking it up with next to no effort at all.

She'd seen him naked so she knew he wasn't heavily muscled, but the man was very clearly strong. He hefted the toolbox into a compartment at the back of the chopper with ease and stacked the fencing wire in there, too, before attaching a pair of ground-handling wheels to the helicopter skids; then, grabbing hold of the back of the chopper, near the tail rotor, he tilted the machine and rolled it forward out of the hangar to the area marked on the tarmac with a large letter H.

Zoe followed, fascinated by the whole process. "I never realized it was as easy as that to move the thing."

Cord laughed. "There are all sorts of tools you can use. I prefer these," he said, gesturing to the removable wheels.

He bent down to remove them from the skids, and after stowing them away back in the hangar, he did a preflight inspection on the chopper. The sun glinted on the bright blue of the fuselage, making Zoe shield her eyes and wish she'd brought her sunglasses.

"There's a spare pair of sunglasses in the glove compartment in the truck if you need them," Cord said as he got to the end of his inspection.

"Thanks."

Zoe didn't waste any time. She went straight to the

truck and opened the glove compartment. The space was very full but she spied the sunglasses quickly and tugged them free. As she did so, a double-folded sheet of paper fell out with them. A funeral service notice, she realized. A stunningly pretty young woman smiled up at her from the front of the notice. She recognized her from a photo she'd seen at the house and assumed it was a relative. Zoe scanned the dates. The girl had died a couple of years ago. Was she the reason for the "memories" Cord had referred to? Instead of relatives, had they been a couple? Feeling as though she was prying into something intensely private, Zoe pushed the notice back into the glove compartment and swung it closed.

As she slid the glasses onto her nose and walked back toward the chopper, she thought about the young woman whose face had imprinted on her so firmly. There was something familiar about her, too, but she couldn't put her finger on when or where she'd seen her. Obviously she couldn't ask Cord. She didn't want to be accused of being nosy, for a start, but she sensed that the subject of the late Britney Collins was a sensitive one.

"Ready?" he asked as she drew closer.

"For sure. Thanks for the shades."

"No worries. I always carry spares."

Zoe's stomach lurched a little as they rose in the air and turned sharply to one side and flew away from the airfield. There was an incredible sense of freedom sitting here in this relatively small bubble and observing the ground racing away beneath them.

"All good?" Cord asked, his voice a little tinny through the headset he'd instructed her to wear.

"A-okay," she replied. "This is really cool."

He flung her another of those grins that made her toes curl. She watched as he competently handled the chopper, dipping and weaving along the contours of the land as they followed fence lines, until he found an area that looked to have been breached. He swiftly turned the chopper around, making Zoe's gut lurch again, before setting the machine down on a level patch of land.

"You do that as if you're born to it," she said after they'd exited the R44.

"I love it. There's a freedom that comes from being in the air that you don't get in a car or a truck. No matter how high performance."

She helped him carry his gear over to the breach in the fence line and watched as he competently made the repairs, handing him tools when he asked for them.

"You're good at this," he commented as she neatly packed his tools back into the box when he was done.

"I used to help my dad around home a lot. With my four older brothers, he had to do a lot of repairs," she said with a laugh.

"I can imagine. Did you enjoy growing up in a large family?"

"It has its drawbacks, but overall it's been good. My brothers are all married now and starting families of their own. It's a bit of a zoo when we all get together, but what can I say…it's family."

She stood up and stretched before leaning against one of the fence posts and surveying the land around them.

"Do you ever feel trapped by all of this?" she asked.

"Trapped? That's a strange way of looking at a large amount of space."

"Well, y'know. The responsibility you have to the land, to the herds, the people you employ. There's so much to consider every day of every month. You're never completely free of it, are you?"

He came and stood in front of her, and she could feel the warmth of his body as he came in close.

"Oh, city girl, you have no idea," he murmured before reaching up to pull something from her hair.

"Was that an insect?" she said with a wary glance at his hand as he tossed something away.

"Just a bit of grass. You're out of your element right now, aren't you?"

"It doesn't bother me," she said, defending herself.

"But you're not comfortable, either, are you?" he pressed.

"I'm never comfortable when I'm not in control. I don't know this world." She gestured around them. "Your world," she clarified.

"And you call yourself a Texan?" he teased, lowering his face to hers. "Let's see if we can't relax you a bit."

He planted his arms on the fence on either side of her and pressed his body against hers as he took her mouth in a sweeping kiss. He'd been thinking about doing this from the moment he first saw her in the kitchen this morning dressed in his old shirt. Last night had been difficult, but even so he hadn't been able to leave Zoe completely alone. He felt raw, as if his nerves were exposed and irritated, and the only thing that would soothe him would be to feel her warmth curled up against him as she slept in his arms.

That had been enough, for then. But now? Now was another story entirely. Now, with the clear fall light bathing the land around them and with the shade trees changing color and beginning to drop their leaves, the sheer satisfaction of being here in his element made him want to pull her into the spell, too.

Her mouth opened beneath his, her tongue meeting his and tasting him with the same eagerness he felt for her. It wasn't long before he knew that kissing her wasn't enough. Would likely never be enough. His desire for her was like a drug in his body, creating a need he couldn't, didn't want to control.

It was both exhilarating and terrifying in equal proportions. Look at how much he'd needed to be with her last night. Even with memories of Britney swirling in the back of his mind, he'd sought Zoe, convincing himself that she needed him more than he needed her. But as he'd lain there, holding her, listening to her steady breathing, absorbing the warmth of her skin, he'd admitted to himself that his need had been the greater.

He'd woken early, determined to put distance between them, but the second he'd seen her again all resolve had been blown to the four corners of the earth. He was glad she'd come out with him today. He'd wanted her to see this, his world, as she'd called it. To understand the call of the land, the beauty that lay before them.

What was the point, though? She was going to be here for only a short time longer. He doubted that Frank would be able to put Sheriff Battle off on the repairs to the equipment for much longer.

He'd take what he could get, he decided. Share with Zoe the perfect synchronicity of their bodies. And when she left, at least he'd have the memories.

Cord tugged her down to the ground and pulled her on top of him. He pushed his hands through her silky hair and cupped the back of her head as he continued to kiss her. She tasted so good, so right, and the way their bodies fit together was equally so.

"What's this?" Zoe asked, pulling slightly away. "Are we checking ground temperatures now?"

He laughed. She was amazing. He hadn't laughed during lovemaking this much, ever.

"Call it whatever you like. I thought it would be a shame to get your blouse all grass stained, hence me being on the bottom," he replied.

"Oh, so you don't want me to get dirty?"

There was a wicked gleam in her eye that totally undid him. "Oh yeah, get as down and dirty as you want."

"Did you bring a condom?"

"Do I look like the kind of man who'd forget something as important as that?"

She cocked her head and grinned. "I'm so glad you like to think of everything."

And then all sensible thought fled as she yanked his buttons undone and bared his chest. Her fingers spread over his skin, her nails lightly rasping over his nipples and sending shocks of delight through his body. He lay there, allowing her access to every part of him, lifting his hips in acquiescence as she tugged his belt free and undid his jeans. When her hands closed over his erection, he jerked against her.

"Whoa, there, cowboy," she murmured. "In some kind of hurry?"

"In some kind of something," he muttered in return.

He clenched his teeth and tensed as she stroked him, her rhythm perfect, and when she wriggled lower down his legs and took him into her mouth, he all but lost it. She licked and tasted him, drawing him into her mouth, then letting him slide free, in a tantalizing, teasing dance. The light breeze was a delicious cold shock against his wet skin. He couldn't take much more of this. He wanted—no, *needed*—to be inside her.

"Condom, front right pocket," he rasped.

Thankfully she was in agreement, because in a matter of moments she'd sheathed him and was pushing her jeans down and standing only briefly enough to remove them and her panties before lowering herself over him again. He could feel the heat at her center as she hovered over him, then reached for his shaft, guiding it to her entrance. And when she slid the rest of the way down he surged upward, meeting her halfway, again and again until the blue sky above them blurred and the only sounds he could hear were their labored breathing and the slap of their skin as she rode him to completion.

She sprawled across his body and he could feel the race of her heartbeat against his chest. He wrapped his arms around her, holding her close, knowing that this was only temporary but wishing it could be so much more. It was at least a half hour later that he felt her shift.

"We'll make a cowgirl of you yet," he teased as she got up and started to tug her clothes back on.

"Certainly has a few highlights to recommend it," she responded just as lightly.

But he could see the shadow that passed across her face. Yes, she was equally as aware as he was that what they shared was transitory. Well, given that fact, there was only one thing for it. They had to make the most of the time they had available.

And he did. Over the next three days he took her everywhere around the ranch with him, even going so far as to getting her up on his oldest, gentlest mare for a rein-led walk. And every night they lost themselves in each other. Of course, he never forgot who and what she was. Not even for a minute. Hard to when she checked her messages daily for updates on the Hamm case and spent a good portion of each evening on her computer. And there was her ever-present handgun. She hadn't worn it that first day they'd gone out in the chopper, but he couldn't avoid seeing its bulk nestled under her blouse every day since.

For now, he felt as though they were living in a bubble,

one where the outside world couldn't get to them. Which was just the way he liked it. Jesse had told him that Janet was coming home from the hospital this week—the infection she'd developed when her appendix burst was now almost clear. By the time she was firmly back on the road to recovery, and Jesse was relieved of the concerns he'd suffered on his baby sister's behalf, hopefully Zoe would have lost the bee in her bonnet about his best friend's possible involvement in the murder case.

He should have known better.

Ten

Zoe had taken control of the kitchen, with Cord supervising her breakfast-cooking skills. It was hard to focus with him standing there, leaning against the kitchen countertop with his hair still damp from the shower they'd just had together. Granted, he was dressed, which should have reduced the impact he had on her senses even after these past few days staying together. But to Zoe's surprise, her interest in Cord Galicia didn't appear to be waning anytime soon. In fact, the longer she stayed here, the harder she found it to focus on her case.

She was just removing bacon from the grill when Cord's cell phone trilled in his pocket.

"It's my dad," he said, checking the screen. "I need to take this."

"No worries, I'll keep everything warm for you."

"Everything?" he asked, stealing a quick kiss from her already swollen lips.

"Go, answer your phone call!" she laughed, giving him a playful shove.

She could hear him talking in the living room. Heard the sincerity and love in his voice as he spoke with his father. The bond was strong there, she realized. It surprised her in some ways, because Cord seemed to be so very self-contained. Not needing anyone or anything.

Zoe broke eggs into the pan and added cream, dill and seasoning before scrambling them all together with a spatula. She was just ladling them out onto warmed plates when the house phone started to ring.

"Can you get that please?" Cord called from the other room.

"Sure," Zoe replied and lifted the handset from the station in the kitchen. "Galicia residence."

"Is Cord available?"

"I'm sorry, he's on another call. Can I take a message?"

"Sure, it's Frank. Can you tell him I can't delay the repair of the sound and video equipment any longer? Nate's getting antsy and I really don't want to be in the sheriff's bad books. Tell Cord we're square now. I put it off as long as I could."

Zoe's brow furrowed in a frown. "Did you say sound and video equipment?"

"Yeah, yeah. Cord will know what I'm talking about. Can you just see he gets the message?"

"Oh, I'll see he gets the message, all right," she answered before severing the call.

Anger rose inside her like a storm surge, filling every nook and cranny of her mind and her body until it seeped from her pores like a palpable presence in the room. She replayed the conversation she'd just had over and over in her head. Each time it remained the same. Each time the result was damning. Cord had tampered with her investigation by deliberately delaying her interview with Jesse Stevens.

She heard a sound behind her and wheeled as Cord came back into the kitchen.

"Sorry about that. My dad sure can talk. He's missing the ranch." He came and stood beside her. "Hey, something's wrong. What's up?"

"You tell me," she said tightly.

"What do you mean? Who was on the phone?"

"Your friend Frank."

She watched his face as understanding dawned. "Ah."

Cord's expression closed up. Gone was the loving, playful cowboy who had occupied her days, and her nights. In place was the silent, careful man who'd greeted her the day she'd arrived in Royal.

"What you did was illegal. You deliberately hindered my investigation," she said bitingly through clenched teeth. "I should arrest you for that."

"Are you going to?"

"No. I don't plan to waste another second on you. Besides, the paperwork would be more than you're worth."

She shoved past him and headed upstairs. He was behind her a split second later.

"Where are you going?"

"To do my job."

She stormed into his bedroom, which they'd been sharing since that day out in the chopper, grabbed her bag and started throwing her things into it. Cord didn't try to stop her. Didn't so much as step in her way. She didn't know what upset her more—the fact he'd done what he had, or the fact that he didn't seem to care now that she knew. Then understanding dawned.

She wheeled to face him, hands fisted and planted on her hips.

"This was your intention all along, wasn't it?" she demanded. "Keep me distracted so I wouldn't question your buddy!"

To her utter humiliation he didn't say a word, but she saw the truth in his eyes.

"You bastard!" she spat.

She snatched her bag from the bed and hammered down the stairs. She paused only long enough to grab her laptop and case from the sitting room and then she was out the door. He didn't follow. He never said a word. And as bitter, angry tears started to track down her cheeks, she realized she'd been taken for a complete fool. Seduced by an oh-so-talented lover. Falling for all the stereotypes she'd sworn she'd never be caught by. Turned out she was just as fallible as anyone else. Worse, she'd been as stupid as some of her colleagues had always expected her to be. She'd lost sight of the case and all because a handsome man had paid her attention.

Well, she thought as she swiped the tears from her face and turned her car toward town, she'd learned her lesson, hadn't she? This interview with Jesse Stevens was happening today, one way or another, and then she was heading home.

She drove directly to the sheriff's office and parked outside. Thankfully Sheriff Battle was in when she asked for him, and he was quick to assure her that the interview room would be ready for her early in the afternoon. He also offered to contact Jesse himself and ask the guy to come in. All of which meant she had a few hours to cool her heels before she could complete her task here and then get the hell out of town.

Zoe headed to the Daily Grind and grabbed a coffee and something to eat. As she sat at the small table near the window and stared outside, she wondered if Cord had eaten the breakfast she'd just finished preparing before the scales had been torn from her eyes. Darn, but she'd been such an idiot. If anything, that hurt more than his lack of sincerity in starting their affair. And, yes, he'd started it. And she'd let him.

She suppressed the tingle that began in her body at the memory of that first night, of being pressed against the motel room door while he did incredible things to her. It had all been fake. A distraction tactic. And it had worked. But no more. She didn't trust anyone, especially not Cord Galicia.

Her mobile phone pinged with a text confirming the interview with Jesse Stevens at one o'clock. She texted back her agreement and finished her coffee. She still had hours to kill. Realizing she needed to burn off some steam, Zoe went for a long walk. While she walked, her phone buzzed. She looked at the screen. Cord. Damn him. She declined the call and shoved the phone back into her pocket, where it began buzzing again. She ignored it, only to have the darn thing continue to go off at regular intervals. In the end she turned off her phone, but she'd worked up a fine head of steam by the time she was shown into the interview room at the station. Sheriff Battle was already there, setting up the equipment. He looked up, his expression growing wary as she walked in.

"You okay?" he asked.

"I'm fine," she said sharply, then sighed. "No, actually I'm not fine, but my day will improve once I get this interview done and get back to Houston."

"Sick of us already?"

She cracked a wry grin. "I do have a job to do. Seems everyone has forgotten that fact."

Nate Battle shrugged. "Looked like you were getting

real comfortable with Cord the other night when he took you back to his place."

She stiffened. "He put me up for a few days, that's all."

He stared at her for a few moments, then nodded briefly. "Jesse should be here any minute. The recording equipment will upload a digital file to your email address when we're done. It'll be waiting for you when you get home."

"Good," she said. "Nice to know it's all working fine now."

"Yeah, about that…"

"Don't worry about it. The problem's sorted."

Yes, the problem was sorted, and she'd begun to accept that she'd had a narrow escape from a dirty, low-down snake. It would have been all too easy to fall for Cord Galicia. She'd deeply enjoyed her time with him on the ranch, had even begun to see the beauty that held him there, although her craving for hot asphalt and skyscrapers still lingered beneath the surface. She shook her head slightly. Nope, she wasn't going back down that memory track. She'd seal it up instead, for good.

A sound at the door made her turn and watch as one of the sheriff's deputies showed Jesse Stevens into the room.

"Good afternoon, y'all," he said, removing his hat and setting it on the desk between them.

Nate Battle didn't waste any time. He launched straight into the formalities, inviting both Jesse and Zoe to take a seat and then turning on the equipment and making the introductory statement for the record. Zoe felt her skin itch as she waited her turn to fire the questions she'd been hanging out to ask. After confirming it was Jesse's voice on Hamm's phone, she pushed him a little harder.

"You were extremely angry with Mr. Hamm when you left that message, weren't you?"

"I was."

Jesse's response was clipped, and she saw the glint of irritation in his green eyes.

"Could you state for the recording why you were angry with Mr. Hamm?"

"Sure. It's common knowledge that over the years I did several favors for the guy. When the shoe was on the other foot and I asked him for help getting an internship at Perry Holdings for my sister, he flat out refused. Seems the big city and his job there made him think he was too good for his old friends back home."

"I can see why that would have upset you," she said, baiting him.

"Upset me, yes. But not enough to murder the guy. I did not kill Vincent Hamm. I was mad at him, for sure, but I took it on the chin and moved on. I told you that around the time they say he was murdered I was three hours away from Houston, attending a stock auction." He reached inside his jacket pocket and drew out a folded wad of paper. "Here," he said, unfolding the papers and stabbing them with his finger. "As requested, my receipts. Motel, gas and copies of sale agreements."

Zoe looked over at Nate, who reached for the papers and carefully scrutinized them.

"It all looks genuine," he said carefully. "Covers the three-day window of time in which Hamm's murder most likely occurred, no question."

"Of course it's genuine," Jesse interjected. "I keep telling you. I'm innocent. Look, I'm sorry the guy is dead. No one deserved to die like that, but maybe he had it coming from someone other than me. Maybe he said no to just one person too many."

"Running my investigation now, are we?" Zoe added acerbically.

"I apologize, ma'am," Jesse said. "Not my place, I know.

But stand in my shoes for a minute and think about this. I would lose my family, my home—everything—if I were guilty of what you're suggesting. Look, if those receipts aren't enough for you, let me take a polygraph. I know you have one here, Nate. Hook me up. It'll prove my innocence."

Nate looked at Zoe with a question clear in his eyes. She took her time answering. On the surface, it would seem that Jesse Stevens was telling the truth. She sighed. Another dead end.

"Sure," she said to both men. "Let's do it."

It was close to four o'clock before the sheriff walked her out to her car. A sheet of paper flapped from under one of her wiper blades.

"Are you kidding me?" she groaned when she spied the parking fine.

Nate laughed and took it from her hand. "Let me take care of it."

"Thanks," she answered and opened her car door. "And thanks for your help today. I'm sure you probably had better things to do."

He shrugged. "There's always something to do around here. Might not be the bright lights and the big city, but it's never dull. You're satisfied now that Jesse's not your man?"

She nodded—a grimace twisting her features. "Yeah, but it puts us back to square one again. I'm sorry, Sheriff. I know you made promises to Hamm's family. I'd hoped we'd be able to bring them some closure by now."

"It's okay. I know you're not going to quit on this."

"Oh, trust me. Quitting is not in my nature. Obviously I need to shift focus. I've gone over and over my notes, but there's something I'm just not seeing. I keep coming back to the crime scene. It's gotta be someone connected to the building, or maybe even to someone connected to Perry Holdings. But where are the damn clues? Hamm must have seen or heard something that had gotten him killed, so why can't I find it?"

"You will. Eventually."

She laughed, but it lacked any humor. "Yeah. Maybe it'll shake loose on the drive back."

"It's getting late. You sure you don't want to stay an extra night?"

"No, definitely not. I need to get back," she said firmly. "I've been away too long as it is."

"Sure. You know, there were a lot of people surprised to see you with Cord at the club the other night."

"So glad I could provide entertainment for their evening," she commented cynically.

"He hasn't been seen out with anyone since Britney died."

"Britney?" There was that name again. Maybe now she'd find out why it had been oddly familiar to her.

"Yeah, they were engaged. Last time anyone saw them together was the night he asked her to marry him at the club a little over two years ago, just before she went to the police academy."

"She was a cop?"

"Yup, Houston P.D. Died on her first patrol. Nearly destroyed Cord when the news came through she'd been shot."

Understanding dawned. "I remember that. I didn't work the case myself, but everyone assigned to it was focused on finding her killers."

"It was a bad time for everyone who knew Britney, but most of all for Cord. His parents even delayed their retirement to help him out."

"And he hasn't been out with anyone since?" she blurted without thinking.

The sheriff shook his head. "Folks wondered if you'd be staying on."

She barked a laugh. "No offense, Sheriff, but Royal's just a little too tame for me."

"That has its benefits," he said with a smile that showed he wasn't in the least offended.

Zoe held out her hand. "Thanks for everything. I'll be in touch."

"Thank you. And that file and the polygraph report will be waiting for you when you get to work tomorrow."

After shaking hands, she got into her car and tapped her address into the map app on her phone. Then with a final wave to the sheriff, she headed out of Royal.

As she drove, her mind began to wander. So Cord had been engaged, and she'd been his first relationship since then. Not that it made any difference. He'd gone out with her only to stop her from interviewing Jesse. She thought back to the day she'd met him, to his dismissive attitude of her being a cop. All the pieces fit. But none of it excused him for using her the way he had.

Eleven

Her eyes were grainy with exhaustion by the time she pulled into her parking garage, but at least she was home. She'd taken only a short break about two hours out of Houston to grab some food and something to drink at a gas station. *Food*, she snorted as she grabbed her bag and laptop. *Cardboard with processed meat and cheese, more like.* She wondered if there was anything edible left in her apartment. Unlikely, but she'd take her chances when she got upstairs.

She exited the elevator and turned down the corridor to her apartment. All weariness fled and adrenaline flooded her system as she spied someone loitering near her front door. She dropped her things and reached for her gun just as the man turned around to face her. Shock replaced the adrenaline as she identified Cord.

"What the hell are you doing here?" she demanded, holstering her gun and snatching up her things again.

"And how did you know where I live, let alone get past security?"

How dare he be here? And ahead of her, too. She'd driven the maximum speed limit the whole way here. Unless he'd been here waiting for her for all the hours it took to interview Stevens. She felt a perverse imp of satisfaction at the idea of him cooling his heels for several hours tweak her lips into a half smile.

"You're not the only one with investigative skills," Cord said with a grin that flashed across his features, then disappeared just as quickly. "I'm here to see you. We need to talk."

"No, we don't. We've done all the talking—all the anything—we needed to do."

"Seems we differ on that topic. Perhaps I should have said, *I* need to talk to you."

"And why should I listen to you? You willfully obstructed my investigation."

"I did."

"We have no more to say," she said adamantly and brushed past him to insert her key into the lock. "Enjoy your trip back to Royal."

"I'm not leaving until we've spoken."

"Then I hope you'll be comfortable sleeping out here on the hallway floor because I have nothing to say to you."

She went inside and started to close the door, but Cord swiftly blocked her action.

"Look, hear me out. Please? I know I was a prize asshole. I apologize for that."

"Good of you, but it makes no difference. I'm investigating a man's death here. You impeded that investigation."

"So arrest me."

They stared at each other in silence for a full minute. Zoe couldn't tear her gaze from his. She could see her own reflection in the darkness of his pupils, saw the determination in every line of his face. His lips, which could do such wicked things to her body, were compressed in a grim line, and the humor that she'd so often witnessed in his expression was not evident today. He wasn't going to leave until he'd said his piece, that much was blatantly clear. She blew out a sigh of frustration.

"Fine, come in. Five minutes and then you're out again. How the hell did you get here, anyway?"

"I flew in."

She stopped halfway through to the kitchen and dropped her bags onto a chair.

"Just like that?"

"The beauty of flying."

"No five-and-a-half-hour drive? No toilet stops in questionable bathrooms?"

He shook his head.

"I hate you," she muttered as she entered the kitchen and opened the refrigerator to stare blankly at its meager contents.

"Even more than this morning?" he said, stepping up close behind her and peering over her shoulder.

She felt his presence acutely, even though he wasn't touching her, and caught her breath so she wouldn't inhale the appealing scent of him. Whatever he smelled like, however good he felt against her body or even inside it, he'd betrayed her.

"Yes, even more than this morning."

"What if I head to the convenience store around the corner and get us some food and cook you dinner? Would you hate me less, then?"

She closed the fridge door with a thud and turned to face him. "No, I wouldn't. It's late, I'm tired, I'm frustrated and I want to go to sleep. Say what you wanted to say and go."

"Not even a coffee?"

She rolled her eyes and moved to the coffee machine. "Fine, and then you go."

She went through the motions, not even fully aware of what she was doing. All she could think about was Cord and the fact he was here, in her world now. Not that it made any difference. She'd closed that door. It wasn't even as if a future together had been in the cards in the first place. Friends with benefits, that was all it was. Heck, not even friends, to be totally blunt.

"I hope you like it black. Milk's off, and I don't have any powdered creamer," she said, pouring him a mug full of the dark brew.

"Thanks, it'll do fine."

He took the mug, his fingers brushing hers. She hated the cliché of it, but there was no mistaking the jolt of awareness she felt as their skin brushed.

"You're not having any?" he asked.

"No, I need to sleep. Gotta get into the station early."

"Right, so I guess my time starts now?"

Cord watched as Zoe nodded and gestured for him to sit in the living room. Before sitting down opposite him, she removed her holster and slid her weapon onto the table between them. A reminder, perhaps, that she was trained in firearms and not afraid to use them. Or simply just a reminder that she was and always would be a cop.

He drew in a deep breath and began to speak. "What I did was wrong."

"Y'think?" she answered caustically and arched one brow at him.

"Not just from a legal perspective, but from a personal one. I've never been the kind of person to cause trouble with the police."

"And yet you did."

She crossed her arms and stared at him. Nope—she definitely wasn't going to make this any easier.

"Look, initially, when I knew you were investigating Jesse, it sent me into protective mode. He's been through a lot."

"And you don't think the Hamm family has been through a lot, too? That they don't deserve some answers as to who murdered their son?"

He shook his head. "I was wrong. I knew Jesse couldn't have been involved. I just didn't want you hassling him. But—" he held up one hand as she started to interrupt "—I had no right to do what I did nor delay your opportunity to interview him. I apologize for all of it."

"Great, I accept your apology. You can go now."

She started to stand.

"Look, just a few more minutes," he begged. To his relief she sat back down again. "I'm fiercely attracted to you, Detective. It scares me."

"Go on."

"I was engaged before, to a girl named Britney Collins."

"I know the name."

"Then you know what happened to her."

"I do."

"I can't go through that again. I can't face every single day knowing a woman I love is putting herself in danger." *Love?* Where did that come from? He was messing this all up, especially if the suddenly shuttered look on Zoe's face was any indicator. "I was never keen on her career choice. In fact, I have to admit that I never fully understood her need or her drive to become one of Houston's finest. But I couldn't hold her back. If I'd asked her, she wouldn't have done it. Instead, she'd have found work in Royal that satisfied her until we had kids, and then she would have stayed home with them. But I knew she wanted more than that.

"Part of me regrets not being selfish. She'd still be alive today if I had. But, in time, she'd have been desperately unhappy. Which brings me to you."

Zoe's eyes widened slightly. "Look, what happened to Britney was awful. It's something every cop and their family dread, but you can't compare her situation to mine. I've been raised in a police family. I've been a cop for nine years. I'm not saying I won't ever get killed on the job, but I am saying I am well trained, and in my role as a detective, I'm not exposed to the kinds of things a frontline officer is on a daily basis.

"But, all of that said, I'm not in the market for a relationship. Especially not a long-distance one. Hell, I'd probably stand more chance of being involved in a car wreck than I do getting hurt on the job."

"Does that mean you're not even willing to try? We have a connection, Zoe. You know it. I know it. Don't you think it's worth exploring to see what happens?"

She shook her head slowly, and he could see regret in her eyes. "No. Your life, everything, is in Royal. Mine is here. We might fit in the bedroom, but we don't fit when it comes to our lifestyles or our careers.

"I know you have an obligation to your family, and that's what drives you on your ranch. It's your home, it's what you do and, from what I could see, you're good at it. It fits for you. This city, the people in it, that's what fits for me. We're oil and water, Cord. We just don't mix. I think you should go now."

He stood, even though every cell in his body was telling him to fight harder, to tell her he could change, make adjustments, that if they both wanted it enough, they could make it work. But deep down he knew it would be futile.

In fact, it would probably only lead to more heartbreak for both of them.

"Thanks for hearing me out," he said, offering Zoe his hand to shake when she'd walked him to the door.

She took his hand and squeezed it gently, but before she could let him go he tugged her slightly off balance, pulling her against him. Without a second thought he cupped her jaw, tilting her face up to his and taking her lips with a kiss that both seared her flesh and said a bittersweet goodbye.

He stood outside the door after she'd closed it. He wasn't giving up. She might think it was over between them, but he had to be 100 percent sure they couldn't make a go of this. Life was too short and way too precious not to fight for what was important. He knew that better than most. And he had an ace up his sleeve that Zoe wasn't expecting.

Cord started walking to the elevator. This round was hers, but he was pretty certain he'd win the next one.

Cord pulled up outside the sprawling home in a suburban part of Houston the next day. The lots were a generous size here, the gardens well established and there was an air of quiet gentility about the area, with echoes of past families having been raised around here. He checked the address he'd been given and looked at the house across the street. So this was where Zoe had grown up. He could just imagine a younger, skinnier version of her shinnying up one of those giant trees or riding her bike along the sidewalk.

He reached for the large colorful bunch of flowers on the passenger seat of his rental car and the bottle of red wine he'd bought and got out of the car. The older woman who opened the door to his knock was smiling widely.

"You must be Cord," she said. "Welcome to our home.

We're so grateful to you for looking out for Zoe while she was out of town."

"Mrs. Warren, lovely to meet you, and it was a pleasure. Can I just say how like Zoe you look, or should that be the other way around?"

"Ah yes, people do say that. Come on out back. The boys and their families are already here. We're just waiting for Zoe."

"These are for you," he said, giving Zoe's mom the bouquet of flowers.

"They're beautiful, thank you. You'll make my husband jealous," she said with a girlish giggle.

"Well, I have brought him a gift, too," Cord said, brandishing the bottle of wine. "So I hope he'll forgive me."

She spied the label. "Oh yes, he'll forgive you, all right. Follow me."

Cord trailed behind her, his eyes catching on a series of family photos that lined the hallway in groupings that appeared to be by various eras within the family. He'd have liked to have lingered and studied the progression of Zoe's childhood to the woman she was today, but Zoe's mom was disappearing through a doorway ahead of him. He quickly followed her through the door and was met by a cacophony of sound. Kids, dogs, family. It looked like there were people everywhere.

This was what Zoe had grown up surrounded by. It was very different from his upbringing as the only child of a close-knit ranching family. Sure, they'd had extended family to visit occasionally, and some of the hands lived on-site. And there had been the Stevens kids as well, but this was something else.

"Jed, come and meet Cord, the guy I was telling you about."

A heavyset grizzled man in his late fifties put down the

tongs he'd been using on the outdoor grill and wiped his hands on the apron he was wearing. The pink frilly fabric looked incongruous on him, but that fact didn't seem to bother him at all as he came over to meet Cord.

"Jed Warren. I'm Zoe's dad. Pleased to meet you."

"Cord Galicia. Likewise. This is for you," Cord said, handing the man the bottle of wine.

"Well, thank you very much. We invited you here to thank you for looking out for our girl, not for you to bring us stuff," Jed said with a grin.

"My mom always said I should never arrive anywhere empty-handed."

"Well, I appreciate this. I really do. In fact, I might just put this on the rack so it doesn't get quaffed by the riffraff here." Jed gestured toward four young men in the backyard who, by their appearance, were obviously his sons.

Zoe's mom linked her arm in Cord's. "Come and meet the rest of the family, and please call me Sarah."

Cord made it through most of the introductions before completely losing track of which kids belonged to what parents, but there came a point when he felt a shift in the camaraderie of the moment to one of pointed observation. It coincided with an intense prickle of awareness running down his neck. Zoe was here. Slowly, he turned around and faced her. Fury and disbelief warred for dominance on her beautiful features.

Sarah Warren saw her daughter and bustled forward.

"Zoe, darling. Glad you could get away from work. Come, have a drink."

"What's he doing here?" she asked bluntly.

Cord saw color infuse her mother's cheeks. "Zoe," she whispered fiercely. "We don't treat our guests like that."

"He's a guest? Seriously? You invited him?"

"Of course we did. He called us, trying to track you

down. Said you'd left something at his house when he put you up after that dreadful motel fire. You remember, the one you didn't see fit to tell your mother about?"

Cord stifled a grin. There was nothing quite like a mother's love and censure all rolled into one telling off. Zoe, it seemed, felt the same way.

"Mom, it wasn't that bad. But I still don't understand why he's here."

"Well, when he called and asked for your address, we just wanted to say thank-you for his hospitality toward you, of course."

The way Sarah spoke, it made her invitation to him so very matter-of-fact, but he could see Zoe wasn't having any of it.

"Right," she said, in response to her mom's explanation. "Well, I can't stay long. I'm waiting for a call to get back to the office."

"Surely you can take a couple of hours away from your work," her mother admonished and grabbed an ice-cold beer from a fridge on the back porch and shoved it into her daughter's hand. "There, now have a drink and play nice."

Sarah went back inside the kitchen, leaving Cord and Zoe mostly alone on the back patio.

"Great place your parents have. Must have been fun growing up here."

"With that lot?" she gestured with her beer bottle to her brothers, who'd lined up on either side of a picnic table to have a drink and a yarn while their wives supervised the children for a while. "Hardly."

"I bet it was fun," Cord said again, this time with a wistfulness to his voice that he hadn't expected.

"Are you stalking me?" Zoe said after a short silence.
"What? No!"
"It certainly looks that way."

"Look, I called your parents' house after you left because you left your computer cable behind. I wanted to know where I could send it. I explained to your mom why you'd been staying with me, and she gave me your address and then when I said I'd be in Houston, she invited me for dinner tonight. I could hardly refuse."

"Oh yes, you could totally have refused." Zoe took a swig of her beer and turned to face him. "And you still haven't given me my computer cable."

"Let's just say I got distracted yesterday. It's in my car now. I was going to leave it with your parents if you didn't show."

"You mean you didn't think I'd be here tonight?"

"Your mom wasn't sure if you'd make it. Seems you don't make it to a lot of family get-togethers these days."

Zoe groaned. "Don't you start. I get enough of that from Mom."

Cord shrugged. "Only repeating what she told me."

He looked at her. There were dark shadows under her eyes, giving them a bruised look and making her look more vulnerable than he'd ever seen her. He couldn't help himself. He reached out to touch her cheek. A slight buzz tingled through his fingertips as they grazed gently against her skin.

"You okay? You look tired."

She shook her head, breaking the contact. "I'm fine. This investigation is driving me insane, though. There's a whole ton of pressure from the top brass to wrap this up, like, you have no idea."

"And I made that worse for you, didn't I? I'm truly sorry. I wasn't thinking."

"Look, I accepted your apology," she said testily and took another sip of her beer.

"I know, but I meant it. Look, I won't stay. I can see that my being here is spoiling it for you."

Cord put his beer down on the table next to them and started to walk away. He was surprised when Zoe grabbed his arm.

"Don't you dare leave. It'll be more than my life is worth trying to explain it after you've gone."

He stopped and looked at her. She was glancing between him and her brothers, all of whom had turned to watch them with varying degrees of interest.

"Okay," he said and picked up his beer again. "Again, my apologies—this wasn't a good idea."

"No, it wasn't, but you're here now, so let's make the most of it. I take it you've met everybody?"

"Yeah. I like your family so far."

She snorted. "Well, the fact that you're still alive probably means they like you, too. Either that or they've decided you're an experiment."

"How so?"

"They're probably taking bets to see how long it'll take me to screw this up."

He raised his brows at her. "You do that often?"

She punched him in the arm. "I get enough cheek from that bunch over there," she said, nodding in the direction of her brothers. "If you're staying, you're my ally, okay?"

He shrugged. "Sure. Does that mean I get to kiss you again?"

In an instant the atmosphere between them thickened and changed into something far more intense. The sounds of the kids playing in the yard, of Jed grilling the meat and Sarah calling her boys to help bring salads out from the house all faded into the background. All Cord could focus on was Zoe's mouth. On the way her lips glistened with a sheen of moisture on the remnants of the lipstick she must have applied a while ago but that had mostly worn away. He wanted to remove the rest of it—with a scrape of his teeth, a rasp of his tongue, with the pressure of his lips.

Heat poured through his body and arousal followed swiftly after. He continued to stare at Zoe, and she remained silent in response. Her eyes had widened slightly, her pupils almost consuming the blue irises that told so much and yet hid so much at the same time. Cord realized that while he knew exactly how to bring her to a screaming climax, he knew very little about Zoe Warren, the woman. And he wanted to. Oh, how he wanted to. What had started as a distraction had wormed its way deep into his psyche and gone way beyond the physical attraction that sparked like fallen power lines between them.

This was so much more, and it was equally as dangerous at the same time.

Twelve

Zoe's breath caught in her chest. One minute they'd been bantering, she on the point of asking him to leave, until he'd gone and offered to do so—and she'd realized that she didn't want him to go after all. In fact, he was the reason she looked so darn tired today. It had nothing to do with the early start back at the station and everything to do with cursing herself for making him leave last night.

The truth was he frightened her. He was intense about everything he did—from seeing to his ranch to stroking her body to flaming life. She couldn't handle it. Didn't want to. And did, all at the same time. Cord Galicia had turned her on her head and she didn't like it one bit. Worse, he was distracting her from her work even when he wasn't deliberately trying to hold her back from doing her job. He'd inveigled his way into every crevice in her mind, meaning thoughts of him—reminders of his scent, the way he moved, the way he tasted—would unexpectedly send ripples of desire through her body at the most inopportune moments.

Last night, after she'd closed the door on him and sent him away—for good, she'd believed—she ended up going to her room and collapsing onto her bed, clutching her pillow to her body like some lovelorn teenager. She wasn't that person, and yet, somehow, he'd made her like that. Made her want him. Worse, he'd made her need him. She'd been unable to sleep in anything more than short snatches, and she'd been short-tempered with her team when she'd gone into the station this morning and they'd ribbed her about her vacation in the country.

There'd been no further progress on her case. She'd reviewed the sound and video files and polygraph results sent through from Sheriff Battle's office, looking for a loophole she might have missed, but they merely confirmed Jesse Stevens was totally clean. She'd even had his alibi checked out, although his receipts had been conclusive in themselves.

And then there was Cord.

She realized that her family was beginning to give them strange looks, as if they'd both missed something going on around them. And they had. While she and Cord had been locked in their bubble, the world had continued around them.

"Aunty Zoe, are you in love?"

The piercingly innocent curiosity of one of her nieces shook her from the spell she'd fallen under.

"What makes you say that, Theresa?" she asked, bending down to the four-year-old's level.

"'Cause you're looking at that man like mommy looks at daddy when she says she wants to eat him all up." Theresa took a deep breath. "And mommy loves daddy."

"Out of the mouths of babes," Cord murmured from behind her.

"Don't encourage her," Zoe said over her shoulder before smiling at her little niece. She rose, taking the little girl's hand. "No, honey. I'm not in love. But I am hungry for dinner. Are you?"

The rest of the evening passed relatively uneventfully. To her relief, Cord gave her some distance and didn't stick to her side. Even so, she was constantly physically aware of his every move. Even the way he tipped his beer to his lips sent a pull of longing through her. By the time her brothers and their wives started to gather up their kids and head home, it was getting late and exhaustion dragged at her.

Cord had been busy in the kitchen, helping clean up, when she decided it was time for her to go. Her mom, bless her heart, shooed Cord from the kitchen, telling him she and Jed could manage just fine from here. As a result, Zoe and Cord walked out together, and instead of her parents standing on the front porch and waving at her until she was out of sight, she had to fight back a tug of humor at her lips when her mom grabbed her dad by his arm and dragged him back inside immediately and shut the front door with a bang.

"Nice touch with the flowers for my mom, Galicia," Zoe said as she walked to her car with Cord shadowing at her side.

"I like to pay my respects. You have a nice family."

"Yeah, as much as I like to complain about them, I love them dearly. I couldn't stand to be too far away. It's not often we can all get together at the same time. We're all on different shift rosters, so whenever there's a free Sunday, Mom puts on an evening like this."

"Family is important."

"It's one of the reasons I'll never leave Houston," Zoe said firmly.

She needed to make it clear that she'd meant what she said back in Royal. No matter how powerful this attraction between them, there was no way it could ever work. Her job aside, she'd slowly die inside if she was that far from the network of her parents and siblings.

"I understand," Cord said quietly, his hands shoved into his jeans pockets as if he had to confine them to stop himself from reaching for her.

A part of her wished he would. Wished he'd take her into his arms and kiss her, right here on the street in full view of anyone. Instead, he tugged his keys out of his pocket.

"Good night, Zoe. It's been great. But I get the message. I'd hoped we could figure it out—make us work somehow—but now, having seen your family and you with them, I truly do understand what keeps you here. It's not just your job, because I know you'd be a great cop anywhere, and it's not the city. It's them, and you don't need to make any apology for that. Family is the glue that holds us together."

"Well, they're a pain in the butt most of the time, but yeah."

"They only want you to be happy. To have what they have."

Unexpected tears sprang to Zoe's eyes. His words cut her to her soul. She wanted that, too, but she wanted to be so much more than that at the same time. Somehow she'd just never envisaged being able to juggle it all. Her job had defined her for nine years, and, yes, she'd put her work ahead of everything and everyone she'd met along the way. With her dad and brothers being in the force, it had made it easier for her to hone her focus, even though they'd always teased her about settling down one day. But, at the same time, they balanced their work and family life without any serious problems.

But it would be different with Cord if they ever did try to make things work between them. He'd already lost a woman he'd loved to her job and in the worst way possible. Zoe had pulled the incident report and skimmed it when she'd gotten into work today. The facts had been chilling. No wonder Cord was so put off by guns and the people who carried them in their line of work.

He was walking away now, and she felt as if she was being torn in two. One half of her urging her to let him go, the other begging her to make him stay, even if only for one more night. The flip side won.

"Cord!"

She was moving toward him before she even realized it. The moment he turned, she reached for him, tugging his face down to hers. She kissed him—hard and fierce and with every ounce of longing that pulsed through her body.

"Come back to my place, please?"

He stared at her a full twenty seconds before replying. She could see the battle that raged behind his beautiful sherry-brown eyes. He closed them a moment, his long lashes sweeping down. They should look ridiculous on a man like him, a man who was so lean and fierce and strong, but instead they only made him look that much more appealing.

"Yes."

It was one simple word, just three letters, and yet it had the power to make her feel as if she'd won the lottery ten times over.

"Follow me," she said and all but ran back to her car.

He tailed her the few short miles back to her apartment building, pulling into the visitor parking he'd used the day before while she put her car in the parking garage. She ran up the ramp to where he was waiting at the front of the building, and she grabbed his hand and tugged him through the front door. She barely acknowledged security when they greeted her; she had only one thought burning through her mind. If this was to be their last time together, it had to be perfect, because it would have to last her forever.

The ride in the elevator was interminable, but finally they spilled out of the car and down the hallway to her apartment. She just managed to wrestle her door open and tumble inside her apartment with Cord right behind her. She grabbed him by his shoulders and pushed him up against the wall the second the door was closed and secured behind them. She tugged at his jacket, then his shirt, exposing the warm, tanned skin of his chest to her gaze, her fingers, her mouth.

He groaned and tangled his fingers in her hair as she kissed him and dragged her lips down his throat, nipping at the cords of his neck, then soothing them with her tongue. Her hands were busy at his belt, unbuckling it and then unbuttoning his fly with a dexterity that amazed her under the conditions. She shoved his jeans down his lean hips and her hand cupped his engorged shaft through his boxer briefs.

Cord didn't waste any time. He tugged at the buttons of her blouse and opened her jeans with equal alacrity, and she toed off her ankle boots and stepped out of her jeans, standing now on legs that trembled. His heated palm cupped her between her legs, and she just about went ballistic on the sensation of heat, silk and moisture against her most sensitive skin.

And then he was lifting her up against him. She hooked her legs around him and held on tight.

"Bedroom?"

"First door on the right past the sitting room," she directed.

He walked them both to the bedroom and dropped her unceremoniously onto the bed, but the second he joined her on the mattress she straddled him again, smoothing her hands in hurried caresses over his shoulders, his chest, his belly.

"You feel so good," she murmured and bent down to kiss him, her tongue teasing his, her teeth nipping gently at his lower lip, tugging it before swiping it with her tongue and kissing him hard.

Her entire body hummed for this man, and she couldn't wait to feel him inside her, stroking her to another amazing crescendo of feeling and sensation, but she could prolong the agony of waiting just a little longer if she could feast her eyes on him and touch him in all the places she longed to. Zoe traced the lean lines of muscle that defined his stomach, letting her fingers edge ever closer to the waistband of his briefs. She skimmed the elastic, then started from the top of his shoulders all over again.

"Detective, is there anything in particular you're looking for? Because you seem to be examining my body of evidence rather thoroughly."

She chuckled and nipped him in the hollow just inside his hip bone. He laughed in response.

"Don't rush me," she growled and pinched the side of his leg in punishment.

"Wouldn't dream of it," he replied.

Cord bunched his fists in her bedcovers and lifted his hips slightly as she slid her fingers beneath his waistband and began tugging his briefs off. His erection sprang proudly free of its confines, and Zoe smiled as she anticipated what she would do next.

"Seriously, Detective? You're just going to look at it?"

Stifling another chuckle, she looked up at his face

and gave him a stern stare. "Like I said, Galicia, don't rush me."

"Or what?"

"Or you might live to regret it."

"Are you going to torture me? I could get used to that."

She ignored the pang his words engendered. Get used to it? Get used to her? That wouldn't happen. She'd made it clear outside her parents' place. And then she'd muddied the waters by inviting him back here.

"Zoe?"

She looked into his eyes, saw the concern there.

"Just dreaming up a suitable punishment," she answered lightly.

She turned her attention to Cord's very enticing body and in particular to one very demanding shaft of flesh. She closed her fingers around the hot, hard rod and stroked him from base to tip before taking him into her mouth. He groaned again, and she teased him with her tongue and her lips until she knew he was almost at the point of no return. She released him from the warm, wet confines of her mouth and blew softly against his skin.

"Detective, I think you need to take me into custody soon or I might not be responsible for my actions."

"Duly noted," she said with a smile as she stretched over him and reached for the bedside cabinet drawer.

She grabbed a handful of condoms and dropped them onto the bed beside them before selecting one and smoothing it onto his straining flesh. Then, without wasting another moment, she straddled him again and guided him into her body, slowly and deliberately taking him inside her inch by slow inch. The expression on his face was one of pure concentration and control, as if he could slip at any moment. She loved the idea that she did this to him and that he let her.

Zoe rocked her hips, taking him that little deeper, clenching against his hardness, then releasing him, setting up a rhythm that increased in tempo until she could control herself no longer. And then she was lost on that wave of pure bliss, her internal muscles spasming and pulling Cord right along with her on that journey to the stars and back again. She collapsed over him, her body slick with perspiration and every nerve shuddering with the power of her climax. Inside her, she could feel him swell and twitch as the last of his orgasm pulsed into satiation and, finally, calm.

Cord's arms wrapped around her and he rolled them onto their sides, and together they slid into sleep, only to wake two hours later and take each other all over again. This time it was Cord who led the way, tormenting her to a point where she felt as though she might shatter into a thousand pieces, before taking her to even greater heights of pleasure.

When Zoe woke in the morning, it was to an empty bed and an empty apartment—and an even emptier heart. She sank onto the sofa in her living room, wrapped in one of her bedsheets, and bent her head and cried for all that they'd shared together and all that they would never have again. She knew now that it went beyond sex. Way beyond it. Somewhere along the line he'd stolen her heart. But it was a love that could never work, she reminded herself. She wouldn't compromise on that which was most important to her. Her family. Her work. And he knew that. Accepted it. Because he'd left without a goodbye, and now it was up to her to deal with that.

Eighteen-year-old Maya Currin synced her playlist to her car and settled in for the drive. The baby of Ryder Currin's kids, she knew if she'd told her family she was coming home, someone would have flown to drive her down or at least accompany her on the long journey from Boston back to Texas. But she didn't want company because she had plenty of thinking to do along the way. Not the least of which was clearing her head of that waste of space she'd called her boyfriend.

How could she have been so stupid to have thought Dirk had truly loved her? All he'd loved was her last name and the kudos that came with being one of the children of the famed oil baron and businessman, Ryder Currin. But she wasn't a real Currin, was she? No, she'd been adopted, and apparently discovering that had been enough for her boyfriend to stop pretending to love her anymore.

She shook her head as she put her car on cruise control after entering the I-81. How could she have been so stupid, so gullible? It was the latter that irked her the most. Her dad had always told her that people would like her for their position, for their money. She hadn't believed him and, believing she was a good judge of character, had delighted in proving him wrong. When she met Dirk, she truly believed every word that fell from his lying lips. Well, more fool her. Her love affair with him, however intense and brief, had momentarily distracted her from her quest to find out the truth about her birth. She'd always known her father knew far more than he'd ever let on, and she'd stopped worrying about it when she'd fallen in love.

But no more. Now she was going to get to the bottom of it. To find out what her birth story really was. She deserved to know. She was an adult, after all. Her father had promised he'd tell her the truth once she was eighteen and he owed her that truth now.

Being rejected for not being a real Currin was one thing. She could get over that and the idiot who'd even had the nerve to say such a stupid thing. But suffering the perpetual sense of disconnection from her father and her older siblings, Xander and Annabel—that was something else.

Yes, she'd known and accepted that Ryder Currin had chosen to raise her with Annabel's mom, Elinah. Elinah, Ryder's second wife, had, until her death when Maya was only five, been the only mother figure Maya had known. As a kid, she'd never questioned why they'd adopted her and brought her up as their own. Her adoption had been private and closed—which had sent up some flags when she'd tried to investigate exactly who her birth parents were. She had a right to know. A right to her history.

Every time she had a question it seemed as though there was yet another secret barring her from knowing the truth. Her father had told her over and over that the truth had no bearing on their relationship, that he loved her and that was all that mattered. But how could she continue to believe him and trust in his love for her when he wouldn't tell her who she really was?

The thought of walking away from the only family she'd ever known sliced through her like a physical pain. It was almost unthinkable, but if she didn't find the answers she sought, she didn't know if she could continue to pretend to be a part of them all. She needed to know the truth, and her father was the only person who could give that to her.

She'd decided this was important enough now to give up a week or more of her classes. Maybe she'd even take a break for the rest of this semester and return to Boston College again in the winter—with the truth in hand and her place in the world all the more secure.

Maya changed lanes and passed a long rig before easing back into the right-hand lane again. While she was eager to find answers, she wasn't exactly in a mad hurry for this confrontation. After all, she'd waited her lifetime to hear what her father would have to say, if he'd even say it, and she wanted to arrive safely and in one piece.

Thirteen

Cord kicked off his boots in the mudroom and walked into the house, heading immediately to the kitchen refrigerator. He snagged a beer by its neck and strolled back outdoors into the loggia. Damn, even here he couldn't rid himself of memories of Zoe.

The entire past week he'd been working every hour he could, even going so far as to repaint the sheds. Anything to keep busy and keep his mind off that woman. Thing was, nothing was working. No matter how tired he made himself, she'd inveigle her way into his thoughts.

He threw himself onto one of the outdoor sofas and leaned back to take a long pull of his beer. He grimaced as he swallowed it. Even that didn't taste any good. A sound from inside the house drew his attention, putting all his senses on alert. He wasn't expecting anyone, and thieves didn't usually bother this far out of town. He put his beer down on the table and rose to his feet, carefully opening the kitchen door and moving swiftly and silently through the lower floor.

He heard a sound again. This time there was no mistaking it. It came from the suite of rooms his grandmother had used. He doubted she'd left her valuables behind after the move to Palm Springs, but, either way, he hated the thought of someone pawing through her stuff. He reached for a tall brass candlestick off the hallway table and gripped it firmly in one hand as he carefully pushed the door open.

"Argh!" his grandmother screamed, and she dropped the clothes she'd been lifting from her suitcase on the bed.

She broke into a voluble stream of Spanish, telling her grandson in no uncertain terms precisely how many years he'd just shaved off her life. Cord threw the candlestick onto the bed and stepped forward to grab his grandmother and hug her tight. She was so tiny she barely even reached his chin, but her strong arms folded around his waist, just the way they had always done, and he felt her begin to calm down.

"What are you doing here?" he asked, still stunned to have discovered she was his intruder.

"Bah, Palm Springs. It's not for me," she said, tugging herself loose and bending to pick up the scattered clothing. "Maybe it's nice for a holiday, but I can't live like that. There's nothing to do!"

"Isn't that the point of being retired?" Cord said as he picked up a stray pair of his grandmother's voluminous underwear and passed them to her.

She snatched them from him with a sniff of disdain. "Retired? That was your father's idea. Not mine. He's my son and I love him but..." She shook her head vehemently. "Palm Springs is slowly driving him loco. I don't know how your mother stands it."

"But wasn't Palm Springs her idea?"

His grandmother made a dismissive snort. "Only after your father started talking about it. You know how he always needs to be led. Oh, he's a hard worker, but he has to be allowed to think things are his idea. When he talked about Palm Springs and retiring, I don't think either of them had the slightest idea of what it meant. Sure, they've made new friends, but it's not—what is it you people say? Their scene?"

Cord sat on the bed and watched as Abuelita moved around the room, putting her things away.

"Anyway," she continued, "I've had enough of being retired. So I came back to take care of you."

"I'm a grown man, Abuelita. I can take care of myself," Cord pointed out with a rueful grin.

His grandmother settled onto the comforter beside him. She raised a gnarled hand to his face, cupping his cheek and forcing him to look deep into her eyes.

"If that is so, my boy, then why do you carry so much pain in your eyes? Is it a woman? Let me talk to her. I'll fix it for you."

Cord laughed, the first genuine joy he'd felt since he'd slipped from Zoe's bed and disappeared into the early strains of morning. The thought of Abuelita fronting up to Zoe and giving her a piece of her mind would be worth the price of ringside seats, for sure, but this was his problem and since it couldn't be dealt with, it would simply have to be left to fade away.

"I see all your easy living hasn't softened your edges," he teased her, bending down to kiss the top of her head.

"Don't try to distract me, Cord. I know when something isn't right here." She pressed a fist to her chest. "Tell me."

"Talking about it won't fix things," he said firmly. "We're too different. We knew it wouldn't work from the start."

"But you still got burned, yes?"

He nodded.

"It's good that you were prepared to open your heart again. I was scared that when you lost Britney, you would never trust yourself to love another woman." She sighed and patted his cheek before taking his hand. "Tell your *abuelita* about this woman. Tell me everything."

"She's a cop," he said on a deep sigh and felt his grandmother's fingers tighten almost painfully around his own.

"Go on," she prompted.

He told her the story of how they'd met. How unhelpful he'd been, how he'd deliberately distracted her from being able to meet with Jesse.

"And she still agreed to see you? Is the girl mad? I would have run a mile from you."

"As I remember, you did run several miles from Abuelo. Didn't he have to come and fetch you to the church on the day of your wedding because you said you'd changed your mind?"

"Pah!" She waved a hand contemptuously. "I needed to be certain he loved me, that is all."

"And he did."

Her face softened on a memory. "Yes, he did. But he would have been ashamed of what you have done to this girl. What did you call her? Zoo-ee?"

"Zoe," he corrected her. "And I was pretty ashamed of myself, too."

"So did you not apologize?"

"I did."

"And she didn't accept it?"

"She did."

"Then I don't understand. What is wrong?"

"She lives in Houston. Her whole life is there. Her family, her career. Everything that is important to her."

"Are you not important to her, too? You young people

today. You want it all your own way. You don't understand compromise. I did not want to leave Mexico, my family, my whole life, to come here to Texas. But your grandfather had a dream, and as his wife it was my role to support him in that dream."

"I know, Abuelita, and he loved you all the more for that. But I don't see how Zoe and I can work this out. I went to her, but she made it very clear that her life is in Houston. She won't budge on that. And I can't leave all this. You and Abuelo built it up for Dad and for me and future generations of Galicias. I can't just walk away. I have a responsibility to our name and to the land."

His grandmother was silently shaking her head. "Your *abuelo* never wanted this to be your prison, my boy."

"It's not a prison. I love my home. I love what it means to our whole family. I'm honored that it now falls to me to look after the legacy."

He said the words with vehemence, but the passion behind them was no longer in his heart.

"That might have been true before your Zoo-ee," his grandmother said with her usual uncanny insightfulness. "But it is not true anymore. I can see why you are unhappy."

"I'm not unhappy," he protested automatically, but even as he did so, he felt the sharp sting of regret pierce his heart. Regret for what might have been had the circumstances been completely different.

But then again, if circumstances were different, wouldn't he and Zoe be different people, too? Would they have come together as hastily as they had? Experienced the heights they'd shared? For all that they had no future together, he couldn't regret a moment of the time they'd had.

Cord had spent a lot of time thinking since Abuelita's return a couple of days ago. And he'd come to a decision.

After his grandmother had gone to bed, he lifted the phone and called his parents.

The sound of his father's voice as he picked up the phone in Palm Springs was instantly calming in the way that only a parent could soothe a child, no matter their age.

"Dad, we need to talk," Cord said after the obligatory greetings had been dealt with.

"This sounds serious. Should I sit down?"

"I can hear the bedsheets, Dad. I know you're lying down already," Cord said with a grin.

"What's up, son?"

"I think you and mom should come back. Take charge of the ranch again. No, hear me out," Cord interjected as his father started to object. "It's not that I can't manage, but I think you left too early. Tell me you're not bored stupid at the end of every day. Tell me you don't miss the herd, the land, the work."

"I don't miss getting up at dawn every damn day," his father grumbled.

"So you start your days a little later. But, Dad, come home where you belong."

"Did Abuelita put you up to this?" Cord's father demanded.

"No, not at all. It's been on my mind awhile. You know I've been diversifying the herd, raising goats, making goat cheese. I want to expand that side of the business, and I can't do it on my own, especially if I'm managing the beef herds and breeding program, too. I need you to come back and work the ranch again. Obviously the choice is yours, but there's a business opportunity that's opened up for me closer to Houston. To make it work, I need you here. If you're certain you don't want to come back, I'll let that opportunity go, because I could never leave this place without ensuring a Galicia is at the head of operations. I respect my heritage too much to do that. What do you think?"

Cord held his breath as he waited for his father's response. His dad's voice was choked with emotion when he spoke.

"I have a good many years left in me, and, yes, while I like the idea of calling my time my own and doing what I want when I want, it took coming here to make me realize that what I want most is whatever's happening on the ranch. But I made my choice, son. I walked away. The ranch is yours now."

Cord gripped the phone so tight he thought he might break it. He forced his hand to relax.

"Dad, walk back. *Mi casa es su casa*, you know that. I never wanted you to go in the first place. When can you get here? Tomorrow?" He laughed, feeling as though a massive weight had been lifted from his shoulders.

"Not quite so fast. We have some things to wrap up here, sell the apartment, pack. Maybe the day after tomorrow," his father joked. In the background, Cord could hear his mother's excited voice. "Your mother is looking forward to seeing you, too, by the way."

"I've missed you guys. We have a lot to talk about when you get back. You see, I've met a girl."

"A girl? What's she li—"

In an instant Cord's mother was on the phone.

"You've met a girl? What's she like? Tell me everything. Well, not everything. But tell me about her."

Cord fought back a smile. No, he would definitely not be telling his mother everything, but he knew it wouldn't hurt to have his mother's perspective on what he planned to do. His feelings for Zoe were too deep for him to take any risks. This had to be perfect, and getting his family on board with the idea was only the first rung on the ladder.

Fourteen

"Flowers for you, Detective," one of Zoe's colleagues announced as he brought a large colorful display of blooms to her desk. "Have to say, they brighten things up around here. Maybe they can lift some of that sour expression you've been wearing these past two weeks."

"My expression is none of your business," Zoe snapped. "Aren't there some follow-up interviews you're supposed to be doing?"

Her fellow detective snapped to attention and executed a sharp salute. "Yes, ma'am. Right on it, ma'am."

She heard him laughing as he left the squad room and fought back a smile of her own. He was a damn fine detective, but he also knew exactly which buttons to push to get her ruffled. You'd think after nine years on the force she'd have developed a tougher hide for this kind of thing, but all it took was something that essentially reminded her she was female to make her even more hard-assed than ever before.

Sour? Really? She was just doing her job. The scent of the flowers tickled her nose and reminded her of what had triggered her current less-than-wonderful mood in the first place. Flowers? Seriously, who sent flowers these days? And why to her work? It wasn't her birthday or any special anniversary of anything. She eyed the arrangement as if it hid a venomous snake somewhere in the cheerful collection of buds and blossoms and spied the envelope that was buried in their midst.

She yanked the envelope out and flicked open the flap, which already bore evidence of having been opened and read by at least one of her colleagues before being brought to her desk. She groaned. She'd never hear the end of this.

I miss you.

The message was short, sweet and unsigned. She felt a flush of heat tinge her cheeks as she read the three words again. There was only one person who could have sent these to her. Cord Galicia. Well, she'd give him a piece of her mind. She snatched her phone off the desk and started to punch in his number before realizing that she actually knew it by heart. What did that say about her?

Slowly, she put her phone back onto her desk, then rose to her feet and grabbed the flowers and walked out to where the captain's personal assistant was sitting.

"Here, Josie," she said, leaving them on the older woman's desk. "These are for you. A mark of appreciation for all you do for us."

The woman eyed them carefully before looking up at Zoe. "Weren't these the flowers that just arrived for you?"

Zoe shrugged. "Busted. But they're no good for my allergies. Would you like them or should I just toss them?"

Josie looked horrified at the very thought. "You will do no such thing. I'll drop them at my mother's care center on the way home. They love a splash of color in their main living room. At least they'll be appreciated there."

Zoe didn't miss the censure in Josie's voice. It was clear the woman didn't believe her excuse about allergies and felt she ought to be grateful someone had sent her such an extravagance, but Zoe didn't do guilt. Life was way too short.

Even so, as she walked back to her desk and shredded the note into confetti before putting the pieces into her trash bin, she couldn't help but cast her eye back at Josie's desk for one last look at the flowers.

The flowers were only the beginning. Over the next few days it seemed that Cord had begun a seduction on her, sending small gifts with a thoughtful message each time. A part of her loved them. Who wouldn't love the sinfully expensive body lotion he'd sent, which paired with her favorite perfume so perfectly, she argued against the inner voice that told her to throw it away. And the small basket of gourmet goodies had been highly appreciated in the squad room at morning break yesterday. In fact, her team was beginning to look forward to the daily deliveries with more anticipation than she did.

But the parcel that arrived today had been the last straw. Despite her best intentions to keep secret the sinfully seductive sapphire-blue silk underwear he'd sent her, the lacy bra and matching thong had slid from their wrapper and onto her desk before she could hide them.

The catcalls and hoots of laughter brought even the captain from his office to see what the fuss was. By then, Zoe had scrunched the pieces into the tissue and summarily dispatched them into her trash bin. Regrettably, the note with the words *I would give anything to see you in these* had been snatched from her hands and circulated around the squad room before she could grab it back.

At this rate she'd never be taken seriously at work again. It had to stop, and very soon she'd make that call to Cord that she'd been putting off. Tonight, she told herself. As soon as she'd followed up with the crime-scene techs on a piece of evidence they'd finally been able to get to that had been extracted from the Hamm murder scene.

She let herself into the lab and went straight to Kane, the tech who'd asked her to come.

"What is it?" Zoe said, coming straight to the point. "Tell me it's good news."

"Well, there's some good news. We're finally working through the last of the evidence that was collected at the murder scene. Obviously you know the scene was severely compromised by the flood—"

"Kane, don't waste my time by telling me what I already know. I need something to go on."

"Well, there's this."

Kane turned his computer screen toward her and magnified the picture displayed there. "As you can see, it's a human hair."

"You've examined plenty of human hair found at the crime scene. What makes this any different?"

"Well, it's not like the others in that it's naturally wavy and, get this, naturally red."

"So we're looking for someone with long, naturally wavy red hair?"

"Very possibly. Now, of course you know we can't determine sex from a single hair, unless—"

"Unless there is a root attached. Tell me there's a root attached."

Kane's face lit up. "Yup. This is definitely from a woman. Obviously we can't determine age, but we can narrow it down to an adult versus a child."

"Did you run the DNA? Did we get any hits in the system? A name, anything?" she demanded, trying her level best not to get excited at the news.

She hoped this could potentially lead her to Hamm's killer, because goodness only knew everything else at the scene had driven them from one dead end to another.

"Not yet. We only just uncovered this information in the last few hours. I thought you'd appreciate knowing straightaway."

"I do. I definitely do. Thanks, Kane. Let me know the minute you have anything else."

"Will do."

Zoe was almost in a good mood as she reentered the squad room, right up until the moment she saw the lingerie she'd thrown into the trash displayed on a crime-scene board behind her desk, with the heading Wanted… by Someone. A slow-burning rage filled her, but she knew better than to let any of that show to her team. She wouldn't give them the pleasure, but she'd sure as heck give Cord Galicia what was coming to him the second she got home tonight. She planned on leaving his ears so blistered he wouldn't bother her ever again. She pulled the lingerie off the board and furiously scored out the heading, then settled at her desk, acting as if nothing of importance was going on. Eventually, this would all settle down. It had to, because there was no future for her and Cord.

"Stop stalking me."

The smile that had been on Cord's face when he'd seen Zoe's caller ID on his phone began to fade. She sounded really pissed.

"I'm merely expressing my affection," he responded, fighting to keep his voice level.

There was one thing about this woman—she could get him from cold to burning hot in about three seconds flat.

The fact that this time the heat had everything to do with irritation and nothing to do with sexual attraction was neither here nor there. No one had ever had the ability to excite or incite him so effectively.

"Well, stop it. It's gone far enough. I thought I made myself clear when I said we have no future."

"You did," he agreed and leaned back against the fence railing behind him.

It was getting dark, and he probably should head inside soon but he enjoyed the peace of the late evening. Would enjoy it even better if he had someone special to share it with.

"Then why do you keep sending me stuff?"

"Tokens."

"What?"

"They're not stuff. They're tokens of my—" He paused for a moment before he said something he'd really rather say face-to-face and not over a phone connection.

"I don't care what they are, and I don't want them. Cord, really, this has to stop. You're making me a laughingstock at work."

Ah, and there it was. There was genuine pain behind her words. It wasn't the gifts she was objecting to—well, maybe not completely—it was where he was sending them. He hadn't thought through the ribbing she'd be getting at work. He'd seen them in a display in town and couldn't think past the mental picture of seeing her on his big, wide bed wearing them.

"You want me to send them to your apartment?" he offered, knowing exactly what the response would be.

She didn't disappoint. For the next several minutes, Cord held his phone away from his ear while Zoe went on a tirade that showed a far more inventive use of expletives and instructions of where to put certain things in a person's anatomy than he'd ever heard before. He was seriously impressed, although there was pretty much nothing about Zoe Warren that didn't impress him. When she finally settled into silence, he put the phone back to his ear.

"I'm sorry. It wasn't my intention to distress you, Detective."

"I'm not distressed," she snapped back. "I'm angry. You're not respecting my wishes. I don't want to see you anymore."

He felt the words like each one was an individual blow straight to his chest.

"But you don't hate me, right?" He couldn't resist digging at her one more time.

Her growl of frustration filled his ear until it was abruptly cut off as she severed the call. He nodded to himself. Yeah, she didn't hate him. She was just driven to do her job to the best of her ability, and she didn't see how she could make time for anyone, let alone him. Well, it was up to him to show her he could fit in her world, and maybe, just maybe, she'd change her mind.

It took a lot less time than he anticipated to get all his plans in motion. Turned out his parents had little emotional attachment to the things they had in their Palm Springs apartment and were happy to leave the place staged with all their new appliances and furniture and leave everything in the hands of the real estate agents. They'd arrived back home a week after his phone call, tired after the road trip but joyful to be back. And he welcomed them with open arms. Abuelita couldn't be more in her element with all her family under one roof again, and Cord wondered how she'd take the news of what he planned to do. To his surprise she'd merely nodded, patted him on the cheek and told him that a man needed to do what a man needed to do.

So now it was a matter of convincing the woman of his heart that she needed him, too. How hard could that be? Cord grimaced as he readied the helicopter for the flight to Houston, in no doubt this would likely be the most difficult thing he'd ever done. He stowed the package he'd painstakingly wrapped for her, one last gift in an attempt to win her heart, and towed the chopper from the hangar.

"You're really doing this, then?" a voice asked him from behind.

Cord turned around and smiled at Jesse. "Damned if I don't."

His best friend raised his brows in surprise. "Seems all rather sudden, don't you think?"

"When you know, you know," Cord said. "And I know if I don't try this one last time, I'll regret it for the rest of my life."

Jesse stepped forward with his hand outstretched. "Then I can only wish you the best, buddy."

Cord clasped his best friend's hand firmly. "Thanks. I need all the help I can get."

He climbed aboard and fired up the chopper as Jesse took the ground-handling wheels back inside the hangar for him. In a matter of minutes he was skyward and headed toward Houston with hope and trepidation warring for dominance deep inside him.

Cord hangared the chopper just outside Houston, the way he'd done on his last visit, and picked up his rental car. Sitting in the parking lot at the small airfield, he dialed Zoe's number.

"I'm going to block you," she said upon answering.

"Then I'm glad you answered this one last call," Cord replied smoothly. "I'm also hoping you'll agree to see me one last time."

He heard the weight of her sigh through the phone.

"Cord, really, stop flogging a dead horse. We can't work. You know we can't, and you know damn well why. Nothing's going to change that."

"One last time, Zoe. Please. We owe it to ourselves," he cajoled her.

"I thought the last time was the last," she answered.

He could tell by her tone she was thinking about it.

"I promise you, this will be the last time I bother you. No more gifts, no more calls, no more touching you—"

"All right!" she interrupted in a fierce whisper. "You win. One last time. When?"

"Can you manage a few hours off today? Say I pick you up at your apartment about two?"

"Cord—"

"Please," he all but begged. "Just this one *last* time, Zoe."

He held his breath as she hesitated.

"Fine, pick me up at two. I'll be ready."

She severed the call before he could say another word, but inside he felt his heart begin to beat again and felt the air around him refill his lungs. He'd never wanted anything as much as he wanted the rest of today to go right.

Zoe paced her living room, waiting for the buzz from security downstairs to say Cord had arrived. She'd left explicit instructions for him not to be let up to her apartment. If she was being totally honest with herself, she didn't know if she could trust herself around him. Since their last night together she'd missed him with a physical ache that no amount of overtime could assuage.

Her apartment phone buzzed, making her flinch. She picked up the receiver.

"Your guest has arrived, Ms. Warren."

"Thank you. Tell him I'll be right down."

Her heart was fluttering in her chest as she entered the elevator to head to the lobby. She clenched her hands into fists and deliberately relaxed each finger in turn, telling herself this reaction was ridiculous. This was their final meeting. The last goodbye. She felt a twist of sorrow deep inside her and pushed it ruthlessly away. This was what she wanted. Closure. An end to the restless nights and the unexpected and totally unbidden memories that flooded her mind at the most inopportune moments. An end to seeing a dark head on a tall, rangy body everywhere she went and wondering if it was him.

And then the elevator doors were sliding open and her eyes were searching for that figure that never seemed far from the periphery of her thoughts. The second her gaze alighted on him, she felt his presence with a physical impact that robbed her of breath and made a hot flush of need rise slowly through her body. She tugged at the front of her leather jacket and strode toward him as if she were totally in control and not at all feeling like she was on the verge of wrapping her arms around him, absorbing him—everything from his heat to his breath to the flavor of him—so she could tuck it away forever.

She came to an abrupt halt about three feet away. He gave her a nod.

"Thanks for making time for me today. I know it probably wasn't easy, especially at such short notice, but I want you to know I appreciate it. Shall we go?"

Wow, heavy on the formal, she noted as he gestured for her to precede him from the building. Not even an attempt to take her hand or kiss her? What was with that, and why the heck was she so upset about it, anyway? It was what she wanted, wasn't it? She came to a stop on the sidewalk and felt him come up behind her, stopping mere inches from her body. She sensed everything about him with a heightened awareness that was going to drive her absolutely crazy if she didn't wrestle it under control.

"Where to?" she asked, fighting to keep the tremor from her voice. Inside, her nerves skittered as he drew up beside her.

"My car." He gestured to the nondescript sedan parked in the visitor's area.

She saw the lights flash as he unlocked it and then stepped forward as he held open the passenger door. She got in, glancing at him as she settled into the seat. He hadn't smiled yet, not so much as a glimmer. That wasn't like him, and the firm set to his jaw made her nervous. This was ridiculous, she told herself. She knew this man, intimately, she reminded herself with a curl of desire licking its way through her body. Whatever he had planned for her, she had nothing to fear except maybe the loss of her own self-control.

And maybe that was what she feared most. She knew he affected her on levels she had never experienced with any of her previous lovers. Heck, even that word—*lover*—was enough to make her entire body tighten in a wave of lust so intense it almost made her cry out.

Cord settled into the driver's seat and started up the vehicle.

"How've you been?" she asked, desperate to break the silence that filled the car so awkwardly.

"Not great. You?"

She sighed. So much for that gambit. "Same," she answered and fell silent again, at a total loss for words.

What did you say to a man whose very presence turned you into a melting puddle of mush, desperate for his touch and to touch him in return? A man you'd turned away from your bed, your life. A man whose absence left a gaping hole in every single day. She turned her head and stared out at the road, watching as they headed out of the city.

"Where are you taking me?" she asked, her nerves stretched to breaking point.

"Airfield."

"What's with the short answers?" she demanded, letting her anger begin to rise in the vain hope it would quell the insecurity that plagued her.

"I'm saving myself," he answered shortly.

"For what?"

He took his eyes from the road ahead and flung her a searing glance. "You'll find out."

"What if I don't want to find out?" she said, taking refuge in belligerence.

This time it was his turn to sigh. "Zoe, just be patient, okay? You granted me this time, and I promise you it won't tax or harm you in any way. For now, we're headed to the airfield. What I want to show you is a short way from town, but I want you to see it from the air, rather than the ground."

"Fine." She crossed her arms over her. "Thank you for at least telling me that much."

She didn't have to wait much longer. At the airfield, Cord pulled into a restricted zone and swiped a card at the security gate before driving alongside the tarmac to where she recognized his helicopter sitting just inside a hangar. Questions tumbled through her mind, but she resolved to hold her tongue as they walked to the chopper, and he dragged it to the helipad and prepped it for takeoff.

Before she knew it, she was feeling that delicious lurch in her stomach as they took to the air. She loved the sensation. The only thing better was sex, and she sure as heck wasn't going to go there. Not when she was doing her level best to remind herself of all the reasons why she and Cord would never work. She began to list them in her mind, taking strength from each one. He lived too far away. He hated her job. He hated the fact she carried a gun. He was traditional and wanted to take care of her, when she was eminently capable of caring for herself. He... Her thoughts trailed off. Okay, so there were four reasons, but they were important enough to be deal breakers as far as she was concerned.

Her headset crackled to life.

"Look down there, to your left."

Zoe did as he suggested. "Looks like a ranch."

"It's a goat ranch. Angora, mostly."

"And the reason you're showing me this is...?"

"It's mine."

She swiveled to face him. "It's yours? But what about your spread in Royal? Who's going to look after that?"

"My parents, and some extra hands."

"But why?"

"Well, you remember the cheese, right?"

"Sure, it was delicious."

"I've been wanting to diversify for a long time, but Dad's a cattleman through and through. So we had an honest talk. Turned out he wasn't enjoying retirement but didn't want to step on my toes by coming back home."

"But why not run the goats on your existing family property, or buy more land closer to home?"

"Because you're not there."

His words hung in the air between them.

"But—" She started to protest, but he cut her off.

"Just hear me out. I can do what I want to do anywhere, especially now that I'm no longer tied to the family spread. Sure, I'll help Dad when necessary, but I don't have to live there."

"But your family, your history. That ranch is everything to you, isn't it?"

"It's not you."

Zoe felt her stomach dip again as he took the chopper down and settled it in an empty field at the top of a rise. Once he'd shut down the engine, they alighted from the chopper, and Zoe stomped after Cord as he moved away from the machine to where there was a great vantage point over the land they'd flown over.

"What do you mean, it's not me?" she demanded, poking him in the chest for good measure.

"Exactly what I said. I've fallen for you, Detective. You have my heart in your custody, and that's where it's going to be for the rest of my life."

"You can't say that. You barely know me," Zoe protested, fear threatening to choke her.

This was all too intense. This was supposed to be goodbye, and here he was, telling her he'd walked off his family's land and bought a ranch close to Houston so he could be nearer to her. Who did that? What craziness had crawled into his brain?

"That's true, but what I do know is that you're a prickly pear with a soft inside. You're diligent in your work, you're a fierce advocate for the underdog, whether they're a good person or not. I know you have the softest lips of any woman I've ever met and that you make love as fiercely as you defend your independence."

"That doesn't tell me why you did this. I made it clear we had no future. I'm not giving up my work to set up house with any man."

"I'm not asking you to give up work, Zoe. I'm asking you for a chance at a future together. I love you."

All the air left her lungs in a massive whoosh. There it was. Those three words. Words she'd craved and yet dreaded at the same time. Words that bound and trapped. She started to shake her head, but Cord closed the distance between them and caught her by her shoulders, forcing her to look at him.

"I love you, Zoe Warren. I want to make a future with you, if you'll let me."

"No," she whispered. "I can't. You want all the things I can't give you. My career is everything to me. You want a family, you want a stay-at-home wife who'll raise your kids and work alongside you on the ranch. I'm not that woman."

"Oh, Zoe, don't be scared. Yeah, I thought I wanted those things. But most of all I just want you. I'd be happy if we never had a family, as long as I knew you loved me and could live here with me. The commute isn't so far into Houston from here. We could make a future together."

"I can't do it, Cord," she said as her eyes glazed with tears. "You hate my job and everything related to it. Yes, it can be dangerous. Yes, my life can be on the line. But I have to keep doing this. Eventually, you'd ask me to give it up. I know you would. Eventually, you'd want to have kids. I don't know if that's ever going to be on my radar. I can't do that to you. I carry a badge and a gun pretty much every day of my life. It's who I am."

"And that's who I love. Don't you see? I *want* to make compromises so we can be together. What we have is incredible and special, and we deserve to be happy together. Please, Zoe, at least give us a chance."

Zoe continued to shake her head. "No, it'll never work. Eventually you'd expect me to change, and I won't do that."

"Or maybe it's just that you're too scared to try," he challenged her. "Too scared to reach for what you know is good. Too scared to be seen as anything but bulletproof

Detective Warren, who feels no emotions but always gets her man. Trouble is, Zoe, your man is standing right here in front of you, but you're too scared to take a chance on me."

"Maybe you're right, but that's who and what I am," she said, lifting her chin and staring him straight in the eyes. "Take me back. It's over, Cord."

Fifteen

Even as she said the words, it was as if a .45-caliber hollow-nose bullet tore through her heart. Cord just continued to look at her, as if unable to believe she was still saying no to what he offered. How could he not see how impossible it was? Sure, she could commute to work from here, maybe even keep her apartment in town for those times she pulled an all-nighter, but she was certain he still hoped that eventually she'd leave her work, put aside the potential danger, and settle down and play happy family. And even if she did that, she knew eventually she'd come to hate it—maybe even hate him. No, it was easier to stand strong, to ignore the allure of what he offered and to let him walk away.

As they transferred from the aircraft to his rental car, she saw him grab a parcel and stow it behind the driver's seat. It was only when they got to her apartment building and she opened her door to get out that he reached for it again.

"Hang on a second," he said, his voice gruff with emotion. "I bought this for you. You should have it. My last gift to you, okay?"

She didn't trust herself to speak. His voice was so desolate, so devoid of hope or joy, and it scored her heart into a million pieces to know she'd done this to him. She accepted the parcel from him and got out of the car, closing the door behind her and walking as quickly as she could back into the lobby. She punched the elevator button with a shaking finger and rode the car up to her floor, her eyes blurring with unshed tears.

When she let herself into her apartment, she gave in to the hideous pain that had begun back at Cord's new ranch and grown in intensity each time she'd said no to him. Her legs buckled and she knelt on the floor of her entrance hall and wept as she'd never wept before.

Once the first wave of the emotional storm had passed, Zoe realized she was still holding the parcel Cord had given her. She plucked at the tape and tore the paper away from a case. One she identified immediately. With shaking fingers, she opened the snaps on the case to expose the brand-new SIG Sauer handgun inside. She recognized the model because it was one she'd been planning to upgrade to. With its reduced-reach trigger and one-piece modular grip, it was a far more comfortable weapon for her to use, when she was forced to.

But it wasn't the gun that made her begin trembling all over again. It was the fact that he'd bought it for her. She knew how much he hated weapons and why. But he'd gone out and bought her the exact model she was planning to buy for herself. More than anything he'd said as he'd tried to persuade her at the new ranch, this spoke volumes as to just how far he was prepared to compromise to have her in his world.

Could she even dare to hope that they stood a chance? That he'd meant exactly what he'd said back there? That they could make a future together? The enormity of what he'd done, of the things he'd said back at the new ranch rained down on her like giant hailstones. She'd been such an idiot. Caught up in her rut of fierce independence, she hadn't stopped to see that she was ignoring everything her heart was begging for. Everything she'd always told herself she'd make time for when the time was right. But when would that time be if she never allowed the love of a decent and good man into her life? If she threw up walls at every opportunity? If all she ever did was take and give nothing back in return? She had to make this right.

Zoe was up on her feet in seconds, and after shoving the new pistol into her gun safe, she grabbed her car keys and headed down to the parking garage. But where would she go? The airfield? What if, by the time she got there, he'd taken off again? The new ranch? Had he even taken possession of it yet? And what if he was flying back to Royal? She had a responsibility to her job to turn up tomorrow. But wasn't Cord more important? For the first time in her life, she put the needs of someone else ahead of her job. She'd start with the airfield, then head out to the ranch, if she could find it on a map. Hell, she was a detective. If she couldn't find an address with the resources available to her, she may as well hand in her badge right now.

And if he wasn't at either place? What then? She started her car and peeled out of the parking garage, driven by a desperate sense of urgency. She'd tackle that when she'd exhausted her local resources, she decided. But one way or another, she would find him.

This wasn't how it was meant to turn out, Cord thought after he'd handed in the rental car and taken a cab to the airfield. He prepped the Robinson for takeoff automatically, trying to ignore the deep sense of loss that had settled inside him. He'd put everything on the line and it had still turned to dust in the wind. All his hopes, all his dreams, shattered. He knew he couldn't do this again. Couldn't put his life and his heart on the line a third time. This was it. The thought of telling his parents and Abuelita that he'd failed was a bitter taste in his mouth. He should have known better than to trust in love again.

The sound of tires screeching to a halt behind the security fencing to the airfield caught his attention and made him look up from his preparations. Then there was the sound of a woman's voice, shouting—no, pleading—with the guy at the security gate. Cord walked to where he could see what all the fuss was about. As he did so, recognition dawned and with it an ember of hope stirred in his chest.

"It's okay," he called out. "She's with me."

"Sir, you know this is an operational airfield. We can't just let people in all over the place."

"I understand. My apologies."

Cord planted his feet firmly on the ground and watched as Zoe pushed past the guard and through the gate, actually running toward him with a look of desperation on her face that fanned that ember to a warm glow. Even so, he didn't plan to make this easy. She'd crushed him. If she truly was back for him, as hard as it would be, he might actually let her fight for it.

"You haven't left yet," she said breathlessly as she drew up in front of him.

"Your powers of observation are on point, as always, Detective," he drawled, not letting an ounce of the emotions that crashed through him surface in the sound of his voice.

"I need to talk to you."

"I thought we were all talked out."

She slid her sunglasses off her face, and he was shocked to see the ravaging evidence of tears there. Zoe was one tough nut. He'd never have expected tears from her. Not in a million years. His every instinct urged him forward, to take her into his arms, to console her and make everything right, but instead he locked his knees and stood firm right where he was.

"Cord, I'm sorry," she started. "I made a stupid mistake."

He kept his peace, not trusting himself to speak.

"Look," she continued, "can we go somewhere a little less out in the open?"

"Nope."

"You want me to do this here?"

"Yup."

"Fine, then." She chewed her lower lip for a second. "I want another chance. I want to take you up on your offer. I want to tell you I was a stupid, prideful, frightened fool who thought she knew what she wanted. But when I walked away from you," she admitted, "I realized how much I really wanted you after all. I'm sorry, Cord. I love you. I guess I was fighting it because it all happened so damn fast. Heck, a few weeks ago I was prepared to arrest you for obstruction and now I want to spend the rest of my life with you."

Every cell in Cord's body shuddered as the impact of her words sank in.

"The rest of your life, you say?" he finally managed to enunciate, hardly daring to believe her words.

"Forever, Cord. I know a love like this doesn't come along often. My parents have it. My brothers have it. I want it, too, with you."

"So, um, marriage? And kids?"

"Yes, marriage and kids…eventually."

He nodded and looked away to the distance so she wouldn't immediately see the gathering moisture in his eyes as the realization of his dreams began to take shape again.

"Today wasn't easy for me," Cord said carefully, still not looking at her. "The last woman I wanted to spend a future with died in the line of duty. The same duty you take on every day you roll up to work."

"I understand that," Zoe said, taking a step closer and reaching out with both hands to turn his face toward hers. "I promise you that I will always do my level best to be as safe as I can possibly be. Beyond that, I have to trust my fellow officers to do their jobs to the best of their abilities, too. You can live with that?"

He allowed his gaze to meet and mesh with hers. "I have to, if I want you in my life, and I do want you, Zoe. I want to build a family with you, the way our parents did with us. I want to grow old with you. I know it's never going to be an easy ride—we're both too strong willed for that. I could never make a life with a biddable woman, anyway. I love your sass, your determination, your strength. Quite simply, I love you."

"Then you'll forgive me for being an idiot this afternoon? For nearly crushing us forever?"

"You may need to make that up to me," he said with a slow, teasing grin beginning to wreath his mouth. "For quite some time."

"I'll do anything you want. Come home with me now. We can make plans."

"Plans?"

"Well, after we…y'know."

"So you liked the gun, then, huh?"

"I love the gun, Cord, but even more than that, I love

what it symbolizes between you and me. And, Cord, I love you even more."

He grabbed her then and kissed her with all the pent-up hope and joy and relief and love that had surged through him the second he'd identified her behind the security gate. And he knew that while they might weather some storms, they'd do it together—stronger for all they'd fought for, better for having each other.

Epilogue

The hot breath of the police was a tangible sensation down my neck. They were getting closer and it was making me nervous. My hands kept sweating, I'd lost weight, my hair was falling out. Thank God no one had noticed yet. I was holding it together when it counted—just.

This craziness wasn't me. It wasn't my fault. I had no choice. Surely they'd see that, wouldn't they? The Sterlings and the Currins, they were the ones to blame. They had everything, and they took even more—the land that should have been my father's, the land that Ryder Currin had coerced out of Harrington York and that he'd made his fortune on.

I thought I'd properly put a spoke in Currin's relationship with Angela. The golden child. The woman with everything. Her daddy's right hand. None of them deserved happiness. Not at my expense.

And then there was that bitch cop who kept poking and

prodding where she shouldn't. It made me laugh when I heard she'd gone out of town on some goose chase to Royal when I'd been right under her nose all along. But she was back now, and more determined than ever.

I had to find my baby before they found out it was me. My child was the only thing keeping me going now. But I'd never find her if I was in prison. Please, don't let me lose my last chance to find my child, to hold her, to love her. To put right the wrongs of eighteen years ago.

Ryder Currin watched as Willem Inwood entered the boardroom and settled at the table with his lawyer by his side. Slimy bastard. He still couldn't believe that this feeble excuse for an executive had abused Ryder's staff and pretty much gotten away with it. And to think it was Ryder who'd given Inwood every opportunity to get ahead at Currin Oil. He'd believed the man to be loyal. The discovery that Inwood was the complete opposite had left a nasty bitter taste in his mouth.

He stared at Inwood, determined not to be the first to speak, taking in the slightly less-than-perfect dark auburn hair, the lanky frame and the dark brown eyes hidden behind his wire-framed glasses.

Ryder had never understood why a man such as Inwood, as insecure as he'd turned out to be, had to turn that insecurity on to his subordinates, instead of learning and growing. Inwood had been a complete failure as an executive on his payroll and it irked Ryder greatly that he hadn't noticed sooner and thereby had a chance to minimize the damage Inwood had wrought.

Inwood tugged at the tie at his collar and stretched his neck. It gave Ryder no small amount of pleasure to see the other man was uncomfortable in his presence. Inwood cast a glance at his lawyer, who nodded as if encouraging him to speak. *Great*, Ryder thought, *let the show begin*.

"I asked you to meet me here today to apologize for my actions. I should never have rekindled the rumors that you had an affair with Tamara Perry, and I apologize for the way I conducted myself while working for you."

"Is that so?" Ryder drawled. "Strange that you didn't seem to think that necessary when I fired you. Nor did you seem to think it necessary when you were haranguing staff and forcing them to falsify paperwork a couple of months ago when it became clear you were incapable of performing your duties properly, let alone adequately."

Hot color flushed the man's face, and his lips twisted into a feral grimace, showing him for the weasel he truly was.

"Look, I didn't need to come here today and put up with your insults!"

His lawyer leaned across and whispered urgently into his ear. To Ryder's surprise, Inwood settled down in his seat.

"I came here to clear the air. I've said I'm sorry. I didn't mean for any of this to go this far. Whether you accept that or not is up to you. But I also need to make something absolutely clear. I didn't kill Vincent Hamm. I never even met the guy. My lawyer will present you with the results of a polygraph that I voluntarily took to prove my innocence."

Ryder watched as the lawyer removed a sheaf of papers from the folder in front of him and slid it across the table. He picked up the data and scanned it quickly before reading the summary at the end.

"So this proves you didn't kill Hamm. But I have a sneaky feeling you know who did, don't you?" Ryder pressed.

Inwood's face paled. The red hue that had suffused his skin earlier now faded to a sickly gray. He shook his head.

"No, you've got it all wrong. In fact—" he pushed up from his chair and stood facing Ryder "—you can go to hell. I'd never give up my—"

Inwood closed his mouth with a snap, as if realizing that he was on the verge of saying something incriminating.

"You'd never give up your what?" Ryder prompted.

Inwood just shook his head and turned for the door. As it slammed behind him and his lawyer, who'd scurried out after him, Ryder leaned back in his chair and whistled softly through his lips. What was it that Inwood had been on the verge of saying? Was it a *who* or a *what* that he would never give up? One thing was for certain—Ryder would soon find out.

* * * * *

COMING SOON!

We really hope you enjoyed reading this book. If you're looking for more romance be sure to head to the shops when new books are available on

Thursday 17th July

To see which titles are coming soon, please visit
millsandboon.co.uk/nextmonth

MILLS & BOON

MILLS & BOON

THE HEART OF ROMANCE

A ROMANCE FOR EVERY READER

MODERN — Prepare to be swept off your feet by sophisticated, sexy and seductive heroes, in some of the world's most glamourous and romantic locations, where power and passion collide.

HISTORICAL — Escape with historical heroes from time gone by. Whether your passion is for wicked Regency Rakes, muscled Vikings or rugged Highlanders, awaken the romance of the past.

MEDICAL — Set your pulse racing with dedicated, delectable doctors in the high-pressure world of medicine, where emotions run high and passion, comfort and love are the best medicine.

True Love — Celebrate true love with tender stories of heartfelt romance, from the rush of falling in love to the joy a new baby can bring, and a focus on the emotional heart of a relationship.

HEROES — The excitement of a gripping thriller, with intense romance at its heart. Resourceful, true-to-life women and strong, fearless men face danger and desire - a killer combination!

afterglow BOOKS — From showing up to glowing up, these characters are on the path to leading their best lives and finding romance along the way – with plenty of sizzling spice!

To see which titles are coming soon, please visit

millsandboon.co.uk/nextmonth

LET'S TALK
Romance

For exclusive extracts, competitions and special offers, find us online:

- **f** MillsandBoon
- **X** @MillsandBoon
- **◉** @MillsandBoonUK
- **♪** @MillsandBoonUK

Get in touch on 01413 063 232

For all the latest titles coming soon, visit
millsandboon.co.uk/nextmonth

MILLS & BOON
HEROES
At Your Service

Experience all the excitement of a gripping thriller, with an intense romance at its heart that will keep you on the edge of your seat. Resourceful, true-to-life women and strong, fearless men face danger and desire – a killer combination!

SHADOWING HER STALKER
MAGGIE WELLS

COLTON'S LAST RESORT
AMBER LEIGH WILLIAMS

KILLER IN SHELLVIEW COUNTY
R. BARRI FLOWERS

COLTON'S DEADLY TRAP
PATRICIA SARGEANT

FUGITIVE HARBOR
CASSIE MILES

MISTAKEN IDENTITIES
TARA TAYLOR QUINN

Eight Heroes stories published every month, find them all at:

millsandboon.co.uk

afterglow BOOKS

Afterglow Books is a trend-led, trope-filled list of books with diverse, authentic and relatable characters, a wide array of voices and representations, plus real world trials and tribulations. Featuring all the tropes you could possibly want (think small-town settings, fake relationships, grumpy vs sunshine, enemies to lovers) and all with a generous dose of spice in every story.

♪ @millsandboonuk
◉ @millsandboonuk
afterglowbooks.co.uk
#AfterglowBooks

For all the latest book news, exclusive content and giveaways scan the QR code below to sign up to the Afterglow newsletter:

SCAN ME

afterglow BOOKS

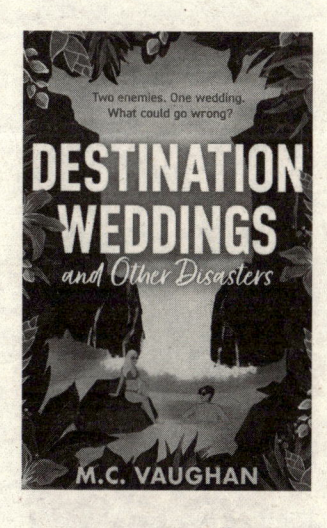

DESTINATION WEDDINGS and Other Disasters
Two enemies. One wedding. What could go wrong?
M.C. VAUGHAN

The Friends to Lovers Project
She has a plan. But he wasn't part of it...
PAULA OTTONI

- ✈ International
- ♥ Enemies to lovers
- (♥) Forced proximity

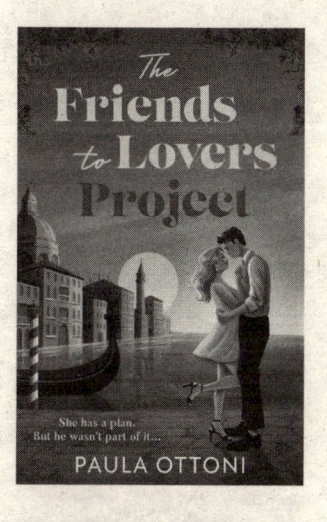

- 👥 Friends to lovers
- ✈ International
- △ Love triangle

OUT NOW

Two stories published every month. Discover more at:
Afterglowbooks.co.uk

FOUR BRAND NEW BOOKS FROM
MILLS & BOON MODERN

The same great stories you love, a stylish new look!

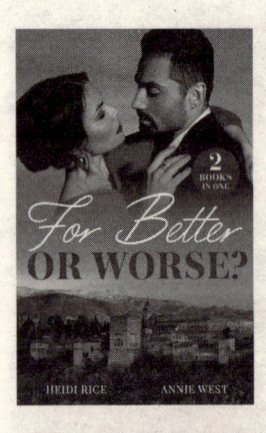

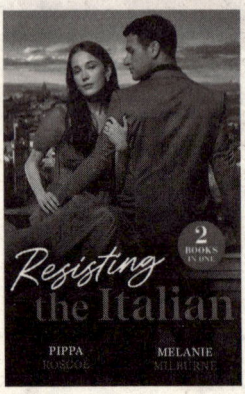

OUT NOW

Eight Modern stories published every month, find them all at:

millsandboon.co.uk

OUT NOW!

SECOND Chance
HIS UNEXPECTED HEIR

3 BOOKS IN ONE

LOUISE FULLER AMANDA CINELLI HEIDI RICE

Available at
millsandboon.co.uk

MILLS & BOON

OUT NOW!

Opposites Attract: Workplace Temptation

3 BOOKS IN ONE

CHRISTY McKELLEN
BARBARA WALLACE
STEFANIE LONDON

Available at
millsandboon.co.uk

MILLS & BOON